AT THEIR OWN PERIL

A MASON COLLINS CRIME THRILLER 7

JOHN A CONNELL

NAILHEAD PUBLISHING

AT THEIR OWN PERIL

A Nailhead Publishing book

Copyright © 2024 by John A. Connell

This is a work of fiction. Names, characters, places, and incidents either are the product of the author's imagination or are used fictitiously. Any resemblance to actual persons, living or dead, events, or locales is entirely coincidental.

All rights reserved. No part of this book may be reproduced or used in any manner without written permission of the copyright owner except for the use of quotations in a book review. For more information: john@johnaconnell.com

ISBN 978-1-950409-24-2 (hardcover)

ISBN 978-1-950409-23-5 (paperback)

ISBN 978-1-950409-22-8 (ebook)

www.johnaconnell.com

AT THEIR OWN PERIL

1

NOVEMBER 1947

Like a rifle shot, a sharp crack had me going for my gun as I spun toward the sound. I got into a shooting stance. My heart raced. My nerves sizzled. A split second later, blood rushed to my face in utter embarrassment. Across the street, a construction worker was unloading plywood from a truck and had dropped a 4x8 sheet to the pavement. Fortunately, the guy hadn't noticed me pointing my weapon in his direction.

I holstered my Colt M1911, the one I'd carried since my army intelligence days during the war. I covered it with my suit coat, turned, and headed up a driveway lined with tall hedges. My cheeks began to cool, my heart rate slowed, but a sharp pain still burned in my gut. That pain was like an old rage that I'd suppressed and was awakening once again.

I lived behind a boarding house in Cambridge, Massachusetts, a nineteenth-century Greek Revival job that had seen better days. At the end of the driveway was the original carriage house that had served as a garage until being converted into a one-bedroom apartment. That was what I called home. It was drafty and groaned with the November winds that already had the sting of winter to them. The lady who ran the boarding house had offered me a bedroom in the main residence, but I preferred the solace of the outbuilding. I didn't like being around people, not since I got back to the States, anyway. I didn't want them to see me flinch at loud noises or tense up for a fight when someone came up to me from behind.

I'd never been jumpy like that. Not during the war, not in occupied Germany, or Tangier, or Austria, or Italy, or Jerusalem. But I suffered from it here, and I couldn't quite figure out what was different. Maybe it had all finally caught up with me. Maybe I knew the answer and was afraid to admit it to myself.

I walked quietly past the house and headed for the door to the garage apartment. I was dog-tired from pulling an all-nighter surveying a house in Medford. My feet were barking from the cheap oxford shoes, and my knuckles throbbed.

I worked as a private eye at the Fred Barnes Investigators detective agency—my boss thought he'd get more business by shortening it to FBI. He didn't. It was still a penny-ante joint, which was about what he paid his private eyes. I'd pulled the all-nighter because my chowderhead boss had put me on an insurance fraud case, which looked like a dead end until the trail led me to the doorstep of an arsonist. I was supposed to notify the local cops of what I was up to, but I didn't want him bolting before they got there. Plus, he'd killed a mother in one of those fires, and I was looking forward to personally curtailing his career. He showed his face about four in the morning. When I confronted him, he pulled a gun on me.

He shouldn't have done that.

It was late afternoon now. I'd spent the day being questioned at the police station, then raked over hot coals by my boss at the agency. Now, I just wanted to pop open a cold beer and put my feet up, ignore the Wanted section and listen to the radio.

I fished the wad of keys from my pocket and slid in the

correct one. The door was already unlocked. Did I forget to lock it on the way out? Did the arsonist I put in the hospital have an accomplice waiting inside to take revenge? My heart was doing the jitterbug, though my nerves were steady. All the worries in the world disappeared as I pulled out my revolver. I crept inside and listened.

A rapid chopping sound had me confused. Then it dawned on me. I holstered my pistol, moved down the hall, and leaned against the threshold to the kitchen. Any remaining tension I had vanished at the sight of her. Laura's back was to me while she sliced up some vegetables. She'd cut her hair short to match the length in the area shaved away seven months ago for brain surgery and decided to keep it that way. I thought the new style made her even more sexy and beautiful.

I cleared my throat. Startled, she sucked in her breath and whirled around. Fear turned to anger, and she threw a handful of cut carrots at me. "Mason, you scared me to death."

She made me smile, even in her anger. I pointed to the knife still in her hand. "I hope you don't plan to throw *that* at me."

Laura put the knife down and moved toward me. She suffered from her own trauma; being in Palestine had left a mark. Her limp was almost imperceptible now; her left leg lagged ever so slightly behind her right, and the fingers of her left hand curled at an odd angle when at rest. A bomb blast in Jerusalem had killed our unborn child and put her in a coma. The doctors had said she may not walk again, but after five months, she'd liberated herself from the wheelchair, and two months later, she was free of the crutches.

She gave me a peck on the cheek. That wasn't enough for me, and I wrapped my arms around her and kissed her deeply. She pulled back from my embrace and examined my jaw.

"What did you do to the other guy?"

I'd forgotten about the bruise. I was hoping to avoid telling her about the encounter. "The door I hit is going to be fine."

"That's a load of bull. What happened?"

"I caught up with a guy who burned down his own house and two others. He tried to pull a gun on me."

"Uh-oh. How bad a shape is he in?"

"Enough for the cops to suspend my PI license."

Laura just looked straight into my eyes. She didn't chide me or counsel me about controlling my temper, like she had done several times before. Her expression was more disappointment. Which hurt worse.

She turned away and returned to the kitchen counter. "Dinner will be ready in about twenty minutes. Why don't you sit down? I'll get you a drink." She pulled out a bottle of scotch from a cabinet.

I sat at the round kitchen table and watched her pour the gold liquid into two glasses.

"Laura, I'm trying to do better."

"I know," she said, her back still to me.

I'd been back since the end of May, and now it was November. Six months in the U.S. after almost three years of war and two years bouncing from war-torn place to place. Laura lived with her parents at her mother's insistence. We both knew that was best; she needed them to heal, a stable place, and not have my mug reminding her of the loss of her unborn child and the physical trauma. She spent about half her nights here, and her mother didn't object, as we were engaged to be married. We'd set aside a date in April, when we figured she would have made a complete recuperation—physically, anyway—and I'd have a steady job. The latter wasn't working out so well.

"We both need some time," I said.

She came over and handed me the drink. We raised glasses and clinked.

"Here's to better days," she said, then swigged her drink.

Without glancing at me, she stood and went back to chopping the carrots. "Father told me he has a friend of the mayor in

Newton," she said in an oh-by-the-way tone. "There's an opening in the police department if you're interested."

That prompted me to down my scotch in one gulp and smack the glass a little too hard onto the table.

Laura spun on her heels. "Are you just going to give up? I've never known you to quit. At least when you're determined to see something through. What scares me is that I don't think you want our life together bad enough to fight for it."

I stood and walked up to her. She let me hug her but kept arms by her side. "I'll fight harder. I promise. I love you too much to ever quit."

I kissed her on the cheek, and she finally put her arms around me.

I said, "Tell your pop I'll go down there for an interview whenever he can set it up."

She hugged me harder. "I know it's been hard. For me, too. But we'll get through this."

I could attest that it had been hard on her. Almost every night that we slept together, I would awake from one of my nightmares to witness her tossing in bed like she was wrestling an alligator. Still asleep, her mouth would move in silent screams. Though she never admitted it, I knew she was reliving the moment the bomb tore at her and stole our unborn child. And it seemed to be getting worse, not better.

The phone on the kitchen wall rang. It made her flinch. I hated the sound. It pierced my ears and raised my heart rate. I wanted to let it go on ringing, but Laura said, "You better get that. It could be the police with more questions."

I reached for my glass, then remembered I'd emptied it. With a growl, I turned and moved to the phone. I plucked the receiver off the cradle. Before I could say anything, a man said, "Mason?"

It took me a second to recognize the voice, especially since the line hissed and crackled like the call came from a distant planet. It was Mike Forester, a major in the U.S. Army's

Counter Intelligence Corps, the CIC, and one of my only real friends. "Mike, it's good to hear your voice." I tried to sound cheery, though I had the feeling this was anything but a social call.

Laura came over and put her ear to the receiver.

"Where are you calling from?" I asked. "The connection's pretty bad."

"Germany. From a pay phone. Look, I haven't got much time. I'm in trouble."

"What kind of trouble?"

"The kind that forced me to call you from a pay phone and ask for your help."

"What do you need? I'll do what I can."

"I've been framed for murder and accused of being a traitor."

That seemed so absurd that it made me chuckle. "You're pulling my leg, right? Have you run out of ways to entertain yourself?"

"Mason, this isn't a joke. I've got the CIC after me for espionage, and the CID for murder. I'm in hiding until I can find a way of convincing both of them I'm innocent."

The CID stood for the army's Criminal Investigation Division, the organization I was part of right after the war.

"I can't believe anyone could accuse you of either crime," Laura said. "You're the most upstanding and loyal guy I know."

"Is that you, Laura?" Mike asked.

"She's standing next to me," I said. "Who framed you?"

"I'm not sure yet. But whoever it is, they did a damn good job of it. If I was investigating me and saw the evidence, I'd shoot me and ask questions later."

"Then get out of there. You've got the resources—"

"Mason, you forget the military runs Germany. They've got eyes and ears at all the exits. Even if I was crazy enough to try walking to the American zone in the west, that's not possible since I've got a bullet hole in my leg."

Laura sucked in her breath. "You got shot? Are you okay? Did you see a doctor?"

"I got patched up, but I'm not going to be running races anytime soon." Mike breathed into the phone. "Mason, you're the best investigator I know, and the only one I can trust. I need your help."

I looked at Laura. I saw her emotions battle it out across her face, from fear to anger to doubt. The same things went on inside me.

I was about to argue why I was a bad choice when Mike said, "I know I'm asking a lot here, but I'm desperate. I hate to play this card, but you owe me. Plenty. I really need your help, buddy."

My throat went dry. I didn't know what to say. Laura prodded me, and I looked at her. She had a neutral expression as she nodded toward the receiver, signaling me to say something. I couldn't face letting my friend down, but neither could I imagine leaving Laura while she was still in her fragile physical and mental state, traveling thousands of miles to the very place, the principal source, of my nightmares.

"Are you there?" Forester asked. "I can't stay on the line much longer."

"Mike, you're going to have to give me more than five minutes with a request like this. How can I get in touch with you?"

"Too risky," Forester said.

I waited for more, but all I got was static. I opened my mouth to say something when he beat me to it.

"I get it," he said in a stoic tone. "After refusing to go back to the States for years, you're starting a new life with Laura."

I avoided looking at Laura. Her look would convince me to stay or go, and I was torn between honoring the two people to whom I owed my life. "Mike, I didn't say no. I just need time to take this all in."

"I need you, buddy. But I know you and Laura have had a

rough go of it. You guys need time to get back on your feet. If you change your mind, take the Nord-Express train from Paris to Berlin—"

"You're in Berlin?" I asked, interrupting him. "What are you doing there?"

"I can't say," Forester said. "Just listen. Okay? Get off the train at the Zoologischer Garten station. Then go to Kurfürstendamm street. There's a café called the Jewel next to the Astor cinema. I'll leave instructions with the owner on how to find me."

I heard muffled voices on the other end of the line.

"I've got to go," Forester said with some urgency. "I hope to see you there, buddy."

The line went dead.

Laura and I stood there for a moment with me still holding the receiver. I avoided her gaze as I returned it to the cradle.

"We'd better get tickets right away if we're going to get there in time," Laura said.

I turned to her. "Going?" The other part of what she said hit me. "We?"

"You're coming along nicely with your English. Pretty soon you'll be up to two-word sentences." With that, she walked back to the counter.

I pursued her. "We're not going anywhere. I just got you back in one piece. I'm not going to leave you, and you're not in any shape to put yourself in danger again."

"You've suffered since coming back to the States. You're grumpy, unhappy, won't hold down a job. You were as solid as a rock overseas. Now you're as jumpy as a cat in a dog pound."

"What's your point?"

"You need to get back in the ring. I've tried and hoped you'd come around to the quiet life, but it doesn't seem to be working. I know you, Mason."

Her words cut too close to the bone, and I lashed out. "And how are you doing with your so-called quiet life? I know you've been looking for a story and talking to editors for international desks of several newspapers."

She seemed taken aback by that. "Have you been spying on me?"

I pointed my finger at her. "Aha! I didn't know until this moment."

She glared at me in a way I hadn't seen from her before, and I felt a chasm widening between us. She turned away and began peeling a potato with such force that I felt she imagined doing the same thing to my head.

I regretted snapping at her. I grabbed up my glass, poured another scotch, and downed it in one gulp. Our situation wasn't working. We were growing further apart. And it was my fault. In her efforts to get well, Laura had been heroic, while I had only made weak attempts at settling into domestic life.

Nothing but being a police detective would satisfy me. A few months after I got back, I tried for a slot as a detective at the Boston PD. They were delighted with my background as an intelligence officer and investigator in the army's Criminal Investigation Division, but then they checked with the Chicago PD, my former employer, and learned I'd been booted out on drug and extortion charges. The same corrupt cops I was investigating had framed me, but that argument fell on deaf ears, and they rejected my application.

After that, I drifted from job to job, never finding my place, never finding peace. I kept waiting for things to get better, always worried I would let Laura down in the end. But then finding out Laura had been bucking for an international assignment, I had to wonder if either of us could be happy in our current situation Stateside. Together or apart. That thought made my stomach twist into one large knot.

We ate in silence, then I listened to a couple of radio programs while Laura read a Taylor Caldwell novel about Cardinal Richelieu. We hit the sack without exchanging a word.

Our unresolved argument, and Forester's disturbing call, kept me up. Forester had saved my hide several times, which he freely pointed out on several occasions. One was just before D-Day. I received orders to go on a mission, parachuting into France and behind the German lines, but the mission's commander was a drunk to the point of being suicidal. Forester tried to cancel the mission, but when that didn't work, he concocted another assignment that kept me from going. Everyone who parachuted in was killed within hours. After the war, he helped me solve a case in Munich and then broke several army regulations to get me out of a British military prison in Austria for assaulting an officer who was trying to rape a local. He helped me get out of Italy before the Brits and Italian police could track me down for various alleged crimes. The real prize was acquiring for me a pass to enter Palestine to find Laura. And just in time, I might add. I owed him my life several times over.

Just after two in the morning, Laura began to moan in her sleep. The thrashing started, her nightly wrestle with an unseen force. But it was worse this time, like she was convulsing, and her moans were mournful and haunting.

I switched on the bedside lamp and checked on her. Her face was twisted in horror. I stroked her hair and whispered comforting words.

She sat up and took shuddering breaths. I held her in my arms while she sobbed. A few moments later, she quieted.

"Jerusalem again?" I asked.

She shook her head and said into my shoulder, "This time, you were holding our baby." There was a deep pain in her voice that made my chest tighten. "I called out to you," she said, "but I couldn't reach you. Then you both disappeared into the flames." She lifted her head and looked at me. "I can't lose you, too."

"I'm not going anywhere."

"I hate that we were fighting," she said. "I get angry at you for the very things I'm feeling. I can't get comfortable with domestic life. I feel like a failure, and I take it out on you."

"You've defied the odds and gotten better—"

Laura laid her finger on my lips. "I want you to just listen for a moment. Yes, I've been looking for an assignment overseas. I didn't tell you because I was afraid you'd get mad. You've tried so hard to fit in, and I hated the idea of pulling the rug out from under you just when you might find your way. What I'm trying to say is, I need this"—she waved her hands—"whatever you want to call us going to Berlin, as much as you do. We do this one thing, help Mike, and maybe I'll get it out of my system."

"You know what you're getting yourself into, but I don't want you to think this is going to be a cure-all for our problems. It could end badly and add to the nightmares. Or seeking danger becomes a kind of addiction."

She held on to me and put her head on my shoulder. "Mason, we *have* to go. Please."

I wrapped my arms tighter around her and began to plan.

2

I watched the outskirts of Berlin come into view after the train emerged from the Grünewald Forest. A sign mounted near the tracks declared we were entering the American sector of occupied Berlin. I was surprised to see that this southwestern section of the suburbs appeared relatively undamaged, considering the constant bombing runs by the Americans and British, and the savage fighting between the Germans and Soviets during the Battle of Berlin, had left a majority of the city in ruins.

Most of the train's passengers were American or British military. There were a dozen briefcase-toting men in business attire and a handful of well-dressed women. I'd scanned the faces several times during the voyage wondering who in civilian clothes might be in intelligence for the West or the Soviets. Berlin was a hotbed of espionage, and being deep into the Soviet-occupied East Germany meant anyone of them could be working for the other side. Who among them might be watching us and hoping we would lead them to Forester or stop us by any means necessary.

Laura was dozing on my shoulder. I smiled as I looked at her, now calm and peaceful. The closer we got to Berlin and the potential dangers, the better she slept. I'd slept better, too. What was wrong with us?

I brushed my hand across her face to wake her. "We're coming into Berlin."

She sat up and looked at the stately houses and tree-lined boulevards passing by our window. "Where are we?"

"According to the map, we're in the Zehlendorf district."

"The rich Berliners seemed to have survived okay," Laura said. "Ain't that always the way?"

I acknowledged the irony with a grunt and continued to look out the window. After scrambling to make all the arrangements, including Laura's father pulling some strings in Washington to get us travel visas, it took us five days to get from Boston to Paris, then a fourteen-hour train ride to Berlin. I hoped Mike Forester was waiting for us at the café, or all this was in vain.

The conductor came through the carriage to announce we would be arriving shortly at the end of the line, the Zoologischer Garten station. Laura nervously gripped my hand, which mirrored my own uneasiness about what might be awaiting us in Berlin. And just to spice things up, the train terminated in the British sector, meaning a sector full of Brit military authorities, where I had to figure I was still on a list of wanted fugitives.

Like Germany, the allies had divided Berlin into four areas of occupation, the Americans, British, French, and Soviets. Conquering Berlin at the end of the war, the Soviets occupied the city and proceeded to wreak havoc on the surviving population for months before reluctantly acceding the western half of the city to the Western powers. Like slices of a pie spreading out from the city center, the western half was roughly divided into thirds: the French with the top third, the British the middle, and the U.S. the bottom. Each sector was administered by its own military government, though there was an Allied Control Council where all four powers made collective decisions over citywide concerns—at least that was the idea on paper. What started out as a cordial détente between the Soviets and Western allies had quickly turned into simmering hostility. The city was one big powder keg, and I wondered when an incident, intentional or not, would light the fuse.

The worst of it was Berlin lay a hundred miles deep in Soviet-controlled East Germany. Surrounded by a sea of red, the only access to the west was through three tightly controlled routes by air, automobile, or train. And only one train, once a day, was provided for civilians to enter or exit.

Laura tapped my arm and gestured toward the window. What started as a scattering of bombed buildings gave way to wide areas of nothing but the skeletal shapes of buildings. Like Munich, the bombs devastated one block, while sparing another. Then came blocks-long areas where nothing existed but piles of brick and stone.

There were signs of order in the chaos. The streets, which were virtually void of vehicles, had been completely cleared, even along the blocks and blocks of rubble. Any available plot of land showed signs of vegetable gardens ready for spring planting. Steam shovels and mine cars on tracks worked alongside teams of people clearing and rebuilding. Shops, restaurants, and bars were open on the ground floors of buildings that remained intact or had damaged upper floors. Throngs of people wandered the sidewalks or waited for the city's local network of S-Bahn trains.

Our train slowed as it pulled into the station. The train jerked to a stop, and we gathered our suitcases. As we waited in line to exit, Laura squeezed my hand tighter. I wasn't sure if it was nervousness or excitement. Maybe a bit of both.

Frigid air hit us when we stepped down to the platform. There was little left of the station's walls or ornate ceiling. A simple structure had been erected as cover against the weather, though it did little to shelter us from the flecks of snow that swirled in the capricious winds.

We followed the crowd of disembarked passengers heading

for the exit. As we moved, I scanned the area for Forester just in case the rendezvous at the café was no longer an option, but steam released from the locomotive created a dense cloud that made it hard to see more than a few feet ahead of us.

A few men lingered in places along the edge of the platform, most of them eyeing the debarking passengers.

"Why do I feel we have targets on our foreheads?" Laura asked.

"*Wilkommen* to Berlin, darling."

We funneled through the doors with the rest of the passengers and reached the street. Behind us was the Tiergarten park and Berlin Zoo. Only a scattering of trees had survived the bombings, and many of those had been cut down by Germans desperate for firewood. Soldiers from the western and Soviet armies circulated among the locals on the cratered park grounds in what was no doubt a large black-market hotspot. When I was in Munich, I'd found it unsettling to see German police in repurposed Wehrmacht uniforms. Now I had the same reaction to seeing groups of soldiers in Russian uniforms, a holdover from unpleasant memories of Vienna. While relations with the Soviets had begun to sour, soldiers for all four armies frequented many of the same places. Tolerance laced with suspicion was now the order of the day.

Ahead was a vast field of rubble and burned-out buildings. One of the few structures to remain intact was a giant flak tower. Built for anti-aircraft guns, its solid concrete walls and four turret-like towers stood like a grim monument to the defeated Third Reich.

"I think Kurfürstendamm is to the left," Laura said.

"You know Berlin?"

"A little. I was here for the '36 Olympics as a rookie reporter. Berlin was beautiful back then, but all the brown shirts and Nazi regalia made my skin crawl. I couldn't wait to get out of here once the games were over."

I followed Laura as we navigated a five-street intersection. We then turned right onto Kurfürstendamm, the famous shopping street before the war. One building gutted by fire bordered another in decent condition. One was nothing but a shattered façade; another housed a clothing store. The randomness of destruction always intrigued me. Shops, cafés, and restaurants were lively spots with a mix of German civilians and Allied soldiers, while British MPs patrolled the streets. I tried not to make eye contact with them, fearing I would attract attention and get detained.

I spotted the Astor cinema a block away and pointed it out to Laura. The café came into view a few steps farther. A wood plank above the door was affixed to the original neon sign—and probably covering up the previous Nazi-appropriate name—with letters painted in swirling script, declaring "The Jewel Café." The windows were covered in adhesive tape to hold the cracked glass together. Otherwise, the place appeared to have changed little from before the war.

Laura and I entered a living-room-sized space decorated in 1920s art déco panels and ceiling. We both sighed with relief at the warmth and rubbed our hands together to get the feeling back in them. It was mostly a British crowd. There were a handful of men in civilian clothes, and a half dozen German girls chatted at one of the wrought-iron tables.

We went up to the man at the counter. He was middle-aged and dressed in black and white, like a Parisian waiter. He smiled and greeted us in British English. "What can I get for the lovely couple?"

"Are you the owner?" I asked.

The man shook his head. "I'm afraid he's not here today. Is there something I can do for you?"

I glanced behind me to see who might be listening, but no one seemed to be paying attention to us. "A friend told me he would leave instructions for us with the owner. Do you know anything about that?"

"I'm sorry, sir, I don't."

"Could you possibly check around? It might be an envelope with Mason or Collins on it."

The barista did a cursory search of the area around the counter and cash register. "Nothing here, sir."

I wanted to insist he look harder, but Laura must have felt the tension and put her hand on my arm. "When will the owner be back in?" she asked in a sweet voice.

"The day after tomorrow," the barista said in a brusque tone. "Now, if you'll excuse me, I have to attend to this other customer." He shifted over to take a British officer's order.

We turned away from the counter and took a couple of steps into the room.

"I guess now we look for a hotel and wait until the owner returns," Laura said.

We headed for the door. Halfway there, a man stood and blocked our way. Without looking at us, he put on his overcoat and said in English with an American accent, "If you're the couple from Boston and here for a mutual friend, follow me." Without looking at us, he exited the café.

Laura looked at me with a concerned look. "Should we?"

I took a moment to weigh the risks. "He knew when and where to look for us. I have to assume Mike gave him the details."

We left the café and spotted him walking up Kurfürstendamm at a brisk pace. He had a confident step and a lean, athletic build. He kept his head down as if avoiding anyone's gaze. Staying ten yards behind him, we let the man guide us. We dodged soldiers, some traveling in packs, some with female companions. There were Germans dressed in their finest, albeit fraying, clothes. Girls with heavy makeup giggled as they eyed the soldiers. Jobs were scarce, and rationing kept the populace lean and hungry, so most did more window shopping than buying.

A couple of blocks later, the man took a right turn. He never looked behind to see if we still followed him. We made the same turn onto a small street lined with rubble neatly piled along the sidewalk, forcing us to stay on the asphalt. The contrast of this grim street compared to the lively Kurfürstendamm was stark. No one walked here. Most of the buildings were only shells. One had lost its front façade, exposing the apartments within. A couple seemingly oblivious to their plight sat at a dining room table with a kerosene lamp serving as both light and heat.

Footsteps behind me made my ears stand up, alert to any danger. Laura must have heard them, too, as she gripped my arm and glanced at me. The pace of the footsteps matched our own, and by the sound seemed to be thirty yards away.

The man we followed made an abrupt turn into the hollow shell of a building. As far as I could tell, nothing but the four exterior walls held the thing in place.

Laura whispered, "Do you think this is a good idea?"

"No, but at this point, we don't have much of a choice."

3

My unloaded .45 pistol was nestled in its carrying case and still packed in my suitcase. Inside were also two magazines, but they lacked rounds, which was the only way I could carry the weapon into France and occupied Germany. Now I wished I'd loaded the thing before disembarking the train. I had my brass knuckles and Ka-Bar knife, also tucked into my luggage. That meant we depended on my instincts and the stranger leading us into a dark and desolate place.

Mirroring the man's path, we entered the same doorless entry and strained to see in the shadows. I braced for an ambush. The rubble had been cleared on the ground floor and looked like it was being prepared for new construction. That made it easier to move through the wide space.

"Where did he go?" Laura said.

The man had disappeared into the darkness.

"Just keep going, steady and calm," I said.

As we passed a large supporting beam of brick, the man said just above a whisper, "Don't stop."

Laura took my hand and squeezed it as we did what we were told. I kept my gaze to the front, while directing my other senses to our rear. Our shoes crunched on a layer of grit, but just below that sound, someone else's footsteps echoed off the bare brick walls.

Those footsteps became quick movements, and I spun on my heels. Our guide sprang from his hiding place. His arm was raised with a blackjack in his hand. But the man following us was ready for the ambush. The follower, a human blockhouse, grabbed our guide's hand with his left and struck him in the jaw and then the stomach with his right. The guide went down.

I charged the assailant as he went for something under his overcoat. I was on him, trapping his hand against his chest. I got in a couple of good punches, but the man seemed unfazed. He returned the favor. We countered each other's blows and kicks, then he got a good one under my chin.

My vision blurred; my head spun. But instead of defending myself from the next blow, I lunged, kneeing him in the abdomen, then head-butting him in the forehead. It was like hitting a concrete wall. I staggered back and fell on my butt.

A quick-moving shadow came up behind the assailant. It was our guide, and he struck the follower on the back of the neck with his sap. The impact made a sound like striking a melon. The guy grimaced, but spun around and struck our guide across the jaw. Our guide went down. After the two blows to the head, the attacker wobbled on his feet but found the willpower to make a run for it back toward where he'd come from. Despite his punch-drunk gait, he disappeared in a hurry.

Laura ran up to me and asked if I was okay. When I answered in the affirmative, she said with a sly smile, "Out of practice?"

I rubbed my jaw and stood. "Seems so. That bull fought like he felt no pain." I helped our guide to his feet and asked, "Who was that guy?"

"Beats me," the guide said.

"Well, make a good guess," I said, raising my voice.

He glared at me with a look of defiance.

"You'd better have some answers," I said. "Not an hour in Berlin, and we're already making enemies."

The guide brushed past me and continued his path into the depths of the building.

I picked up the pistol the attacker had lost in the scuffle. "A Tokarev. Soviet Army issue." I handed Laura the pistol. "Hold on to this until we can find you something more your style."

"That was a Soviet agent?" Laura said.

"Could be," I said. "Or he was carrying a Tokarev to make it seem like he was. That's something we should ask our guide. Just as soon as he decides to speak to us."

Near the back wall of the building, the man turned right and exited a small opening. We did the same and caught up with him. I wouldn't pepper him with questions until we got some place where I could pry the answers out of him. We continued down a narrow alley in silence until coming out onto another small street. The man walked up to a 1930s Rolls-Royce and opened the back door.

Laura got in. Before doing the same, I stared at the guy for a second and tried to judge if I could—at least temporarily—trust him with our lives. He'd softened his expression and nodded toward the back seat. That was enough to persuade me to sit beside Laura, while the guide got behind the wheel and drove off.

I leaned forward to get close to his ear. "Start talking."

The man completed a left turn. "My name is David Ellenberg. Lieutenant. CIC. Mike Forester and I are friends."

Laura leaned forward next to me. "Where is he?"

"Not sure. My guess is somewhere in East Berlin."

"He's in the Soviet sector?" I asked, surprised.

"Near as I can figure," he said.

"Are the Russians detaining him?" Laura asked.

"Last I heard, no."

"And when was that?" I asked, getting impatient.

"Two days ago."

"What the hell is he doing on the Soviet side?"

Ellenberg made a couple of quick turns while checking his rearview mirror. I looked back to see if I could spot someone following us. We appeared to be the only car on the road for the moment.

I turned back to our driver. "You haven't answered my question."

"It's complicated," he said and turned onto a wide boulevard.

I got the impression we were going back toward the center of the city. "Where are you taking us?"

"A secure place."

"What is so complicated about Mike's situation?" Laura asked.

"I'll explain everything once we reach our destination," Ellenberg said as we approached a large sign that read: *"You Are Now Entering the American Sector"* in English, French, and Russian. Then something about no firearms except for on-duty soldiers and to obey all traffic laws. I wondered how long it was going to take for me to break one or all of those regulations.

Two American MPs stood next to a barrel fire near the sign, warming their hands. Ellenberg slowed and rolled down the window. Both MPs barely glanced at him and waved us to proceed. Ellenberg drove away.

"Kind of a lax checkpoint," I said.

"There are hardly any restrictions crossing the three Allied sectors. The Soviet one is another matter."

Entering the American sector did nothing to alleviate the city's bleak atmosphere. There were still blocks of brick and dust. Teams of Trümmerfrauen, the women who stacked bricks salvaged from the ruins or loaded mine cars with rubble, were on every block and reminded me of my days in war-torn Munich and Frankfurt. Still, it was a relief to see American GIs on the streets and U.S. flags flying. Outdoor cafés and clubs for soldiers had sprung up, and Berliners were out in numbers rivaling the busy Kurfürstendamm.

We remained silent as Ellenberg navigated a series of small streets. I noted every turn until he slowed down on one street with mostly burned-out houses. He drove through a ruined gate and pulled into the enclosed front yard of a damaged stone house. He parked under a portico that was out of sight from the road and stopped the engine.

"Where are we?" Laura asked.

"Someplace safe," Ellenberg said.

"Your vagueness is getting on my nerves," I said. "You'd better be ready to spill everything once we get inside."

Ellenberg said nothing and got out of the car.

4

Laura and I retrieved our suitcases from the car's trunk and followed Ellenberg across the property of tangled bushes and scattered debris. The three-story house looked to be from the early 1800s and sported a turret and rough-cut stone walls, making it look like a small castle. We mounted the stone portico steps to a massive front entrance adorned with bas-relief columns.

A link of chain was wrapped around the handles of the double doors and kept in place by a padlock. Ellenberg used a key to release the lock and let the chains tumble to the ground. He pushed open the doors, and the rusted hinges groaned under the weight of the thick wood. Inside, the foyer ceiling had collapsed. The floor was littered with chunks of wood and masonry. The dusky sky of late afternoon was visible through the hole extending from the upper floors to what remained of the roof.

Laura wrapped her coat tightly around her. "It's colder in here than outside."

"This is your safe house?" I asked Ellenberg.

Our companion remained silent and headed for a pair of closed doors to the left.

"More like Dracula's castle," Laura said as she looked around.

The man pulled back pocket doors of solid oak, and we followed him into a rectangular room that had fifteen-foot ceilings and ornate wood detailing on the walls and ceiling. The warmth of a fire in the man-sized, stone fireplace greeted us. The only furnishings in the grand space were two sofas that faced the fireplace and the small end tables that flanked them.

"I need a stiff drink before we get started," Ellenberg said as he headed to one of the end tables and picked up a bottle of cognac. "Anyone want to join me?"

We both agreed, and he poured the amber liquid in three of the four glasses stacked by the bottle. "They're clean, if you were wondering." He carried over the three glasses and raised his in a toast. "To absent friends."

I downed the drink, then stared at our companion. "Now's the time to start talking."

Ellenberg shifted his look from me to Laura as if assessing how much to say. "The last time I spoke with Major Forester, he told me he was going into the Soviet sector. Then he went dark. Whether he's there now or not, I don't know. Whether he's still hiding out or imprisoned by the Russians, I don't know that either."

"Was he on a CIC mission?" I asked.

Ellenberg put his glass down, then went to the fireplace and added some logs, which seemed to me as an obvious attempt to buy some time to weigh his answer. "He went there to rescue a local asset. Either she was abducted or was running from something. Or someone."

"She?" I said in surprise.

"Did he get involved with a female spy?" Laura asked.

"He didn't say it, but that's the impression I got," Ellenberg said. He threw another log into the fireplace, stood, and walked over to the end table to pour himself another drink. "The woman isn't—at least as far as we know—a Russian agent. Her name is

Sigrid Graf. She was an asset for Nazi intelligence and worked on the Eastern Front during the war. She was born to German parents living in Odessa. They moved back to Germany at the beginning of the war, and because she was fluent in Russian and knew Soviet culture, she was a perfect candidate to work behind enemy lines. When Germany fell, Soviet intelligence—the MGB—picked her out of a prison camp and forced her to work for them. That is until she escaped to the West."

"The CIC cleared her?" I asked with a tone of suspicion.

Ellenberg downed his drink and put the glass on the table. "Not the CIC."

"Army intelligence?" Laura asked. "You mean G-2?"

Ellenberg eyed Laura for a moment and gave her a weak grin. "I'm not even supposed to be talking about this. It's all very hush-hush. But under the circumstances, you need to know this stuff. And if Mike Forester trusts you, then I will, too." He paused for a moment. "G-2, and by extension the CIC, made an arrangement with the former chief of Wehrmacht intelligence on the Russian front during the war. His name is Reinhard Gehlen. When Germany fell, Gehlen offered his services in exchange for his freedom. After some persuading, G-2 gave him the green light, and Gehlen recruited all his old Nazi intelligence buddies to form an organization to track down Soviet spies and their German assets infiltrating into the West. Their expertise in Soviet intelligence and an extensive network of informants were too good for G-2 to pass up. The brass swept their Nazi pasts under the rug and kept the organization's existence a secret. We didn't find out about the organization until some of their agents started horning in our territory."

"So, this woman was vetted and hired by Gehlen's organization," I said.

"There's no way to verify that, but that's seems to be the case."

"Falling in love with a German asset isn't grounds for treason," Laura said.

"I don't know where the information is coming from," Ellenberg said. "The story is that Sigrid was a double agent, and that Mike has been passing along classified documents to her."

"Mike?" I said. "Not a chance."

"I wish I shared your certainty," he said.

I walked up to the end table and poured myself another drink. I held up the bottle to Laura, but she declined.

"What about Mike's murder charge?" Laura asked.

"One of Gehlen's agents was found with his throat cut behind the American Forces radio station in the Dahlem district. Two witnesses from the radio station put Mike at the scene at the time of the murder."

"Jesus, Mike," I said to my absent friend. To Laura, I said, "He sure got himself in a bind this time." I took a sip of the cognac while weighing a possible strategy. "Do you know what Mike was investigating that it prompted someone to frame him?"

"Nope. Mike and I are friends but in different departments. He was running clandestine operations. I analyze intelligence reports and sometimes interrogate ex-Nazi officials. In fact, his partner is one of the agents hunting him down."

That news hit me hard. The accusations must have been serious enough for his partner to join in the hunt.

"There's no word about Mike's girlfriend, Sigrid Graf?" Laura asked.

Ellenberg shook his head. "Forester may have had some idea of where she is, but he didn't share that with me. I'm sorry I don't have more."

"More that you're willing to share with us, that is," I said.

He looked at me with a neutral expression. There was something in his eyes that told me I was right, but he simply buttoned his coat and said, "I've got to go. But you guys can stay at these fine accommodations until you can make plans for your trip back to the States."

"We didn't say we were going back," I said.

"I don't see what you two can do for him. Berlin is under martial law with four different military governments. You're civilians and not going to get very far on temporary travel visas. Go home. I'll do everything I can to help Major Forester. You have my word on that."

His words sounded hollow. Laura must have felt the same, because neither of us said anything in response. Ellenberg turned away from us, mumbled a goodbye, and exited the room. Laura glanced at me, then turned her gaze to the roaring fire. I guessed she was as stunned and deflated as I was.

"Maybe we should take Ellenberg's advice," I said, giving her a way out.

She kept her gaze on the fire while lighting a cigarette. "The hell with staying in this place. I vote we get a hotel room. A bath, food, and a little rest will help us think clearly."

"You mean, we should think about how to get out of here?"

"No, how to help Mike."

I smiled. "A hotel it is, then."

5

We finally found a hotel west of the Tempelhof airfield, the airport used by the American forces. Walking the ruined city at midnight, past buildings standing like tombstones, past Berliners huddled around fires or aimlessly wandering the streets to keep warm, was like moving through a form of purgatory.

The dismal experience, the long trek, and the cold had taken their toll on both of us, but particularly on Laura. She stared in silence at the rubble-strewn pavement as if willing herself to keep going. She didn't complain; her pace never faltered. Still, I admonished myself for agreeing that she come along. She wasn't ready. But then again, I wondered about myself. Was I ready to face the hunters and the hunted in the ruins of the Reich?

Every urban airport I'd ever known had a cluster of hotels around it. The Tempelhof airfield was no different, but only one hotel was left standing. It was a four-story turn-of-the-century building solid enough to withstand the onslaught of bombs that fell all around it. A couple of MPs had directed us to the place, saying the army used it for transiting soldiers and government officials coming through the airport.

I didn't even register the name of the place. We lumbered up the steps and entered a lobby that hadn't changed since the turn of the century. The patina of age overlaid everything. Four GIs sat in a corner, drinking and playing cards. A middle-aged man with a broad face and bulbous cheeks occupied another chair. He looked as Russian as they come and eyed us as we passed. No one was at the reception desk. I tapped the bell and waited. A large portrait of General Eisenhower hung on the wall behind the counter. I imagined the owner had tacked it up there to replace the one of Stalin from when the Soviets took over, which had replaced one of Hitler. A sleepy-eyed elderly man with a prodigious mustache came out from behind an equally gray curtain and checked us in.

"Got anything to eat around here?" I asked.

"Cheese and sausages," the man said in a thick accent.

"We'll take it. And some beer."

He handed us a room key. "Wait here."

I turned to look at the broad-faced man in the chair. He was lighting his pipe while observing our reflection in a large mirror above a fireplace. I memorized his face in case we ran into him again. The hotel manager pushed through the gray curtain and walked up to us with a platter of cheese, sausages, bread, and two mugs of beer. We thanked him and clambered up the two flights of stairs to find our room. Music from radios and boisterous voices came from several rooms. Two soldiers guffawed as they passed us in the hallway. Despite the racket, it was good to be out of the cold darkness.

The room had two swaybacked twin beds, but they looked inviting all the same. After depositing our luggage and my backpack on the floor, we sat on the edge of one of them and put the tray of food between us. I attacked the bread and cheese, then swallowed it down with a long swig of beer.

Laura grabbed one of the sausage links. "You certainly know how to show a girl a good time."

She didn't intend it that way, but the remark hit me in the gut.

She tapped me on the forehead with her sausage. "Stop feeling guilty. I'd prefer this to twiddling my thumbs back in Cambridge."

"This isn't an adventure, Laura. It's serious. We're already in over our heads on this one."

"Since when did you start thinking I was that naïve? I'm aware of the difficulties."

"Even in Vienna, even when we were civilians, Mike and the CIC had our backs. This time the CIC, the entire U.S. Army, won't take lightly to us snooping around. And trying to do the same in the Soviet sector? I say we cut our losses and get out of here."

"We haven't even started yet," Laura said and glared at me. "This is Mike we're talking about. I've never known you to give up so easily …" Her voice trailed off, and she looked as if a thought had come to her. "You're doing this because you think I'm not strong enough if we get into trouble. That I'm not ready emotionally."

"I didn't say that," I said, knowing it sounded insincere.

"You didn't have to. That hang-dog expression of yours says it all. So, stop. We're staying." She took an aggressive bite of the sausage and continued to glare defiantly at me.

I took a chunk of cheese and munched on it while I weighed what to do.

"This is when you say something," Laura said.

I took my time responding by nursing my beer. "How about this? We spend a couple of days looking into the case. See how bad the roadblocks are before we go any farther."

"I'll agree if we establish, right now, that any decision has to be mutual."

I nodded and held up my mug. "Then it's settled."

We clinked glasses and drank, though I had a tough time

swallowing past the lump in my throat. All I could think of was that image of Laura just as the bomb went off in Jerusalem.

∼

Laura and I were forced to stand in the S-Bahn train car as it rolled slowly south. We were packed in tight, making it difficult to lift my hand to scratch my nose, and the closeness was a good reminder that most Berliners had little access to running water for baths.

The train rolled over another unstable spot on the tracks due to the hastily repaired line, causing everyone to be jostled. The Soviets had taken one set of tracks from all the S-Bahn lines and shipped them back to Russia, leaving only a single track to serve trains in both directions.

My adrenaline bumped up a notch when the swaying crowd revealed the man who had been eyeing us too closely ever since we'd boarded the first train. To reach our destination, we'd changed trains twice, and the man was still with us, suspiciously choosing the same car. It wasn't the human blockhouse who had followed us yesterday. This guy was trim and stood out on the packed car with his gray wool overcoat that didn't have a blemish. His matching suit that was well-pressed. Both of which would be out of reach for the average Berliner these days.

"We could have walked faster than this," Laura said, bringing me out of my ruminations.

"Your feet will thank you. Besides, we're here."

The train came to a stop at the Lankwitz station. We wedged ourselves past the other passengers and exited the train onto a rickety platform along with thirty or so others. Laura moved toward the exit, but I touched her arm to stop her and checked the platform for our unwelcome companion.

"Did you see someone?" she asked.

"I could say it was a coincidence, a guy riding the same trains. But I don't believe in coincidences."

The man stepped off the train at the rear of the car, causing more adrenaline to course through my system. He avoided looking our way. He turned his back to us and started walking toward the south exit.

"He doesn't look your average Berliner," Laura said.

"Someone put a tail on us."

We watched him descend a short ramp farther down the platform then shuffled along with the rest of the crowd to the nearest ramp. We pushed through the turnstiles and checked the map, which informed us to head southwest.

The noonday sun had barely cleared the treetops in a cloudless sky, and the temperature hovered above freezing. Laura pulled her coat tight around her and clicked her tongue when an icy wind blew into our faces.

"I figured a Boston girl would be used to arctic weather," I said.

"I don't like the baked beans, either, so send your commentary to the Department of I Don't Care."

Following the map, we made a couple of quick turns and found the street we were looking for, Gallwitzallee. Our gray-suited shadow trailed us a block back. He didn't seem to care when I glanced behind several times to verify his presence. Eight minutes later, we approached the Oliver barracks, a complex of buildings that had housed a German anti-aircraft regiment but was now the property of the U.S. Army. A sign on one building announced the location of the 16th Constabulary Squadron.

Laura and I looked back to watch the follower turn down a perpendicular street and disappear out of sight.

Laura said, "Either he just wanted to see where we were headed, or getting close to the MP barracks scared him away."

I just grunted, and we approached the driveway. A lone MP stood between a guard kiosk and the boom barrier blocking access to the complex. He eyed me with suspicion, though Laura got most of his attention. He couldn't have been more than twenty-two, yet he puffed out his chest like the safety of all Berlin rested on his shoulders.

"What's your business, sir?" the guard asked.

"We'd like to see the chief CID investigator."

"I can't let you in without written orders, sir," the guard said. "Is this an emergency?"

"No. My name is Mason Collins. I was a chief investigator for the CID in Garmisch—"

"Was. That means you're not now."

"No, but—" I stopped when the guard shook his head.

"Sorry, that don't qualify."

"I thought as a courtesy, me being a former investigator, you'd at least call the CID office about my request."

The guard smiled as if enjoying his little bit of power. "Does the chief know you?"

The kid was getting on my nerves. "Now, how am I supposed to know that if I don't know his name?"

Laura touched my arm, reminding me to keep my cool.

I guess my growling scared him, because he nervously glanced toward the closest building as if looking for backup. When no one came, he said, "The chief is Mr. Cuthbert. He's a real ball breaker, so I'm not about to call him to say there's a stranger at the gate wanting to speak to him. His office number is in the army directory. You can call him yourself. Now, unless you have some legit business, I'd advise you to move on."

Laura gave me a little tug. "We should leave, Mason." She smiled at the guard. "Thank you, soldier."

The guard grinned at Laura, which faded when he glanced back at me. Laura tugged on my sleeve a little harder, persuading me to turn and walk away. At that same moment, a black Buick sedan pulled up to the barrier.

"Mr. Collins?" someone said behind me.

I turned to see a man sitting in the driver's seat of the Buick. He wore civilian clothes and squinted at me with one hand shading his eyes. I didn't recognize him at first, but when he broke into a big, toothy grin, I remembered him from my time in the CID in Garmisch-Partenkirchen.

"Arnie Wilson?"

Wilson got out of the car and strode up to us. "Well, Mason Collins, as I live and breathe. You're still alive."

As we shook hands, I said, "Not without a couple of close shaves and new scars."

He tipped his hat to Laura. "You must be the woman reporter Mr. Collins was so crazy about."

"The same," Laura said and shook his hand. "Laura McKinnon."

Laura had given him her maiden name, which made me all warm inside. While technically her last name was Talbot after marrying her now-deceased husband, she frequently used her maiden name when she wanted to feel closer to me.

I asked Wilson, "You're stationed in Berlin?"

"Yup. Got bumped up to warrant officer back in Garmisch, and they sent me here."

"Good. You earned it."

Wilson grinned again, making his freckles bunch up on his cheekbones.

"What are you two doing in Berlin?" Wilson asked. "Stirring up trouble or getting into it?" He chuckled at his own wisecrack.

"You just charge right in there, don't you?" Laura said with a smile.

Wilson's face dropped. "Sorry, ma'am, I didn't ... What I mean is, I heard about the hornet's nest you two kicked up in Vienna."

"Don't worry about it," Laura said and tapped me on the arm to say something.

"We don't intend to turn this into Vienna," I said. "We're trying to help out an old friend in the CIC."

Wilson's smile faltered. "It wouldn't be Major Forester, would it?"

"Did your detachment catch the case?" I asked.

"Yes, and if he's a friend, you should know the case against him is pretty ironclad."

"I've known him for five years," I said. "He's been nothing but a good man and a loyal agent. He's been framed. I'm sure of it."

Wilson glanced back toward the compound as if worried his boss or another investigator might be spying on him. "I don't know what you could do being on the civilian side of things."

"We could use your help," Laura said.

Wilson looked like he'd just bit into a lemon. "I don't know, ma'am. That's not my case. The chief has it, and he's not one to share. A real hard-ass, if you ask me."

Tall and lanky, I remembered him as a baby-faced kid who seemed to be right out of high school. Now he was thirty, and the three years in Germany had erased that childlike demeanor. Despite the grins and the ah-shucks attitude, he exuded a world-weariness I hadn't seen in him before.

"We're not asking you to show the files," I said. "I knew there were two witnesses. Maybe you could pass along their names."

He looked pained as he shook his head. "You know I can't do that, sir."

"You don't have to call me sir," I said. "I'm not your chief anymore."

He thought for a moment, then glanced behind him as if checking to see if anyone might be listening. "I tell you what. How about I run you through the crime scene?"

"Anything could help," I said.

"It'll have to be later this afternoon. Meet me behind the AFN radio building at five. I have something to look into around there, so that'll cover my tracks."

A car pulled up to the guard gate from the direction of the parking lot behind the building. A guy got out from behind the wheel and looked our way. The man wore an officer's uniform with chief warrant officer emblems on his collars. He was older and had the face of a marine drill sergeant. "Wilson," he said. "Get your ass over here."

I felt like I'd seen or known him before but couldn't place him. That flash of memory of the man wasn't flattering.

Wilson clenched his jaw and closed his eyes, and he kept his back to the chief for a moment in an act of defiance.

"Maybe do what the chief says before he starts asking questions," I said. "Just a suggestion."

Wilson plastered on a smile and tipped his hat before turning toward the car.

As Laura and I headed back toward the train station, she said, "He seems like a good guy, but wound a bit tight. Do you think he's going to be any help?"

"When I worked with him, he had just come up from the MP ranks. Young, inexperienced, but smart. The other junior investigators called him the 'Professor.' Those qualities made him someone I could always depend on. But my guess is, he's still finding his way in this new position. He'll play by the book."

"So, not much, then."

"We have to come up with another angle."

"I have an idea," Laura said and picked up her pace.

6

I nursed a beer while watching Laura charm the pants off a fellow reporter. The Rainbow Corner, a Red Cross spot set up for servicemen of all stripes, was in a baroque setting that I imagined had been an upscale restaurant and show venue before the war. There were a few diners having a late lunch. Most of the patrons sat at the L-shaped bar, which overlooked a space for dining, dancing, and a stage. I sat at the bottom of the L, while Laura and the AP reporter sat at the longer section.

I'd given Laura a ten-minute lead to make sure the guy didn't think we were together. It was her idea to approach him, which I wasn't too crazy about. He was leaning in, doing his best to be seductive. He'd speak, and she'd chuckle. He was in his fifties and a real ladies' man, lean, handsome, with a suave salt-and-pepper beard and perfectly coiffed hair. If he leaned in any more, I was going to get up and scare him within an inch of his life. I knew Laura could control the situation; it just made me more comfortable fantasizing about dropping the guy down a notch.

I took another sip of my beer and tried to relax. But I forgot to swallow when Laura and the AP reporter stood, and she grabbed her things. And I nearly spit out the beer when they walked out of the club. I shot up from my bar stool and headed for the exit. Laura had one hand behind her, and she waved for me to back off. I slowed my pace but continued. The club had a connecting hallway to a hotel. With me in tow, they crossed the lobby and stopped at the bay of elevators.

Laura glanced to her side and spotted me. I stopped, and she shot me a glare. She reached into her overcoat pocket and pulled out the brass knuckles I'd insisted on giving her. She held them at her side and wiggled them to appease me. The man holding her arm was oblivious to the action. I doubted she'd use them, but the display eased my anxiety all the same.

I returned to the bar and my unfinished beer, but when I got there, a man sat on the stool next to mine, despite there being plenty of empty ones. His back was to me, but there was no mistaking him; it was the man in the gray suit who had followed us on the S-Bahn train. He turned to face the bar once I had settled onto my stool.

I waved down the bartender and pointed at the gray-suited man with my thumb. "This guy needs a beer. It's on me."

"I don't want one," the man said in English with a German accent.

"Sure he does," I said.

The bartender nodded and headed for the stack of mugs.

"What's a kraut doing at an American bar?" I asked, using the slur to get a rouse out of him.

He continued to stare straight ahead, seemingly unfazed. "Your slight has no meaning. I know you were born in Augsburg."

"You seem to know about me, so how about telling me who you are, and why you've been tailing me?"

"I know of your reputation. And that reputation seems to have gone to your head. You are audacious and reckless, but no longer have any authority. If you are looking for trouble, you will find far more than you are prepared to remedy."

"Oh? Enlighten me." I took a sip of my beer.

The bartender returned and placed a mug of beer in front of the stranger.

The stranger slid it over to me. "I am here to warn you. Stop your efforts to help your friend."

"Who sent you to give me this warning?"

"Does it matter? There are several, let's say, parties who have an interest in your friend. None of those interests are good for him or you."

"My guess? You work for Reinhard Gehlen's team, and he wants this problem and my friend to disappear. I imagine a fledgling organization like Gehlen's can't afford to get into hot water with G-2 or the CIC."

"Think what you like," the gray-suited man said and got off his stool and put on his overcoat. "Remember, do not get involved—"

I shot up from my stool and got in his face. "I don't like being threatened. And you just got me more interested. I catch you following me again, and I'll put you in the hospital."

The man tried a defiant grin, but it didn't quite get there. He stepped around me and marched out of the room.

I sat and returned my attention to the rejected beer. Just in case he'd slipped something into it, I pushed the mug aside. After lighting a cigarette, I pondered what had just occurred. It seemed likely that the gray-suited man was from Gehlen's organization. Digging deeper into them went on my priority list. I wouldn't put it past a bunch of ex-Nazis to be ruthless in their efforts to stop an investigation into Forester's plight. Why? I didn't know. But without the protection of army intelligence or the CID, Laura and I were out in the cold.

One thing became clear: Forester's predicament went beyond accusations of murder and treason. Far more was at stake than tracking down a fugitive from justice.

∽

I recognized the sound of Laura's assertive walk before I turned to watch her approach. She sported a satisfied smile, which might have concerned me, except she held up a press badge and wiggled it in victory.

"I take it you're working for the Associated Press, now."

She sat on the stool next to me. "Not really working *for* them, but I've got an assignment. And you're my photographer. We'll need to get you a camera. I'm sure we can pick up one cheap on the black market."

"I assume you didn't have to use the brass knuckles to get that job."

"Nah, he's harmless. Donald and I go way back. He's one of the good ones. He gave me an angle no one else in the press pool wanted, a piece about the life of a typical soldier in Berlin." She held up two badges. "Behold. Military Privilege Cards. They give these to accredited press reporters. Now, we have access to military areas we couldn't get into on our charms. Including shopping at the PX and entering the officers' clubs."

"That's impressive," I said. "Are you going to have time to write that article?"

"I can knock out that piece easily between running into bad guys."

She picked up the stranger's beer, held it up in a salute, and moved it toward her mouth.

I stopped her and gently lifted the mug from her grasp. "That was someone else's. No telling what's in there. Besides, we should get going if we want to get to the AFN radio station by five."

7

Laura pulled her coat tightly across her chest. "Too bad Mike didn't wait until summer to get in a jam."

We'd arrived at the northeast corner of the American Forces Network radio station and were waiting impatiently for Wilson to show up. He was late. I didn't say anything, but I feared he'd decided helping us was too much of a risk. Apparently, the AFN building was some rich guy's mansion before the army took it over to broadcast news and music to the soldiers. The architectural style was ultra-modern, with travertine slabs and spartan surfaces, all at right angles. The street corner we were on overlooked the rear gardens, and across the street was an open field that the locals used for growing food, though what crops could grow in the frigid temperatures, I didn't know.

Two people standing on a corner in the dark and cold could seem suspicious, but we'd encountered no one in the last ten minutes. The main street passing in front of the station had some foot and car traffic, but not here.

"I doubt this is going to lead to anything," Laura said.

I got what she meant: standing out in the cold in the middle of the night just to see a muddy field was hardly worth the effort.

She continued, "I know it's only been twenty-four hours, but aside from a trickle of information and getting press passes, we haven't made much progress."

"Does this mean you've changed your mind?"

"No," she said firmly. "I'm just airing my frustrations."

"I was debating when to tell you. But speaking of progress, while you were up in the AP guy's hotel room, a German sat next to me at the bar and warned me to stop helping Mike or face dire consequences."

She turned to me with a scolding look on her face. "Why didn't you tell me this before?"

I shrugged. "I don't know. Maybe it was because I didn't want you to get spooked."

"You know me better than that. Everyone's convinced Mike is guilty. That makes me want to dig even more. And it means whoever is behind this whole thing is scared enough to make threats. Maybe they didn't cover their tracks as well as they could have." She slugged my arm. "Me, get spooked."

Her reaction made me smile, and I fell in love with her a little more. "Sorry."

"You should be."

Car headlights appeared at the north end of the street and headed toward us. Moments later, a Buick pulled up next to us, Wilson waving for us to get in. I sat in the back, and Laura took the front passenger's seat. She rubbed her hands next to the heater vent.

"I'll let you two warm up a bit before showing you the spot." He pointed to the field on our left. "It's about twenty yards from the fence line."

"What was the victim doing in the middle of a field in the dead of night?" Laura asked. "Isn't there a curfew for Germans?"

Wilson turned in his seat. "Who said the victim was German?" He looked at me. "Did Forester tell you that?"

"Another source," I said. "And before you ask, I'm not going to tell you his name. He's not in any way involved."

Wilson stared at me for a moment, then turned back to the field. "What we can figure from the forensics is that the victim died between midnight and four a.m."

"Back to Laura's question," I said, "do you have any idea what the victim was doing in that field?"

"No. Two sets of shoe prints went in, and one set came out. Best I figure, the murderer chose an isolated spot to execute the victim. Only it wasn't as isolated as he thought."

"Where were the witnesses?" Laura asked.

Wilson pointed toward the rear of the AFN building. "They were in the garden. One of the program directors and a girl he'd picked up at a bar. What they were doing back there in the freezing cold, they wouldn't say."

"Jeez, I wonder," Laura said sarcastically.

I said, "That's quite a distance from the garden to the field to see much of anything on a dark night."

"I'd agree with you, except the program director got a good look at the murderer when he exited the field and got in a car, which was parked about where we are now. That's what? Twenty yards? Close enough to give the sketch artist a solid description. Plus, we found the knife used to cut the man's throat at the scene and got a good print off the handle. That's what led us to Forester."

"A knife? At the crime scene? Mike Forester has years of experience as an intelligence officer. He's not about to leave evidence at a crime scene."

"You'd be surprised what someone, even an experienced officer, will do after killing a man up close like that."

I shook my head. "Not Mike. He was trained by British SOE commandos."

SOE stood for Special Operations Executive, the British clandestine organization with commandos operating behind enemy lines during the war.

"Maybe. But when we went to his billet, we found his shoes. They had mud on them, and the size fit the footprints in the muddy field. And no one has seen him since the night of the murder. If he was innocent, why did he flee?"

"What did the German police say about the victim?" Laura asked.

"That he was an ex-intelligence agent with the Wehrmacht during the war. He spent some time in a British POW camp before being released. As far as they could tell, the victim had been leading a quiet life in Berlin since then."

Laura glanced at me.

Wilson noticed. "What? What have you two heard?"

"Not much except that he could have been a recent intelligence asset for the Army's G-2."

"You heard that from the same source?"

I nodded.

Wilson seemed confused and looked out the windshield. "That adds another angle to motive. Maybe some kind of rivalry, or the victim threatened to expose Forester as a traitor."

"Mike didn't do it," Laura said. "He was framed for the same reason you think was his motive."

"You have any proof of that?" Wilson asked. When Laura and I offered nothing, he said, "I take it from your silence that you don't."

"Arnie," I said, "I've been a cop for a lot of years, and my instincts say Forester is innocent."

"Being a former cop, you know you're going to need more than your instincts to clear Forester."

"What is the program director's name?" I asked.

"It's bad enough I'm giving you as much information as I have. You approach a witness, and it'll come back on me. And that goes for the girl, too."

The headlights of a car lit up the interior of our car as it approached us.

"Are you expecting anyone?" I asked.

We all looked back as the car got closer. It slowed, prompting me to feel for the pistol in my belt. With the lights in my eyes, I could only make out that there were two people in the car, both wearing men's hats. Just before reaching us, it turned right, onto the side street running along the AFN building.

"Probably a radio employee coming for the late shift," Wilson said and turned to face forward. "You two want to check out the spot?"

I said nothing as I watched the red taillights continue up the side street. I wasn't convinced the car's passengers were station employees and could only guess who might have tracked us down this time. My gut told me it was time to leave. "Not worth it."

8

The morning sun hovered low on the horizon and lit up the freezing mist hanging in the air. The droplets froze to the few remaining trees left standing in the Tiergarten park and seeped through the overcoat I'd bought secondhand to blend in better with the crowd. I was meandering through a crowd of black-market vendors and buyers. Laura had split off to look at jewelry someone was selling to put food on the table, a common theme throughout the market. I was in search of a good camera. One that a press photographer would be expected to have at the ready.

The customers were mostly soldiers from each of the four Allied powers, with the Soviets outnumbering the Americans, British, and French, three to one. The burned-out Reichstag loomed in the background. To the right of that stood the blackened and scarred Brandenburg Gate, which delineated the border between the British and Soviet sectors. The main checkpoint between the two drew most of my attention. I wanted to see how the MPs from both armies controlled entries and exits.

An elderly man sporting thick spectacles and wearing a threadbare overcoat stood next to a makeshift booth made by resting a wood plank on two empty oil barrels. He had a handful of cameras balanced on the plank. They were mostly too bulky to be practical or looked like they'd been dropped from a B-17 bomber, but among them was a 35mm Leica. I knew the camera; it took great pictures and was small enough to fit in my pocket.

I pointed it out and asked in German if I might examine it. The vendor eyed me with suspicion, making his bushy eyebrows obscure his pupils. I figured it was because he assumed I was German and would steal it. The locals had little to nothing, let alone enough cash to buy such a luxury item. He gave me a weak nod, and I picked it up. The body and lens looked to be in great shape, and everything worked. I took $25 out of my pocket and showed it to him. That amount of American dollars would buy him a great deal.

To my surprise, he shook his head. "That's not enough?" I asked.

"I can't use that money, sir. It is illegal for Germans to exchange. Either you're not German, or you're a criminal."

"American," I said and put the money back. I had some Reichsmarks, the only currency allowed for Germans, but that currency was close to worthless. Instead, I pulled out three packs of Lucky Strike cigarettes. I'd bought the packs as a bartering tool, and that amount of cigarettes could buy him a couple of weeks' worth of food or fuel.

The man's eyes widened, and he took the packs with care. A big grin crossed his face as he presented me with the camera.

"Do you have any film to go with this?"

"That depends," the vendor said with a sly smile.

I could probably pick up film at one of the PXs, the stores set up for military personnel, but I wanted more than film from the man. I pulled out the half pack I'd been smoking and handed that to him. He grinned and handed over three metal cassettes of 35mm film.

"Is life getting any better for you these days?" I asked as I loaded a roll into the camera.

He scoffed. "Worse. Winter is already upon us, and we have less food and fuel for fires than we did just after the war. Too many refugees." He leaned in and lowered his voice. "Too many damn Russians. Who is to say what might happen if those bastards force the Western armies out of Berlin? And if we have it bad, our comrades in the east have it worse." He shook his head at the dire situation.

"Are you able to visit friends or family on the Soviet side?"

"Until recently, yes. You can still enter easily enough, but getting out is another question. There are so many of my countrymen trying to escape to the west, but the Russians have made it difficult for Germans to leave. My only sister and her husband and young son are trapped over there, and I'm afraid to go see them because I'm not sure I could get out again."

I wished him luck and went to find Laura. She found me first and held a pretzel in each hand. She offered me one, and we wandered across the street. We then headed over to the Soviet War Memorial, a Greek-style stone structure with six minor columns flanking a taller one sporting an oversized Soviet soldier. To me, the whole thing was a way for the Soviets to thumb their collective noses at the Germans and Western allies. That and the massive Soviet flags and two-story-high posters of Stalin plastered on building walls.

We sat on one of the shallow steps and under the shadow of the Brandenburg Gate. From there, we had an up-close view of the main checkpoint. There were close to twenty British soldiers with Jeeps and an armored car gathered around the western side of the checkpoint. Not to be outdone, the Soviet side had more than eighty soldiers supported by machine gun emplacements, several armored cars, and a T-34 tank. Beyond them were men in black overcoats and fur hats watching as people—both Western soldiers and civilians—crossed over to the Soviet side after showing their papers.

I pointed out the men in black. "Probably Soviet intelligence." I tilted my head at a British soldier and a young woman who had just crossed over the Soviet side. "Watch that couple."

As the two headed down the wide boulevard of Unter den Linden and deeper into the Soviet sector, a man in black peeled off from his place against a wall and followed them.

"Crossing isn't going to be much of a problem," Laura said and took a bite out of her pretzel.

"It's the secret police that worry me. Not to mention the herds of Soviet soldiers and a network of informants."

"Even if we evade the secret police and informants, how are we possibly going to find Mike?"

"We're not. If Mike doesn't want to be found, we're not going to do any better than the Soviets."

Laura tore off pieces of her pretzel and threw them to the birds.

"That's breakfast," I said.

"It's stale, and I'm not hungry anymore."

I tried my pretzel and spit it out. "Tastes like paper."

"Maybe it is."

I tossed the entire pretzel to the birds. "Well, I'm hungry. And I'm cold."

Laura mocked me by stroking my shoulder and sticking out her lower lip. "Ah, poor baby. Do you want to go home?"

"Boston? Not a chance. I'm having too much fun."

I choked off a chuckle. The man in the gray suit was standing to the side of the monument steps, smoking a pipe as he pretended to read a newspaper. I was tempted to give him a few knocks before demanding some answers. Instead, I pulled out my camera and pointed it at him.

"Hey, asshole," I yelled.

The man turned to me and realized what I was about to do,

but before he could turn his head away, I snapped his picture. He stared at me and looked as though he was debating whether to attack or back off. He chose the latter and headed for the south end of the park.

I got up from my seat and descended the steps.

Laura followed me. "What are you doing?"

"I'm going to follow *him* for a change."

9

The gray-suited man didn't look back as he wove through the black-market crowds in the park. He moved at a leisurely pace and didn't waver in his southerly direction. I had to assume he was aware we were following him.

"You know he could be leading us into a trap," Laura said.

"Yes, that's possible. Or he's simply taking us on a wild goose chase. Either way, I want him to know that this following game can work both ways."

"This won't solve anything," Laura said as she kept up with me.

"I'll only take it so far. And that's why I want you to hang back."

"That's not going to happen."

I said nothing in return and picked up my pace. North to south, the park was a good five city blocks wide and spread westward seven or eight blocks. We passed the edge of the black market two blocks from the southern edge. A few naked tree trunks, too large to be easily cut for firewood, stood sentinel over the wasteland of mud and bomb craters.

Our quarry's curiosity seemed to get the better of him, and he looked back, then sped up his walk. He had a sixty-yard lead and was closing in on the park's boundary. Beyond lay buildings with burned and scarred facades. I might lose him if he made it to those ruins.

"Damnit, Mason, slow down."

I looked back and saw Laura was having trouble matching my speed. Her left leg lagged slightly behind her right. I slowed while keeping my eye on the man. He crossed the aptly named Tiergarten Strasse that bordered the southern edge of the park and entered a small street narrowed by the piles of rubble pushed up against the foundations of the buildings.

I reached the head of the side street. Only a murky light reached ground level. The gray-suited man walked alone, past the blackened cavities that were once doors and windows. I hesitated to let Laura catch up. By that time, the man was midpoint in the block and was continuing his quick pace.

I had about two minutes before he reached the end of the street. I stopped. "Stay here."

"What are you going to do?" Laura asked in a hushed tone.

I pulled out my .45. "I want some answers."

I hurried ahead, ignoring Laura's angry whispers for me to stop. The man was fifty yards from the end of the street, which ended at a T intersection. A ruined factory sat on the other side. A good place to disappear.

I broke into a trot. My footsteps echoed off the barren walls. I had just enough time to wonder why he hadn't looked back or made a run for it, when someone behind me said in German, "Stop right there," then the click of pistol hammers being cocked. By the sounds, I figured there were two shooters ten feet away and at opposite corners.

"Drop your gun," a man behind me said in English with a German accent.

I squatted, laid my .45 on the ground, then straightened and raised my hands.

In front of me, the gray-suited man stopped, did an about-face, and walked toward me. He had a self-satisfied smile on his face. "I warned you not to interfere."

"You plan on killing an American? That's a big risk. You and your pals must be covering up something pretty damning."

The gray-suited man stopped a few feet from me and kicked my pistol to the side. "If we wanted you dead, it would already be done."

The man was maybe a good intelligence agent, but he was a lousy gunman. He stood too close to me, giving me the opportunity to disarm him. It was the other two I had to worry about. "Another intimidation tactic? Now you've really got me interested."

The man jammed the barrel of his pistol into my stomach. The blow knocked the wind out of me, and the pain forced me to bend over.

"Did you ever think you would die in a graveyard?" the man asked.

I straightened and readied myself for a bullet.

"Put down your weapons!" Laura yelled from behind me.

The gray-suited man looked over my shoulder. The momentary distraction was my chance. I grabbed his wrist and yanked the gun out of his hand. In the same movement, I got behind him, wrapped my arm around his throat, and kicked the back of his knees, forcing him down. I squatted, using the man as a shield, and trained the pistol on his two companions.

I recognized the two shooters. They'd been lurking at the bar the first time the gray-suited man had approached me with his warning. One was a tall, lanky guy with a bird's beak for a nose. His barrel-chested partner sported a pumpkin-sized head, cow eyes, and a permanent five o'clock shadow.

Relief and pride flooded over me. Laura stood just inside the hollowed-out building on my right. She pointed her pistol at the beak-nosed man's head, while positioning herself so the man's body blocked any clear shot the pumpkin-headed companion had for her. She must have crept through the ruins while they were concentrating on me. I wasn't sure she could or would pull the trigger, but the gunman didn't know that, either.

"Throw your weapons over here," I said in German, just to make sure they understood.

With the gray-suited man trapped in my grip and our pistols trained on the two gunsels, they had no other choice but to comply. Pumpkin man threw his pistol on the ground near my feet, but it took Laura jamming the barrel of her gun into the beak-nosed man's temple to persuade him to do the same.

I wagged my gun barrel toward the park. "Get lost."

They looked at the gray-suited man for guidance. I squeezed the man's neck tighter, cutting off his breathing. Reluctantly, he nodded to his men. They hesitated a moment longer, then backed up the street and toward Tiergarten park.

"Keep an eye on them," I said to Laura.

I aimed the pistol at the gray-suited man's head and waited until his companions were out of sight. "Who are you?" I loosened my grip so he could speak.

He fought to get air past his swollen neck. Laura came up and retrieved my .45. She had turned pale, and her hands trembled. She needed something to think about other than how close she'd come to shooting a man.

"Cover him while I go through his pockets," I said.

She glanced nervously behind, then trained her pistol on the gray-suited man. "We should get out of here."

I jerked the man by his collar. "Maybe we should take you with us. Go to a quiet spot and see what we can get out of you."

He said nothing.

I belted the pistol I'd taken from him, reached in his overcoat, and pulled out his wallet. In it was his ration card, one that allowed more food than the regular German. He also had a denazification certificate declaring him exonerated from any suspicion of being a Nazi. Having possession of such a card meant he had unrestricted movement throughout the city, that he could work and obtain certain privileges compared to the rest of the population.

"Ernst Leiter," I said, reading his name off the certificate and putting it in my pocket. "If that's your real name. All the right papers to go anywhere unmolested. Perfect for a spy. You were Wehrmacht intelligence and worked with Reinhard Gehlen during the war, right?"

The man remained silent.

"Aren't you guys supposed to be spying for our side?"

"He murdered one of our own," Leiter said. "Anyone who wants to help him is getting in the way."

I jerked his collar again. "There's more to it than that. What are you and your comrades trying to cover up?" I pulled him backward to put a strain on his knees and spine.

The man grunted through the pain but said nothing.

"Mason," Laura said with urgency in her voice.

She was right; we had little time before a Brit MP patrol or civilians would happen upon us. I was still wanted by the British police and couldn't risk arrest. At least not yet.

I leaned into Leiter's ear. "Tell your boss to back off. I'm not going to stop, and if you persist, I will take you down." I shoved him hard, and he fell face-first onto the pavement.

While Laura kept her pistol on the man, I gathered up the two discarded pistols, removed the magazines, and ejected the rounds from the chambers. I pocketed the magazines and rounds, then threw the two pistols into a ruined building on my right.

"You're a lucky man," I said. "Next time I'll make sure we're someplace quiet."

Laura and I started backing out of the street and away from the park. As we did so, I said to Leiter, "You move, and I won't hesitate to shoot."

Laura turned to walk forward, while I continued to back

away. Once we were a good thirty yards from him, Leiter jumped up, glared at me, then headed in the opposite direction.

Laura bumped my arm, and I turned to face forward. A middle-aged woman and two teenaged girls had turned the corner and were walking towards us as they talked and giggled. I took Laura's arm as if we were out for a stroll. I tipped my hat at them as we passed.

We turned left on the perpendicular street and headed west and away from the Soviet sector. Laura shuddered just once, then took a deep breath to calm herself. "That went well, I think," she said. Her sarcasm wasn't from bitterness or fear, but from a place of determination and defiance.

"That was closer than I'd like," I said. "I won't underestimate them again."

"It seems to me they underestimated us."

"Yes, and that makes them more dangerous," I said and glanced at her to see if that might have spooked her, but her expression remained calm and resolute.

She stopped and turned to me with a scowl on her face. "That was a stupid thing to do. Do you need a brush with death to make you feel alive? If that's the case, then leave me out of it. You got that?"

She was right. "I've got it," I said.

"Good. Don't ever do something like it again."

She made a move to slug my arm, then stopped. She let out a sigh of exasperation and turned and walked away. I paused a moment and thought about what she said. I had better come up with an answer to her question sooner rather than later.

We emerged from the ruins and onto the sprawling Potsdamer Platz. Several streets intersected the area at odd angles and formed a wide square bordered by numerous stately buildings that had been severely damaged by the bombs and artillery. We crossed the plaza and headed for a contingent of American MPs standing by the entrance to the American sector.

Laura said, "I'd like to know why Leiter and his comrades are so afraid we might prove Mike is innocent."

"Well, assuming Forester is innocent—"

"What do you mean 'assuming'?"

"Bad choice of words. *Since* Mike is innocent, the most logical murder suspect is someone from the Gehlen Organization. I'm not sure where the treason charge comes in, but they have to be connected."

"And Mike was getting too close to the truth," Laura said.

I grunted and glanced back to see if Leiter or his goons were following. Aside from a handful of pedestrians and several vendors selling wares laid out on makeshift stands, the plaza was relatively empty. It appeared that Leiter and his buddies had given up. For now.

We got ready to show our papers, but the MPs paid no attention to us, and much to my relief we exited the British sector.

"What's next?" Laura asked.

"Solving the murder should lead us to the traitor's identity."

"The AFN radio station?"

"Let's see what we can get out of that witness," I said and steered us toward the underground U-Bahn train station.

10

It was midafternoon when we arrived at the American Forces Network building. Laura had insisted we stop at the Tempelhof airfield officers' mess for lunch. I had protested, but hunger won out, and now my belly was warm and full, which was something neither of us had enjoyed the last few days. We passed under the awning declaring the American Forces Network and showed our press passes to an uninterested private at the porticoed entrance. We entered the glass doors and encountered another bored private at the reception desk.

We displayed our press passes, and Laura said in her sweetest voice, "We'd like to see the program director."

The private looked up from his comic book. When he saw Laura, he gave her a big grin.

"Private?" Laura said.

He blinked and said, "Which one?"

"Whoever's on duty this afternoon."

"That'd be Lieutenant Hodgson, ma'am." The private stood and leaned over the counter a little too close to Laura. "I bet he'd enjoy your company." His coy smile faded when Laura returned a stony expression. He pointed toward a glass door. "You'll find him in his office. Go past the studio and then three doors down."

I let Laura go first and hesitated at the counter. "At ease, soldier," I said to the private, then followed Laura through the glass door.

A red light above the studio door signaled that someone was on the air. A glass window looked onto the room, where a soldier was monitoring a recorded message. Two soldiers sauntered in the hallway, both of whom ogled Laura, then eyed me with envious looks as we passed. We found the door with "Program Director" stenciled on it in white paint. Laura knocked, and a male voice told us to come in.

We entered a small office clogged with papers. File cabinets dominated one wall, and a large corkboard that was plastered with notes and a weekly chart hung on the opposite.

A young man with blonde hair and rounded facial features sat at a desk buried in papers. He looked like an Ivy-league kid fresh off a college campus, his skin baby fresh, his confidence borne of a privileged life. He gave us a puzzled look. "What's this all about?"

"Lieutenant Hodgson?" Laura asked.

"Yes. Who wants to know?"

His sneering made me dislike him instantly. He was the lord of his little domain, and he intended to wield whatever tidbit of power his position could provide.

Laura flashed him her press pass, and I followed suit.

"We're from the AP press office, and my boss asked me to write a piece about the good work the AFN is doing. We'd like to ask you a few questions and see if we could get a tour of the facility."

He self-consciously patted down his hair, though it did nothing to tame the cowlick at the crown. "Me?" he asked with a growing smile. "Well, sure." He straightened his tie, stood, and went up to the corkboard.

Laura followed him over and acted interested as he ran through his duties, how he single-handedly kept things from falling into chaos. I got out my camera and began clicking a few pictures. He hammed it up for the lens, while Laura peppered him with questions and wrote down his responses in a notepad.

"You mind if I get a few photos of the facility?" I asked him.

He looked annoyed at being interrupted and waved his hand for me to get lost. "Just don't go into the sound booth while the red light is on. And don't disturb anyone. It's hard enough getting them to do their work."

I assured him I wouldn't and exited the room. In the hallway I nodded at a private holding a bundle of recording tapes as he passed, then waited for him to disappear before heading for the back of the building.

After passing a couple of offices with clacking typewriters, I pushed through a heavy door and stepped out onto the rear patio. Outdoor furniture and an iron firepit were arranged on the patio's tiled surface and overlooked a large backyard. A dry water fountain stood in the middle of the garden and was bounded by neglected flower beds.

I looked toward the area where Wilson said the witnesses had claimed to see the killing and Forester get into his car. The scattering of trees obscured the view, so I stepped off the patio and slowly headed for the rear four-foot wall of limestone. To get a clear view of the street and the field across from the property, I had to step all the way up to the northeast corner of the wall. A thin layer of snow lay in patches on the ground. The soft earth would have left some traces of footprints, but I observed none. I shifted right along the wall and searched for shoe prints or any disturbance that would indicate someone's presence. Nothing.

I headed back to the center of the garden and the fountain. A single iron chair sat to one side, its legs imbedded in the mud. There I found quite a few imprints of different size shoes, and what looked like a woman's heeled shoes in the mud and snow. A pack's worth of cigarette butts lay about. Probably a favorite hangout for the staff to do whatever they needed to do in private. I took some photos of the area and the view of the field from that position.

"What are you doing back here?" someone said behind me.

I turned to see a private on the patio with a cigarette in his hand.

I walked up to him. "Just taking in the view."

Another kid, at least to my eye. And this one looked like he should still be in high school, probably fresh off the debate club or the marching band.

He pointed at my camera. "You're supposed to be taking pictures of the inside of the facility, aren't you? There's nothing to see back here."

I took out a cigarette and lit it. "To be honest, I had to get away from your pompous boss."

The private laughed, then caught himself. "The lieutenant told me to fetch you. He wants pictures of the place."

"With him front and center, I bet," I said and took a puff as if biding my time. I glanced back toward the field, then put on my best oh-by-the-way voice. "I was curious. I heard about the murder taking place over there. Must have been scary knowing it happened so close to the building. Were you here that night?"

He hesitated. "I was in my office."

"Who was out here? I heard one of the AFN people witnessed the killing."

"Are you fishing for dirt? 'Cause I could get into a lot of trouble talking about that night."

"I'm just a photographer. I'm not paid to write gossip columns." I took a drag off my cigarette, prompting him to do the same. "What I don't get is why talking about a murder none of you had anything to do with could get you into trouble."

The guy shrugged. "Maybe someone wasn't supposed to be doing something when they saw what happened."

"Lieutenant Hodgson, perhaps."

He started to nod but caught himself. "I didn't say that."

"No, but he's your commanding officer. That's the only guy around who could get you into trouble." I tried a new tack. "Look, forget I asked. I was just curious. I was in the army until a couple of years back and know how it is with officers."

"Were you in combat?" the private asked, intrigued.

I took another puff as if reluctant to say. "Normandy to the Battle of the Bulge. I was a POW for a while."

"Gosh," is all the private could say.

"I don't like talking about it," I said, which was true. I never liked talking about my experiences, but I hoped this time it might get the private on my side. "Just to say that I get it. I've had my share of pain-in-the-ass officers." I gave him a pat on the arm.

The private glanced at the door, then said, "It was the lieutenant, all right. He was back here messing around with some German girl."

I chuckled. "It must have been awfully damn cold out here."

"They were out here because bringing a German girl—any girl—to the station is against regulations. Man, if he caught me or one of the other privates out here doing the same thing, he'd have us thrown in the stockade."

Laura poked her head out and waved for me to come inside. I wished the soldier luck and entered the hallway. She was with the lieutenant, who was bending her ear with the operations at the network. She glanced back at me and rolled her eyes.

The lieutenant glared at me when I came up to them. "What were you doing out there?"

"Just needed some fresh air," I said and thrust my thumb toward the back door. "The garden and fountain. You guys got a nice setup."

He continued to glare at me until signaling for us to follow him. "We can get a look at the studio."

As we walked, I said, "I heard you were near the fountain when that murder happened. You must have gotten an eyeful."

Lieutenant Hodgson stopped and spun toward me. "Who did you hear that from?"

I shrugged, acting innocent. "From a couple of CID guys at a bar. They said you saw the murderer. That must have been spooky."

The lieutenant pursed his lips together as his eyes wandered. "I told them I didn't want to be identified."

"Why?" Laura asked in an innocent tone.

I said, "Because he was out by the fountain with a girl and could get in trouble for going against regulations."

The lieutenant's face turned red. "This interview is over. I want you two out of here this instant." He turned and walked away.

Laura and I pursued him.

"I was out by the fountain, Lieutenant," I said. "You can't clearly see the field or the street from there."

Hodgson waved away the question. "I'm not saying anything."

"Did someone tell you to lie? Or are you afraid of the real killer?"

Hodgson ducked into his office and slammed the door. We stood quietly and listened. We could hear him dialing the phone, then asking the operator to connect him to the CID detachment.

"We certainly hit a nerve," I said.

"Now we're on the CID's naughty list."

11

It was close to seven p.m. and pitch black by the time we made it back to the hotel. We were footsore, cold, and hungry. We'd been forced to walk back because the trains had stopped working due to a power outage. The street was quiet. Even the Tempelhof airfield had fallen silent, probably from the same lack of electricity.

Laura groaned when we saw no lights in the hotel windows. "I was hoping for a warm room."

"During the war, we endured—"

"Oh, shut up," Laura said, obviously exasperated by my war stories. She'd endured wartime hardships too as a war correspondent.

We reached the three steps leading to the entrance, but stopped when the glow from a cigarette revealed a man leaning against the wall. The light illuminated his face for an instant and long enough to see it was Ellenberg.

"You make a habit of lurking in dark doorways?" Laura asked.

Ellenberg launched off the wall and stepped up to us. "Too many times, if you ask me." He tilted his head toward the door. "Can we talk inside?"

"It's probably colder in there than it is out here," I said. Just as I finished my sentence, the lights came on in the building and the surrounding area. "I stand corrected."

"Oh, thank God," Laura said and hurried into the hotel.

We said nothing while I ordered food and several beers from the hotel manager and continued our way up to the room. I got the space heater going, then Laura and I immediately sat on the bed and started attacking the sausages, sauerkraut, and limp green beans.

"Sit down," I said. "Have a beer."

Ellenberg remained standing and glared at us. "You two were supposed to leave town."

"I don't recall it being an order," I said between bites of a sausage.

"You should have at least taken it as a dire warning."

"Is that the second or third time we've been direly warned?" Laura asked offhandedly.

"I've lost track," I said.

Ellenberg tried to show calm, but his apoplexy got the better of him. "Who else threatened you?" he asked, raising his voice.

Laura held up her sausage and wiggled it. "You know, I'm getting tired of these things."

"We'll find something else tomorrow," I said.

"What are you guys playing at?" Ellenberg yelled.

I finally took my gaze away from the sauerkraut and looked at him. "You want information? How about you volunteer some?"

"I gave you what I have."

"I have to disagree. For instance, what's so important that you decided to stand out in the cold and dark to wait for us? You obviously want something badly."

"I'm trying to help Forester," Ellenberg said, "so anything you two have dug up could be important." He stepped over to the desk under the window, grabbed his beer mug, and took a long swig.

He was nervous about something, and more than just disobeying his superiors by helping Forester.

"You're as tense as a high-voltage wire," I said. "What's going on?"

He spun on his heels to face us, causing his beer to slosh in the mug. "I know you were in contact with German agents. What did they want? What did they say?"

"We *suspected* they were Gehlen agents," Laura said, "but you've just confirmed it."

Ellenberg slammed his mug onto the table. "You're avoiding the question."

"They warned us to stay out of the way," Laura said. "I think they want us to leave town worse than you do."

"Ernst Leiter," I said. "Do you know him?"

Ellenberg shook his head. "What about him?"

I held up the German agent's identity paper. "I took this off him when he and two of his buddies tried to ambush me."

I found it interesting that Ellenberg showed little reaction to my ambush remark. He took the paper and scanned the document. His eyes appeared to lock on the man's ID photo, and a flash of recognition crossed his face. He masked it well, but I noticed it nonetheless.

"You *do* know him," I said.

"I told you the CIC has no direct involvement with the Gehlen Organization. That's G-2 territory."

"Then why are agents from the Gehlen Organization so concerned about Mike Forester?" I asked. "Even if the CIC can't officially recognize the organization, you guys all swim in the same pond. And I know the CIC has looked the other way when using ex-Nazis as assets. So, don't try bullshitting me. Even if you don't know his name, you've seen him around." I stood and came up close to him. "Tell us what you know."

"I hate to break it to you, but you're in no position to be calling the shots. In fact, you're in a very tenuous position."

"Is that a threat?"

Ellenberg growled and slipped past me to get some distance. "I'm not your enemy, but you two are making plenty. What makes you think you can fight against army intelligence and German agents?" He put on his hat and headed for the door. "I'm the only friend you've got, and you're treating me as an adversary. Get out of town now, while you still have the chance." He slammed the door as he exited.

"Temperamental, isn't he?" Laura asked.

"He's scared," I said as I belted my pistol. I slid my knife in my boot, pocketed my brass knuckles and the camera, then pulled on my overcoat. "I'm going to find out why."

"You want to follow him? I suppose you plan to run alongside if he has a car."

"I'll figure something out. You should stay here."

Laura jumped up from the bed. "Not on your life." She pulled on her coat and met me at the door.

12

Laura and I exited the hotel and spotted Ellenberg heading west on foot. He was a city block ahead and nearly swallowed by a misty rain that had already soaked us to the bone. We hurried along the sidewalk so as not to lose sight of him.

We kept back far enough to just make out his silhouette. I was prepared to duck into a doorway if Ellenberg checked his surroundings, but he continued at a leisurely pace as if lost in his thoughts. He took a couple of turns, left and right. Whether his meandering path was to check for a tail or to stick to small streets, I didn't know.

This went on for ten minutes until Ellenberg turned left onto a wide boulevard. We did the same a moment later, and the contrast from the blackened ruins was stark. Neon signs glowed in the damp haze, and music spilled out onto the street from the various nightspots. There was a ten p.m. curfew for Germans, and they seemed to be taking advantage of the final forty minutes of freedom for the evening. Groups of couples or packs of excited teenagers were out circulating among the cafés and bars. With soldiers of the four armies and well-dressed civilians adding to the lively atmosphere.

Ellenberg suddenly picked up his pace, obliging us to do the same.

"Do you think he knows we're following him?" Laura asked as we weaved through the crowds and dodged the drunks and umbrellas.

"Could be. Or he doesn't want to be noticed by another intelligence agent prowling the same territory."

A block later, Ellenberg stopped in the middle of the sidewalk, and this time he checked his surroundings. Laura and I took a step to the side and used the throng of people to mask our presence. He entered an establishment that had a pink-and-blue neon sign of a martini glass and, in script lettering, "Conga Lounge."

We waited a few moments by the door to give our quarry a chance to get settled.

Laura looked around at the crowds and lively joints. "It's like we parachuted into another city."

"The economics of booze, darlin'."

We stepped through the door and found ourselves in a mass of people standing in groups with drinks in their hands. Swing music emanated from a jukebox near the bar. Couples danced in the middle of the room and were packed so tight that they had to sway or hop in place.

As we nudged our way deeper into the room, I asked, "When's the last time we danced like that?"

"Christmas 1945. The Officers' Club in Munich."

"Almost two years?" I asked with fake incredulity, and gestured at the tangle of dancers. "How about we give it another try?"

Laura tapped my arm and used her chin to point at an area on the other side of the bar. I followed her gaze and spotted Ellenberg sitting in the back corner at a table just big enough for a couple of mugs of beer. He faced a tall, lean man in his forties, with intense eyes and a jutting chin. They seemed to be in a heated argument, Ellenberg waving his hands and the older guy jabbing his pipe for emphasis.

"Let's go say hi," I said and headed for the corner, ignoring Laura's objections.

I grabbed two unoccupied chairs and brought them over to Ellenberg's table. "Mind if we join you?" I asked.

Laura and I sat before either man could refuse.

Ellenberg shot to his feet. "You were following me. Get out of here if you know what's good for you."

"Sit down, David," the older man said.

Ellenberg continued to glare at us, then he yanked his chair forward and sat.

"Aren't you going to introduce us to your friend?" Laura asked Ellenberg.

Ellenberg clamped his mouth shut, but the older guy focused his deep-set eyes on us. "Bill Hardin. Captain in the CIC. And I know who you two are. Forester's friends."

"You must be his partner," I said. "So much for having your partner's back."

"Not when he's a traitor, I don't."

"If you'd been around Forester as long as I have, you'd know that's not possible."

Hardin took a puff on his pipe. "A man will do foolish things for a lady's love."

"Mike is the most level-headed guy I know," Laura said. "Not to mention steadfastly loyal."

"I've seen plenty of good men crack," Hardin said. "Especially in a place like this. It's not like during the war, when you knew friend from foe. You're always looking over your shoulder. The weapon of choice is poison or a dagger. I'd say it got to Mike, and he looked for solace in the wrong place."

"If you're so sure of Mike's guilt, you must have some solid proof," I said.

"Two witnesses who swear that Fraulein Graf is a double

agent," Hardin said. "And Mike was passing on documents for her."

"Witnesses, meaning Gehlen agents," I said.

Hardin's expression remained neutral, but he glared at Ellenberg like a disappointed parent, which I figured was anger and surprise that the junior CIC agent had let that tidbit slip. He returned his look to me. "Who the witnesses are is none of your business."

"Was one of them Ernst Leiter?" Laura asked.

"You're wasting your time if you think I'm going to confirm knowing anyone named Leiter."

"Mentioning him certainly gave your friend here a scare," I said.

Ellenberg's face turned red, and he blurted out, "I wasn't scared. I was mad at you for trying to interrogate me like a common criminal."

Hardin held up his hand to quiet his companion.

I took Leiter's ID out of my pocket and laid it on the table in front of him. "This is Leiter, though I'm betting he's using that name as an alias. Who is he?"

Hardin betrayed nothing in his expression as he took a few puffs off his pipe, then slid the photo back to me.

I tapped my finger on Leiter's photo and told him that the man was following us and finally tried to ambush us on a deserted street. About how Lieutenant Hodgson at the AFN couldn't have possibly witnessed Forester stabbing someone or getting into his car. "It seems everyone wants us to stop, even to the point of not-so-subtle threats. Our friend is being framed to cover up the real murderers and traitors. We won't stop until we get to the truth."

Like a buddha, Hardin studied Laura and me as he savored his pipe as if at peace with the world. But his eyes betrayed him; I could see the wheels were turning in his mind as he calculated his next move.

Ellenberg fidgeted in his seat until exploding with impatience. "Okay, you two have said your piece. Now, get out of here before I have the MPs drag you out."

Hardin's gaze shifted to Ellenberg. He removed the pipe from his mouth and let out a cloud of smoke. "David, how about you call it a night? We'll continue our conversation in the morning." Ellenberg opened his mouth to speak, but Hardin held up his hand again to stop him. "Now, now. You've been running yourself ragged. I'm sure you'll think clearer after a good night's sleep. I don't want to pull rank on you, but I will. We'll talk in the morning."

Ellenberg exchanged looks with the three of us like choosing which one of us to attack first. Finally, he grabbed his hat, pushed back from the table, and walked away.

Hardin nursed his pipe until Ellenberg disappeared into the crowd. "Ellenberg's an excellent analyst and interrogator, but he's too high-strung for this kind of work."

I had a feeling the analyst's nervousness was caused by something to do with the whole Mike Forester affair, but I kept my mouth shut. I wanted to keep Hardin talking. Laura must have picked up on my thinking and said nothing.

Hardin looked at me. "Mike thought highly of you. And he told me that he'd tried to convince you several times into joining the CIC. So, I'm taking what you've said at face value. While I still feel Mike went off the deep end, what's happened to you so far has got me thinking." He shifted in his seat as if his next thought made him uncomfortable. "If you can come up with more that can support your theory, I'd like to hear it."

"More proof is what you mean," Laura said.

Hardin sat back and peered at us down the bridge of his nose. "If you can get it. But it's not going to be easy."

"Let's start with what you and Forester were investigating when this whole thing blew up in his face," I said.

"You know I can't divulge that information. What I can say is that we were running down rumors of a high-level former Nazi working as a double agent in U.S. intelligence."

"Which agency?" Laura asked.

"The problem, dear madam, is that there are several competing agencies, G-2, our CIC, and then there's the new civilian Central Intelligence Agency sending out covert agents under the benign name of Office of Special Operations. And we're all stepping on each other's toes for the same assets and information."

"That's a long way of saying you don't know," I said.

Hardin shrugged and tapped the burned contents of his pipe into an ashtray.

I tried another line of questioning. "What can you tell us about the agent murdered near the AFN?"

Hardin reloaded fresh tobacco into the bowl. I figured all this fussing was a way to stall for time while he weighed his response. We waited while he used his lighter to get the pipe going again.

"Victor Heissmeyer," Hardin said. "A former captain in the Sicherheitsdienst, the intelligence arm of the SS. He worked in the east, mostly Poland and Russia. He was released from a POW camp about three months ago outside Frankfurt."

"Then he became a Gehlen agent?" Laura asked.

"The CIC is not privy to a list of G-2 assets, so I couldn't say for sure."

Laura leaned forward like I would during an interrogation. "But it makes sense, since he shared the same intelligence territory as Gehlen."

Hardin shrugged and smiled like a Cheshire cat.

"Was Heissmeyer the target of Mike's investigation?" she asked.

"*A* target," Hardin said.

"Where is the Gehlen network headquarters in Berlin?" Laura asked.

Hardin chuckled. He seemed to enjoy being on the other end

of an interrogation. "I don't know, and I wouldn't tell you if I did. Besides, I wouldn't recommend you go poking around there anyway. That would be a quick way to end your stay."

"Is that what happened to Mike?" I asked. "He got too close, and they framed him for murder?"

Hardin looked at me. "You said the witness at AFN couldn't possibly have identified Mike as the killer. But there's still the bloody knife with his fingerprints on the handle. Unfortunately, Mike went out on his own the night of the murder, following a lead, as he put it. I wasn't there. What I suspect, it has something to do with exposing Sigrid Graff as a double agent, and Mike wanted to hush Heissmeyer up."

"Could have been self-defense," I said. "Heissmeyer may have led him out into that field in an ambush."

"You can speculate all you want," Hardin said. "Until you find Mike, or come up with evidence proving the CID wrong, then Mike will continue to be the prime suspect. And it doesn't help his innocence by disappearing." He made a move to stand. "That's all I'm willing to share this evening."

"What about Sigrid Graff? Do you have any information on her?"

"That's G-2 territory. And Mike didn't say anything to me, other than he was infatuated by a German girl."

"Can you put us in touch with someone at G-2?" I asked.

Hardin stood and put on his overcoat. "No." He reached into his pocket and handed me his card with his phone number and address. "I do encourage you to continue. And if something else of value comes up, I'll let you know. In the meantime, I'd like you to keep me informed. I trust you'll do that discreetly."

He said goodnight and left us at the table.

"I wasn't expecting him to be so chatty," Laura said.

"Me neither. But if I was a betting man, I'd say he's giving us just enough information to help him track down Mike."

13

It was midmorning when Laura and I finally left our room and went down to the small lounge at the back of the hotel for some breakfast. We nabbed some trays and shuffled along the buffet tables. The breakfast array was impressive, a bounteous mix of American and German dishes. And fortunately so, as the room was packed with hungry soldiers. Still, the soldiers had nothing on Laura when it came to healthy appetites. She had piled on so much food that her plate was no longer visible.

"You sure you're not pregnant?" I asked her.

"Don't be nasty," she said.

We balanced our plates in one hand and used the other to grab some coffee, then found the last free table near a drafty window. I had a fork of scrambled eggs to my lips when the young woman presiding over the buffet fare came up to me.

She said in decent English, "Sir, you have a phone call."

"Me?" I asked. "Are you sure the caller asked for Mason Collins?"

"Yes, sir."

I turned to Laura.

"Don't look at me," she said. "I left my crystal ball in the room."

I tossed my napkin on the table and stood. "I haven't had my coffee yet."

"If it's Ellenberg, you might want a stiff drink instead."

I wove through the tables and passed through the hallway to the lobby. I picked up the wall phone. "Collins."

"Lieutenant-Colonel McCormick, G-2," a man said on the other end of the phone. "I understand you've been trying to get in touch with me."

I hesitated. I'd called my former commanding officer in G-2, who I'd served under during the war, and asked him to contact G-2 in Berlin on my behalf. I really hadn't expected he would honor my request. And I definitely hadn't expected to wind up speaking to the commander of the Berlin detachment.

"Are you there, Collins?"

"Yes, sir. I appreciate you—"

"I normally don't talk to civilians," the colonel said, interrupting me. "But your records show you were an exemplary officer in G-2, a combat veteran, and a prisoner of war."

"Thank you, sir. I would like to ask you a few questions, if that's possible."

"About you helping Major Forester?" McCormick said, more as an accusation than a question. Before I could answer, he said, "Meet me at Recreational Field Four on Siemensstrasse at eleven hundred hours."

He hung up before I could respond. I returned the receiver to the cradle and stood there for a moment, unsettled that G-2 was aware I was trying to help Forester buck a treason charge and, most disturbing of all, knew exactly where we were staying.

Laura was where I'd left her, downing coffee and consuming a prodigious plate of cheese, eggs, and apple pancakes. Neither one of us had eaten much since lunch the day before, and she was attacking the food with such intensity that she didn't notice me until I sat down.

"Is that your second helping?" I asked.

"What if it is?" she asked with a mouthful.

I stole one of the apple pancakes off her plate. She nearly got me with her fork, but I was too quick. I chewed it quickly and downed it with my lukewarm coffee.

"So?" Laura asked. "Was that Ellenberg?"

"A lieutenant-colonel at G-2."

Laura stopped chewing and looked at me in alarm. "What does he want?"

"It's more what I want from him. He heard about me asking how to contact someone in authority at G-2. It seems he took it upon himself to reach out to me."

"Does half of Berlin know we're staying here?"

"Seems so," I said. "He wants to meet at eleven."

Laura pushed her plate containing the rest of her food over to me. "I lost my appetite. Finish it, and we'll go."

"First, we find another hotel," I said with a forkful of egg.

"Why? I was just getting used to this dive."

"Too many people know where we're staying. I was up most of the night keeping watch. And I noticed you were pretty restless. More than you have been since we got here."

She let out a noncommittal grunt.

I sopped up the last of the eggs with a piece of bread and stuffed it in my mouth. "The bellhop recommended a hotel that's not too far from here. Off Potsdamer Strasse. He warned me that it's near the red-light district and is busy with nightclubs, but the hotel is livable."

Laura stood. "Today is off to a lousy start."

"And the day's just started."

∼

We packed our suitcases and hoofed it over to the hotel the bellhop had recommended. It turned out to be a charming place that had survived the Allied bombing raids. There was a handful of upper-echelon military and civilian administrators hanging around the hotel lobby. We were close to the Allied Control Authority building, where high-level brass and military government officials from all four Allied armies met to argue over the general administration of the city. Of course, it might also have had something to do with the hotel's proximity to the red-light district.

After checking in and dumping our things in the room, we took the same lurching S-Bahn train as we did to see Wilson at the CID. This time we walked north once debarking at the same station and more or less followed that direction until coming to a recreational field reserved for U.S. personnel. There was a set of wooden bleachers in the center overlooking a muddy field with football goalposts at either end. A baker's dozen of young soldiers in football uniforms were doing passing drills. A tall man stood on the sideline and held an umbrella while shouting at the players. Although an unadorned bomber jacket covered his uniform, he still wore his officer's service cap, lest no one mistake him for a lowly enlisted man.

"Does he want to talk or have us try out for the team?" Laura asked with anger in her voice.

We'd walked a good forty-five minutes in a cold misty rain to get there. The wet had seeped through my worn-out shoes, and my feet were numb. We headed for the bleachers and sat on the top row. McCormick glanced back at us, then continued to tell the players to get the lead out of their asses.

Laura shook the rain off her umbrella and closed it. "His office would have been dryer."

"He knows we want to talk about Forester," I said. "My bet is, he chose this place to be away from prying eyes."

"That could be good or bad."

"My thinking exactly."

The tall man called for his players to take five. He then turned and started climbing the bleachers. He looked to be in his mid-forties and negotiated the rows of seats like a track star. With his lean physique and chiseled features, he could have doubled for Errol Flynn.

He gave us a politician's smile as he shook our hands.

"Thanks for taking time away from your rigorous schedule," I said.

He kept on smiling, though I could tell my sarcasm hadn't gone unnoticed. "This is the way I relax. I enjoy motivating people to do their best, even if it involves some pain."

We exchanged stares for a moment. Laura cleared her throat to break up the standoff.

"I wanted to meet you," McCormick said. "Especially after everything you went through as a former intelligence officer during the war. I had hoped to see some action, but I was chained to a desk in Washington for most of the fighting."

"Trust me, it's overrated," I said.

McCormick eyeballed Laura. "And you, young lady, had your share of the war if I'm not mistaken."

Laura bristled at being called a young lady, but she said nothing and gave him a half smile.

The colonel sat with an exaggerated sigh. "There are stories going around about your activities in Berlin."

"None of them good, I expect," I said.

He let out a fake chuckle and patted my shoulder. His patronizing tone was already getting on my nerves.

"No, not really," he said. "But I admire people who are that loyal to a friend. Even if he is a murderer and a traitor."

"We're here to prove both accusations are wrong," Laura said.

"Okay," the colonel said dismissively. "How about we start with the murder? Aside from the evidence he knifed Heissmeyer, when Heissmeyer was picked up by the German police a week earlier on suspicion of murder, Major Forester took it upon himself to get the charges dropped. Kind of odd, don't you think?"

That was news to me, and I felt like someone had slugged me in the gut.

"I see this information surprises you," McCormick said.

"Did he give a reason?" Laura asked.

"Forester told the German police that Heissmeyer was working for him. That it was vital the German be released for security reasons. What those reasons were, I don't know."

"It's strange that Major Forester is being accused of murdering the very man he had released," I said.

"He couldn't very well murder the man in a German jail," the colonel said.

"Come on, Colonel, he's smart enough to know that the release would be on the record. It doesn't fit."

McCormick flashed another condescending smile. "We'll be sure to ask him why when we catch him."

The man's attitude had me weighing the merits of telling him to stick it where the sun don't shine and walking away. Laura must have detected my mood and diffused it by asking, "Who was Heissmeyer's alleged victim?"

"Another German. Otto Gumbel. A middle-aged gentleman who'd escaped from East Berlin with his wife the week prior. We know that because he registered with the Red Cross to obtain food and shelter. A metal worker, if I remember. We checked his background the best we could; the Soviet authorities are not very forthcoming on information on *any* matter, let alone illegal emigres. Forester interviewed him, then let him go. Heissmeyer murders Gumbel, and Forester murders Heissmeyer. That tells me something was going on between them."

"Would it be possible to question Gumbel's wife?" Laura asked.

McCormick shook his head. "She disappeared. Presumably farther west."

Laura and I looked at each other. I wanted to make sense of this information, but decided to wait until we were alone. McCormick betrayed nothing of what he was thinking until a brief smile crossed his face.

"Intriguing set of circumstances, isn't it?" McCormick said, smiling, clearly enjoying himself.

"I'll remember to chuckle after I clear my friend's name." I said that a little too forcefully, and Laura nudged me with her elbow.

She was right to do so; that last retort was a feeble attempt of taking back control of the interview. Hardin had said Forester was investigating Heissmeyer, which would make it more likely he was guilty. Things were adding up in the wrong direction. I tried another approach. "Another source told us that Victor Heissmeyer was a former captain in the intelligence arm of the SS. That he worked in Poland and Russia. We suspect he was part of the Gehlen Organization."

McCormick's smile faded. He took a moment to respond. "The what organization?"

I turned to Laura and pointed a thumb at the colonel. "This guy's playing cute while German agents working for G-2 go around trying to kill us."

Laura jammed her elbow in my ribs.

McCormick shot to his feet and glared down at us. "I didn't ask you here to be insulted. And may I remind you that you're only tolerated in Berlin by the good graces of the U.S. Army."

"So you can use us to flush out Forester for you," I said.

Laura pushed me back to talk around me. "Sir, we're only trying to get at the truth. If Major Forester is guilty of treason, we won't hesitate to see he's brought to justice. But it is a fact that German ex-intelligence agents are rumored to be working for G-2. Maybe it's been hushed up, I don't know, but they're trying to stop us by any means necessary." She shoved her hand in my coat pocket and pulled out the photo of Leiter. She held it up for McCormick. "This man and his cronies have followed us and harassed us, warning us to stop investigating Forester or face the consequences."

McCormick took the photograph from Laura and examined it.

Laura continued. "Now, why would these Germans be so concerned about what we find if it poses no threat to them? Major Forester was chasing down rumors of a high-level former Nazi working as a double agent in U.S. intelligence. Maybe I'm mistaken, but I think that should concern you and the rest of G-2."

McCormick eyeballed Laura, then turned his attention back to the photo. "I've seen this fellow around."

"Ernst Leiter," Mason said.

"Yeah, that's it. But I have no direct knowledge of him or of this Gehlen Organization. We're a small detachment here. Headquarters in Frankfurt might have made decisions I'm not privy to." He handed the photo back to Laura. "Look, I can't give you details of the espionage charges for security reasons. This is top-secret stuff. All I can say is that we suspect very important documents have been exchanging hands. The biggest concern right now is that anytime we put an asset in the east, they wind up missing or dead. You'll have to take it at that." He let out a long sigh and gazed at the horizon. "The only other thing I can share with you is that Leiter was arrested by the German police for assault a couple of weeks ago. We immediately received orders from Frankfurt to have him released from custody. No explanations." He looked at us with a grim expression as if conveying something he shouldn't. "It may be nothing, but you may want to go by the Rote Lantern on Rothenberg Strasse. He and two others were arrested at that bar."

The football players began to reassemble on the field. "I've got to get back to my boys," he said. He took a few steps down, stopped, and turned back to us. "I promise you I will look into this. If I hear anything, I'll be in touch." He climbed off the bleachers and stepped out onto the field.

McCormick barked commands at his men, while Laura and I headed for the street.

"It takes a pro to smile while lying through his teeth," I said. "He's got an agenda, and I'd like to know what it is."

We stepped onto the street.

"I need a drink," I said.

"Rote Lantern?"

"Why, Miss McKinnon, you read my mind."

14

It was after four p.m. by the time we reached Rothenburg Strasse. The temperature had dropped close to freezing and brought in a fog that was transforming into snow. We were near to the U.S. military government offices and, interestingly enough, a thirty-minute walk to the AFN building.

"Four hours of walking in this cold is for the birds," Laura said. "We have got to get a car. And I don't mean stealing one."

I said nothing. Getting one legitimately would be tough; stealing was my best option. The problem there was that aside from the cars used by the military and military government officials, there weren't very many private ones on the road from which to choose. An idea came to me about where to get one, and I decided I'd work on that once we'd finished scoping out the bar.

The buildings on this section of the street were severely damaged though still standing. I stopped us fifty yards from the Rote Lantern and stood in front of a secondhand store. The bar was on the ground floor of a burned-out brick building. It didn't look very stable to me, but it was perfect for an out-of-the-way place for riffraff—and clandestine intelligence operatives—to meet and scheme. I scanned the area for a lookout, and I didn't want to run into one of our ambushers until I was ready. A young couple lingered near the bar's doors, talking and smoking. They were just teenagers, but I didn't want to take any chances.

"There's got to be a rear entrance," I said.

Laura motioned to an area behind us. "I saw a small alley a half block back."

We retraced our steps until we found the alley and used it to reach a courtyard formed by the rear facades of several buildings. Piles of rubble, some towering over our heads, took up most of the space. A maze of paths had been cleared for access to the various buildings. The rear entrance to the Rote Lantern was in the middle of the block that ran along Rothenburg.

I tried the doorknob. It was unlocked. I pulled out my .45 and put one in the chamber. Laura did the same with the Tokarev and slipped it into her overcoat pocket. Her face was tight from nervousness, though her eyes expressed determination.

"Ready?" I asked.

She nodded, and we entered a dark, narrow hallway. It was crammed with beer barrels and empty crates and smelled of a mix of sauerkraut, spilled beer, and urine. Up ahead and to the right of the door, someone was clanking pots. I peeked around the doorway into the kitchen. A woman had her back to us, and we slipped past. On our left was a broom closet, then the open door to the toilet. By the noxious cloud emanating from the closet-sized space, it hadn't been cleaned since the end of the war.

At the end of the hallway, we came up to a swinging door. I opened it slowly, and we entered the main room. It was almost as dark as the hallway. The walls of aged mahogany absorbed any light the wall sconces might offer. Two dozen square tables populated the large space, with booths around the perimeter. Only a handful of customers were scattered among them. No one appeared to be Leiter or the other two ambushers. And no one seemed to pay us any mind. The bartender sat on a high stool and listened to a radio broadcast in German about the U.S. loosening restrictions on German industry and what the Soviets might do in retaliation.

He looked up at us and didn't object to us coming in the back way. I chose a booth two down from the back hallway, and we sat side by side with a good view of the front door and room. The only light illuminating our table was a small wall sconce just above our heads. I reached up and unscrewed the bulb, putting us in shadow.

"Who said spying couldn't be romantic?" Laura said.

I signaled for the bartender, and he sauntered over to the booth. He was a big man with the face of an old boxer, a push-broom-sized mustache, and black wiry hair.

"The bulb must be blown," he said in German. "You two want me to change it?"

"No need to bother," I said.

He altered his gaze between the two of us. "No smooching. This is a respectable place."

"We're here for the beer. And if you have something to eat, we'll have that, too."

"Potato soup."

"We'll take some."

The bartender headed for the kitchen, leaving us alone. An elderly man entered through the front door with his cane in the lead. He took two steps in and stopped. He looked straight at us as if our unfamiliar faces aroused his suspicion. A moment later, he doddered over to a table near the cast-iron wood-burning stove.

"We're too visible from the front door," Laura said. "Move to the other side."

"We won't see anything from there."

She nudged me to move. "Trust me."

We shifted over to the seats with our backs to the entrance. Laura rifled through her purse and pulled out a small hand mirror. She positioned it so that we had a partial view of the room, and with a slight shift in the mirror's position, we could see the front door.

"Now we're in business," I said.

She put the mirror facedown when the bartender came back with two bowls of the chunky mustard-colored soup. He returned to the bar, and we waited patiently while he poured out two beers from the tap and came back with the mugs. We thanked him, and he went back to his seat in front of the radio.

Laura took a few spoonfuls of her soup. I asked with my eyes if it was any good. She made a face that said it wasn't too bad. "It's hot and I'm hungry." She put her spoon down and looked at me. "I thought coming here was a good idea. Now I'm not so sure."

I downed a swig of beer. "Sometimes you've got to improvise."

"That's another way of saying you're not sure, either."

I shrugged. "You never know when it might pay off. But I worry I put you in danger by coming here without a plan."

She leaned into me and hissed. "I'm not your feeble sidekick. I can take care of myself."

"It's not that. I have a history of kicking a hornet's nest just to see what comes out. It's gotten me into trouble. Plenty. I nearly got Wolski killed in Munich. Abrams in Garmisch. And maybe if I'd left well enough alone, that bomb in Jerusalem wouldn't have put you in the hospital. I put people in danger without thinking about it."

"Stop second-guessing yourself. And stop whining."

She was right, but I still got mad. "You want to know the truth? Ever since we got here, I thought it was a bad idea. I'd never forgive myself if something happened to you. That's selfish, I know, but that's how it is. I want you to rethink about going home. This case went from helping a friend to stepping into a cesspool of crooks and killers. Neither one of us signed up for this."

"You can go back, if you want," Laura said in a flat tone. "I won't stop you."

She'd managed to put me in my place. That settled, we nursed our beers for another hour while we watched a few customers come and go. To cut the tedium, we ordered and consumed a second bowl of the soup, which was clotting my intestines.

Just as I thought this expedition was a waste of time, the front door opened, letting in a blast of frigid air. Laura seized the mirror and angled it to give us a view of the entrance. A single man entered and pulled off his homburg hat. Though the lighting was dim, we recognized the man's lanky frame and a nose like the beak of a predatory bird.

"One of our ambushers," Laura said in a hushed tone.

The man studied the room, then headed for a booth on the opposite side. Two people saw him coming and hurriedly vacated the booth just before the man got there. He sat on the bench facing the door and out of our line of sight. This odd ritual continued when the bartender dispensed a beer without asking and carried it over to the man. They exchanged a few words, then the bartender wasted no time in returning to the radio and tuning it to a station playing classical music. He then filled three more mugs of beer and brought them over to the booth.

As the bartender returned to his place behind the bar, the man leaned forward and scanned the room. Laura and I leaned back against the wood partition to block his view. We looked at each other. I didn't know why I chose that moment to kiss her, but I did, and we stayed that way until another wave of cold air announced that someone else had entered the bar. Laura picked up the mirror, and we watched three men walk over to the same booth. Laura stopped breathing, and I felt a hot surge of adrenaline course through me.

15

Leiter and the second ambusher, the one with a pumpkin for a head, took the bench across from the first ambusher. We didn't recognize the third companion. He walked as if on a military parade ground, his chin up, his chest extended. His stature was medium, his body trim, somewhere in his forties. Just before sitting, he tucked his hat under his arm, revealing a high forehead and receding black hair that had a touch of gray at the temples. Despite his age, he still had choir-boyish looks that contrasted with his dead eyes. I imagined him smiling while sending his victims to the grave. The others seemed to defer to him, making plenty of room on the bench for him to sit.

"I've seen that man in a photo somewhere," I said. "I just can't place it."

"Try to take his picture," Laura said.

"It's too dark in here."

"It's worth a shot. Do a long exposure."

When I looked at her with a quizzical expression, she reached into my backpack and pulled out the camera. She fiddled with the dials like a pro, set it on the table, and aimed it in Leiter's and his buddies' direction. She pushed the button, and the shutter clicked. After a long moment, it snapped closed.

"I picked up some photography tricks while in the field," she said. "A long shutter speed to help with the bad lighting. If they move too much, it'll be fuzzy. We might get something usable."

Laura tried a couple of different shutter speeds while I kept an eye on the bartender to see if he noticed what we were doing. No doubt he was loyal to the men in the booth. Whether they paid him well or he was afraid of them, I didn't know.

Laura got off two more shots and was about to try a fourth when the door opened again. I slid the camera out of view. Laura picked up the mirror and trained it toward the front of the room.

We both stiffened when we saw the soft-featured young man hesitating at the door. It was Lieutenant Hodgson from the AFN radio station.

"What's he doing here?" Laura whispered.

"Playing a very dangerous game."

Hodgson spied Leiter's group and moved nervously toward them. He put on an air of confidence as he approached, though it only made him look more vulnerable to the pack of wolves leering at him from the booth.

No one from Leiter's group spoke. Hodgson stood next to the table and zeroed in on Leiter. I was hoping we could overhear the conversation but, as if reading my mind, the bartender raised the volume of the music. Hodgson said something, and Leiter responded. Then the young lieutenant pulled a folded piece of paper out of his overcoat and laid it on the table next to Leiter's gray-haired companion. Hodgson then did an about-face and scurried for the exit like he couldn't get out of there fast enough.

Leiter pocketed the folded paper, and the group went back to drinking beer and chatting in low tones. The bartender lowered the music and glanced at us just as Laura set the mirror down on the table. He regarded us with suspicion but betrayed nothing of what he was thinking.

"Well, well, well," Laura said. "What do you think our little lieutenant is doing with that charming cabal?"

I was about to suggest that we leave and try to pick up Hodgson's trail, but the pumpkin-headed thug stood up and headed our way.

"The toilet," I said. "He's going to walk right by us."

I slipped the .45 out of my belt and hid it under the table. Laura stashed the mirror and camera in her purse, then removed the Tokarev. The man turned left to go around the bar and passed us without glancing our way. In relief, I let out the breath I was holding. But it was premature. The man halted. When he reached into his jacket, Laura and I raised our weapons. He twirled as he brought his pistol up. He saw our weapons, and his arm froze halfway.

"A wise decision," I said in German. "Now, I want you to toss your pistol into the booth beside you."

The man complied, but the action alerted the rest of the group. The gray-haired man remained where he was, but Leiter and his second gunman rose from their seats and moved toward us. While Laura kept her pistol aimed at pumpkin man, I turned and pointed mine at Leiter and his beak-nosed companion.

"That's far enough," I said in German to make sure they understood me. When they stopped, I said, "Keep your hands where I can see them."

They extended their arms from their hips. I glanced at the bartender to see if he intended to make trouble, but he stood at the far corner of the bar with his back against the wall.

"You've made a very grave mistake, Herr Collins," Leiter said. I must have betrayed my surprise, as he smiled and said, "Yes, I know your name. And Miss McKinnon's. And it's only a matter of time before we find where you're hiding."

I wagged my pistol at the pumpkin-headed man. "Get over and join the others."

The man didn't move until Leiter said, "Dietrich." As pumpkin head moved next to the others, Laura maintained her aim at the man's chest.

"Now what?" Leiter said. "Are you going to shoot us?"

I slid out of the booth and made room for Laura to do the same. I gestured for Laura to head for the back hallway.

I backed up while keeping my eyes and my .45 trained on the group. "I wouldn't advise anyone to try coming after us."

Leiter leered at me as I backed through the swinging doors. "We'll see you again."

"Pray you don't," I said and let the doors swing closed.

Laura covered me at the rear door while I continued down the hall in reverse. She opened the door and waited.

"Ready?" I asked her.

"Ready."

I spun around, took Laura's arm, and we burst through the door. We ran along one of the paths between the piles of rubble. Night had fallen, and the mix of snow and fog had become thicker. She steered for the alley, but I pulled her in another direction.

"They'll be waiting for us on the street," I said and pointed in the opposite direction. "This way."

We raced for the center of the courtyard to try for the rear entrance to a building on the opposite side of the courtyard. But when the door to the Rote Lantern's rear exit burst open, we ducked behind one of the tallest piles of shattered concrete and wood. At least two pairs of footsteps crunched on the path. I peeked through a gap in the rubble. I couldn't see the bar's rear entrance, but had a clear view of two diverging paths that disappeared into the murky darkness.

By the sound of the footsteps, I could tell the two had split up. I figured the other members of the group waited on the street. I glanced at Laura. She was coiled tight but vigilant for movement in the opposite direction.

Footsteps grew louder. I looked through the gap. On the path that led straight to us, the silhouette of a man stood motionless thirty feet away as if listening, his pistol pointed straight ahead. The mist and darkness obscured his face.

I tried to track the other agent's footsteps, but either he had headed for the street or was quietly stalking in another section of the courtyard.

The man in my line of sight stiffened and turned his head toward me as if he'd detected us somehow. He swung his body into a firing position. I sucked in my breath. He was aiming straight at me.

He took two steps forward, and I got ready to return fire. Suddenly, he froze and looked to his left. I jumped when a pistol fired twice and lit up the surrounding mist. The flashes illuminated the man's face for a heartbeat, but all I could see clearly was his eyes wide in shock. He tumbled to the ground.

Laura let out a chirp of surprise. She shifted over to stand at my back and tried to peer through the same opening. Both of us had stopped breathing. Someone unseen was out there in the darkness. A moment later, the faint sound of rushing footsteps echoed in the courtyard, then they faded, leaving us in silence.

"Did you see what happened?" Laura whispered.

I shook my head while still listening intently.

From the street, tires screeched, men shouted.

I sensed we were alone in the courtyard and ventured out from our hiding place. Laura followed right behind me. We crept forward to where I'd last seen the man fall and found him lying on his side with his back to us.

I squatted and turned the body on its back. Even in the dim light, I could see that it was Leiter. A dark pool of blood stained his suit jacket, and more seeped from a wound in his temple.

"Did you see the shooter?" Laura asked in a hushed tone.

"He was hidden behind another pile of rubble."

"Damnit, what's going on?" she asked with exasperation and fear in her voice.

Even if I could have answered that question, I didn't have a chance to respond; four American MPs rushed up to us with their guns out.

16

To pass the time, I tried to count the number of days I'd spent in jail cells against my time as a cop. The ratio between the two was closer than I liked. Here I was again, behind bars. The only positive thing to come out of it was that I'd finally made it inside the 16th Constabulary building.

Laura and I had been separated when the MPs arrested us outside the Rote Lantern bar. She was somewhere in the building, probably in a secure room since the jail cells were populated by men—soldiers and a few American civilian administrators. My cellmate, a surly corporal, was in for assault and drug possession. He'd tried to pick a fight with me, but that hadn't ended up well for him, and now he sulked in a corner. I stood at the front, leaning against the bars of the door.

A couple of junior investigators had already interviewed me. They drilled me about how I happened to be standing over a dead man with a gun in my hand. That had gone on for three hours, them trying to make me sweat and me answering truthfully.

My ruminations were interrupted when the main door opened, and two MPs marched up the aisle. They stopped at the cell door. One of them ordered me back up to the bars. He extended his arms through the bars and handcuffed me, while the other guard unlocked the door.

They walked me out of the holding cells, across a modest area with desks, now vacant. We proceeded out into a courtyard, where Jeeps and motorcycles were parked in neat rows, then entered another wing of the building complex and across a lobby. I got stares from some of the other MPs. They acted more curious than hostile. I figured the word must have gotten around that I'd been a chief investigator for the CID and was now a detainee.

The MPs pushed me through the open door of a small room and deposited me in a chair. To my relief, it turned out to be Wilson's office. Aside from mine and another chair, the desk and a filing cabinet were the only things in the room. Wilson kept his eyes on his typewriter as he filled out a form.

"Close the door," Wilson said to the MPs as they left. He leaned forward and squinted at the form. "I swear they want us to go blind filling out this damn paperwork."

"I asked to see you hours ago," I said.

"I was busy. And a suspected murderer doesn't get to dictate terms."

"Oh, come on, Arnie. I'm sure you got Laura's version of what happened, and it jibes with my account. And you'll have to let us go once it's determined that the weapon used to shoot Leiter wasn't mine. I'm sure that's already happened. Now you don't know what to do with us."

Wilson finally turned away from his typewriter. "The chief investigator wants me to kick you out of the country. But I stuck up for you, thinking you might help advance the investigation."

"Hand you Forester on a silver platter, you mean."

Wilson ignored the remark. "And then you get involved in a shoot-out, with one German citizen getting murdered, not to mention harassing Lieutenant Hodgson at the AFN. Under false pretenses, no less. What I told you about the investigation didn't include permission to interrogate a witness."

"Neither Hodgson nor the German girl could have witnessed Forester at the scene, and I can prove it."

Wilson lowered his head in exasperation.

I continued, "He and the girl were frolicking by the fountain in the middle of the rear garden. From where they were standing, they couldn't have seen what happened in the field. Or Mike getting into a car and driving away any more than if they were inside the building. Who put Hodgson up to that? You?"

Wilson raised his head. His anger had changed to weary introspection. "I told you that isn't my case. It's the chief investigator's. But I did hear the autopsy came back on Heissmeyer. The coroner said the knife wounds don't match the weapon we found with Forester's fingerprints on it."

"You know that the German police picked up Heissmeyer on suspicion of murder a few weeks before his death, right? And Mike Forester authorized his release?"

Wilson cursed under his breath and fell back in his chair.

"I guess you didn't," I said. "Your chief is holding out on you. And here's something else to brighten your day. While we were at that bar, Hodgson came into the Rote Lantern and handed a folded piece of paper or papers to the man who was subsequently murdered."

Wilson looked confused, so I explained what Laura and I had learned about the network of former Nazi intelligence agents working for the U.S. About how one of them, Ernst Leiter, threatened our safety if we didn't stop searching for Forester. And when we didn't comply, he and two of his cronies tried to ambush us. Based on a tip—I wasn't going to mention it came from McCormick at G-2—we went to the Rote Lantern to see what the agents might be up to, and that was when Hodgson showed up.

Wilson waved his hands. "I don't want to hear about Hodgson

and ex-Nazi agents. That has nothing to do with Heissmeyer's murder." He said it with little conviction behind it. "In any case, I'm not the lead investigator. My hard-ass boss is."

"Run it past him. If he's any kind of competent investigator, he'll take it under consideration." I touched each finger as I made a point. "Mike Forester was working with Heissmeyer, who was suspected of murder, then Heissmeyer gets bumped off. Mike is framed for it by a witness who's in cahoots with German agents. Agents who, in turn, will do just about anything to stop Laura and me from getting any deeper."

Wilson fell silent, but I could tell his wheels were turning. He picked up a pencil and started tapping it on the desk. Finally, he shook his head. "Something stinks. The chief seems hell-bent on pinning the murder rap on Forester."

"Who's the chief?"

"Harry Cuthbert. Chief warrant officer. The same rank you had in Munich. Why?"

I chuckled, though there was bitterness behind it. "I heard about him through the grapevine. Story was, he was a junior investigator in Frankfurt when I was in Munich, and he was charged for shaking down Germans and selling exoneration documents to ex-Nazi officials for a high price. They busted him down to an MP but, somehow, he'd wiggled out of the charges."

Wilson tossed the pencil onto a pile of paperwork. "Yeah, I heard the same thing. Since the army has sent most of the experienced investigators back to the States, they reinstated his rank and sent him to Berlin." He sighed and leaned in. "Cuthbert wanted me to give you a rough time, then put you and Laura on the next plane out of here." He glanced at the door, then said in a quiet voice, "I'm not going to do that, but I need you to keep a low profile. Get arrested again, and I won't have a choice."

"Does that mean you're going to help?" I asked.

"I figured getting you out of here is help enough."

He tried to be the tough guy, but I could tell he was plenty rattled. When I worked with him, he preferred walking the straight and narrow. Defying his boss was a daunting move.

"Any leads on who killed Leiter?" I asked.

Wilson stared at his paperwork as he said, "Nope. And we printed the negatives from your camera. Those photos didn't help either. Mostly dark and fuzzy. We're keeping the originals, but you can have copies."

He looked conflicted enough to make me think he saw something in the photos.

I figured he needed just a nudge to give a little more. "Look, Arnie, I get you're stepping out on a limb, and I appreciate it. But I could use a lead. Something. Anything."

Wilson picked up the pencil and wrote something on a small notepad. He pulled the paper off and handed it to me. On it was a name and address. "That's Sigrid Graf's roommate. We think she was the last one to see Forester and Graf. We questioned her pretty hard, but she didn't give up much. Maybe you'll have better luck."

I pocketed the paper and thanked him. He called the guard waiting outside the door and told him to release us and return our belongings, including our weapons and camera. He pushed a manila envelope over to me. "There are copies of all the photos you guys took."

I thanked him for the envelope and stood.

Wilson said, "Remember, you end up in here again, and there's nothing I can do about it." He shook my hand. "I might as well wish you luck, 'cause whatever luck you had at the start has definitely run out."

17

The blue of the dawn sky glowed outside our window. Neither of us had slept much. Rather than pass the time staring at the ceiling waiting for the day to start, Laura had rented the hotel manager's typewriter to work on the article she'd promised her Associated Press buddy. It was good watching her fingers fly over the keys. She hadn't written a thing since the bomb in Jerusalem. The article's subject was banal, but she still attacked it with gusto.

The photographs Laura and I had taken at the Rote Lantern were laid out on the bed, and I scanned them while the typewriter clacked in the background.

The German man who sold me the camera must have forgotten he'd left a half-exposed roll inside, because there were a handful of photographs of him with a woman his age. They were smiling as they stood arm in arm next to a car parked on a dirt road. Then others of them picnicking under a blooming apple tree. Most of the photos we'd attempted to take at the bar were too dark or blurry, but three were salvageable. They captured the entire booth, with the two Germans sitting close to the wall falling off into darkness, but there was just enough detail in each to recognize Leiter and the mysterious dead-eyed man. I chose the best of the three and walked over to the dresser and taped it to the mirror among the notes I'd made for each of the players in the mind-numbing game of who's who. It helped connect some of the dots, but the whole affair still made little sense.

The room fell silent. Laura had stopped typing. She stared at the wall, her fingers poised above the keyboard, as if frozen in time. I thought she was searching for the right words, but then she wiped her cheeks with the sleeve of her bathrobe.

I walked over and put my hands on her shoulders. "That story boring you to tears?"

She tried a smile, but it came out lopsided. "When I went downstairs to rent the typewriter, I called my parents."

"I'm sure you miss them," I said.

"That's not it. I was hoping my father would answer, but my mother did. We got into a screaming match. She accused me of being irresponsible, acting like a child. Which is what she always does." She turned to look at me with her red eyes. "I'm not crying because I'm sad. I'm angry. I've never been good enough for her. A constant disappointment. I'm sick of it. She always makes me feel small."

"Sorry to say it, but your mother just wants to control you. She's got nothing else in her life—"

She shot up from her chair. "It's more complicated than that." She stepped over to the photos I'd taped to the wall.

"Complicated isn't the first thing I think of when it comes to your mother," I said to make light of it.

She turned to face me. "This isn't a joke. I can't stand the idea of going home. My mother just sucks the life out of me. And don't say I'm overreacting."

"I'm on your side. Remember?"

Her expression softened, though she said nothing and turned back to the photos. I joined her without getting too close.

She leaned in and scrutinized the one I'd just put up. The act calmed her. Her shoulders relaxed; her breathing returned to normal. "At least one of them worked, but it's not clear enough to use as an ID. Maybe we can have someone play with the exposure and blow it up."

"In the meantime, we planned to go see Sigrid Graf's roommate this morning," I said.

She sighed while still looking at the photos. "I need better walking shoes. That's got to be a four- or five-mile walk."

An idea came to me, and I looked over at the photos still lying on the bed. I went over to the wardrobe and pulled on my jacket.

"Where are you going?" Laura asked.

"Meet me out front in ninety minutes. That should give you enough time to finish your article."

I left before she had time to respond.

∼

As I strolled through Tiergarten park, I kept my fedora tilted low on my forehead and the collars of my overcoat up against my cheeks. No telling who of Leiter's gang—now minus the man himself—was on the lookout among the black-market shoppers. It was clear and cold, with the sun just rising above the Brandenburg Gate. There were fewer customers than last time and, more importantly, no cops. Half the vendors were just setting up, including the one I was looking for, the elderly man who had sold me the camera.

He stopped when he saw me approach. Ice had formed on his mustache whiskers, and he'd stuffed his worn shoes with newspaper. "No returns," he said in German.

"The camera works fine," I said. I shook my pack of cigarettes to offer him one.

He took it and nodded a thanks. As he lit his cigarette, he eyed me with suspicion. After a moment of reflection, he seemed satisfied about whatever bothered him and pulled a flask out of his overcoat. He held it up to offer me a snort.

"It's eight in the morning," I said.

"It'll warm your insides."

It was a little early for me, but I wasn't about to decline the peace offering. I accepted the flask and took a sip of the schnapps.

"I assume you didn't come here to socialize," he said and took the flask. "I only sell cameras. If you want girls or drugs, you've come to the wrong place."

"No, it's nothing illegal. I want to rent your car."

The man chuckled. "What makes you think I have a car?"

Instead of showing him the photos of him and his wife, I said, "I'm an ex-cop and can tell a lot about a person." I pointed at his time-worn wool overcoat. "For instance, the way you dress tells me you were well-off before the war. Probably a professor or teacher, and an amateur photographer on the side. A Berliner by your accent. And you live alone. I bet you've got a car locked up somewhere and holding on to it until the authorities let you drive it again."

The vendor turned away from me and started to set out his cameras for display. "I taught medicine at Friedrich Wilhelm University. That is until the Nazis burned twenty thousand books and expelled the Jewish professors. That's when I walked out. I made ends meet with portrait photography until everything went to hell."

"Mason Collins," I said and shook his hand.

"Anton Lehmann."

"Have you ever thought of going back to academics?"

The man stopped what he was doing and thought for a moment. His face expressed nostalgia that turned to bitterness. "Perhaps. But not that university. It's in the Soviet sector. I can't abide the Russians any better than I could the Nazis. I guess I wasn't too subtle about my feelings, because they kicked me out of my flat. I crossed over to the west and haven't looked back."

"You must know the Soviet sector pretty well," I said.

"Like the back of my hand. Why?"

"I might need your expertise."

"You won't catch me putting one foot over there."

A couple of Russian soldiers came by to look at his cameras. Both of them had five or six wristwatches on their wrists, which was a common sight. Soviet soldiers were finally getting their wartime back pay and had money to spend. Money they couldn't spend in the motherland. I stood by and watched the haggling until one of them walked away with a Zeiss Contax camera. While doing this, I was concocting a plan on how to persuade him to be our guide into the Soviet sector.

When they were gone, Lehmann turned to me. "You want to rent my car or not?"

"For a couple of weeks, yes."

"And what will you pay me in the bargain?"

I removed my backpack, squatted, and opened it just wide enough for the man to see a bottle of cognac I'd bartered from a Russian soldier for my watch and a carton of cigarettes. "Hennessy XXO."

Lehmann's eyes widened as if seeing a pot of gold. He waved his hand and nervously looked around. "Close it. Someone will steal it."

I buttoned up the backpack and stood. "Do we have a deal?"

Lehmann agreed, and I helped pack up his cameras. He then led me to a row of single-story warehouses several blocks from the Tiergarten park and close to the Landwehr Canal. About half the single-story buildings had been damaged by a bombing raid. The others were scarred by bullets or fire. A third of the way down, he stopped in front of a brick building the size of a car repair shop. The battered double doors were secured by a rusted chain and an ancient padlock. A sign pasted on the door declared the building condemned and forbade entry.

"You keep it here? The place looks like it could fall down any minute."

"It discourages looters," Lehmann said. "Besides, I live right across the street." He pointed to a two-story building that looked like it had once been a clothing store. Its façade had a small hole through the front wall and brick chipped away from small-arms fire.

He removed the padlock and chain and pulled the doors open. I took several steps inside. The interior walls were blackened from fire. At the far end, several ceiling support beams lay at various angles. Debris was everywhere, except for a cleared path leading to the back wall, where a large rectangular object sat covered in a soiled canvas tarp.

We approached the shrouded car. Lehmann pulled off the tarp. A cloud of dust billowed around it, and it took a few moments for it to clear. The car was an Opel Admiral in dark green. Though a little worse for wear, it was in good shape considering the surroundings.

"A convertible. Why, you old playboy, you."

Lehmann looked at it with affection. "My wife and I picked out this car together. We drove everywhere before the war." His smile faded. Melancholy took its place. "She was home when a bomb hit our apartment. I lost her and everything else. This car is the only thing I have left that could remind me of her."

"I'm sorry, Anton."

He patted the sweeping fender. "She's in excellent shape. I worked hard to keep her that way, even with the constant bombardments and the battle for Berlin. It's a miracle the Russians never found her. Fate has kept us together." He looked at me with a stern countenance. "You had better take good care of her. She's all I have left."

I nodded in agreement, though I wondered with all we were facing if I could keep that promise.

18

Laura stood under the awning covering the front entrance of our hotel. Her arms were crossed, and she kept swinging her head from side to side with impatience in expectation of me walking up the sidewalk from either direction. I'd promised to be back in ninety minutes, but two hours had passed. I hoped driving up in the Opel might save me from her wrath.

I pulled up to the curb. I figured the reflections off the windshield obscured her view of the interior because she eyed the car with suspicion. She put her hands in her overcoat pockets, one of which contained the Tokarev pistol. She leaned over to get a look at who had stopped at the curb. Her face widened with surprise when I leaned over and rolled down the window.

"Need a lift, lady?" I asked.

She walked up to the window and scowled at me. "You said you wouldn't steal a car."

"I didn't. Hop in."

She got in and sat in the passenger's seat. "I suppose you just came across the car with a sign that said 'take me' on the windshield."

"I'm renting it from the vendor in the Tiergarten park. The guy who sold me the camera."

Laura gave me a skeptical look as she rubbed her hands near the heater vent. "A man holds on to a car when he can barely get enough money for food to eat?"

"It's all he's got left to remind him of his late wife."

"So he rents it to a guy who makes a habit of attracting bullets?"

"I avoided that particular subject," I said. "Shall we go see the roommate?"

"Just as long as you keep the heater on full blast, I'll go anywhere."

I put the car in gear and took off. We drove down mostly deserted streets, passing only an occasional Jeep or army-green sedan and headed west, then crossed over into the U.K. sector. We were now in British territory, which made me sit a little lower in my seat. I started to regret renting such an eye-catching vehicle. I was hoping to avoid attracting attention, especially from the Brit MPs, but thankfully the ones we passed only gave us curious glances.

Laura checked our location on a pre-war map she'd picked up in the hotel and directed me to go north on Kaiserallee. Then she had me turn left onto Bismarckstrasse, a wide boulevard that once accommodated snarls of traffic but was now virtually empty. "This car makes us stick out like a sore thumb, you know."

I pointed at the windshield, which was getting pelted with freezing rain. "Exhibit A in my defense for acquiring a car."

Laura offered no rebuttal. Instead, she looked at the stream of pedestrians huddled against the wind and cold—Exhibit B, I would have said. We passed a mix of intact and damaged buildings interspersed with piles of rubble.

After several blocks, I steered the car left onto a narrow street flanked by the skeletal remains of apartments.

Laura pointed to a four-story building. "There's number eighteen."

I parked at the curb and scanned the building. Half the front façade was missing and exposed the living rooms of several apartments. Most were empty, but two still had neatly arranged furniture and wood-burning stoves vented to the outside.

"It's not even full winter yet," Laura said.

"We might have to get tough with this girl. Are you ready for that?"

She shot me a glare and got out of the car.

"What?" I asked her as I got out.

"Don't ask me that again."

I threw up my hands. "Sorry. Duly noted."

Laura checked the information on the note that Wilson had given us. "Beatrice Schweitzer. Apartment 10."

I looked up at the upper floors. "Let's hope the building holds together until we're done."

A couple of boys of about ten stood together by a subway vent to stay warm. I pulled out a partial pack of cigarettes and waved it at them. They ran up as they stared at the prize.

"Keep a watch on this car," I said to them in German. I gave them two apiece. "There's more for you when we get back. Got it?"

The boys nodded and stood next to the car.

"No touching," I said, and we headed for the building.

We navigated several large chunks of concrete to get to the entrance. I pushed through a wooden door barely hanging on its hinges, and we entered the once-elegant and expansive lobby. Drips of water sounded in the gloom. Daylight leaked through the cracks, giving us enough illumination to find the winding staircase of wood and marble. There were man-sized holes in the back wall and debris piled in a corner. The doors to the bank of mailboxes were all open and empty, with the names gone or removed.

I signaled for us to climb the stairs and did so quietly. On the second floor, there were four apartments. The one facing the street had no door and the outside wall was gone. The door to the back apartment was open and void of contents.

Laura stepped up to the one opposite the staircase and used her flashlight to search for the number. She rubbed the soot off the numbers etched on each door. "Seven. Schweitzer's apartment must be on the fourth floor."

We made it to the third-floor landing when a woman above us said, *"Wer ist da?"*

I looked up to see a woman in a thick bathrobe standing at the staircase railing and aiming a Luger at our heads. She appeared more frightened than menacing.

"We just want to talk to you," I said in English, hoping being American would make us less threatening. "It's concerning our friend Mike Forester and Sigrid Graff."

"Are you from the American CID?" Schweitzer asked in accented English. "Because they already asked me a lot of questions."

"We're not military," I said. "We're civilians."

She waved her hand at us. "I do not want to talk about it. Go away."

"It's just a few questions," Laura said. "We can talk wherever you feel safe. You can even keep that gun on us."

Laura's tender tone seemed to have an effect on the woman. Schweitzer shifted her gaze between the two of us as if deciding whether or not to trust us. Finally, she waved for us to continue.

We climbed the last flight of stairs and stopped a respectful distance from her. She panted heavily from lingering fear while still holding the gun on us. She looked to be in her mid-thirties and had long black hair and blue eyes, giving her a striking appearance despite her disheveled hair and the trauma written on her face. Her ratty bathrobe swallowed up her thin frame, which I guessed had fit her in the past, before the extreme rationing, before the poverty.

We introduced ourselves, and she confirmed her name was Beatrice Schweitzer. She looked Laura up and down, as if studying her clothing and demeanor.

"How do you know Mike?" she asked as if it were a test.

Laura and I briefly told her of our histories with Forester, and about him calling us at our home in Boston.

"You came all this way to help him?" she asked skeptically. "In this rathole?"

"He saved me more than once," I said.

Laura said, "And he helped Mason track down someone who murdered my late husband and tried to kill me."

"That sounds like Mike," she said and lowered the gun. "Come in."

We followed Schweitzer into her scantily furnished apartment. Two beds and a dresser were positioned on one side, along with a single vanity that was crammed with makeup. A wooden table and three chairs sat near a coal-burning stove. The stove was vented by a salvaged pipe that stuck out of a window overlooking the street. Aside from the laundry hanging from a rope tied across the beds, the place was tidy and decorated with dried flowers.

She put the pistol on the kitchen counter, then turned to Laura and studied her again. "This is my first time meeting an American woman." She self-consciously patted down her hair. "I like the way you cut your hair short."

Laura thanked her, and Schweitzer gestured toward the beds. "I'm going to freshen up," she said and looked at Laura. "That's what you say, right? Freshen up?"

"Yes," Laura said, "but you don't need to bother on our account."

Schweitzer mouthed Laura's words as if committing them to memory. She pointed to the chairs. "Please, sit, while I change."

I took the chair with its back to the beds so that Schweitzer could change in privacy.

Laura sat and said, "Your English is very good."

"I learned so I can work as a secretary and interpreter at British police headquarters. My teacher said I have a gift for languages."

"Is that how you met Sigrid?" I asked.

"Yes. She was an interpreter there too. She left that job six months ago. We became friends and decided to be roommates."

I could hear her brushing her hair as I scanned the room. An ashtray was overflowing. Some butts had traces of lipstick, and some didn't. Two glasses sat next to a schnapps bottle. A framed 8x10 photograph of Beatrice and another woman posing in an office was displayed prominently on a small cabinet by the sofa. They were shoulder to shoulder, their heads resting against each other, as they smiled for the photographer.

"The other woman in the picture," I said. "Is that Sigrid?"

"Yes. I wouldn't say happier times. But better."

Sigrid had a swimmer's body and was a few inches taller than Beatrice. In her late thirties, she had long curly brown hair that framed a high forehead and strong cheekbones. Her penetrating gaze and Mona-Lisa smile gave her a bewitching air. I could see why Mike had been smitten.

I continued to scan the room and noticed a pair of men's shoes sticking out from behind a curtain covering a small wardrobe. "How long have you and Sigrid been roommates?"

"About a year."

"Do you have any other people staying here?" I asked.

The woman said nothing. The only sound was the rustling fabric as she dressed. I looked at Laura and wiggled my eyebrows. Laura looked confused, and I tilted my head toward the shoes.

"Beatrice," Laura asked, "is there someone else staying here?"

"That is not your concern," Schweitzer said sharply. She

marched over to the chairs and sat, now coiffed and wearing a pair of pleated pants and a pink sweater. She shifted her gaze between Laura and me and furrowed her brow. "I have a boyfriend who comes by. Okay? But I don't know what that has to do with Sigrid or Mike." She lit a cigarette with trembling hands.

"Have you seen Sigrid in the last week or so?" I asked.

She sighed with impatience. "As I told the men with the CID, I haven't seen her for two weeks. I came home from work, and she was gone. Along with half her clothes. She has relatives in Hamburg. I thought she must have found a way to get to the west. I had to answer the same *verdammte* questions to the counter-intelligence agents."

"Do you remember the CIC agents' names?" I asked.

"The aggressive one said his name was Hardin. The other one didn't speak to me."

Laura and I exchanged a look. At the bar with Ellenberg, Hardin had claimed knowing nothing about Sigrid. What else was he hiding from us?

"Do you know what Sigrid does for work?" Laura asked.

"She doesn't talk about it. She is never here that much. The best kind of roommate." She took a long drag on her cigarette. "I know she works as a spy." Alarm came to her eyes. "For the Americans," she blurted. "Not those Russian bastards."

"She's not in the CIC," I said.

She glowered at me. "Did I say she was in the CIC?"

"Then who does she work for?"

She became rigid in her chair. "I told you she doesn't talk about it. Is this now an interrogation? Because I have done nothing wrong."

"Beatrice," Laura said in a soft tone, "the more information we have, the better chance of helping Sigrid and Mike."

Schweitzer's expression softened, though she still puffed nervously on her cigarette.

Laura asked, "Do you know if she was working with some German agents who gather information for the Americans?"

She glanced at the door as if fearing someone would burst into the room. "Yes."

I took Leiter's photo out of my pocket and showed it to her. "Do you know this man?"

She fidgeted in her chair. "I've seen him a couple of times."

"Can you tell us where or with whom?" Laura asked.

"When I met Sigrid at a bar a few times. The Rote Lantern. He and another man were there on two occasions. I didn't like Leiter. His friend was okay. At first. We were together for a week until I found out he was a liar and a violent drunk."

"What is this other man's name?" I asked.

"The guy Mike was supposed to have murdered. Victor Heissmeyer." She pointed her cigarette at us. "But I am sure Mike didn't kill him. Sigrid told me Mike was a tough guy on the job, but he was kind and gentle with me. If I didn't think Sigrid would ring my neck, I would have tried to steal him away from her." She flashed a contrite smile.

"Do you have any idea why Heissmeyer was killed?" Laura asked.

"No, but he deserved it. He was not a moral man. He could put a knife in someone's back before breakfast. I warned Mike about him, but he said he had no choice but to work with that swine."

"Do you know what Mike and Sigrid are accused of?"

Schweitzer's expression remained neutral, but her hands gripped the arms of the chair. "That CIC agent, Hardin, told me it had to do with treason. That they were both in terrible trouble."

I said, "Sigrid is accused of being a double agent, and Mike of passing on American intelligence to her for the Soviets."

Schweitzer let out a groan and shot to her feet. She walked over to the bottle of schnapps sitting on a small table.

"What do you know about that?" Laura asked.

Schweitzer poured herself a drink and gulped it down.

"Beatrice?" Laura said, prompting her to answer.

She held tight to her glass as she stared at a blanket covering the broken window. "I won't let you put me in the middle."

"The middle of what?" Laura asked.

"Things get bad for you, and you can leave whenever you want. I can't. There is no place I'm safe. The police find me dead, it's just another German corpse in this dead city."

"Who might come after you if you talk?"

"Ernst Leiter, for one."

"Ernst Leiter was murdered last night."

Schweitzer spun around and looked at us. The color was gone from her face. "You know that for sure?"

"We were there," I said. "Someone shot him in the head and escaped in the fog."

"He's dead, Beatrice," Laura said, pressing her. "What information would have made Leiter try to kill you?"

"He and Heissmeyer threatened to cut Sigrid's throat."

"You said you only saw him a couple of times at a bar."

"I lied, okay?" she said. "I thought that beast was still alive." She poured another drink and gulped down half of it. "They came to the apartment. They didn't know I was here, and I saw Heissmeyer hold her while Leiter held a knife to her throat. He told her if she talked, they'd kill her."

"What were they afraid she'd say?"

"I didn't hear most of it. Once I saw that knife, I hid. The only thing I could make out was something about getting Mike into a field by the AFN building. When they left, I asked Sigrid about it, but she refused to tell me. We argued, and she left. That's the last time I saw her."

"Is that the last time you saw Mike, too?" I asked.

"No, he came to the apartment the next morning. He was filthy and exhausted. There was blood on his coat and his face. I tried to convince him to stay, but when he learned of Leiter threatening Sigrid, he rushed out. He was very upset." She drained the glass of schnapps. The rapid intake of booze was having its way with her; she swayed and held on to the table for support.

I pulled out the photo I'd snapped at the bar. I showed it to her and pointed at the dead-eyed man. "Do you know him?"

She squinted at the photo, then pushed it away. "No."

Laura and I exchanged looks, and we silently weighed how far to push Schweitzer, whether to insist she answer more questions.

Laura turned back to Schweitzer. "Beatrice, we're almost done. Just a couple more questions."

Schweitzer shuffled over and dropped into the chair.

Laura said, "You got upset when we mentioned the accusations against Sigrid and Mike. That makes us think you know more than you're telling us. Are any of the accusations true?"

Schweitzer shrugged. "I don't know. Maybe. Sigrid only told me that those other men were pushing her to do something she didn't like."

"Leiter and his comrades?" I asked.

She nodded. "They threatened her if she refused. She was more frightened than I'd ever seen her. She said she was only making small gestures to keep them from doing worse."

"What about Mike?" Laura asked.

"He loves Sigrid," Beatrice said. "He wouldn't do anything to betray his country. If he was involved, then it was to keep Sigrid safe."

I felt a twinge in my stomach. Like anyone, Mike was capable of doing something stupid for love. Going after Sigrid in East Berlin was a good example. "If Sigrid did go to the Soviet sector, do you have any idea where that might be?"

"Why would she do that?" Beatrice asked. "She was happy to get out of that place."

"The latest intelligence for Sigrid is that she went there, and Mike followed her."

Schweitzer stamped out her cigarette and lit another. "She wouldn't be that stupid."

"Beatrice," Laura said, "what if she's on the run and in fear for her life? If she's a suspected double agent, then it would be next to impossible for her to escape to the Allied zones of occupation."

"I was a cop and an intelligence agent," I said. "I know she won't get past the American or Soviet authorities if they want her bad enough. Trying to cross over the border guarantees she'd be arrested. She's either hiding here or in the Soviet sector, and the latest intelligence says she's over there."

"What do you want to know for?" Beatrice said, her tone hostile, her words slurred. "Do you plan to go over there and rescue her?" She chortled at the idea.

"That's the only way we can see helping her and Mike," Laura said.

Her amused expression faded. She took a drag off her cigarette. "She has an old boyfriend who lives in the Nikolaiviertel near the Nikolas church. If you can call it living."

"Do you have an address?"

"Third pile of rubble on the left," Schweitzer said in a sarcastic tone. "There is nothing in that district but ruins."

"How about you take us there?" I asked.

"Me? Are you joking? I wouldn't go to the east with a gun at my head."

"Don't you want to help Sigrid?" Laura asked. "I thought you were very close."

Schweitzer started to say something, but I beat her to it. "We'll pay you."

She stuffed another cigarette in her mouth and lit it. After a couple of shaky puffs, her glower faded and was replaced by something resembling avarice. "How much?"

"You can't use American dollars, and Reichsmarks are worthless. Two cartons of cigarettes."

"Make it four."

I looked at Laura as if Schweitzer was driving a hard bargain. A carton of cigarettes at the PX went for a dollar, but the same carton could be sold to a Russian for up to $200. Though she wouldn't be able to exchange the cigarettes for cash, they would be worth a small fortune on the black market.

Laura nodded.

"Done," I said. "We do it tonight."

19

It was a few minutes before nine p.m. when we approached the Osthafen train station. We were to meet Beatrice at the west end, but she was nowhere in sight. The U-Bahn station had been severely damaged by bombs and was no longer in use. Its jagged ruins, like ink-black bones, stuck out in the velvety darkness. Remnants of the elevated tracks disappeared into the mist formed over the Spree River. We were close enough that I could smell the dampness and hear a barge chugging up the frigid waters that divided the American sector and the Soviets.

We crossed a wide area cleared of debris and stood next to one of the thick pillars that held up the covered portion of the station. There were few people around, and those who passed scurried home before the ten p.m. curfew. I lit a cigarette and scanned the shadows.

"You think she got cold feet?" Laura asked.

"Maybe." I looked at my watch under the glow of the lighter. "We'll give her fifteen minutes, then we'll get out of here."

"Can't say I'd blame her," she said. "If we get in any trouble, I'd rather it be in an American jail than a Soviet one."

I could have mentioned something about us backing out, but

I held my tongue. Not unless I wanted another bruise on my arm. She looked calm and determined. I would never have any qualms about going on a dangerous mission with her. Schweitzer, on the other hand, was an unknown. And I didn't like unknowns, especially when it came to sneaking into hostile territory. A payday motivated her, and that would only get her—and us—so far.

Laura nudged my arm and directed my attention toward the opposite pillar. Schweitzer was walking our way. She wore a black stocking cap and a black coat. Her face was taut with nervous tension. Her eyes flitted in every direction, as if someone might jump out at any minute. She stopped a few yards away and motioned for us to accompany her.

We took a path under the elevated track as we headed east, only stepping out of the darkness to avoid piles of rubble from damaged sections of the deck above. Within a few minutes, the outline of a bridge loomed ahead of us. I knew from looking at the map earlier that it was the Oberbaum Bridge, a turn-of-the-century Gothic structure of brick-red stone and sporting two turreted towers that rose out of the middle of the river. A roadway and sidewalk ran beneath and parallel to the elevated trestlework. War had mauled the whole thing, but the mighty towers still stood in defiance of the violence that had occurred around them.

We climbed a short set of stairs to the deck and remained under the bridge's trestle. The cold fog coming off the river enveloped us and reduced visibility to mere yards.

We reached the middle span when a Soviet patrol boat crossed under us. Its searchlight swept the trestle, the light casting odd shadows from the arches. A few other pedestrians walked along the bridge, but they seemed more interested in avoiding the patrol boat than acknowledging us.

"Are there guards on the other side?" I whispered to Schweitzer.

"Not usually. This area is so damaged, few people live here. The Russians don't seem interested in patrolling here anymore."

"How do you know for sure?" Laura asked.

"I've used this way to get into the Soviet sector several times."

That set off an alarm, and I stopped. "I thought you wouldn't go to the Soviet side even with a gun to your head."

Schweitzer smirked. "That was before you offered to pay me." When we returned stares, she said, "I smuggle things to the east. And sometimes people who are wanted by the Soviets pay me to guide them to the west. The money the Brits give me isn't enough to live on. I have to make a living any way I can."

I looked at Laura, and she shrugged. "We've come this far."

"If you want to stay healthy, you won't double-cross us," I said to Schweitzer.

"I want those four cartons of cigarettes."

I motioned for her to continue, and we stayed a few paces behind her.

We came to the end of the bridge and turned left to follow the right bank of the river. Schweitzer led us north, toward the center of town, taking small streets and weaving through ruins. It took us fifty minutes to reach the Nikolai quarter, as we had to dodge several Soviet mobile patrols. Heavy clouds obscured whatever moonlight we might have used to navigate the tangle of rubble. Only the closest buildings were visible, rising like stalagmites in a dark cave.

We rounded a high mound of brick and stone, and the rectangular tower of the Nikolai church came into view. The walls of the structure still stood, though the entire roof was gone. Schweitzer led us past the church and entered a street with only a handful of shattered buildings at random intervals. Between them were mounds of bricks, concrete, and wood.

She stopped and pointed at a brick building with just two walls remaining. Wooden scaffolding held one side in place, which gave me little comfort.

"In there," she said.

"Lead the way," I said to her.

She looked at both of us. I couldn't tell if she was scared or tempted to make a run for it. Finally, she turned and entered the ruins through one of the missing walls. We went in right behind her. Instead of a roof, the charcoal sky was exposed and transformed the jagged walls into a tortured silhouette. Laura had a flashlight pointed at the ground, while Schweitzer and I used our lighters. The floor spanned sixty feet in each direction.

Schweitzer followed a path through the heaps of debris. If there were people hiding in these ruins, they'd done a good job of covering their tracks.

"How could anyone live here?" Laura said in a soft voice.

"Are you sure we have the right building?" I whispered to Schweitzer.

The woman ignored the question and motioned toward an opening. On closer inspection, it proved to be a staircase leading down to the basement level. I pointed for her to go first and positioned my .45 for a quick draw if we ran into an ambush.

Our feet crunched on the concrete staircase going down. Laura trained her flashlight forward, as there was no other source of illumination. I strained to listen for any movement that was not our own, and half expected a light at the bottom. Some sign people lived down there. The stale air grew thick with odors of decay with each step.

I was starting to regret not turning back while we were still on the bridge. I pulled out my pistol and held it at my side. Near the bottom, I noticed a faint glow from somewhere to the left of the staircase. Then the faint odor of burning wood. Hope rose in my chest; we might actually find Mike down in this dungeon.

20

I urged Schweitzer to quicken her pace, and we reached the bottom of the stairway in seconds. A dozen or more people sat around several small fires and makeshift tents in the back half of the large space.

They all looked startled when we first appeared, then frightened as Laura and I hurried toward them and called out Mike's and Sigrid's names. No one responded. Some people stood as if getting ready to run. I put my pistol away and assured them in German that we were only looking for two lost friends. Laura and I went from person to person, asking if they'd seen or heard anything about Mike Forester or Sigrid Graf.

I spoke to an older man who sat on a block of concrete next to a soiled mattress. His eyes had that thousand-yard stare, and he didn't acknowledge me at all. But then his eyes fixed on a spot some distance behind me. His eyes widened in fear.

I looked to where he'd fixed his gaze and sprang to my feet. Three men stood in a line at the bottom of the stairway. Their guns were drawn and pointed in my direction.

"Laura," I said in a warning tone.

Laura was on the opposite side of the encampment, speaking with a woman. She turned and sucked in her breath.

I recognized the beak-nosed man and Dietrich from Leiter's group at the Rote Lantern. They said nothing and seemed to be waiting for the man in charge. With Leiter gone, I wondered who would emerge from the shadows.

Schweitzer's shouts of protest echoed down the stairway. She had slipped away unnoticed while Laura and I had circulated among the residents. Now she was being forced down the stairs. A moment later, she tumbled off the last step and onto the ground. Her assailant emerged from the stairway. It was the dead-eyed man we'd seen with Leiter at the same bar.

The man yanked Schweitzer to her feet and forced her across the room before giving her one final shove.

She stumbled and fell next to one of the fires. She screwed up her face in anger and kicked dirt in the man's direction. "I did what you told me to do. Now let me go!" she yelled in German.

"You haven't told me where we can find Major Forester and Sigrid Graf," the dead-eyed man said. "You do that, and you can leave." He pulled out a Luger from a holster and aimed it at me. He said in English, "If you will please throw your weapon on the ground next to me. You as well, Miss McKinnon."

It was bad enough having five guns pointing at us, but the man knowing our identities left me cold. I pulled my .45 out of my waistband with my thumb and index finger, placed it on the ground, and kicked it over to the man. Laura did the same. I glanced at her to check if she was okay. She looked defiant, not scared. I suppressed my fear that it might be the last time I saw her and concentrated on any way to get out of the situation in one piece.

"You were warned not to interfere," the dead-eyed man said in German. "I will ask you only once. Where are Major Forester and Sigrid Graf?"

I said loud enough for everyone to hear, "Decorated intelligence officers for the Third Reich now work for Russia. The one country every German was taught to despise."

The dead-eyed man pulled the hammer back on his pistol.

"What is it about Forester that has you guys so desperate?" I asked. "Does he know you're all double agents? Was Leiter just following orders when he warned me, and then he found out you're working for the Russians? Is that why you shot him?"

"Even suspecting us of being traitors means that you have to die," the dead-eyed man said.

"And what do you propose to do with all these witnesses? Shoot them, too? Because when the U.S. Army finds out you murdered two Americans, they won't leave any stone unturned. They'll find these people and ask them. When they find out it was you, they'll see you all hang."

Schweitzer let out a growl and dived for Laura's pistol lying near to where she sat. She managed to get the gun in her hands and bring it up to fire, but the dead-eyed man seemed to be waiting for her to do that. He fired three shots into her. Schweitzer crumpled to the ground. One of the rounds passed through her and struck a woman standing nearby. She cried out and collapsed. Another round had smacked the wall just behind Laura. Rage boiled within me, and I had to refrain from retaliating. I would have been dead before getting anywhere close to my .45.

Undaunted, Laura knelt next to the wounded woman. A couple of other people joined in to help the unconscious woman and ignored the agents' warnings. They waved their guns and moved toward the group. I glanced at my pistol lying at the dead-eyed man's feet, but he was watching me with a gleeful smile.

Someone at the top of the stairs yelled something I couldn't make out. Gunfire broke out from above. Everyone's eyes turned toward the sound.

The dead-eyed man barked an order at his men, and they ran up the stairs. More yelling. More gunfire. The dead-eyed man rushed over to the bottom of the stairs. He barked orders, then disappeared into the stairway.

Firm hands gripped me from behind. I jerked away and turned to see two of the basement's residents urging me to follow them. Two men already had the wounded woman in their arms, while several women were silently pulling Laura in the same direction. I hurried over to Laura, and we followed the group toward the far corner of the basement.

To my surprise, the lead men disappeared into what appeared to be the wall. Others followed. Laura and I moved with the crowd into a hole formed by the collapse of the building's structure. We were in a primitive tunnel and moving in complete darkness. The residents seemed to know the way without light as we climbed down piles of rubble.

Only fifty feet in, the dead-eyed man's shouts reached our ears. He was giving orders for his men to pursue us.

Everyone increased their pace, climbing down faster until reaching a tunnel of concrete a few inches higher than my head. Rancid odors assaulted my nose. We were in the city's sewer system.

Wading through knee-deep, black water, Laura and I ran with the rest of them. I didn't ask where we were going and hoped they weren't taking us deeper into the Soviet sector. We were in a straight section of pipe, and our pursuers would have a clean shot when they made it into the sewers. The men carrying the wounded woman slowed our progress. I pitched in and took some of her weight. The effort of pushing through the water had many of the people out of breath. Some of the older people had to be half carried by the younger ones. I tried to see if Laura was managing okay, but I could only make out the shadows of those next to me.

It seemed like an hour had passed, though it couldn't have been more than a few minutes, when I discerned a charcoal-gray light farther up the tunnel in front of us. Everyone else must have spotted the same thing, as it seemed to urge them to increase their speed.

Not far behind us, I could hear our pursuers splashing in the water. The beam of a flashlight swept across our backs. I glanced back. The agents were sixty yards behind us but closing fast.

One of them called out, "Halt!" A pistol shot followed it. The blast echoed in the tight space. A bullet smacked into the ceiling above us.

A few cried out in alarm, and we all put on the speed, our legs kicking through the water in a desperate race to safety. The gray light grew larger and stronger. It was the ambient glow of the sky and city.

Hope vanished when I saw that an iron grating blocked the end of the tunnel. The banks of the Spree River were just on the other side. So close, but we were trapped.

The lead men hit the grating and pushed with all their strength. To my relief, the grating gave way and hinged out, as if it had been rigged for such an emergency.

We all poured out of the tunnel. With the last person through, I helped the men push the grating back into place.

Several shots rang out from within the sewer. Bullets zipped past us or ricocheted off the iron. One man screamed with pain and staggered back. More shots rang out. We wouldn't be able to hold the grating closed once the gang was upon us.

I looked around to see if we could use anything to block the exit. But there was nothing. Then a man rushed up with a large beam of wood. He jammed one end into the boulders at the base of the exit, and together we shoved the other end against the bars. More bullets rocketed past us as I pulled on the grating to make sure it was secure. It held. Our pursuers would have a tough time freeing the beam.

The other men with me urged us to hurry, and the group scrambled along the sandy soil of the riverbank.

I raced over to Laura. "Are you okay?"

She nodded. She was out of breath and visibly in pain, but she continued to help one of the elderly women keep up with the rest.

A middle-aged man with matted gray hair walked alongside us. "I'm sorry about your friend," he said in German.

"A friend wouldn't have led us into a trap," I said. "But she didn't deserve what that man did to her. And I'm sorry we put you all in danger."

"Why were those men after you?" he asked.

"We are trying to help a friend, and they want to kill him."

"Those men are vermin."

"Do you know any of them?"

The man shook his head. "Though I think the one who did the talking was a high official. Gestapo or SS. I don't know."

That fact tickled something in my brain. A face. A name. But it still wouldn't come. And it seemed obvious this man was the high-ranking Nazi officer Forester was hunting. I looked back from where we came. No one followed.

I said to the man, "You all seemed to know exactly where to go."

"Most of us use the sewer system to move around the city. That way, the authorities do not molest us. There are branches that connect directly to the Western sectors."

Laura had me ask the man in German why they didn't find places to stay in the American or British sectors.

The man let out a bitter chuckle. "As if the living conditions there are any better." He glanced at both of us as if weighing whether to continue. "We move from place to place because most of us are wanted by the authorities. Not for being Nazis, but for mostly petty crimes. I beat a Russian soldier for trying to rape my wife. And a British officer for trying to do the same thing to my daughter. Others for black market activities. Some for stealing food from your army's depots or restaurants. We are not angels. Simply people trying to survive."

The searchlight beam of a Russian patrol boat swept along the bank as it moved down the river. It came toward us, and we all rushed to the embankment and crouched along the incline. The light passed above our heads and moved on.

The middle-aged man approached several others in the group and discussed what to do next. A plan was apparently agreed upon, and the gray-mustached man walked back to us. He held out his hand. "This is where we leave you."

I shook his hand and thanked the rest for saving us. They waved as they climbed up the embankment and disappeared into the shadows. Once they were out of sight, Laura and I embraced, holding each other for a long moment. Life had almost ended for both of us. The relief was overwhelming, but I was tormented by the feeling it wouldn't last long.

21

It was past one a.m. when Laura and I reached our hotel. We'd been silent the whole way, from retrieving the car to driving back to the hotel. By the time we climbed the stairs, Laura was noticeably limping, favoring her right leg. We both fell onto the bed from physical and mental exhaustion. I took her hand and stared at the ceiling, following the cracks in the paint as I tried to suppress thoughts of how close we got to being gunned down in the ruins.

"Don't ask, okay?" Laura said. "We're going to finish what we started."

"I know better than that. But we could use a few days of doing nothing. To recover, I mean."

"It's just my hip. It has never seemed to heal right."

I turned on the bed to face her. "Your hip will be fine. On the other hand, we escaped being dead by the skin of our teeth."

Laura launched off the bed and backed up against the dresser. She crossed her arms and glared at me. "Don't you think I know that? It's not the first time I've had a close call."

I sat on the edge of the bed to face her. "Laura, all I'm suggesting is taking a few days off."

"There's that patronizing tone again. You're implying that I can't cope with the stress. I'm too fragile. I was in a bomber squadron taking flak over Germany. On the front line in the Vosges when the Nazis shelled our position. So stop trying to get in my head."

I knew she was tough. I'd heard her stories about being a correspondent during the war. She could take it with the best of them, but her standing there in the bedroom with her arms wrapped tightly around her chest, it looked like she wanted to crawl out of her own skin.

I held up my hands in surrender. "I'm sorry. Okay? Maybe it's me. I'm scared I'll lose you, and I couldn't take that. Look, I'm not saying we should go home. Just take some time—"

"To what? Go to the movies? Have a candlelit dinner?" She pointed her finger toward the window and the city below. "Not while Mike is still out there, wounded and in danger."

I got up and walked over to the small table by the window. All we had left was a quarter bottle of vodka. I poured myself a drink. "You want one?"

She said yes. I poured both drinks and handed her one. I sat back on the bed and raised my glass in a silent toast. We both drained the glasses and stared at each other for a moment.

She unwound her arms, sat next to me on the bed, and slugged my arm. "I got rattled, but I'm not scared. I'm mad as hell."

"Yeah, me too," I said. "I'm too bushed to show it."

Laura put her head on my shoulder. "The only thing that scares me is how much I would have enjoyed shooting that bastard in the face."

I chuckled and put my arm around her. "Will you marry me?"

She answered with a chuckle of her own. "Maybe."

We sat there for a while in silence, until Laura said, "We haven't talked about Beatrice's claims. That Leiter and Heissmeyer had forced Sigrid to do bad things, whatever that entails. And maybe Forester did some, too, out of his love for Sigrid."

"She led us into a trap," I said. "I wouldn't trust anything she said."

"It's still the elephant in the room."

I said nothing. Forester might have done some stupid things to impress his girlfriend, but he wouldn't have gone so far as to be a traitor to his country. At least that was what I was hoping.

Laura must have guessed my thoughts, because she adeptly changed the subject. "Now we know those Gehlen men are double agents."

"And I'm fairly sure that Nazi creep shot Leiter."

She lifted her head from my shoulder and looked at me. "Maybe even Heissmeyer."

"And get this: the German guy we were talking to after the escape said that the dead-eyed bastard is a former high-raking SS or Gestapo officer."

"And you think he's the same one who Mike was hunting," Laura said.

"Yup. At least we have a few pieces of the puzzle falling into place."

"Yeah, but someone is cheating and making the puzzle bigger."

"Here's another piece, but I don't know where it fits. Framing Mike for the murder would have been a neat trick for a German, even a former intelligence agent."

"And the supposed witness to the murder is an American."

"Framing him for spying would need someone with juice in the Allied intelligence community to pull it off."

"An inside job?"

"That's what I'm thinking."

"I don't trust anyone we've met in intelligence."

"Best to avoid them," I said.

"Then we go to Wilson at the CID," Laura said, then pulled me on top of her on the bed. "But first …"

"So ordered."

~

Getting to the CID offices at the Oliver barracks by car was a lot more exasperating than by the S-Bahn trains, but at least we were warm and dry. The dated map we had was of little help navigating the tangle of streets, some without signs, some blocked by rubble or construction vehicles. An inch of snow had fallen during the night and was turning to slush from the noonday sun.

We'd both slept late into the morning. I hadn't stirred the whole time and, as far as I knew, Laura didn't either. I could have attributed it to the heavy bout of sex, but nights without waking up to nightmares were becoming the norm for us in Berlin. Maybe I should have been worried that danger around every corner had us sleeping like babies, but I put off questioning our sanity for another time.

Laura pointed to the left at an intersection, and I steered the car onto Siemensstrasse.

"We go three streets, then turn right," Laura said.

I was about to make a wisecrack about her getting us lost several times when a black sedan pulled out of an alley right in front of us and stopped. I hit the brakes, almost T-boning the sedan. I hit the horn. Another sedan pulled up behind us at an angle. We were boxed in.

I went for my .45 on the seat. Laura put a hand on my arm to stop me. I looked up to see Hardin getting out of the sedan to our front with two other men in civilian clothes. In the rearview mirror, two more men appeared, similarly attired and with pistols at their sides. One of them was Ellenberg.

Hardin approached the driver's side while the others stayed

where they were. I turned the crank to lower the window, and Hardin bent at the waist to look into the car.

He tried on a smile as he tipped his hat to Laura, but it looked evil. "We've been looking for you."

"A dangerous way to say hello," I said.

"Dramatic, though. Don't you think? You were easy to spot in that fine-looking automobile."

"What do you want besides worsening our day?"

"We're due for a talk. Taking this route, I figured you're on your way to see the CID, and I wanted to get a crack at you first."

"We're listening."

He shook his head. "Not here. I'd like to invite you to my place."

"Said the spider to the fly," Laura said.

Hardin chuckled. "You wouldn't pass up a chance at some turkey and dressing, would you?" When we returned puzzled looks, he said, "Don't tell me you've been so busy gallivanting around town that you forgot. It's Thanksgiving. We'll have a little chat, then commune over a great American tradition."

"How can we resist?" I asked sarcastically.

Hardin patted the car door. "That's the spirit. You follow us over. It's not far." He started to walk back to his car, then stopped, turned, and held up his index finger. "Now, don't try anything funny," he said cheerily.

22

With Ellenberg's sedan behind and Hardin's in front, our mini caravan wove through Berlin's streets in a northwesterly direction. We wound up just south of the OMGUS building, the U.S. military government headquarters. I mimicked Hardin's car and pulled into a curved driveway that served a sprawling mansion on the aptly named street of Kronprinzen Allee. Ellenberg's car parked behind ours, and everyone got out. The three-story house consisted of white stucco walls and a steeply pitched red roof. It took up half a block and looked like it could accommodate a company of soldiers.

Hardin met Laura and me by our car and motioned for us to follow him. The double doors opened before we reached the portico. An elderly man in a black suit stepped out of the house and stood at attention like he was welcoming a lord home from the hunt.

We stepped into an entrance hall as big as my house in Cambridge, and a woman in a maid's outfit took our overcoats. She was around twenty-five and smiled at Hardin in a way that told me they were more than servant and employer.

"Let's gather around the fire," Hardin said.

The three other men in Hardin's entourage remained in the hall while Laura and I followed Hardin through an eight-foot-tall entrance. Ellenberg silently trailed behind us. It was a stately library, all carved wood paneling and walls of books. Laura and I sat on a plush leather sofa, facing a fireplace worthy of a castle. Hardin and Ellenberg took opposite and equally plush club chairs.

The woman servant softly padded into the room.

"Anyone care for a drink before we proceed?" Hardin asked.

"Let's get on with it," I said. "Bad form to drink with our abductors."

"Relax, it's a holiday," Hardin said and looked at the young woman. "Emma, bring a bottle of the Puligny-Montrachet and four glasses." He turned back to us. "The previous occupants kept a marvelous wine cellar. It'd be a shame for you two to miss out on such a treat."

When Emma left, Hardin plucked a pipe from its stand and began loading it with tobacco stashed in a wood-carved tobacco humidor.

"I had a CIC friend in Garmisch who lived like this," I said. "He was up to his neck in felonious acts."

Ellenberg had been silent until I said that. "There are more CIC officers than Lieutenant Hardin living here." He closed his mouth when Hardin shot him a warning glare.

"Who might that be?" Laura asked.

After a long moment, Hardin turned his attention back to us. "The CIC requisitioned this house for some of its officers operating autonomously, away from the politics and distractions at headquarters."

"Autonomous," Laura said. "Interesting word choice. Wouldn't unaccountable be more accurate?"

"Laura—" Hardin started to say.

"Mrs. Talbot," Laura said, interrupting.

"Mrs. Talbot," Hardin said and gave her a patronizing smile.

"Even though we're having this discussion in pleasant surroundings, the reason you are here is very serious."

"How so?" I asked.

"We know you went to see Beatrice Schweitzer," Ellenberg said. "Now she seems to be missing."

"And we know you went to the Soviet sector in the middle of the night," Hardin said. "Where, coincidently, a firefight took place. And now the Soviets are combing the ruins looking for the perpetrators."

Emma returned with the bottle of wine nestled in a standing wine cooler and a tray with four wine glasses. We remained silent while she placed the cooler by Hardin's chair and the tray on the table in front of us.

When Emma left the room and closed the door, Hardin held up the bottle. "David, would you do us the honors?"

Ellenberg stared down Hardin for a moment, conveying his displeasure, then rose from his chair and walked over to the bucket.

"Beatrice Schweitzer was murdered last night," I said, then watched for Hardin's reaction. I got little from him, but Ellenberg stopped pulling on the corkscrew and jerked his head in my direction.

"How do you know this?" Ellenberg asked.

"We were there," Laura said. "Beatrice agreed to lead us to some ruins in the Soviet sector on the chance that Mike Forester or Sigrid Graf were holed up there. Instead, she led us into a trap."

"Trapped by whom?" Hardin asked.

"Leiter's gang," I said. "Without Leiter, of course. Their new leader seems to be a hawk-faced guy, who's rumored to be ex-Gestapo or SS. A high-ranking one. Odd coincidence that Forester was also hunting a high-ranking Nazi goon."

"I'm sure you heard about Leiter being shot at the Rote

Lantern," Laura said. "And we suspect this former officer is the one who murdered him."

The two CIC men fell silent. The only sound was the crackle of the fire.

Ellenberg removed the cork from the bottle with a pop and poured wine in the four glasses. He offered Laura and me one, which we took, then placed on the coffee table.

"What makes you think—" Hardin started to say.

"We've shared some of our info," I said, interrupting. "Now, it's your turn."

Hardin leaned forward, his smile replaced by a predator's glare. "I'm rapidly losing my patience." He pointed his chin at Ellenberg, who stood and exited the room.

A moment later, the three other CIC agents accompanied Ellenberg into the room. They took up positions behind us, and Ellenberg returned to his seat.

"So much for holiday cheer," I said.

"There's still a chance for conviviality," Hardin said. "Cooperation is key, of course. I know of your reputation while in the army. A hothead, but a good investigator. You and Mrs. Talbot could make valuable additions to the team."

"Our cooperation depends on who's offering it," I said. "In my book, everyone's a suspect until proven otherwise."

"That makes two of us. That's why, until proven otherwise, I still consider Forester guilty. That's why I suspect you two of collusion. Why I take everything you say with a heavy grain of salt. I insist you answer my questions. Once I'm satisfied, I'll answer yours. Deal?"

"With three guns at our backs," I said.

Hardin shrugged, and that annoying smile of his returned. "Now, what makes you think that this ex-Gestapo guy shot Leiter?"

"The man is a cold-blooded killer. He was ready to murder the two of us and the fifteen potential witnesses, innocent Germans who just happened to be sheltering there."

"And you believe this ex-Gestapo man and his three gunmen are agents working for the Gehlen organization?"

"Double agents," I said. "They might work for Gehlen on paper, but the Soviets keep them on a short leash."

"You have proof of this?"

"Why else would they be so desperate to stop Forester and bump off anyone who gets in their way?"

"The short answer is you lack any evidence," Hardin said.

I ignored the comment and continued. "According to Beatrice Schweitzer, Leiter and Heissmeyer showed up at their apartment and threatened Sigrid at knifepoint not to talk. About what, Schweitzer didn't know. Then Heissmeyer murders a man called Otto Gumbel and, in turn, gets murdered himself." I left out the part where Forester supposedly worked with Heissmeyer and got him off the murder rap. "According to the CID, the autopsy revealed that Heissmeyer's knife wounds don't match the knife found at the scene with Forester's fingerprints on it. We proved that their two eyewitnesses couldn't possibly have seen Forester in that field or entering his car. The question is, if Forester didn't do it, then who did? Why? And why try to frame Forester unless they wanted to put him away for what he knows?"

Hardin took a sip of his wine and sucked in air to savor it. Finally, he said, "So far, what you've told us doesn't prove they're double agents. It could be any kind of criminal enterprise. Robbery. Drugs. Murderers for hire."

"Framing Forester for murder *and* espionage are connected," I said. "And we've already found enough evidence to prove he's innocent of the murder."

Ellenberg said, "It sounds like you two are trying to find anything that will discredit Forester's espionage charges."

"What we're saying is that Major Forester was framed for both crimes to cover the tracks of the real traitor. His accusers are the Gehlen agents, and those agents are doing whatever it takes to get Forester out of the way. Do anything to stop us from getting to the truth."

"You think the real traitor is an American?" Hardin asked in a deadpanned voice.

"I don't think Leiter's group could operate with immunity any other way."

Hardin looked at Ellenberg, who had remained silent in his chair. "What's your assessment?"

"It's all conjecture and circumstantial evidence," Ellenberg said. "I think these two will concoct anything to get their friend off the hook."

Laura turned to Ellenberg. "And you seem awfully eager to believe alleged German double agents."

Ellenberg scowled at Laura and opened his mouth to speak, but Hardin cut him off. "That's enough. This is serious business, and I don't need it reduced to hurling accusations." He waved at the three agents standing behind us to leave. When they exited and closed the door, he asked, "Do you have anything else to add?"

Laura said, "When we were at the Rote Lantern, watching Leiter's gang, a programmer from the AFN, a Lieutenant Hodgson, slinked in and handed Leiter something."

"It was too dark to make out more than it being folded papers," I said. "He's also the one who claimed to have seen Forester at the scene of Heissmeyer's murder and his getaway."

Hardin puffed on his pipe as he studied me. He glanced at Ellenberg, who subtly shook his head. "We've been watching Hodgson," Hardin said.

I must have betrayed my surprise, because Hardin gave me a gratified smile.

"He squealed so hard about you two haranguing him—his words, not mine—that we decided to look into his activities."

"And?" Laura asked.

"He keeps company with some, shall we say, disreputable German women. So far, nothing beyond that. His alleged association with those agents is new to me."

"Do you have any idea who the ex-Gestapo guy is?" I asked. "Mid-forties, medium height and build. Black hair and graying on the sides. Dead eyes." I held out the photo from the bar for him to see.

Hardin had a talent for concealing his emotions, but after my description and the photo, he looked a deer caught in the headlights. He recovered a second later and said, "I see where you came up with the dead-eyes description."

"You know who I'm talking about, don't you?" I asked.

He snuck a glance at Ellenberg, then said, "I've heard a similar description bandied about."

"That's the man Forester was searching for," I said. I didn't know if that was true; I was fishing for an answer. "And he must have enlisted—or coerced—Heissmeyer to help. That's why Heissmeyer was murdered, and Forester framed for it."

"You appear to be living up to your reputation as a tenacious investigator," Hardin said.

Ellenberg said, "That reputation includes behaving recklessly and disregarding army regulations. That's why he was kicked out of the service."

I ignored Ellenberg's comments, though Laura looked like she was ready to throw her drink in his face.

Hardin sat forward and took a sip of his wine. "This high-ranking ex-Gestapo man Mike was chasing down, I don't know who he is, or whether it's even true, but I tried to dissuade Mike from pursuing it. I thought he was chasing a ghost based on idle gossip."

"Maybe it's time you *did* look into it," Laura said. "Mike obviously got close enough to be framed for murder. And isn't it ironic that he's been accused of the very thing he was investigating, by the very group we think is run by this cold-blooded killer?"

"Or maybe you don't want to," I said. "Like I said, it'd take an inside man to pull this off."

Hardin froze before taking another sip of his wine and scowled. "You'd better be careful with those innuendos. They'll bite you in the ass. Having said that, I don't like the idea of an American selling out his country. That gets me very angry. Like you, I'll stop at nothing to get at the truth. And I'll roll over anyone that gets in the way. Including you. Is that clear?"

23

We'd declined Hardin's offer of having Thanksgiving dinner with him, as neither of us wanted to endure another minute in the presence of His Bloviating Majesty or his sidekick, the Court Jester. Instead, we decided to partake in the holiday festivities hosted by the army brass.

We parked our borrowed car in the lot across from the Harnack-Haus. A stone's throw from General Clay's headquarters, the military governor of the entire American occupation zones of Germany. The hotel-sized building of beige stucco with red brick accents was once a meeting place for scientists and other luminaries. The U.S. Army moved in after the war and turned the undamaged building into an officers' mess and entertainment venue.

I launched out of the car, tossed our weapons in the trunk, and slammed the lid shut.

"Try to relax," Laura said. "Don't let Hardin's arrogance get under your skin."

"I wanted to knock that smirk off his face. I almost lost control when he brought in his muscle to intimidate us. Did you ever wonder why gunsels always show up in threes?"

Laura took my arm and smiled like a contented cat. I knew she was mad, too, but it let me know she was determined to have a good time. I took a deep breath and led her toward the entrance.

We were ready to show our Military Privilege Cards to the pair of soldiers guarding the door, but they didn't seem interested, and we walked in. The spacious lobby of marble was abuzz with soldiers and couples dressed in their Sunday best. We were wearing the same street clothes we'd put on that morning. Laura looked sharp enough in her wool plaid suit with pleated pants, but I had on rumpled khaki pants and my leather jacket that had been through shoot-outs, brawls, and a bomb blast. Laura elbowed me and glanced at my head. I pulled off my fedora and tucked it under my other arm.

We followed the music across the lobby and entered a large auditorium set up with three long rows of tables. There were around two hundred people eating, standing at the open bar, or dancing in front of the thirteen-piece band. The band played "Moonglow," not as good as Artie Shaw, but decent enough. The slow number kept the mood subdued in deference to the upper echelons of the army brass. The music had my shoulders relaxing and my fingers snapping. Right then I just wanted to take hold of Laura, steer her out onto the dancefloor, and forget the rest of the world.

"Looks like a full house," Laura said.

I pointed out two open seats at the far end of the middle row. Getting there would require navigating the roving waiters, groups standing in the aisle, and people seated with their chairs pulled away from the table. Laura was apparently famished, because she pushed past me and braved the gauntlet with steely determination. All I had to do was follow in her wake.

A drink was what I needed, and I glanced at the bar. My gaze landed on Wilson, who was standing among the customers packed elbow to elbow. He gave me a weak smile and nodded his head. I nodded back and caught up with Laura. We got there seconds before another couple and claimed the chairs. Laura's gaze locked on one of the waiters circulating with trays of food.

"Didn't you have breakfast?" I asked.

"What about it?" she growled. "Your ability to not feel hunger annoys the heck out of me."

I held up my hands in surrender. I knew better than to argue with her when she skipped a meal.

I stood and had to lean into Laura to talk over the band. "Flag the waiter down. I'll get us some drinks."

She waved me off, not wanting to be disturbed while using what mental powers she had to coax the waiter to come take her order. I wove past the few chairs at the end of the row and dodged dancers at the perimeter of the dance area to get to the bar. I joined Wilson, who seemed to be waiting for me.

"You being here saved me a trip to the CID," I said.

"It's my day off," Wilson said. "Unless you want to talk about life, dames, or booze, I'm not listening."

He was already a little tipsy, swaying as if standing on the deck of a gently rocking boat.

"A good investigator never has a day off," I said.

He cupped his hand near his ear. "What was that?"

I relented and let him talk about needing to relax from the daily grind, of policing bored soldiers tempted by the black market, drunken brawls, and taking out their frustrations on the local citizenry. My attention wavered. I nodded occasionally while scanning the room. I suddenly felt a pair of eyes on me and looked in that direction.

One of the waiters stood near the opposite wall and was staring at me with a furrowed brow. As soon as our eyes met, he looked away and stepped into the throng of dancers.

Wilson tapped my arm with the back of his hand. "I guess I'm boring you."

That forced me to take my eyes off the waiter and look at Wilson. "Just admiring some of the ladies."

"Can't see why. Your lady puts the rest to shame."

I muttered my agreement and glanced back at the dancers. The waiter was no longer there. A quick scan of the room had the same result. I'd lost him.

"Let me buy you a drink," Wilson said.

"I thought it was an open bar," I said.

"Take it as a symbolic gesture."

"For what?"

Wilson took a sip of his drink before answering. "An apology for treating you like a suspect."

"What changed your mind?"

He waggled a finger at me. "It's my day off."

"In that case, two beers," I said.

Wilson turned to the bar and waved for the bartender. I took the opportunity to search the room again. The suspicious waiter was nowhere in sight, but I did notice Laura shoving a fork of food into her mouth while motioning for me to come. She then pointed to a plate of food sitting next to hers.

Wilson turned to me with the two beers. He held his up for a toast, and I clinked his mug with mine.

"Cheers to those who wish us well, and may the others go to hell," Wilson said and took a long draw of beer.

"You here alone?" I asked him.

"Yup. I don't much like big to-dos, but I thought, why the hell not? Walked over to have a few drinks for free."

"Glad to hear you walked, Arnie," I said.

"Have a house right across from OMGUS. Can you believe that? They must want to keep an eye on me or something."

I glanced over at Laura, who gestured even harder for me to come. "My better half is calling. Food's getting cold. I better get over there before she eats mine, too."

"Why don't we talk tomorrow?" he asked.

I nodded and started to go, then turned back to him. "Oh, and by the way, Sigrid Graf's roommate was murdered in front of our eyes the other night."

Wilson's face widened in shock. He opened his mouth to say something, but I beat him to it. "It's your day off, remember?"

Wilson yelled after me as I walked away. I couldn't hear what he was saying over the music and the diners competing for the loudest voice in the room. I imagined what he said wasn't pretty.

I joined Laura. She was finishing up her plate of food and eyeing mine. I shifted my plate away from her and waved a mug of beer in her face to distract her. I'd barely had the chance to take a bite of the cold turkey before she plucked a slice off my plate and inhaled it.

"I don't know why I'm so hungry," she said. "The tension, I guess."

"Talking to Hardin will do that," I said. "It's either stick a fork in some food or in his neck." I concluded that my food wouldn't get any warmer and started shoveling it in.

"Everyone we've talked to has had that same effect on me," Laura said. "Evasion, half-truths, like they're hiding something. They all seem guilty in my book."

I looked up from the table and caught a glimpse of the kitchen door swinging open. In that moment, I saw the suspicious waiter huddled with our favorite AFN producer, Lieutenant Hodgson. They appeared to be in a heated argument. I nudged Laura with my elbow and nodded toward the kitchen. We both watched for a moment as a couple of waiters entered or exited, then the door swung shut.

"That waiter with Hodgson made a beeline for the kitchen after he spotted me," I said.

"You think the waiter is a lookout for the German agents?"

I was about to answer when Hodgson came out of the kitchen and hoofed it toward the exit.

"Let's see where he goes," I said and used my hand to stuff a slice of cold turkey in my mouth. Laura gave me a chiding look.

"What?" I said.

We got up from the table and fought our way toward the doors.

I glanced at Wilson, who was tracking our movement with the best hawkish glare he could muster under the influence of several drinks.

24

Laura and I kept our distance as we trailed Hodgson to the parking lot. He looked behind several times, forcing us to duck between parked cars. After one last glance to the rear, he got into a dark green Mercedes Cabriolet. The motor roared to life, and he drove out of the lot, making a right onto Van't-Hoff-Strasse. We rushed to our car and took off after him.

He drove at a leisurely pace along the narrow street, then turned right on a broader street that was divided by a center island. We were the only two cars on the road, obliging me to hang back farther than I wanted. Up ahead, he took another right on Berliner Strasse.

I gave the car some gas to catch up.

"He doesn't seem to be in any hurry," Laura said.

"Probably thinks he's in the clear," I said.

Ten minutes later, Hodgson pulled over to the curb in front of a PX dispensary. I did the same a half block behind him. He got out of the car and rushed up to a woman who was about to close up shop for the day. Hodgson waved his hands at the woman in a pleading manner. At first the woman shook her head, then finally relented after Hodgson groveled and clasped his hands together in prayer. The woman let out a visible sigh, then opened the door and let Hodgson enter.

"Should we follow him?" Laura asked.

"If he doesn't come out in a few minutes."

We only had to wait three for Hodgson to reemerge with a bundle of flowers in one arm and a bottle of wine in the other. He was all smiles as he waved his thanks to the shop manager and hopped in his car.

"Our pudgy program director has a honey on the side," I said.

"Something tells me he didn't woo her with his charms."

Hodgson guided his car onto the street, and I followed him, keeping my distance. Four blocks later, he pulled to the curb again next to a cluster of apartment buildings.

"This time we follow him," I said.

We got ready to exit the car, but paused when Hodgson remained behind the wheel and honked the horn. A moment later, a young woman emerged from one of the buildings, carrying a suitcase. Hodgson climbed out of the car and opened the hatch of the rear storage compartment.

"You think he's making a run for it?" Laura asked.

I shrugged. "We'll know soon enough."

The woman couldn't have been over twenty and had the looks of a model. She carried her overcoat so as not to cover up the tight dress accentuating her voluptuous figure. The only thing that betrayed her sophisticated air was her struggle to walk in her high heels.

"What do you call a gold digger in German?" Laura asked.

"Don't know, but I bet she has him hook, line, and sinker."

She and Hodgson kissed, then hugged. He put the suitcase in the storage compartment and slammed the lid shut, while the woman got in the passenger's seat. Hodgson almost skipped to the driver's side, hopped into the car, and took off.

"They look like newlyweds leaving for their honeymoon," Laura said.

"Not before we ask him a few pointed questions," I said, and hit the accelerator.

Hodgson continued south for a few blocks, then turned left into a web of small streets with a scattering of houses and apartment buildings bounded by open fields. The army had created a basketball court in one of them, where a handful of soldiers were shooting hoops. A couple of army brass were exercising horses on a grassy area set up for dressage.

After two more turns, Hodgson slowed and turned into the driveway of a two-story house with red shutters and a tiled roof. A low stucco wall enclosed the property. I found a spot that offered a good view of the front without the risk of being spotted.

The program director and his date got out of the car. Hodgson went to the rear compartment and opened it, while the woman watched. After getting the suitcase, they both headed for the front door, hand in hand.

"He's not leaving town," Laura said. "That solves one problem."

"Not yet, anyway," I said. "I don't get it. After spotting me, the waiter went to Hodgson, which I figured was a warning we were there. Then Hodgson hotfoots it out of the club. If our presence spooked him, he's not acting like it."

"What do we do now?" Laura said. "We can't go up to the house like a couple of peeping toms."

I didn't have a good answer and said nothing. Hodgson and the woman stepped up to the front door. While Hodgson fished around in his pocket, the woman put her hand to her mouth and pointed toward the car. She rushed back, opened the passenger's door, and leaned in. Hodgson grinned at her as he put the key in the lock.

He opened the door and stepped inside. A ball of fire enveloped the doorframe. A millisecond later, the blast rocked our car. The woman, who was halfway to the door, flew backward. She hit the ground and rolled. She screamed as she sat on the lawn and looked on in shock.

Laura sucked in a withering breath. Her mouth opened in a silent scream as she tried to breathe. She was my first concern, and I spoke in a calming voice while stroking her back. Moments later, she finally took in long gulps of air. She tried to speak as her chest heaved, but the words wouldn't come. She frantically pointed toward the house.

I got the message. I jumped out of the car and raced over to the woman. She was dazed but appeared uninjured aside from singed hair and a few cuts and bruises. She wailed, "Benjamin!" and gestured toward the front door with her open hand.

The blast had caused a small fire that was consuming the curtains. It would soon spread. I took the chance and raced for the front door. Inside, Hodgson was six feet into the living room. He was dead, torn apart by whatever bomb had been rigged to take him out upon his return. Blood and parts of him formed a gruesome circle around his torso.

There wasn't much time. Not only because of the fire, but the MPs or German police could show up any minute. Laura yelled for me to hurry from the front lawn.

I looked around and returned my gaze to Hodgson. Maybe ...

I knelt by his left side and touched his chest. "Sorry, buddy." I rifled through his pockets. Nothing in front. I grimaced and turned his mangled torso on its side and checked the back of his pants. There, in his left rear pocket, was a spiral-bound notepad like cops and reporters used. I slipped that in my jacket pocket.

Flames had jumped to the furniture and wallpaper, engulfing everything. Smoke filled the living room, obscuring my view and burning my lungs. My skin felt like it was sunburned. I was out of time. Searching the house for anything else was now out of the question. Growling in frustration, I grabbed up the woman's suitcase and staggered outside.

I gasped for air as my lungs spasmed. I sprinted over to Laura and the woman and knelt next to them. With tears in her eyes, Laura shivered as she rocked the woman. The woman sobbed uncontrollably until she spied her suitcase sitting at my side. The waterworks dried up. Her brow furrowed. With a growl, she broke away from Laura's embrace and lunged for it.

Her desperate move made me suspicious. I plucked the suitcase off the ground, stood, and took several steps back. The woman's aggression startled Laura out of her shock, and she looked up at me. It wasn't a reprimand but a sudden realization.

She said to the woman, "We have to get out of here before the police arrive."

"Benjamin!" the woman pleaded as she held out her hand toward the burning house. It seemed theatrical to me, and by Laura's sober expression, she felt the same.

"He's gone," I said in German. "If you don't want to be arrested by the police, you'll come with us."

The woman glanced at the suitcase one more time, then nodded. She grabbed her purse and stood with Laura's help. As Laura guided her to the car, she seemed hypervigilant, as if contemplating whether to attack us or make a run for it.

The house was fully ablaze by the time I sat behind the wheel and Laura got in back with the woman. As I drove off, I looked at Laura. The bomb explosion had brought back her trauma. She was resilient, but everyone had their limits.

And I wondered if a bomb with our name on it was waiting out there, somewhere.

25

As I drove north on Potsdamer Strasse, I watched Laura and Hodgson's paramour in the rearview mirror. Laura's gaze met mine. I knew she could tell by my eyes that something was up and to get ready for an opportunity. I dodged horse-drawn carriages and army vehicles while keeping watch on our passenger.

"Where are you taking me?" the woman asked in British-accented English.

"Someplace safe," Laura said.

"Safe to you," the woman said.

"What's your name?" Laura asked the woman.

Good, I thought. She was distracting the woman with small talk.

"Greta Schaller."

"Do you live near here?" Laura asked.

The woman looked out the side window to get her bearings, taking her attention away from the interior of the car.

"Purse," I said.

Before the woman could react, Laura grabbed the purse from Schaller's grasp. The woman lunged for it, but Laura pinned her to the back of the seat and popped open the bag. Schaller went for the door handle. I hit the accelerator to discourage her from jumping. Schaller hesitated just long enough for Laura to pull a .22 pistol out of Schaller's purse and put the gun barrel against the woman's cheek.

"Stop," Laura said. "Get back in the car."

Schaller eased into the seat and pulled the door closed. She crossed her arms and glowered at the city passing by out the windshield.

"Your English is quite good," Laura said. "Where did you learn to speak it?"

She huffed as if annoyed at the question. "My mother is English. She left my father and went back to England when Hitler came to power." She snapped her head toward Laura with fire in her eyes. "What do you want from me?"

"Ask a few questions," I said.

"I don't know anything."

"If you don't try to escape or scream out, you'll be fine," Laura said.

"And if I refuse to answer your questions?"

"All I want you to do now is keep your mouth shut," I said. "We're almost there."

I remembered the path Ellenberg had taken the first day we arrived. Once I passed a cemetery with shattered brick walls, I turned off Sachsendamm and took two lefts to end up on a small street that ran near the southern end of the Tempelhof airfield. I recognized the battered gate among its burned-out neighbors.

I pulled into the semicircular driveway and parked under the portico. It was dusk. Snow flurries had started to fall, and the turreted stone house looked foreboding in the fading light. I got out and opened the back passenger's door on Schaller's side. Dread darkened her face, and it took some prodding on Laura's part to get her to move. With Laura at her back and me at her side, we headed for the front door. The door was locked, and it took a few tries with my lock picking tools to get it open.

The three of us entered, and I locked the door and threw the large bolt as extra security. As far as I could tell, the place hadn't been visited since Ellenberg dropped us off that first day. Our footprints, and only ours, were still visible in the dust. Schaller scanned the area, presumably to scout for an escape route. She wasn't a typical woman of the street. My guess was she'd had some training, which made me wonder what we were going to do with her once we finished the interrogation.

The pocket doors were open, and we filed into the expansive living room. The sofa and chairs stood watch over the fireplace. The half-empty bottle of cognac from our previous visit still sat on the small table along with the three glasses. Laura went directly to the table and poured herself a drink. Her hands shook as she lifted the glass.

"You want one?" she asked as if just remembering I was in the room.

I shook my head, and she downed the liquid.

"Take a seat," I said to Schaller and motioned toward the sofa.

"I expected instruments of torture," Schaller said defiantly.

"Answer our questions, and this can all be a pleasant conversation."

Schaller sat. Laura put the suitcase on the coffee table, and the woman reached for it. I caught her hand and shook my head. She sat back and scowled at me.

Laura popped the latches and opened the suitcase. "Well, well, well."

While keeping one eye on Schaller, I glanced over at the contents. The case was filled to the brim with money.

Laura shuffled through the bound packs of bills. "Occupation Reichsmarks, Swiss francs, and U.S. dollars. The currencies of choice for making a getaway. And look at this." She held up two U.K. passports. She leafed through both. "One for Hodgson and one for our guest. Both under fake names. Very professional. Even some of the pages have exit and entrance stamps. Visas."

"Where did you get the money?" I asked.

Schaller stared at the fireplace with a defiant look.

I sat in the chair to Schaller's right. "You two must have done something big to earn that kind of cash."

She offered no response.

Laura closed the suitcase and sat in the chair to Schaller's left. "Did the Gehlen agents or the Soviets pay for your services?"

"Do what you want to me," Schaller said. "I'm not answering your questions."

"Whoever arranged the payment also double-crossed you," I said. "Obviously, their intention was to have your burned corpse lying next to Benjamin's." I used Hodgson's first name to make it personal.

It had no effect on her.

"Or maybe you knew about the bomb and forgetting your purse was a way to avoid getting blown up. You were using Hodgson to get the money. Then you concocted a method of getting rid of him so you could keep all the money for yourself."

Laura stood. "I might as well start the fire. We're going to be here for a while." She went over to the fireplace and put some fresh logs on the iron grate.

"What do you mean, a while?" Schaller asked.

"We're not going anywhere until you start talking," I said.

"People are going to be looking for me."

"Who would that be?" Laura asked as she wadded up newspaper and put it under the kindling.

"Dangerous people."

"My guess is, they only care about the money," I said. "Not you."

I let that sink in for a few moments. Laura put a match to the wadded newspaper and kindling, then backed away from the fireplace after getting a small blaze going. "Maybe we can offer them a trade. Fraulein Schaller and the cash for information."

"That's a fine idea, Miss McKinnon."

Schaller shot to her feet. "You can't do that!"

"Sit down," I said in a threatening tone.

She ignored the order and stomped her feet. "They won't bargain with you. They'll just kill us all and take the money."

She made a run for the door, but I caught her by the arms and shoved her down to the sofa.

"You're not going anywhere," I said. "If you don't calm down, I'll tie you to a chair and gag you."

Schaller tried to appear defiant, but she trembled from fear.

"You're working for those double-dealing German agents," I said, almost yelling.

"That's not true!"

"Who else would scare you that badly?" I asked.

Schaller scowled at me, then shifted her gaze to the fireplace. The veins in her neck pulsed hard and fast. A cheek muscle quivered. She was frightened out of her mind. I needed one more push.

I put on my hat and slipped on my jacket. "That's it," I said and turned to Laura. "She's more valuable as a trade." I seized her arm and pulled her up.

Like a trapped animal, Schaller growled as she twisted and squirmed to free herself. She swung her fists at my arms and kicked my legs. Finally screaming out, "No! Stop!"

Picking up my strategy, Laura stepped over to us and put a hand on Schaller's shoulder. "Mason, wait. Give her a chance." She almost had me convinced of her sincerity.

I growled and let Schaller go. The woman dropped to the sofa and hunched down as if claiming it as safe territory. Laura sat on the edge of the chair and faced her. She put on a sympathetic look but said nothing, waiting for the woman to speak and save herself. I remained standing, giving her the impression I might snatch her up at any minute and drag her away.

"The money came from the agents," Schaller said.

"What used to be Leiter's gang?" Laura asked in a soft tone. She nodded.

"Is the money for work Hodgson did for them?" I asked.

"Probably," Schaller said. "I don't know."

"What kind of work?"

"Passing on documents," Schaller said. "I don't know what kind of documents. Secrets, I suppose, because the gang paid well." She looked up at me in alarm as if she'd said something wrong. "I was only a courier. I had nothing to do with stealing documents."

"Where did Hodgson get them?" I asked.

"I don't know," she said.

When I returned a skeptical look, she blurted out, "I swear!"

"How long has this been going on?" Laura asked.

"We've been together three months. What he was doing before that, I don't know."

"When did you begin working as a courier for him?" Laura asked.

"A week after we started being a couple."

"It didn't take much persuasion for you to take on such a dangerous job," I said.

"We loved each other. I would do anything for him."

"I'll tell you what I think," I said. "The gang instructed you to seduce him, so you could keep an eye on him, control him."

"That's not true," Schaller said with little conviction in her voice. "I fell in love with him the first time we came together."

The woman recoiled when I leaned in and got in her face. "You lie again, and we'll put you in the trunk and go for a little drive."

Schaller turned to Laura, silently begging for her to protect her.

Laura glanced at me, and I straightened, backing off one step. "Greta," Laura said, "tell us the truth. I won't stop Mason again if you continue to lie."

"Did Leiter tell you to seduce Hodgson?" I asked in a stern tone.

She rubbed her hands as she stared at the fire. A long moment passed, then she said, "Not Leiter. Hermann Trisko. My boyfriend. Or he was my boyfriend until he ordered me to have relations with Benjamin."

"But Trisko was taking orders from Leiter?"

Schaller shrugged. "I don't think he would dare sneeze without Leiter's permission."

"What about Hodgson?" Laura asked. "Was he taking orders from Leiter or any other member?"

"I don't think so," Schaller said.

"What do you mean, think?" I asked. "Did he or didn't he?"

"They wouldn't go near him."

"We saw him go into a bar and pass something to Leiter," Laura said.

"If he did, that is the first time I've heard about it," Schaller said. "And I was with him most of the time he wasn't at work. Leiter and the rest acted as if he was untouchable. Hermann said that's why he wanted me to get close to him. It was the only way they could keep a watch on him."

I looked at Laura, puzzled. She returned an incredulous expression. Why was he considered untouchable? A softie like Hodgson wouldn't intimidate a ruthless group like Leiter's. Unless he was only the front for another powerful man. Someone who could wield the power of the U.S. Army.

"Did Hodgson have any interactions with higher-ranking U.S. military personnel outside of work? Was he afraid of any of his superiors? Late-night rendezvous or phone calls?"

"I observed none of those things," Schaller said.

I let out a sigh of frustration and took another step back, letting Laura take over.

"Greta," Laura said, "after Leiter was killed, another man took over as leader. He's rumored to be a former high-ranking Gestapo or SS officer. What's his name, and what position did he hold?"

Schaller hunched down even lower on the cushion. "I don't know."

"Yes, you do," I said.

Schaller glared at me. "What are you going to do with me after your questions? Huh? Have me arrested? Just leave me on the streets? Either way, they will kill me for what I'm telling you."

"We'll protect you," Laura said.

"How?" Schaller asked with desperation in her voice. "This is the only place you felt safe to take me, isn't it? Those agents will find all of us and kill us! Leiter was murdered. Benjamin murdered. I heard many rumors about others. That's why Benjamin wanted to leave. It is too dangerous."

I opened my mouth to say something, when a beam from a flashlight swept across the stained-glass window overlooking the front yard. A split second later, someone pounded on the door.

Schaller screamed and dived flat onto the sofa. "They're here!"

26

Laura jumped to her feet and whirled around toward the flashlight beam projected on the window. We both went for our firearms at the same time.

"Stay here and cover her," I said to Laura.

I rushed to the pocket doors and peered into the foyer. I loaded a round into the chamber as quietly as I could.

"Mason Collins, we know you're in there," a man said from the other side of the door. It was Hardin of the CIC. "Open this damn door."

I looked back at Laura. She had obviously recognized his voice, too, because she slipped her pistol into her coat pocket. Schaller was out of sight, and I figured she was digging herself deep into the sofa cushions. I belted my .45, then remembered the notebook I'd taken off Hodgson's body. I slipped that up my sleeve and went to the door. I turned the lock, pushed back the bolt, and opened the door.

Hardin stood on the other side, flanked by two of the armed agents who'd stood over us in Hardin's living room.

"Not very neighborly to come calling with those guns drawn," I said.

"We understand you're harboring a murder suspect," Hardin said.

"That's not how I see it," I said. "Given more time, we could have cracked the case. How did you find us so fast?"

"I had agents keeping tabs on Hodgson. Remember?" Hardin said with his usual smirk. "Now, if you'll step aside, we'll be about our duties."

I did as he asked, and the three CIC agents entered.

Ellenberg came up behind Hardin and peered over the man's shoulder. "Not very bright, hiding a suspect."

Now I knew how Hardin and his boys had found us. "You're nothing but a big disappointment, David."

Ellenberg seethed but remained behind Hardin. I put my hand on Hardin's arm to stop him from proceeding to the living room. "She's just a kid. And she's shaken up from the bomb blast and losing her boyfriend. Go easy on her, would you?"

"I'll be as easy with her as I imagine you were," Hardin said. He turned and went into the living room, with Ellenberg tailing him.

I followed them in. The two gun-toting agents already had Schaller on her feet. She struggled to get out of their grasp, but the two men held her tight as she sobbed and pleaded. Laura stood directly in front of them in an act of defiance.

Hardin made a beeline for the suitcase as if he knew what it contained. He opened it and whistled. "Hodgson knock over a bank?"

"You know what it's for," I said.

"No, I don't," Hardin said. "Enlighten me."

"It's payments for the secrets Hodgson was passing on to the gang of German agents. There are two passports in there, too. Things got too hot, and Hodgson and Fraulein Schaller were planning to leave town."

"That should be enough to clear Forester," Laura said. "Hodgson was the traitor, not him."

"Just because Hodgson might have been selling secrets doesn't mean Forester is innocent," Hardin said. "After all, Forester murdered Heissmeyer behind the AFN building. To me, that says they were colluding. Heissmeyer found out, and Forester killed him."

"Stretching the facts to fit your fiction?" I asked. "Forester didn't kill Heissmeyer, for one thing, and you know we can prove it."

"Maybe Fraulein Schaller can shed more light on things for us," Hardin said, and motioned for the two agents to take her away.

Schaller screamed and jammed the thick heel of her shoe into the foot of one of the men. The man lost his grip, and Schaller wiggled out of the other's hands. She rammed into Laura, and they both fell onto the coffee table. The two men yanked on her arms. She fought and growled as they half carried her out of the room.

"Take it easy," Hardin yelled after the men. "I want her in one piece." Once the commotion had died down, he said to us, "You two are coming with me. I'm bringing you in." He took steps toward the foyer and noticed we weren't behind him. "You can make this easy or hard. I don't intend to arrest you unless you refuse to come on your own accord. You can even keep your firearms."

I looked at Laura, who shrugged. Resisting wouldn't accomplish anything other than us winding up behind bars. We gathered our things and followed him out of the house.

The three of us froze in surprise. Lieutenant-Colonel McCormick stood with two other uniformed men with captain's silver bars near two army squad cars. Four MPs already had Schaller in handcuffs, and one captain held Schaller's suitcase. Hardin's men stood off to one side and looked to him for guidance.

"What's the meaning of this?" Hardin said to McCormick.

"Is there a 'sir' in there somewhere, Captain?" McCormick said.

"Sir," Hardin said caustically, "this is a counter-intelligence investigation, and these people are suspects. I'm bringing them in for questioning."

McCormick tilted his head back to look down his nose at Hardin. "I have orders from Frankfurt that anything relating to the Gehlen Organization is under G-2 authority."

The two of them faced off like rams ready to butt heads in a fight over territory. I knew about the rivalries between the CIC and G-2, but this was the first time I'd seen it play out in person. Stepping on each other's toes had made American military intelligence a messy business. Throw in the fledgling CIA stirring the pot, and it almost rose to the level of a cat fight.

"How could you have information linking Fraulein Schaller to an organization you claim doesn't even exist?" I asked McCormick.

"I don't have to share classified information with a pain-in-the-ass civilian," he said. "And when headquarters says jump, I jump."

"How could G-2 headquarters possibly know about Fraulein Schaller's involvement so soon after the bombing?" Laura asked.

"Madam, you seem to forget that G-2 is the intelligence branch of the army," McCormick said, raising his voice. "Now, no more questions." He pointed at Laura and me. "You two are coming with us."

"They're in my custody," Hardin said.

"Not anymore, they're not," McCormick said and motioned for two of the MPs to move on us. "Confiscate their weapons."

"We seem to be quite popular," I said to Laura as we handed over our pistols to the MPs. Each one took a pistol, and the one next to me started to pat me down.

The MP started at my shoulders. I had the small book I'd taken from Hodgson's burning house still tucked in my shirt sleeve. I didn't want McCormick to get his hands on that. "There's a knife in my boot."

The distraction worked. Instead of finding the book, the MP went for my pants leg. He removed the knife. "Anything else?" the MP asked with an annoyed expression.

"Brass knuckles in my jacket breast pocket," I said.

He shot me a glare, then rifled around in the leather coat's breast pocket, nearly tearing the interlining.

"Take it easy," I said. "This jacket and I have been in some tough scrapes. I don't want some ape damaging it."

The MP locked his jaw and made a fist, ready to knock my jaw into center field. At least he'd neglected to find the book.

"That's enough," McCormick said. He turned and stepped up to the car. He said to the MPs, "Now that they're disarmed, they ride with me."

The MPs escorted us to the rear passenger door of McCormick's sedan. The two captains got in front, while Laura and I climbed in the back with the colonel. Hardin glared at the sedan as the captain made a three-point turn and steered it onto the road.

We were silent for several blocks until McCormick said, "You two are lucky I came along when I did."

"What's that supposed to mean?" Laura asked.

He raised an eyebrow in surprise, as if we should have known. "I suspect Hardin was going to run you two out of town. Or worse."

"You suspect him of working with Gehlen agents?" she asked.

McCormick shook his head. "I suspect he's working with Forester. Either he or Forester planted the bomb, killing Hodgson, in order to cover their tracks."

I closed my eyes and took a deep breath; either the man was ignoring the facts, or he was that dull-witted. It wouldn't be the first time a high-ranking officer was a few cards short of a full deck. Laura noticed my agitation and nudged me to say something. I couldn't. I was tired of repeating what we'd discovered just for it to fall on deaf ears.

"What are you going to do with Fraulein Schaller?" Laura asked while nudging me once more.

"Question her," McCormick said. "Whether or not she knew she was passing on secrets or was just a patsy in Forester's and Hardin's schemes, she's still guilty of espionage."

"Do you have any concrete evidence to back up those accusations?" I asked.

"When did you conclude that army intelligence is obliged to share anything with you two?" McCormick said. "Suffice it to say, the information getting into Soviet hands is seriously compromising our national security. The Soviets seem to know OMGUS's moves before they're implemented. Within days, any asset we send east disappears or their corpse is found floating in the Spree. We need to nail these bastards before they can send anymore classified material to the Reds. And that's where you two come in. I want you to keep searching for Forester. And maybe, in the process, you dig up something on Hardin."

"In other words, put us on a long leash," I said. "Then grab us all up when we find what we're looking for."

McCormick shrugged. "I wouldn't have worded it quite that way, but yes. Better than doing time in jail."

It was fortunate Laura sat between me and the colonel. I was ready to explode. "Jail? For what?"

McCormick leaned forward and jabbed his index finger at me. "Do you really want me to go through the list? Because it's substantial. It's past the time you two could just pack up and leave. That ship has sailed. Get the job done or be arrested." He tapped on the driver's shoulder. "Pull over."

The captain did as he was told and stopped at the curb in front of a block of buildings that were nothing but rubble.

"This is where you get out," McCormick said.

"Our weapons," I said.

McCormick nodded to the captain in the front passenger's seat, who held the pistols out for us to take. "Are you going to keep the money for yourself?" I asked as I slipped the gun into my belt at the small of my back.

"Get out now, or face the consequences!" McCormick yelled.

We did, and the sedan raced away a second after Laura closed the door.

As we watched it disappear, Laura said, "Greta whispered something in my ear when she tackled me."

"I noticed."

She turned to me with a grim expression. "She begged for help, then said the money wasn't for Hodgson."

"Then who?"

"That's all she was able to say before the two goons pulled her off of me."

I groaned a reply and rubbed my head to keep a headache at bay. I was too exasperated to do more.

Laura grabbed the lapel of my jacket to keep me focused. Her expression was firm but soft. "Snap out of it. Hardin, McCormick, and Ellenberg are all after the same thing and covering it up in the process."

"I'd put my money on any one of them. They're all conniving rats."

Laura pulled her coat tight around her torso. "Why don't we talk about this somewhere else? Anywhere that's warm. We have a long, cold walk ahead of us to get the car."

I thought to myself, *A long walk with targets on our backs*, but I didn't share that with her.

"Welp, here's another nice mess you've gotten me into," I said, quoting from Laurel and Hardy, trying to lighten my mood.

Apparently, Laura didn't think that was funny. She gave me a deadpanned look and pulled me down the sidewalk by my earlobe. "Come on, Ollie."

27

We'd recovered Lehman's Opel at the abandoned mansion and were driving back to the hotel with the heat on full blast to get the feeling back into our hands and feet. Laura's eyes kept closing, and her head nodded to the south, only to come awake with each bump in the road. The same urge to sleep pulled on my eyelids, but I wanted to swing by one more place. I made a quick turn.

Laura snapped awake and looked at me with half-lidded eyes. "Whatever you're up to, can't it wait until morning?"

"I thought, since we're in the neighborhood …"

She looked out her side window. "The AFN?"

"That's right. Hodgson's office."

"It's after ten, and the bed is calling my name," she said.

"Ten's as good a time as any," I said.

"You're a cruel, cruel man. You know that?"

I made a final turn and pulled over to the curb across from the rear gardens of the building. I fished my lock-picking tools and a flashlight out of my backpack and put my hand on the door handle. "I won't be long."

Before Laura could object, I got out of the car, jogged over to the waist-high stone wall, and leaped over it. The back garden was pitch black, but lights from the windows gave me enough illumination to find the walkway and the back door. It took me a couple of minutes to jimmy the lock and get inside.

An Eddy Howard song about an adobe hacienda echoed in the hallway from a speaker hanging on the wall. Most of the doors I passed were dark, though light glowed from the control room and a front office. I took quick strides up to Hodgson's office door. The small window showed the room was dark. Nobody was home.

I knelt at the doorknob and picked the lock in a few seconds, then slipped into the room and flicked on the flashlight. I plucked a file folder off the desk, taped the corners, and stuck it over the window.

The room looked like someone had already rummaged through Hodgson's things. File cabinet drawers hung open, and papers littered the floor. The police probably, though I didn't put it past whoever had killed him to have arrived first. Still, there might be something they overlooked, and I started with the desk. I lifted the blotter and checked the bottoms of the paperweight. The top drawer contained the usual office supplies, matches from various bars, and a photo of a young woman who, I assumed, was the girl back home. I leafed through the file folders in the side drawers but found nothing relevant. Some folders had labels, though whatever had been in there was now gone. Apparently, I was too late for the most salient documents. But who had taken them?

Rifling around, I noticed that the wooden tray for pens and pencils was loose. My scalp tingled when I lifted it and found a folded sheet of tracing paper. I held it up to the light. An array of dots appeared to be drawn in random patterns. An odd thing and odder still to hide it. I pocketed that and turned to the corkboard on the wall. Hodgson had pinned up a *Stars and Stripes* article about him at the AFN. There were some photos of him and various high-ranking officers, him grinning and the officers tolerating the intrusion. Mounted alongside those were a couple of invitations, one to the Thanksgiving Day banquet and one for the upcoming Christmas extravaganza at the Tempelhof Club. I discounted those, as anyone working at the AFN could see them. While a clever individual might hide vital information in plain sight, Hodgson was not in that category. To the left of the maps, a clipboard hung off a hook and appeared to be the daily programming notes. I lifted the clip and took a handful, folding them up and stuffing them in the same pocket.

I froze when two men passed the door as they talked about getting drunk and seducing frauleins later that night. I ducked down behind the desk until the voices faded.

Next, I searched the file cabinet drawers. They had been ransacked and yielded nothing of importance. At least nothing the other searchers hadn't taken. I checked my watch. Ten minutes had passed. It was time to get out of there while my luck still held. I removed the file folder taped to the window, returned it to where I'd found it, and got out of there.

∽

It was closing in on midnight by the time we got back to the hotel. All the way up the stairs to the third floor, I kept checking ahead and behind, as I half expected yet another ambush by Hardin or Ellenberg. Or Wilson, since I felt sure the CID was abuzz over Hodgson's killing.

We made it to our room. Fortunately, no one was waiting for us in the dark this time. I took it as a minor victory. I leaned on the closed door and let my body unwind. Laura flopped onto the bed with a heavy sigh. "I'm out of gas."

Reliving the trauma of the explosion and the revolving door of irate intelligence officers had taken their toll on her strength.

She patted the bed next to her hip. "Come lie with me."

"If I get cozy, I'll fall asleep."

She raised her head to look at me. "That's the idea." She dropped her head on the pillow.

"How's your leg?" I asked. I'd noticed her limping had gotten worse the longer we had walked in the cold.

"I'll live."

She knew my silence was more than having nothing to say. She raised herself on her elbows and frowned. "We couldn't get out of here even if we wanted to. McCormick made sure of that."

"I could find a way."

"No."

"It's not just your leg," I said. "I know that bomb going off at Hodgson's hit you pretty hard."

"Damnit, Mason. I'm fine. I just …" She paused. "That explosion made me think of losing our baby. Those thoughts aren't going away, whether we're here or home."

Fair enough. I resolved to let it go, for now.

"Which one would you pick as Hodgson's ringleader?" I asked, changing the subject.

"Any one of them."

"Maybe I have a clue up my sleeve," I said and removed the notebook from my jacket. I held it up to Laura, then noticed one corner of the cardboard backing was stained with blood.

"You got that off Hodgson?"

I nodded and sat on the bed next to her. I opened the front cover. The first page was filled with scribblings: short notes, numbers, and what appeared to be times and places, as if he'd hastily jotted down future appointments. Some were in a kind of shorthand only he would understand.

"It's like trying to read a doctor's prescription," Laura said.

I turned to the next page, then the next. Front and back of each page. More of the same. No order or pattern, only that it seemed he had written everything chronologically.

"Counting front and back, there are at least fifty pages of this stuff," I said.

I looked at the last page, as I presumed those were his final entries. It stopped about halfway down with Hodgson writing, "Get flowers." There was one with the address for the officers' club's Thanksgiving party at the Harnack-Haus. Above that entry were some comments about the next day's programming at AFN and his list of holiday music. Before that was "the 28th" followed by a short phrase: "Kevin celebrating 15 years in the service."

"An odd thing to put in his notepad," Laura said. "A code of some kind?"

I leafed through the preceding pages and found other phrases: "Quincy has six siblings"; "Martin and Nancy 4th anniversary"; "Oliver his first newborn."

I said, "If these entries are a code, maybe by going through the whole thing we could figure out his thinking."

Laura yawned. "That could take hours." She fell back onto the bed.

I pulled the folded tracing paper from my pocket. "I found this hidden under a pencil tray in his office desk drawer."

With a grunt, Laura sat up to see what I was talking about. I unfolded it and laid it on the bed. It had been unfolded and refolded many times. At eighteen inches square, the sheet had nothing on it but the dots I'd seen earlier. No notes or other markings, just what looked like punctures on a dartboard.

"Well, isn't that interesting," Laura said in a sarcastic tone.

I waved a dismissive hand at it. "Why go through the trouble of hiding this if it didn't mean anything to him?"

She flopped back down onto the bed. "Maybe it slipped under there. It's drawer science. A realm where chaos reigns."

I folded it up with the promise to get back to it when my brain was rested. I then pulled out the program charts that I'd put in the same pocket.

"It might mean something when our heads clear, but in the meantime, I'm going to get some ..."

The lights went out.

I got up and checked the switch for the overhead light. Nothing.

"They cut the power again," Laura said.

The power grid was still fragile thanks to the bombings. The repair work often required cutting a section, or it happened when a section became overloaded. The Soviets had dismantled anything mechanical, from entire factories to the city's infrastructure, in the early days of the occupation, and the allies had worked overtime to get everything up and running again. The hotel's neighborhood experienced more than its share of outages.

Fortunately, the gas heater still worked. While most of the room fell into deep shadow, the radiator bathed Laura in a warm glow.

"Isn't this romantic?" I said.

Laura shook her head. "Don't even think about it."

I slipped off my jacket, stepped up to the foot of the bed, and lowered myself so I was above her, taking most of my weight with my hands. "Pretend we were having a candlelit dinner. We've finished off a bottle of champagne, loosening our desires and giving in to the moment."

Laura laughed. "Have you been reading romantic novels on the sly? Thought you'd try out those corny lines on me?"

"Did it work?" I asked in a hushed tone.

"No," she said and wrapped her arms around my neck. "My advice? Stick to what you do so well."

We kissed long and hard. She pulled me down and turned so we were both on our sides. Undressing each other was slow and gentle. The same was true with our lovemaking. The world was gone. Only the two of us and the soft thrum of the radiator. I didn't want it to end.

28

I thought sunrise had stirred me from sleep until I opened my eyes and saw that it was still night and the electricity had been restored. The overhead lamp and bedside lamp both conspired to ruin my much-needed rest.

I checked my watch. It was 1:50 a.m. I sat up in bed and looked at Laura. She was still out, though her eyes were doing calisthenics behind her lids, and her lips quivered as if in conversation. Probably a bad dream, but a far sight better than the ones in Boston.

I stood and poured water from the pitcher into my glass and gulped it down. A few snowflakes passed close enough to the window to reflect light. I turned off the overhead light but left the bedside lamp on, then went over to the window to see how bad it was snowing. There were just a few flurries dancing in the wind and floating down onto the pedestrians milling about the bars and strip clubs.

The power outage had done little to subdue the festivities outside. The whole street, as far as I could tell, was lit up by neon lights, beckoning potential clients, the majority being in uniform. A few cars cruised by. Big band music drifted up.

Then my gaze landed on a sedan parked across from the hotel. Someone sat inside, smoking a cigarette. A man in civvies and a homburg hat. He wasn't interested in the girls flanking the doors and luring in customers. He just sat there, sometimes eyeing the hotel entrance. I instinctively took a few steps back from the window.

Either he was part of a surveillance team or the driver of a getaway car.

I went for my .45 in the nightstand drawer, put one in the chamber, and slipped over to the door. I listened with my ear pressed to the cool wood. Not a sound. I got my pistol ready and opened the door enough to stick my head outside. I waited a good five minutes, long enough for any potential shooters to mount the stairs. All was quiet.

"Mason?" Laura said sleepily.

I shut the door and moved over to her. "There's someone downstairs watching the hotel."

I didn't have to say more. She jumped out of bed, slipped on her robe, and got her pistol from her bedside table.

Stepping up to within a few feet of the window, I looked down at the sedan. That was when I spotted another guy standing in the recess of a door to a shop. At that moment, he was distracted by a soldier and a woman in the throes of passion ten feet from him. I turned off the bedside lamp and ducked back when he turned his head to look up at our window.

"How many?" Laura asked.

"Two, from what I can see. There could be one inside."

Laura peeked out the window on her side of the bed. Red and blue neon from the street threw a weak light into the room and onto her face. She shifted to the edge of the bed and out of sight. "Can you tell who they are?"

"No, but I'm going to find out," I said. I pulled on my clothes and shoes, coat and hat. I then belted my pistol in the front and closed my coat to conceal it.

As I moved for the door, Laura said, "Be careful."

I nodded at her and exited the room. I kept to the inside wall of the stairway as I descended the steps in case there were shooters lying in wait. For the last flight of stairs, the walls fell away and opened up to a view from the lobby. I stopped and bent low to scan the front room. It was empty. The front desk was closed, the lights dimmed.

I took the rest of the stairs and turned left, away from the lobby, and headed for the side exit. The night we'd checked in, I'd scoped out the escape routes, something I'd gotten into a habit of doing since being on the run in France and Morocco. The exit opened onto a narrow alley. I turned right to the street behind the hotel and made a loop around until ending up a block to the rear of the observers' car.

I unbuttoned my coat and put my hand on the pistol grip. With measured steps, I moved toward the observer standing in the doorway. A few drunken couples staggered past me. Music blasted onto the street when several soldiers exited one of the bars.

I got within fifty feet of the man and fought the urge to shoot first and ask questions later. But there were too many people, and I risked hitting a bystander.

The observer in the doorway spotted me, then my hand on the pistol. He flicked his cigarette onto the sidewalk. I recognized him as the beak-nosed gunsel who had appeared in the basement in East Berlin. The one who'd held his gun on Laura.

He eyed me as if unsure of what I might do. What my rage told me to do. His hand moved slowly toward something inside his coat as he stared directly at my eyes.

I pulled out my .45 and pointed it at him. A woman screamed. A couple dived into a bar. Others froze at the spectacle.

"*Ich bitte Sie, Ihre Waffe zu ziehen,*" I said to the agent in German, taunting him to go for his gun.

The man stared at me for a moment, then dropped his hand

to his side and strode over to the car. He got in, and the driver peeled away. Part of me was relieved, but the other part regretted he hadn't gone for his weapon and given me an excuse to gun him down.

Movement from our hotel entrance prompted me to look in that direction. Laura, fully dressed, stepped onto the sidewalk. She watched the car drive away with her hand deep in her coat pocket, presumably holding the Tokarev.

I buttoned my coat, crossed the street, and pulled her into the alley. The witnesses to the altercation had disappeared and replaced by other revelers who seemed unaware that anything had occurred.

Laura stared into my eyes. "I recognized the one on the street. I wanted to shoot him, Mason," she said with a pained look on her face. "It would have given me a great deal of satisfaction."

I nodded knowingly.

"What does that say about us?" she asked.

"It says that we're damned fed up with ex-Nazis threatening to kill us," I said.

"That, and forcing us to find another hotel," Laura said.

"Good enough reason, right there, if you ask me."

A Jeep with four MPs pulled up to the curb on the opposite side of the street.

"We'd better use the side door," I said and led her to the entrance in the alley.

Once inside, we moved through the hallway and mounted the stairs.

Halfway up, Laura said, "I'm too rattled to sleep any more tonight."

"Good, because we're going to pack up and leave."

"Now? It's two in the morning. No hotel's going to take us at this hour."

"I've got a better idea."

29

I knocked on the front door. I waited, then knocked harder. The door rattled in the frame.

"Are you sure we've got the right place?" Laura asked.

"Hope so," I said and knocked again.

Laura and I huddled under the awning of the front porch to stay out of the misty rain. The porch belonged to a single-story house, which was part of a much larger property dominated by a sprawling mansion. I'd already knocked on the mansion's door, but no one had answered. Being unoccupied, I figured the mansion had been converted into offices, as we were right across from the headquarters of the Berlin section of the Office of Military Government, United States, or OMGUS.

A light came on and illuminated the bay window curtain. The front porch light followed it, and then someone fiddled with the lock. The door opened. Wilson stood inside wrapped in his bathrobe and squinted at the light.

Surprise registered in his bloodshot eyes, then his entire face twisted in anger. "What the hell?" He glanced down at our suitcases. "What the hell?"

"We need a place to stay," I said.

"You came here in the middle of the night to tell me that?" he asked, then realization worked its way through the fog of his hangover. "Oh, no you don't. Not here."

"Arnie, we've run out of hotels," I said.

"Two of the German agents just chased us out of the last one," Laura said.

"So, you picked me?" Wilson said.

"You're the only person we can trust in this snake pit of a town," I said.

He glanced at both of us. Our expressions must have been pathetic enough for him to groan and step aside. "You guys could have picked a worse night, but I can't think of one off the top of my head."

Laura and I entered and stopped a few feet into the living room.

"You were already one drink away from hammered this afternoon," I said.

"Yeah, well, that didn't seem to stop me," Wilson said as he closed the door.

The place was all in wood, from the walls and ceiling to the furniture. Mounted stuffed heads of deer and boar took up a considerable amount of wall space.

"Interesting place you got here," I said.

"What? You don't like late medieval?" Wilson said and walked over to a leather sofa and dropped onto a cushion. He rubbed his eyes and let out a yawn.

Laura and I put our suitcases by a table and sat in plush leather chairs flanking the sofa.

"This is just temporary," Wilson said. "A bird colonel and his family took over the place where I was staying—" His thought was interrupted by another yawn.

"How about I get some coffee in you?" Laura said.

Wilson groaned as he pushed himself to his feet. "I'll make some."

We followed Wilson into the kitchen. Laura and I sat at a square table for four, while Wilson shuffled over to the counter. He added water to the percolator, then measured out some ground coffee, and put the percolator onto the stove. Once that ritual was completed, he came over and sat across from us.

"Why don't we talk about that little bombshell you dropped on me this afternoon?" he said.

Laura gave me a quizzical look.

I shrugged and said, "You mean Beatrice Schweitzer being murdered?"

"I'm sure you have enough to make this a long night, but let's start with that one."

Laura and I took turns recounting our talk with Beatrice. About how Leiter and Heissmeyer had threatened both Sigrid and Beatrice to keep their mouths shut. About what, she didn't know. That she'd overheard Leiter talk about making sure Forester showed up at the field behind the AFN building only a couple of nights before Heissmeyer was killed. "That proves Forester was set up to be framed."

"Pity Schweitzer isn't around to give her testimony," Wilson said.

"Then she offered to take us to a location where we might find Forester," I said. "In the Soviet zone."

"Which turned out to be a trap," Wilson said.

"How did you know?" Laura asked.

"Forester isn't here, is he?"

"Beatrice led us to a basement in the Soviet sector," I said. "Then Leiter's gang showed up minutes later." I pulled the bar photo from my breast pocket and gave it to Wilson. "This is one of the photos you had developed."

"Yeah, I saw them," Wilson said.

"The guy on the left is the one who shot Beatrice. He appears to be the new leader."

He looked at it again and shook his head. "Okay, but it's

blurry and dark, and the face is in profile. There's no way anyone could make an ID from this."

"According to one of the Germans we escaped the basement with, he was a high-ranking SS or Gestapo officer. He's now the new leader of Leiter's group."

"Our guess is that Forester was trying to track down this man when he was framed," Laura said.

Wilson stared at the photo and said nothing in response. I took that as a good sign; he was starting to believe what we'd been saying all along. We let him digest the new information. A dog barked in the distance. The percolator gurgled on the stove.

Laura broke the silence. "We feel certain that same ex-SS officer and the gang are responsible for Hodgson's death."

Wilson looked up in surprise. "The chief says that explosion was caused by a gas leak."

I shook my head. "The blast was too localized. And it happened just seconds after he opened the door."

Wilson furrowed his brow. "Don't tell me you were there."

"We followed …" I said.

Wilson interrupted me by groaning and falling back in his chair. "What is it with you two? How is it that you just happen to be around every time there's a killing?"

"That's a bit of an exaggeration," Laura said.

"Not much," Wilson said. "Leiter, Schweitzer, and now Hodgson." He let out a long breath and sat upright. "I had my suspicions about Hodgson's death from the beginning. But someone seems interested in sweeping it under the rug. Okay, you two were following Hodgson …" He waved his hand for us to continue.

"I spotted him at the Thanksgiving party," I said. "He was having a heated argument with a waiter, who I think is a German plant. After that, Hodgson stormed out of there. We decided to see where he might lead us. He picked up his girlfriend and drove to his place. She went back to get something she forgot in the car, while Hodgson unlocked the door. As soon as he stepped inside, the bomb went off. By the looks of it, a tripwire was rigged to an explosive and an incendiary device."

"To burn evidence as well as kill," Wilson said. "I'll bet my bottom dollar you still went in there and rummaged around."

I looked at Laura, then noticed the coffeemaker had stopped percolating. I got up and went to the stovetop.

"Your silence answers my question," Wilson said. He went over to a cabinet by the sink and pulled out three mugs. "What did you find, aside from Hodgson's corpse?"

He stared at me as I poured coffee into the three mugs.

"Mason, what did you find? You can trust me."

I suppressed a cynical chuckle, wrangled the mugs, and went back to the table. Wilson sat across from me. I took the notepad from my jacket pocket and held it up. "I found this on Hodgson's body." I laid it on the table in front of him. "Have a look, but it stays with us."

Wilson opened it and leafed through the pages. "A lot of gibberish. Some addresses we could check out. There could be some coded messages in there, or nothing at all." He closed the notepad. "You know I can't let you keep this. It's evidence in a murder case."

"I figured you'd say that," I said. "That's why I didn't want to show it to you. Your fearless leader isn't going to do a damn thing with it. In his mind, he's solved this case and doesn't want to hear anything that might make his job more difficult. Might as well toss it in the river."

Wilson said nothing in response. He had to know I was right. "I'll make you a deal," he said. "You can hold on to it for a few days before I turn it in. But it stays here."

"Sounds like we get to stay," Laura asked.

"Did I ever have a choice?" Wilson said.

"You're a gentleman and a scholar," I said.

Wilson scowled at me. "Don't push it."

A brief silence fell on the room as we all took sips of the coffee.

"Now, what about Hodgson's girlfriend?" Wilson asked.

I made him wait until I had another sip. "We took her."

Wilson closed his eyes and put his face in his hands. "I'm losing count of the criminal acts you two have committed."

"Do you want to hear what she said or not?" Laura asked.

He lifted his head but said nothing.

Laura and I alternated telling the tale of following Hodgson, him picking up Schaller, and her carrying a suitcase. How we trailed them to his house, Schaller supposedly forgetting something in the car, and the bomb exploding upon Hodgson opening the door.

"Either she was supposed to die in that blast, or she was part of the setup," I said. "Lure him to the house, then grab up the suitcase and take it to the German agents."

"My vote is for the latter," Laura said.

We spoke about taking Schaller to the abandoned mansion and finding a large stash of money in various currencies inside. She claimed the money came from the German agents as payment for Hodgson passing on classified documents.

"Here's a real stumper," I said. "According to Schaller, the German agents considered Hodgson untouchable."

Wilson screwed up his face in confusion. "If he was untouchable, then who planted the bomb?"

"Ah, there's the rub," Laura said. "There are two possibilities. Either the German agents did it to take back the pile of money. Or whoever was controlling Hodgson did it because Hodgson risked exposing the operation."

Wilson glanced at both of us. I could tell his brain was working overtime to put it all together. "Let's assume Schaller was telling the truth, that the agents considered Hodgson untouchable. Then someone with a lot of authority was controlling him."

"And the only people with that kind of juice are American officers," Laura said.

"That's a long list," Wilson said and slumped in his chair. He fumbled in his bathrobe pocket and pulled out a pack of cigarettes. He noticed my look of surprise. "What? You don't keep cigarettes in your bathrobe?" He pulled one out and lit it, then shook the pack at us.

Laura declined, but I took one and let him light mine with the same match.

"The list is shorter than you think," I said. "Before a couple of G-2 goons took Schaller away—"

"Wait, wait, what?" Wilson said, interrupting.

Laura told him that Hardin and Ellenberg from the CIC had come to arrest her, only to be intercepted by McCormick of the army's G-2 and two of his captains. "McCormick took us, Schaller, and the suitcase with them. McCormick let us go on the condition we hunt down Forester."

Wilson rubbed his forehead and mumbled, "Jesus. There goes any chance of getting any more out of Schaller."

"Anyway," Laura said, "before they took her away, Schaller whispered to me that the money wasn't meant for Hodgson. Unfortunately, that's all she could tell me before she was dragged away."

"I thought she was frightened of getting picked up by someone in Leiter's gang," I said. "But she seemed more scared of Captain Hardin and Lieutenant Ellenberg of the CIC and Lieutenant-Colonel McCormick in G-2."

Wilson shot up from his chair and paced. He'd pause just long enough to take another puff off his cigarette. Finally, he said, "I should be able to get hold of their files. The ones that aren't classified, anyway. Requesting those will raise alarm bells."

"What about your superior?" I asked and snapped my fingers. "What's his name?"

"Cuthbert?" Wilson asked and shook his head. "He's not going to step on any toes. He's only interested in keeping his nose clean until his time is up and he leaves for a choice law enforcement job Stateside."

"Solving a high-profile case like this could give him high marks," I said.

"Mason, you know better than anyone. Investigating the CIC or G-2 will get you nothing but trouble." He waved his hand. "No, that's out."

"Do you have the authority to send junior investigators out on stakeouts?" Laura asked.

"Yes, but not enough to keep an eye on all three," Wilson said. "Besides, Cuthbert has already labeled Hodgson's death as accidental. Requesting junior officers for surveillance duties is going to be tough."

"Going through some personnel files won't get us anywhere," I said. As I pondered everything, I walked over to the stove and poured another cup of coffee. "Look, I'm pretty sure whoever was running Hodgson killed him out of fear of being compromised. Now the killer has a decision to make. If he's scared, he'll lie low. If he's greedy, he'll pass on the documents himself or find another patsy."

"The guy had to have balls, setting up a spy ring while working for the CIC or G-2," Wilson said. "He won't go crawling back under a rock. The money's too good."

"That could bring him out into the open," Laura said. "How about we pick just one of the trio to put a tail on?"

"Hardin is the most logical," I said. "He's worked hard to maintain Forester's guilt."

"McCormick is the one who took Schaller and the money," Laura said.

Wilson sat with a heavy sigh. "I'll do it myself. We keep this between us."

"Laura and I will check out the addresses in Hodgson's

notepad," I said. "We'll start at the back of the notepad and work our way forward."

"That could take days," Wilson said.

"We might get lucky," I said.

"You better count on something other than luck," Wilson said. "Like I said, yours ran out a while ago."

Laura shrugged. "With our luck?"

She had a point, and I readied my .45. We got out of the car and headed for the entrance. The single MP at the door glanced at our press passes and waved us in. The ballroom was closed for decorating, so the management had set up tables and chairs in the lobby. Early diners, mostly in uniform, occupied about half of them. Three buffet-style tables ran along the back wall, one with cold items and one with warming trays; the last featured a prime rib carving station. A couple dozen patrons sat on stools at the bar. A pianist played the Cole Porter tune "Night and Day" with a few people standing around the piano, singing the lyrics.

"There won't be as many waiters tonight," Laura said.

"Then we'll just have to do with a couple of drinks," I said and held out my arm.

Laura took it, and we headed to the bar, pretending to be guests at a swanky cocktail party. We found two empty stools and ordered drinks, her a martini, and a scotch for me. While the bartender prepared the drinks, we both surveyed the room. A couple of waiters circulated among the diners, bringing drinks or clearing plates. The line had grown for the prime rib station as more people filtered in. A captain sat a few stools down from us and set a full plate of food down on the bar. The odors made my stomach growl loud enough for Laura to hear it.

"No time for that now," she said and pointed her chin toward the buffet tables. "Is that him?"

I looked in the direction of her gaze. The waiter we'd seen arguing with Hodgson stepped up to a second prime rib station to help serve the influx of hungry diners.

The bartender brought our drinks. We clinked glasses and set to watching the second carver as we sipped our cocktails. He looked to be in his mid-thirties with blond hair and towered over his carving colleague. His delicate, almost feminine facial features seemed out of place compared to his muscular frame.

"That's him all right," I said.

"He's good with that knife," Laura said. "All that and pretty, too. That is, if a girl liked Nazi poster boys."

"Why, Miss McKinnon, if I didn't know you better, I'd be jealous."

"He might have pleasing features, but judging by that permanent scowl on his face, I think he'd rather carve the customers than that hunk of beef."

I downed my drink and stood. "I'd say it's time to give him a better reason to frown."

"Where are you going?" Laura asked.

"Talk to the pretty Nazi," I said. "Watch my six, would you?"

Laura sipped on her martini to give me a head start. I got in line for the prime rib station but didn't pick up a plate. I kept watching the knife-wielding Nazi as I shuffled along, but he kept his eyes on carving the meat and doling out slices. My stomach pleaded with me to grab a potato or dip a finger in the horseradish sauce while I waited, but all that would do was tease my brain.

The woman ahead of me received her slices of beef and headed for the tables. It was my turn. Pretty Nazi kept his eyes on the beef, and I kept mine on the substantial knife he skillfully wielded. He lifted a forkful of pinkish meat to lay on my plate. With a furrowed brow, his gaze went from my empty hands to my face.

He froze, his eyes registering surprise.

"I have Greta and the suitcase," I said in German to make sure he got the message. "I bet you guys would do anything to get them back. But it will cost you."

I stepped away and headed for the restrooms, taking my time, while keeping my gaze forward and hoping the waiter would take the bait. I trusted Laura was watching at a discreet distance in case the waiter had lost his cool and jumped me then and there.

The restrooms were at the end of a short hallway in the far

back corner of the room. I registered the rear exit at the end, then pushed through the restroom door. The room was sizeable, with six sinks and the same number of urinals and stalls. As soon as the door swung shut, I rushed to a stall. Leaving the door open, I pulled out my gun and waited. Minutes passed, but no waiter.

The door swung open. I got ready to attack, but two men came in, talking about the latest fiasco of a meeting at the Allied Council between the four allies. That the Russians had walked out in protest over discussions concerning the currency issues. I softly closed the stall door and waited until they had finished their business and walk out again.

The bait hadn't hooked the Nazi fish. More than likely, he'd run to his boss to report what I'd said. I belted my pistol and exited the stall. Since I was there, I went over to a urinal.

The door blew open, and the waiter was on me in an instant. He swung the carving knife and narrowly missed my throat.

I jumped back and hit the wall. He swung at me again, but I deflected his arm and got in a right jab to his chin. That barely slowed him down. He slashed at me again and cut into the sleeve of my suit coat. A searing pain shot up my arm.

He tried a backhanded swing. I caught his arm and tried to knee him in the crotch, but he pulled his hips back.

I wrapped my free arm around his neck, trapping his knife arm to his chest. We both tried headbutts, but neither of us could land a good blow. We spun around, both of us delivering weak hits to the face.

My back collided with a stall door. We both fell into the enclosure. My legs buckled when my calves hit the toilet.

He freed his knife arm and raised it to plunge the blade into my chest. Near the arch, I heard a hollow thud from behind him, and his eyes went wide in pain and surprise. Another thud put him out, and he collapsed onto me, pinning me half-standing against the toilet.

Laura stood outside the stall door, holding her pistol by the barrel. She had a self-satisfied grin on her face.

"You could have come in a little sooner," I said, out of breath.

The restroom door swung open.

"It's closed for cleaning," Laura said in a loud voice.

"Jesus," a man said, retreating, and the door swung shut.

I grunted from the strain of pushing the unconscious waiter off my legs and had to step over him to exit the stall. "We've got to get him out of here."

"How are we supposed to do that?" Laura asked. "We'll have to go past a hundred people. Then there's the MP posted at the door."

"There's an exit to the right," I said. "At the end of the hallway."

Laura groaned her displeasure, but she helped me lift the waiter's limp body by his armpits. We dragged him to the door, leaving a small trail of blood as we did so.

"Ready?" I asked.

Laura took a deep breath and nodded. I pushed through the door first, with Laura on the other end. A guy who looked like he'd had one too many cocktails stood a few feet from the door.

"This guy can't hold his liquor," I said to the man. "Got to get him to the hospital."

Fortunately, the exit was just ten feet to our right. Laura and I dragged him the rest of the way. I hoped it wasn't locked. I kicked with enough force that the latch popped out of the strike plate and the door opened. We pulled him down a service corridor and out into an alleyway.

"How are we going to get him to the car?" Laura asked between breaths.

"I'm working on it," I said, even though I didn't have the slightest idea how. More troubling, I didn't know what to do with him if we managed to stash him in the trunk.

31

I looked both ways in the alley. To the left was a driveway, and beyond, the entrance and parking lot. To the right, the road took a sharp turn past a small lawn bounded by high shrubs.

"That way," I said, pointing toward the lawn.

We both strained to drag the man's heavy body the thirty yards to the edge of the shrubs. Our captive moaned when we dropped him to the ground.

"Go get the car," I said. "And hurry."

As Laura rushed toward the other end of the alley, I sat on the ground and lifted the waiter with his back to me. The man's groaning went on for a couple of minutes as he came out of his stupor. I wrapped his neck in a headlock and waited. He sucked in his breath and kicked and grabbed at my arms. I squeezed his neck. His struggles became more violent. I tilted my head back when he tried to put his fingers in my eyes. I clamped down harder. A moment later, the fighting stopped, and he fell limp in my arms. I checked his pulse and breathing. He'd passed out, but was fine.

I heard the roar of the Opel engine as it sped up the alley. It stopped next to me, and Laura got out. Even though she'd never done anything like this before, she knew the drill and opened the trunk. She helped me lift the dead weight of the guy, and we carried him to the back of the car.

I stopped. With the spare tire in the trunk, there wasn't enough room for the waiter. I lowered his shoulders to the ground and went for the tire. I knew Lehman would be really upset if he saw me, but I couldn't worry about that now and put the tire in the back seat as gingerly as I could. I hurried around the back, and we hoisted the waiter. Even with the tire gone, we had a tough time jamming him inside. We finally succeeded and slammed the lid closed.

"The air in there won't last long," Laura said.

"We won't be going far," I said.

As Laura went around to the passenger's side, she asked, "You know where we're headed?"

"Nope," I said and got behind the wheel. I hit the accelerator and zipped around the curved portion of the alleyway and ended up on the street. With no exact destination in mind, I turned left, then left again, and headed north on Berliner Strasse.

Our captive waiter started pounding on the trunk lid.

"Well, he's awake," Laura said.

I grunted a response.

Laura turned in her seat. "Mason, if we have to stop anywhere around people, they're going to hear that noise."

Adrenaline was still pumping through me, and the pounding set off my temper. I spotted a narrow road that led to an area of ruins. I hit the accelerator and turned, making the tires squeal in protest. I figured Laura knew not to question my judgment, because she just held on and watched for MPs or German police.

I pulled into an alleyway. The far end was blocked off by a towering pile of debris from the surrounding buildings. I slammed on the brakes, came to a stop, and got out, leaving the engine running. I pulled my pistol out of my belt and stood by the trunk. The waiter continued to bang on the lid despite the rough ride. With the muzzle of my pistol hovering just above the trunk lid and aiming for an abandoned building, I pulled the trigger. The blast from the gun was deafening in the eerie silence. The man stopped.

"Not another noise, or I'll empty my gun into the trunk," I said.

The fury in my voice must have convinced the man that I was serious, because he fell quiet. I belted my pistol and got back in the car. Shoved the gearshift into reverse and backed out of the alley at full speed.

"Beating the car half to death isn't going to make things better," Laura said. "You promised to take care of it. Plus, you're going to attract the wrong kind of attention."

She was right, and I eased off the accelerator pedal.

"We could have gone into those ruins to question the waiter," Laura said.

I shook my head. "There's still a chance someone lives in there. We need a place that's inconspicuous. A place with items we can use to restrain him. Somewhere we can make some noise without being heard."

"Warm would be nice, too," Laura said.

"Definitely a bonus," I said and made a left onto Kaiser Allee.

∼

Twenty tense minutes later, I parked the car in front of Beatrice Schweitzer's apartment building. I shut off the engine, and we surveyed the street. It was close to eight p.m. With no working streetlights, the area was pitch black.

"Night works in our favor," Laura said.

I got out and went around to the trunk and pulled out my .45. With one last scan of the area, I readied my pistol, unlocked the trunk, and lifted the lid.

The waiter sucked in fresh air as he shivered and coughed. He seemed weak from the ordeal and lack of oxygen. Blood from where Laura had struck him had dried and matted his hair. Laura covered me with her pistol, while I pulled the man out of the trunk. I closed the lid and pushed the man against the car. I put the muzzle of my .45 under the waiter's chin. The man tried to shrink away from the muzzle, but he stopped when I pressed it harder into his flesh.

"Not a sound," I said in German.

The waiter nodded. I yanked him by the collar of his suit coat and shoved him toward the building entrance. Laura led the way through the darkness. Though I was behind him, I could tell he was looking for a way out, and I pulled even tighter on his collar to dissuade any thoughts of escape.

Laura got the door open, and we entered the lobby as dark as a coal mine.

"Lighter in my pocket," I said.

Laura had to feel her way down to my pocket. She found the lighter and ignited the wick. Compared to the utter blackness, the tiny flame seemed bright. I followed her to the staircase, and she started climbing the steps.

I pulled back the pistol's hammer. "This gun's got a light trigger," I said in English. "Try anything, and your brains will end up on the wall."

"Then you better not trip," the waiter said with a heavy accent.

I figured he spoke English; it just took the threat of a bullet to get it out of him. I gave him a nudge, prompting him up the stairs.

Moments later, we reached the third floor. The waiter stiffened when we reached the door to Schweitzer's apartment.

"So, you know this place," I said.

The man said nothing as Laura opened the door, and we went inside. She put her purse on a chair in the corner and lit two lanterns, one on the small dining table and one near the beds. I shoved the waiter into one of the three chairs and pointed to the laundry still hanging on a length of rope between the two beds.

"Get that rope, would you?" I said to Laura. "And something for a gag."

Laura closed the ragged curtain and did what I asked. She returned with the rope along with a long wool stocking and two pairs of panties. I looked from the panties to her.

She shrugged. "For the gag. They're clean. I think."

I handed her the .45, and she held the gun on our captive while I started lashing him to the chair. The man remained stoic as I secured his arms and wrapped his torso, binding him to the back of the chair. I pulled everything tight, purposefully restricting his breathing.

"Why are you doing this to me?" the waiter asked. "I've done nothing wrong."

"Then you have nothing to worry about," I said.

"I do not have any information, if that is what you are looking for," he said.

I ignored the comment and finished with the last knot, binding his legs. I got up off my knees. Laura laid the pistol on the table next to me but out of our prisoner's reach. She went over to the potbellied stove.

"There's no coal," she said. "I'll have to use the wood that's here."

I was only half listening as I searched the waiter's suit coat. I found his wallet and pulled it out. A search behind a flap of leather revealed his ID.

"Well, well," I said to Laura. "Guess who we have here. Greta Schaller's beau, Hermann Trisko."

Laura stopped loading wood into the stove and came over to look over my shoulder. I searched the wallet pocket meant for cash and discovered another photo. I looked at Laura to see her reaction. The 2x2 photo was of Trisko and Beatrice Schweitzer.

"Now we know who her mysterious boyfriend was," I said.

"Poetic justice, bringing him to Beatrice's place," Laura said.

"What does this mean, poetic justice?" Trisko said.

"She refused to say who you were because she was so frightened of Leiter and Heissmeyer. You did nothing to keep her from those two killers, and now she's dead."

Trisko appeared genuinely surprised. "What? Beatrice is dead?"

"Oh, come on, Hermann. Do you expect us to believe you didn't know? It was your lunatic leader who pulled the trigger."

He twisted his face in anger. "You're lying!"

"You can deny it all you want," I said. "We were there when that ex-SS officer gunned her down in cold blood."

Trisko clamped his mouth shut and looked away from us with a defiant expression.

"You know what comes next," I said. "We're going to ask you some questions, and we expect answers." I rubbed my hands together. "It's damn cold in here. We should get that fire going." I walked over to the stove and knelt in front of the firebox. Laura had already loaded enough kindling and wood, and all I had to do was put my lighter to it. Once the fire took hold, I lifted a metal poker sitting next to the stove and held it up for Trisko to see it. "This will do nicely." Out of the corner of my eye, I could see him looking my way. I put the tip of the poker in the pile of burning wood and shut the door most of the way.

Laura shifted her gaze from me to the poker sticking out of the stove. She said nothing, but she must have known what I had in mind.

32

Laura dragged another wooden chair from the other side of the table to sit in front of Trisko. "I can see that the news of Beatrice's death upset you. Your boss murdered her. You don't owe him any loyalty."

Trisko looked away to avoid Laura's eyes. His expression remained stern, but I could see it soften. Laura's approach seemed like a good way to start, so I stood off to one side, crossed my arms, and kept quiet.

Laura leaned over with her elbows on her knees in a relaxed posture. "I can't promise we'll just let you go, but I assure you, no harm will come to you if you answer our questions."

Trisko remained as he was.

"What were you doing at the Harnack-Haus?" Laura asked.

He said nothing.

"Spying? Trying to recruit assets? There to relay covert messages?"

Trisko stared at the far wall with his stoic expression.

"You must be cold," Laura said and walked over to Beatrice's closet.

"I thought the woman Hodgson was panting over, Greta

Schaller, was your girlfriend," I said. "That's what she claimed, anyway."

Trisko shrugged. "That was just to encourage her to do what we wanted."

Laura took one of her overcoats off a hanger, moved behind Trisko, and draped the coat over the man's shoulders. He recoiled as if the coat had disgusted him, and he tried to shake it off his shoulders. It was a smart move on Laura's part. It told me, and her, that he had loved Beatrice and felt guilty for her death.

"No?" Laura asked. She removed the coat. "I didn't realize you had such strong feelings for Beatrice. That was unthoughtful of me."

The man seemed confused. He had steeled himself for a brutal interrogation, and then Laura treated him with kindness.

She sat in front of him and leaned in. "What's the leader's name? The one who gunned down Fraulein Schweitzer?"

Trisko turned his head to look at Laura. "What difference does his name make?"

"I'll turn that around," she said. "If it doesn't make a difference, then why conceal his identity? The only reason to do that is if he's on a list of war criminals. Is he, Hermann?"

"We know he took over from Leiter," I said. "My guess is he's the one who murdered Leiter to make that happen. Did he pull the trigger?"

"I wasn't there, so I don't know."

"He certainly didn't have any qualms about murdering Beatrice," Laura said. "And if the Soviets hadn't shown up, he would have killed us and the two dozen innocent Germans who just happened to be there seeking shelter."

"The man is a cold-blooded murderer," I said. "Fits the profile of a sadistic SS commander."

"I will make sure he is punished, but I will not betray my countrymen to you or any other foreigner."

"At least one high-ranking American officer knows who he

is," I said. "How about you tell us who's been calling the shots, shielding your group from the rest of the Allied intelligence agencies?"

"Reinhard Gehlen is our commander. No one else. Who he takes orders from is unknown to me."

"Your group has been operating outside Gehlen's authority," I said. "We know that. The CIC knows it. That is, unless Gehlen's also a double agent."

"He would never work for the communists," Trisko said. "Never."

"But you guys are," I said.

"That's a lie!"

"Maybe you didn't know what your colleagues were doing," I said. "Though I find that hard to believe." I held up my hand and raised a finger for each point. "Hodgson had a deal with Leiter to trade secrets for cash. We know this thanks to Beatrice. Hodgson was in possession of a large sum of money when he was killed. According to Greta, that money was from the Soviets for services rendered. And Beatrice also said that your group considered Hodgson untouchable. Meaning he was being protected by someone with power. You see? All this adds up to a bunch of German ex-intelligence officers working both sides and taking orders from someone high up in American intelligence."

"Why would you be taking Beatrice's word for all of this?" Trisko said. "She was not part of our team. She knew nothing."

"Hermann," Laura said, "if you're so passionately opposed to the Soviets, then you have no reason to keep information from us."

"I hate Americans only a little less than I do the Bolsheviks."

"Then why be with Gehlen's organization?" Laura asked. "He and his team are helping the Americans."

"The lesser of two evils. Isn't that the expression? Besides, I am nothing if I am not an intelligence officer. I could not go back to living as a civilian, begging you Americans or British for work just to keep from starving to death."

"Let's leave that for a moment," I said. "Who killed Victor Heissmeyer?"

"I don't know. I wasn't there."

"You don't seem to be anywhere when your buddies are committing crimes," I said. "That's convenient. What exactly is it you do for the organization?"

"What we all do. Hunt for German communist spies working for the Russians in the Allied sectors."

"Do you see the irony here?" I asked. "That some of your pals are working both sides?"

Trisko growled and fidgeted in his chair. "Heissmeyer was a cruel man with no honor. I celebrated his death. Leiter told me he had the man killed because he was working for an American counter-intelligence officer."

"Major Forester," Laura said.

"Yes," Trisko said. "Leiter said that this Forester had information on Heissmeyer and was threatening him with it if he didn't betray us."

"What did Forester have?" I asked. "That Heissmeyer had murdered Otto Gumbel?"

He glanced at me as if surprised at the mention of Gumbel's name. He recovered quickly and looked away. "I will answer no more of your questions."

Laura stood and went over to the dresser. Her back was turned, and I couldn't see what she was doing, but a moment later, she turned to us and walked back to the chair. She sat and propped a framed 8x10 photograph of Beatrice on her lap. She didn't say anything, and just stared at Trisko.

Trisko tried to keep his expression neutral, but his face began to twitch. His knees bounced with agitation. With one final leg bounce, he exploded, convulsing in his chair. "Get that out of my sight."

Laura flinched at the violence but held her ground. "We don't know where her body is now. It could still be in the basement of the ruins in the Russian sector. Forgotten and rotting."

Trisko growled like a taunted wild animal. Laura had found a pain spot no physical torture could reveal. Tears filled the man's eyes as he struggled with his bonds.

"The man you won't name murdered her," Laura said. "He shot her three times, smiling the whole time." Laura continued telling the story of our encounter with the dead-eyed man and the other men from his team. She recounted it with a soft voice that contrasted the horror of it. How Beatrice tried to put up a fight. How she did what they asked but was killed anyway. How those men were ready to kill everyone, and how we made our escape. "We had to leave Beatrice behind, still dying in the dark basement." She told everything in a way that made the hairs on the back of my neck stand up.

With each detail, Trisko's struggles became weaker, and by the end of Laura's tale, he cried out like we'd just put hot needles under his fingernails. He hung his head and muttered Beatrice's name. We remained silent; there was no need to say any more. After a few minutes, he quieted. He raised his head with a look of resignation on his face. "He wasn't Gestapo. He was a major for the SD, the Sicherheitsdienst, the intelligence division of the SS. His name is Wilhelm Pfeffer. He performed his duties in Poland and Hungary. Even though he was simply obeying orders, many European countries want him for war crimes."

"Obeying orders, like the mass murders of Jews and Polish resistance," I said.

Laura seemed perplexed and turned to me. "Wouldn't he be on the American list?"

"Could be he was," I said. "But then someone at either the G-2 or the CIC plucked him off the street and suppressed his record. Gave him a new identity, and put him to work."

Trisko said, "He bragged about how he had evaded capture several times by hiding his identity."

"So, Major Forester was trying to identify Pfeffer," I said.

Trisko nodded.

"What about Otto Gumbel? Why did Heissmeyer kill him?"

"Because Gumbel recognized Heissmeyer from the war and accused him of doing terrible things with Pfeffer in Poland. He threatened to go to the authorities about his so-called war crimes."

"And Forester was using Heissmeyer to get to Pfeffer?" I asked.

"I only heard Leiter talk about he and Heissmeyer luring Forester into a field to kill him."

"But Forester fought back and killed Heissmeyer," Laura said.

I looked up at Laura. "Then Leiter goes running to whoever in American intelligence is running the spy ring."

"Then Forester is framed, and Leiter is killed for his failure," Laura said.

"Does that sound about right?" I asked Trisko.

"I have given you enough. That is all I have to say."

"Not quite," I said. "I'm going to ask you one more time. Who is the American giving the orders?"

"If an American is giving orders, I do not know who it is. They tell me what to do, and I do it."

"Like knifing me in the Harnack-Haus bathroom?"

"There is a standing order to kill both of you," Trisko said. He smiled and nodded at Laura. "You should have taken better care of your lady friend. Now she has a target on her forehead."

Enraged, I rammed my fist into his stomach. Air burst out of Trisko's lungs. He doubled over and grunted in pain. "The nice-guy routine is over," I said to Laura. I took one pair of panties and stuffed it into his mouth even as he tried to catch his breath from the blow. I tied the stocking over his mouth and walked away before succumbing to the temptation to beat him within an inch of his life.

Laura followed me to the kitchen. I stopped at the counter with my back to the room. She stood behind me and said in a lowered voice, "You just guaranteed that we won't get any more out of him."

"I don't care if he went after me. But when he grinned at the idea of killing you..."

"He got to you because you still feel guilty for bringing me along," Laura said.

She was right, but I wasn't going to take the bait and changed the subject. "Extracting any more out of him would require inflicting pain. I'm not prepared to go that far for what few tidbits we could get."

"What do we do with him?" Laura asked. "We certainly can't let him go. And I don't want to kill him."

"Once his gang finds out we got him to sing, they'll do the dirty work for us. We leave word at the Rote Lantern about his complicity, then dump him on the street."

We both looked at Trisko, bound and gagged.

Laura snapped her fingers as an idea came to her. "What about taking him to Wilson's? Trisko might pass on the same information. At least enough to convince Arnie of Mike's innocence and get him to search for Pfeffer. I bet Arnie's place has a basement."

I turned to look at her and smiled. "Wouldn't he get a kick out of that?"

The creaking of the door's hinges had us turning around in alarm. A woman stood in the doorway and aimed a 9mm pistol directly at us.

It was Sigrid Graf.

33

"*Wer sind sie? Was macht ihr hier?*" Graf asked us who we were and what we were doing there.

"Sigrid, we're Mike Forester's friends," I said in English, figuring she could speak the language. "Do you know where he is?" I glanced at my .45 lying on the table, then at Laura's purse, which contained her pistol, sitting on a chair near the window. We were a good fifteen feet from her and over twenty to our weapons.

"I advise you not to move," Graf said. "I am an excellent shot."

Trisko kept trying to say something through the gag and gestured toward the ropes binding him.

Graf glimpsed at Trisko. A wry smile formed on her face. "Hello, Hermann." She returned her attention to us and stayed by the door, presumably taking a moment to figure out what to do next. She looked like she'd been through the wringer. Her hair was disheveled, her clothes wore a layer of dust, the soles of her thick-heeled shoes were separating from the toe caps.

"Mike never told me he had American civilian friends," Graf said.

"You had already disappeared when he called us for help," Laura said.

"Anyone who claimed they would help has, instead, betrayed us," Graf said and took two steps into the room. She shut the door while keeping her gun on us.

"Ask Mike," I said. "I'm Mason Collins and this is Laura McKinnon."

"Asking him is not possible," Graf said. "I don't know where he is." As an aside, she said in a glum voice, "He's dead for all I know."

"We were told you were in the Soviet sector," I said.

"I was," Graf said and left it at that.

"You don't know if Mike is alive or dead?" Laura asked. "Whether he's trapped or really on the run?"

Trisko let out a desperate moan and jerked impatiently in his chair, his eyes pleading with Graf.

Graf kept her focus on us. "When my friend told me she had seen the three of you enter my apartment, I wondered to what end. Now I know. What are you doing with Hermann?"

"Asking him questions," Laura said.

Graf glanced at Trisko. She smiled and turned her attention back to us. "The iron rod in the stove tells me he hasn't been very cooperative."

"He said enough," I said.

Graf gave a faint nod to say she understood. Whether that was a good or a bad thing, I didn't know. She pulled out a switchblade and popped it open. "Let us free you from bondage," she said to Trisko.

Without taking her eyes or her pistol off us, she moved sideways toward the man. Trisko stopped struggling and appeared relieved. He was out of breath from the exertion and struggled to take in enough air through his nostrils. He eyeballed my pistol as Graf moved around him. His intent was clear. My mind raced, searching for a way to defend ourselves.

He raised his arms the best he could for Graf to cut the rope. She bent slightly at the waist to speak into Trisko's ear. "This is for Beatrice."

In one swift move, Graf pulled the blade across Trisko's throat. A highly trained commando couldn't have done it with more deadly accuracy. The man had only enough time for a chirp of alarm before he became unconscious from the rush of blood spilling onto his black suit. He slumped lifelessly in the chair.

Laura sucked in her breath at the shock of it. I remained silent and fixed. Sigrid's move had surprised me, and I found it hard to resolve her beauty and the savage act. It brought a vivid memory of the beautiful yet lethal woman assassin who had hunted me in Jerusalem. My knife was tucked securely in my boot. If she attempted to do the same to us to avoid the noise of a pistol shot, I was ready to fend off an attack.

Instead, she looked down on Trisko with a mix of anger and regret. "Beatrice wouldn't be dead if it wasn't for Hermann bullying her into working for them. I told her that was dangerous, but she loved Hermann too much to listen to me. He deceived then betrayed her."

She used Trisko's suit coat to clean the blood from the blade and put the knife away. She then picked up my .45 and put it in Laura's purse. "If you don't pursue me, I will leave these downstairs in the lobby."

"Sigrid," Laura said, "we want to help Mike. Please, tell us where to find him, and we'll make sure he gets home safe."

"I told you I don't know where he is," Graf said and moved toward the door.

"But he went into the Soviet sector to find you," Laura said.

That made her stop. "Then he failed. I haven't seen him for over two weeks."

"He was framed for murdering Heissmeyer and spying for the Soviets," I said. "We have proof he's innocent."

"I'd like to believe that," she said. "Isn't it a shame that I don't believe or trust anyone? I have to worry about myself right now. I would advise the same for you two. Leave this apartment and make sure you eliminate any fingerprints." She wagged her head toward Trisko. "He's going to stink."

"Sigrid," I said, "the new leader is Wilhelm Pfeffer. He murdered Leiter and Beatrice."

"I'll see he pays," Graf said.

"You want revenge?" I asked. "We'll help you. Tell us where we can find him and the rest of his gang."

Graf snickered. "Do you think it would be that easy? Like they all live in a clubhouse with a sign above the door? They were trained to be ghosts."

"Then where would the group meet?"

Graf walked up to the door. "I have no time for this." She stopped with her hand on the doorknob. "You might try the Rote Lantern. But with Trisko missing, they'll be extra cautious." She opened the door. "Remember. You only get your weapons back if you stay here until I'm out of the building." She pointed the gun at us once more for emphasis before she exited.

As the sound of her steps on the stairs echoed in the hallway, Laura and I walked over to the window. Laura turned to look at Trisko, and I did the same.

"I wonder if she really killed Trisko out of revenge," Laura said.

"You mean, maybe she wanted him to stop talking," I said. "A good possibility."

"I wouldn't have pegged Mike to be attracted to a woman like that," Laura said.

I shrugged. "Maybe she's a sweetheart most of the time and only murders people on special occasions."

Laura furrowed her brow at me. "You're pretty flippant for a guy who's just lost a valuable informant."

"How many informants have we found then lost?" I asked. "I'm getting numb to it."

The sound of the entrance door slamming echoed up the staircase, and we looked out the window. The beam of a flashlight swept the sidewalk. Then the light went out, and a shadowy figure disappeared into the darkness.

34

"We can't go in there without some official help," Laura said.

"You mean Wilson," I said.

"That's exactly who I mean."

Laura and I sat in the parked car and stared at the front entrance to the Rote Lantern. We'd retrieved our weapons in the lobby of Sigrid Graf's apartment building and decided to scope out the bar. It was just shy of midnight, but despite the late hour, I'd expected the place to be busy with GIs looking to continue their pickling process. A nightclub farther down the street and a competing bar behind us had customers coming and going, but not the Lantern. The lights were out, and it was dead quiet, aside from two goons standing guard, one near the front entrance and one across the street. We'd already gone around back only to discover that the back door had been chained shut, probably thanks to our previous appearance and Leiter's subsequent demise.

"Wilson is too by the book," I said. "He won't go in there without permission, and he's not going to get that from his lazy bum of a boss."

"I'm not going to do a repeat of tonight. We can't keep abducting people on the off chance they'll talk."

As much as I wanted to charge into the Rote Lantern, truss up the bartender like roast chicken, and make him sing, I saw the logic in her argument. We were just one baby step away from being thrown in prison or kicked out of the country.

Reluctantly, I started the car and did a U-turn in the street. That probably got the guards' attention, but I didn't care. I pressed on the gas and headed east.

Twenty minutes later, I turned into the driveway of Wilson's place and switched off the engine. I was surprised to see that the house was dark. I was thinking about that so much that I dropped the car keys as I pulled it out of the ignition switch. With a curse, I leaned over to feel for them in the dark.

An explosive pop came from behind us, followed by a snap like something ripping through the air. The glass around the speedometer shattered. It happened so fast that I only heard the crack of the rifle as a faint echo a split second later.

"Get down!" I said and grabbed Laura and pulled her down. "Sniper."

Laura breathed hard but didn't panic. I grabbed my .45 from my waistband while Laura fumbled through her purse for hers. We lay on the edges of the seats and floorboard, waiting for another shot.

"He should have waited until we were at the front door," Laura whispered.

"Lucky for us, he didn't."

"That rifle shot must have attracted a lot of attention," Laura said. "Do you think he's still out there?"

"He's just waiting," I said. "The sound delay from the gunshot means he's about a hundred yards away."

"That's almost to the OMGUS building," Laura said. "The MPs must be running around looking for him. Let's make a run for the house."

"Too risky," I said and weighed our options. "If he's any good, he'll have already relocated to get a clear shot. Or he'll keep us pinned until a team moves in for the kill."

"That's not helping," Laura said.

Each of the options had risks, but I had to pick one. I started the car from my prone position, using my hand on the accelerator.

"What are you doing?" Laura said with panic in her voice.

"Stay low and hold on." I used my hands to push in the clutch and put the gear in reverse. I hoped we would back straight out of the driveway. I eased the clutch and pushed on the gas. The gear engaged and we sped backward.

A bullet slammed into the back window and blew a hole in the windshield. The car jumped as it hit the curb and bounced in the street. I launched into an upright position, jammed the car into first, and turned the steering wheel.

A third round hit the driver's window with a smack. The air cracked from the force of the rocketing bullet passing a fraction of an inch from my face. It pierced the passenger's door just above Laura's head with the sound of a hammer. She cried out in alarm. I hit the accelerator, and the tires squealed as I raced down the street.

Laura sprung from the floorboard onto the seat and took in deep breaths. "I guess the word got out that we had Trisko."

"And they knew where to find us," I said.

"Who do you think tipped them off?" Laura asked. "Sigrid?"

"I think the answers lie in where the shots were coming from," I said.

"OMGUS? The American traitor? Still, that's awfully reckless even for an officer."

"It's far more plausible than one of Pfeffer's goons sneaking around a heavily guarded American installation with a rifle."

Laura was quiet for a moment. "Then we must be hitting close to the bone. Whoever the traitor is, he's getting desperate."

I steered the car onto Hindenburgdamm and headed southwest.

"The CID?" Laura asked.

"Unless you have a better idea," I said. "Get me to Gallwitzalle."

With her hands still shaking, she removed the map from the glove box and opened it up. I gave her my lighter to better see the details.

She found a route after a couple of blocks. "Turn left," she said and pointed. "That will take us over the Teltow Canal."

I did what she said and crossed the bridge. The moment I got to the other side, an army sedan pulled away from the curb and began following us.

"Looks like we have company," I said.

Laura looked behind. "He's catching up to us, fast."

I hit the accelerator. The Opel engine was peppy, but it was no match for the Buick, and on a straightaway, the pursuers shortened the distance. I made treacherous sharp turns to keep them from gaining too much ground. I had no idea where we were.

Laura thought quickly under pressure and kept us going in the right direction. She barked out several turns, each time at the last moment, finally taking us into a grid of residential streets.

"We're going to have to backtrack to cross over the railroad," Laura said. "Turn now."

I did so and wound up on a wide boulevard that ran relatively straight.

"You sure there's not another way?"

"Not unless you want to go farther south."

The army sedan used the wider street to close the distance. Two shots from a pistol. Both slammed into the rear with loud bangs.

"Herr Lehmann is going to be very disappointed with the condition of his car," Laura said.

"Yeah, well, the idea is to live through this so we can see his sad face."

"There!" Laura pointed.

I hit the curve too fast. The car fishtailed, and the rear wheels hit the curb. The engine sputtered, and I had to nurse the pedal to keep it alive. It roared back to life, and I hit the accelerator. As we gained speed, I glanced at the rearview mirror. The pursuers' sedan experienced the same problem, hitting the curb and losing ground.

Laura directed me into another tight grid of residential streets. I pushed the Opel to the limits. The acrid odor of burning tires and hot brakes filled the interior. The engine temperature was hitting maximum.

"Tell me we're getting close," I said.

"Three turns, two streets," she said. "Next one ... now!"

I took the turn. Our pursuers raced past without doing the same.

"They've figured what we're doing," I said. "They'll try to cut us off."

"Then go faster," Laura said. "The last couple of blocks, there's another wide street without curves."

I pushed the car to sixty miles per hour, blowing past parked cars in a narrow street. I prayed no one was out for a leisure stroll and happen to walk in front of me. As I crossed the intersection of small streets, we were hit by headlights. The army sedan was racing right toward us. I held on and increased my speed. Even clipping us at these speeds would have had us tumbling end over end.

The sedan just missed us. A shot rang out and the rear window shattered. I kept going.

"Last turn," Laura said.

We turned right onto Gallwitzallee. I don't know how the pursuers did it, but the sedan had already made the turn one street up and was now bearing down on us. I got the speed back up to sixty and held tight to the steering wheel. The entrance to the CID detachment headquarters was two blocks up. The two guards stepped away from the barrier to watch us approach with their hands on their holsters.

"We can't stop for the guards," Laura said.

I didn't respond, keeping all my concentration on driving. We came up fast on the short driveway and the barrier. I honked the horn several times to warn the guards to get out of the way. At the last minute, I hit the brakes and jerked hard on the steering wheel. The car fishtailed, but I maintained control and hit the accelerator again.

The guards dived out of the way, and I struck the barrier. It crumpled and spun off its support. I immediately slammed on the brakes, bringing the car to a halt only feet away from one of the MP Jeeps.

Outside the windshield, four MPs came charging out of the building and moved toward us with their guns drawn. Laura pushed our pistols onto the floorboard. I jumped out of the car with my hands up while doing my best to point to the street. The sedan rolled past. I tried to see inside, but the interior was too dark. A second later, it sped up and disappeared.

"We were being shot at," I said to the guards. "Somebody in that staff car tried to kill us."

The two gate guards rushed up. One of them grabbed me by the back, slammed me into the side of the car, and started cuffing me.

"They're getting away, damnit!"

The other gate guard yanked Laura's door open and pointed his pistol at her. "Get out with your hands up."

Laura did as she was told, and the MP pushed her against the car and cuffed her.

"Take it easy, boys," I said.

That was the guard's cue to force my bound hands upward,

making my shoulders cry out in pain. Another MP patted me down.

"Pistols in the car," I said and told him where to find my knife and brass knuckles.

A third MP started searching the car, while the fourth kept his gun on me. Two of the MPs lifted a cuffed Laura off the car and half carried her toward the rear entrance to the building.

The guard pinning my arms shoved me forward using the same upward pressure on my shoulders.

We were in deep trouble, but we were at least safe. For now. I knew it wouldn't last.

35

The MP shoving me toward the CID rear entrance seemed to think it would be funny to use me as the battering ram to get the back doors to swing open. The only thing that saved my face from the worst of it was bowing my head and allowing my skull to take the brunt of the blow. I held my temper and my mouth. Aggravating them might blow back onto Laura, so I fantasized about meeting him in a future back alley.

The MPs halted a few yards into the hallway when Wilson came charging toward us with a murderous look on his face. I didn't know if his wrath was directed at us or the MPs until he zeroed in on the MP corporal manhandling Laura. "What's the meaning of this?"

"These two nearly took out Grimes and Boyle with a car," the MP corporal said. "Not to mention damaging the gate, reckless driving, and possession of firearms."

Wilson looked at me for a rebuttal.

"We were being pursued by some shooters in an army sedan," I said.

"We didn't hear any shots, Chief," the corporal said.

"Go look at the car," I said to Wilson. "There are five bullet holes that I know of."

"Could have happened anywhere, anytime," the MP said.

"Yeah, sure, we drive around with busted windows and ram police barricades all the time," I said.

"Shut up, both of you," Wilson said. He looked at the corporal, who I figured was the one in charge of the group. "Take them to my office. I'll go inspect the car."

"But we got to book them," the MP said.

"Do what I said!" Wilson said.

Wilson's face was red with anger as he glared at me before stepping around us and heading out the door. Laura yelped in pain. I spun around. The movement was too fast and violent for the MP holding me to react, and I broke free of his grasp.

I got in the corporal's face. "You hurt her again, and I'll put you in the hospital."

I said it with such rage that the MPs backed off an inch. The corporal released Laura and nodded to his companion to lead the way. The cop grabbed my arms from behind and put his mouth near my ear. "I can't wait to get you alone in a cell."

"Private!" the corporal said. "Get going."

The rest of the group accompanied my future tormenter down the hall. He stopped at Wilson's door and stepped aside to let Laura and me enter. Once in the office, I asked the corporal, "You going to take these cuffs off?"

"Our orders were to take you to the chief's office. Nothing else." He started to close the door, then said with a sadistic smile, "We'll be waiting for you."

When the door slammed shut, Laura looked at me. "If you say 'another fine mess,' I'll put my foot in your mouth."

"That'd be a neat trick with the handcuffs."

Laura growled in frustration and turned away from me. I walked around Wilson's desk, put my back up against it, and opened the top drawer with my cuffed hands.

"What are you doing?" Laura asked.

"He's got to have keys in here somewhere," I said, and my fingers blindly rummaged through the drawer's contents.

The door opened, and Wilson stepped in. "You're not going to find them in there."

I turned to face him. "You've got a couple of wise guys for MPs."

Wilson pulled a wad of keys from his pocket. "They're sensitive to people trying to run them over." He unlocked Laura's cuffs and moved to me. He unlocked mine, dropped the cuffs on the desk, and pointed at the two chairs. "Sit down."

Laura rubbed her wrists and shot Wilson a glare before she sat.

I snapped my fingers after realizing what one of the MPs had said. "One of your MPs called you chief," I said as I sat. "Cuthbert get in trouble again?"

Wilson got behind his desk and roughed up his chair before taking a seat. "Shaking down wealthy Germans. Seems he got greedy and went after some bigshots. They raised such a stink that General Clay himself got involved. The provost marshal came down on Cuthbert hard. Now he's on his way back to the States and Leavenworth. Some of the MPs aren't happy about it. Cuthbert was cutting them in on the takings."

We congratulated him on the big promotion, but his sour disposition didn't change. He slid a cigarette out of the pack, lit it, and threw the pack to me. "That *was* a nice car. Where'd you steal it?"

"I didn't," I said and helped myself to one of his cigarettes. "I rented it for a bottle of Hennessy and a couple of cartons. I'll see that it's fixed."

"Once you get out of the stockade, you mean. *If* you get out."

"Oh, come on, Arnie. That wasn't attempted manslaughter, and you know it. A sniper took potshots at us in your driveway—"

Wilson sat up straight in his chair. "What?"

"We made it back to your place after a rather interesting day, when the sniper started shooting. We only managed to get out of there by the skin of our teeth. We were on our way here when a couple of trigger-happy goons started chasing us in an army sedan. That's where the other bullet holes are from."

"If we'd waited to convince the guards to open the gate," Laura said, "those goons would have shot us. Maybe the guards, too."

"You brought them to my house?" Wilson asked flatly, but there was simmering anger behind it.

"Now wait a minute," I said. "The only people who knew we were staying there are Laura, me, and *you*. So, who brought who?"

Wilson slammed his fist on the desk. "If I'd wanted a sniper to take you out, I wouldn't have picked my place."

"Boys, please," Laura said. "You both know it's not one of us. Arnie lives across the street from OMGUS." She looked at Wilson. "That's where the shots came from. You said it yourself; they probably want to keep an eye on you by putting you there."

"That implies …" Wilson stopped.

I nodded. "Like we've been saying. Someone high up in American intelligence is orchestrating this whole drama."

Wilson looked from me to Laura. He leaned to one side and opened a lower drawer of his desk. He took out a bottle of bourbon and put it on the desktop. "I've only got two glasses." He put those on the desk, filled them to the brim with the liquor, and put the glasses in front of us.

"Aren't you having any?" I asked.

Wilson answered my question by taking a long gulp from the bottle. Laura and I finished ours and put the glasses on the table.

Wilson gathered everything, put it all back, and slammed the drawer closed. "Now, was that you two creating the incident at the Harnack-Haus?"

"What incident is that?" I asked.

"You know which one I'm talking about," Wilson said, raising his voice. "The missing waiter after a bloody melee in the bathroom. I interviewed several witnesses who described you both to a T."

Laura and I glanced at each other.

"You mean the one where a German waiter attacked Mason while he was relieving himself?" Laura asked with an air of innocence.

Wilson peered at me. "He didn't attack you for peeing in the urinal."

"I might have mentioned that we had Greta Schaller and the suitcase full of cash," I said. I told Wilson that the waiter was the one who had a heated discussion with Hodgson at the Harnack-Haus, which prompted Hodgson to hightail it out of there and the subsequent bombing.

"And I suppose you two took the opportunity to abduct yet another German citizen and put him through the ringer," Wilson said.

"His name was Hermann Trisko," Laura said. "He was a member of Leiter's gang."

"Was?" Wilson asked.

"We'll get to that in a minute," Laura said.

Wilson grimaced like someone had hit him in the stomach. He opened the top drawer and popped a couple of aspirin, then went into the bottom drawer again, took a swig of bourbon to swallow the pills. He slammed it closed again and put his elbows on the desk as if bracing for worse news.

I took that as a signal to continue. "He gave us a name of the ex-SS officer who's running the gang. Wilhelm Pfeffer. He was a colonel in the SS intelligence arm, the SD."

That made Wilson sit up and pay attention. "Isn't he on every list of wanted Nazi war criminals?"

"The same," I said.

Wilson hit the button on his intercom. When the man acknowledged, Wilson said, "Get anything we have on a Colonel Wilhelm Pfeffer. That's an SS rank of Standartenführer in the SD, the Sicherheitsdienst."

"Now, sir?" the voice said.

"Now, Corporal."

When Wilson turned his attention back to us, I said, "Pfeffer's the one who shot Beatrice Schweitzer in cold blood and ordered the murder of Ernst Leiter. Why, I don't know, but I figure Leiter was skimming off the top, or he had second thoughts about working for the Soviets."

"Was Pfeffer who Forester was tracking down?"

"He knew the man was a high-ranking SS officer, but not his identity," Laura said.

"And Forester was using Heissmeyer to help him find Pfeffer?" Wilson asked.

"That's right," I said. "But when Leiter found out, he ordered Heissmeyer to lead Forester into a field outside the AFN building and kill him."

"But Forester got the best of Heissmeyer," Wilson said.

"Or someone else knifed Heissmeyer and framed Forester for it," Laura said.

"And you got all this from Trisko?" Wilson asked. When Laura confirmed it, he asked, "Did he admit to anything about the Hodgson bombing?"

"No," I said. "But we've been over this; everything we've heard suggests Pfeffer's gang didn't do it. To them, Hodgson was untouchable."

Wilson sat back in his chair and stared at his desk for a moment. I felt sure he was trying to digest this. Investigating an officer several ranks above his would be perilous for his career, not to mention risking reassignment to some backwater posting. Finally, he said, "To get to a high-ranking officer, we're going to need to find Pfeffer and use him to provide a link."

"If you put out a bulletin to every department, it could alert whoever's calling the shots, and Pfeffer will just go underground."

Wilson paused again. He tapped a pencil on the desk surface as he gazed at the wall. "All right, we do it on the sly, but only for a few days." He stopped his pencil tapping when there was a knock at the door. Wilson invited the person to enter, and a young MP corporal came in and deposited a file on the desk. He left while Wilson scanned the documents inside.

He read the top page out loud. "Born in Dresden, he joined the Nazi party in the mid-thirties and rose in rank over the next five years. Most of his postings were in Poland and the Russian Front. He was head of the department hunting down partisans, which he accomplished through torture and murder. Reprisal killings of entire villages. He also supervised the roundup of Jews and mass executions. His worst war crimes were committed during the crackdown on the Warsaw uprising, participating in mass rape and murder. Torturing victims, then mutilating them in—"

He slapped the file folder down on the desk and reared back in his seat, as if the printed words had shocked him to his core. "How could this guy be still walking around? Why hasn't he not already been hanged and buried in an unmarked grave?"

"The Russians don't care about what he did to the Poles," I said. "My guess is, as far as what he did in Russia, the Soviets value his infiltration in the Gehlen Organization more."

"And I wouldn't put it past American and British intelligence to look past his war crimes to beat the Soviets at their own game," Wilson said. He took a deep breath in an obvious attempt to relieve some of his outrage. "I'm not sure I want to know the answer, but where is Trisko now?"

"Tied to a chair with his throat cut," I said.

Wilson eyed the bourbon drawer but remained as he was. "You know what? I'm going to stay completely calm. My mom used to say, 'think positive thoughts.'" He paused a moment, presumably doing just that, then he put on a smile that was more of a grimace. "Please, proceed."

"Sigrid Graf was the one who killed him," Laura said. Her voice was muted, like a kid confessing a bad deed. I figured she thought the same as I did, that it all sounded like the ravings of a lunatic.

"Sigrid Graf, as in Mike Forester's girlfriend?" Wilson asked. "The one who Forester went into the Soviet sector to save?"

"The same," I said. "She claims to have returned from the Soviet sector just a couple of days ago. That she never saw Forester and doesn't know if he's alive or dead."

"Someone tipped her off that we were using her apartment," Laura said. "She showed up and held us at gunpoint. She killed Trisko for betraying Beatrice Schweitzer, or to shut him up. We don't know which."

Wilson rubbed his temples. "You guys should write up a playbook, so I can follow along."

"You want to get at the heart of it?" I asked. "Help us find Wilhelm Pfeffer and whoever is pulling the strings."

"Have you got any leads?" Wilson asked.

"Sigrid's parting words were to look hard at the Rote Lantern," Laura said.

"Isn't that where you guys had a run-in with the German agents and Leiter got shot?" Wilson asked.

"It is," I said. "And we know the place is on G-2's radar because McCormick sent us there."

Wilson looked at his watch. "It's coming up on one o'clock. Too late to do anything tonight."

"Curfew hasn't stopped these agents before," I said. "They could be in there right now, plotting their next treachery."

"You want me to lead a raid on a German tavern that's closed up for the night? And if we find anyone, what do we charge them with? Curfew violation?" He shook his head. "Nothing's going to happen if we wait until tomorrow. This is all shaky as it is, and I'm going to have to answer to the provost marshal if we wind up with nothing."

I glanced at Laura with an I-told-you-so look. She said to Wilson, "We want to go with you when you lead the raid."

"As observers only," Wilson said. "In the meantime, you can't go back to my place. *I* can't go back to my place. I'll set us up in two bedrooms reserved for non-law-enforcement personnel." He stood. "I'll escort you personally. We should get some shut-eye. It'll be a busy day tomorrow."

Wilson gave us our weapons, and we followed him out into the hall. The MPs glowered at us when they realized we weren't bound by handcuffs. It took Wilson some forceful persuasion to get the corporal and his cohorts to disperse. He then led us to another building in the complex and up some stairs to the third floor. He talked about following Hardin around for part of the day without results. I didn't listen. I was busy studying the layout of the place, noting the placement of guards, areas to avoid, and possible escape routes.

Wilson stopped at a door. "Well, this is yours." He pointed down the hallway. "I'm three doors down. I'll see you at oh seven hundred." He said good night and headed for his room.

Laura and I went inside the small bedroom. It was minimally furnished with two twin beds, a dresser with a mirror above it, and one bedside table. Outside the small window, blowing rain and sleet pelted the glass.

I stood by the door and listened. Laura went deeper into the room and checked her reflection in the mirror.

"Looks like I used an eggbeater on my hair," she said. She turned to look at me. "You're supposed to say that I look beautiful all the same."

I put my index finger to my lips and put my ear to the door. Wilson's door clicked shut. I couldn't hear anyone else stirring in the hallway.

Laura came up to me and got in my face. "Let me guess. We're not going to enjoy Wilson's hospitality."

"We can't wait for him to cobble together a half-assed raid," I said.

Laura glanced back at the storm outside the window. "Nice night for a walk anyway."

36

Laura and I stood on the covered patio of the Oliver barracks' motor pool administration building. The rain swirled all around us and disappeared into darkness beyond the reach of the light. The barracks' compound spread out before us, but none of that was visible. I knew it was a collection of low buildings, including the 16th Constabulary building, on an area of land of about size of three football fields. In front of us was the parking lot containing Jeeps and sedans with white stars painted on their sides. There were a couple of armored cars—I sorely wanted to take on those, but I'd have to live out that fantasy another time. I had keys to one particular sedan among the ten haphazardly parked in the sizeable lot.

We peered into the black maelstrom to see if any guards might be around to observe us. Our ponchos flapped in the wind, both of which I'd stolen from a supply room on the ground floor below our sleeping quarters. We'd also helped ourselves to two helmets with "MP" in large white letters painted on the sides, two flashlights, two nightsticks, and a hefty pair of bolt cutters.

"Ready?" I asked.

Laura nodded, and we stepped out into the rain. With our heads bent low against the wind, we made it to the closest sedan. The key didn't do a thing to the door lock. Despite the inclement weather, I figured a couple of MPs on patrol would make their rounds soon, so we hurried to the next, then the next. On the fourth try, the key worked, and we got inside.

"Let's hope the gate guards aren't too anxious to venture out in the rain," Laura said.

"I'll try one of the exits to the rear," I said and started up the car.

I headed for the far side of the large parking lot and a gate wide enough for trucks and armored cars. Fortunately, there was no barrier, but there was a guard kiosk. As we got closer, the soldier became visible in the small window. He was huddled next to an electric heater and reading a magazine under the single light. He turned when he saw our headlights.

"Keep your head low," I said to Laura as we approached the guardhouse.

I was counting on the guard not paying much attention to a vehicle leaving the barracks and assume we were two MPs going out on a routine patrol. The dark and the rain would do the rest. He stood at the narrow door and watched us. I turned my head slightly and waved a salute. He strained to see past the foggy windows, then finally waved a salute back and stayed where he was.

I let out the breath I was holding and pulled out onto a small street that was no more than an alleyway. Listening to my gut, I turned right and followed the road around a curve. A hundred yards later, it dumped us onto Eiswald Strasse, one of the streets that bordered the constabulary compound. Getting to the main road required us to go past the main entrance with the broken barrier and the hapless guards, but they paid little attention to us.

Laura sighed with relief when we turned north onto Gallwitzallee. I pressed on the gas and headed toward the center of town. I would only relax when I was sure the shooters' sedan hadn't been waiting for us to exit the barracks and pick up our trail. Maybe the MP sedan and our helmets were enough to cover our tracks. After several blocks, it became clear we were alone.

Thirty minutes later, I parked the car a block from the Rote Lantern. The street was quiet and dark. The rain had transformed into a thick drizzle.

"I don't see the lookouts," Laura said.

"We can't risk going in the front," I said. "We use the back like we'd planned."

We gathered the flashlights, nightsticks, and bolt cutters into a small canvas bag. After checking our pistols, we got out and surveyed the surroundings once more. All was quiet. We crossed the street at a quick pace. We had to pick our way through the pitch-black alleyway leading to the rear courtyard. When we exited the alley, we turned on our flashlights and navigated the piles of debris that were like islands in a sea of mud.

We reached the back door to the tavern and stashed the ponchos by the base of the building. Laura put her helmet back on, and I looked at her quizzically.

"You never know," she whispered.

I shrugged and fished the bolt cutters out of the bag. With a little effort, the tool made quick work of the rusty chains. They clattered as they tumbled into the mud accumulated at the door. We froze and listened in case the noise alerted someone. Nothing stirred.

The back door opened with a single creak from the hinges, and we stepped inside. The short hallway was as black as the alley. Laura pulled the door shut, and we paused to listen and let our eyes adjust.

A groan of wood came from beyond the swinging door that divided the hallway from the main room. Another one sounded behind the first. Someone heavy was coming down the stairs from the second floor.

I pulled Laura into the broom closet and huddled against the wall by the open door. I held my pistol high and waited. A groan from the swinging door was followed by heavy breathing. The double barrels of a shotgun appeared first. Held chest high, it slowly floated past, and then the bartender filled the doorway.

I put the muzzle of my .45 against the man's skull and pulled back the hammer. The bartender flinched and made a move to turn. "I wouldn't do that if I were you," I said in German.

The bartender stopped mid-turn. He panted like a locomotive.

"Not a sound," I said. I put my free hand on the shotgun barrel and eased the weapon from his grasp. I handed it to Laura, who aimed it at the man's belly. We exited the broom closet and faced him. His eyes registered surprise when he recognized us. His expression turned to contempt as if to show us he had no fear.

"*Gehen hinein,*" I said, urging him toward the closet using the pressure of the muzzle on his temple.

He hesitated a moment and glanced at me as if to read my intentions, whether I was going to simply subdue him or execute him among the rancid mop and buckets. Further pressure convinced him to do as I told him, and he stepped into the closet.

"Stop there and get on your knees," I said in German.

Because of his size, he had some difficulty kneeling in the tight space. With one final grunt, he accomplished the task. "I have money," he said in German. "It's not much, but it's upstairs in the bedroom dresser."

"We're not here for the money," I said. "Who else is here?"

The bartender flinched but said nothing.

"Answer me," I said as I shoved the muzzle harder into the back of his skull.

"No one," the man said without conviction.

I glanced at Laura, pointed at my eyes, and tilted my head

toward the hall in a silent command to watch for anyone trying to sneak up on us. Laura went into the hallway.

"Now," I said to the bartender, "I'll give you one more chance. Who else is here?"

"Johann!" the man yelled.

I struck the man just behind his ear with the handle of my pistol. The man fell on his left side. He was dazed but not out. There was no time to tie him up. It took two more blows with the pistol to the base of his skull to knock him out. I slipped into the hallway to stand next to Laura. She held the shotgun toward the main room and shook her head, telling me there was no sign of movement. I moved ahead, stooped low, and breached the swinging door, gun first.

Using the bar as cover, I listened for footsteps coming down the stairs. I heard shoes on wooden stairs, but the sound wasn't coming from above. The sound came from below and grew louder. I tried to peer in the shadows, searching for a door to the basement.

The pounding stopped before I got a fix on the location of the sound. There had to be a door behind the bar. A broad mirror was flanked by floor-to-ceiling shelves and covered the back wall. I stood and leaned over the bar to see if there was a trapdoor. A split second later, the shelf on the far side swung open. A man in silhouette stood just inside the hidden door. He blindly fired two shots from his pistol. He'd come up from a lighted basement and shot before his eyes had adjusted to the darkness.

I dived to the floor and fired from a prone position. The man cried out. His body made a banging noise as he tumbled down the stairs.

Laura charged out from the hallway. "Mason!" She ran up to me and started searching my body for a wound.

I took her hands and held them. "I'm fine," I said and headed for the door to the basement.

Laura accompanied me, and we began descending the stairs

side by side, me with my pistol at the ready and her holding the shotgun waist high. The air was thick with the smell of mildew and wet earth. A light threw a dim glow on the molded brick walls and dirt floor. The shooter lay at the bottom of the stairs in a twisted heap.

The bottom half of the stairway was exposed to the room below, and I paused. If there were more gang members where he came from, we were vulnerable. I gestured with my hands for Laura to stay. She pushed them away and glared at me. I pointed at my chest and held up my index finger, then all five fingers, telling her to wait five seconds. She bit her bottom lip and nodded.

I took in a deep breath and bounded down the stairs, taking three steps at a time. I hit the ground and threw myself into the dirt while aiming my pistol toward the center of the room. A single chair sat in the middle, and the only person waiting for us was a woman bound to it.

Laura rushed down as I got to my feet. We both walked up to the woman, expecting she was dead. The scene hit me hard. It reminded me of the woman I had tried to rescue in Italy and failed.

Laura shouldered the shotgun and lifted her head. "Sigrid?"

Sigrid opened one swollen eye. Her face was bruised and bloody. What looked like cigarette burns dotted her neck and cheeks. She moved her lips to say something, but no words came out.

"Those bastards nearly killed her," Laura said.

I pulled the Ka-Bar knife out of my boot and cut the ropes binding her. She slumped forward and would have fallen if Laura and I hadn't caught her. "Let's get you out of here," I said.

We both lifted her gently. She cried out in pain and held her ribs. Her knees buckled. I let her collapse in my open arms and cradled her, lifting her and walking toward the stairs. Laura went ahead of me and dragged the dead shooter out of the way. The man rolled onto his back. I recognized him as one of our ambushers, the beak-nosed man, the one who'd held a gun to Laura's head in the basement in East Berlin.

Sigrid groaned with each step. She was muscular and heavier than she looked, and it took some effort to get her up to the ground floor. On the final step, I turned to let Laura get past me. She cocked the hammer of one barrel and led the way.

Just as I cleared the swinging shelf, the bartender growled as he charged directly for us. Laura raised the shotgun and pulled the trigger. The lead shot disintegrated a portion of the bar. Shattered wood flew in all directions. Sigrid jumped into my arms. The blast had my ears ringing. But it did the trick. The bartender froze in his tracks.

Laura pulled back the hammer on the second barrel and aimed it at the man's head. "Take one more step, and I'll blow your head off."

Whether the bartender understood English or not, the rage in Laura's eyes and the tone in her voice were enough to convince the man she was serious. He raised his hands and backed away. Laura and I made it past the end of the bar, and she motioned with the barrel for the man to back up toward the front door. We put our backs to the swinging door and pushed into the hallway. I went first and kicked a doorstop in place to hold it open. I wanted to give Laura a clear shot in case the bartender decided to make another charge, but the bartender seemed content to stay where he was.

I got the rear door open and backed out into the courtyard. My muscles were straining from carrying Graf as I half jogged out of the courtyard and down the alley. Laura kept guard to the rear. Near the street, I hesitated to let Laura lead the way with her weapon. We hurried across the street. She opened the rear passenger door, and I laid Sigrid on the seat. I pulled out my pistol to cover Laura. Once her door closed, I got behind the wheel, started the engine, and took off.

"Now what?" Laura asked breathlessly. "I don't think Wilson is going to let us put her in a room at the CID. And she needs medical attention."

"All good points," I said. "When I have an answer, I'll let you know."

37

I steered the car through several random turns while I pondered what to do next. We ended up on Hindenburgdamm going southeast. The only other traffic on the road was the occasional MP patrol or army sedan, and I was grateful to be in an official MP vehicle.

Laura silently watched the road and tried to keep track of where we were on a map. I figured a part of her silence came from the same place as mine, assessing our troubling situation: AWOL with the CID, in a stolen army vehicle, after breaking into a bar and gunning down a man and making a getaway with a fugitive wanted by U.S. intelligence.

"We've got to ditch this car," I said. "There could be patrols looking for us by now."

"We have to get Sigrid medical assistance," Laura said.

"You got any suggestions where to do that?" I said a little too harshly.

"No," Laura muttered. "But ditching this car isn't going to help us. You propose we flee on foot?"

I spotted a side street on the right that was lined with big houses, and I turned at the last moment.

"Where are you going?" Laura asked.

I ignored the question and cruised down the narrow street, glancing in driveways. Five houses down, an early thirties Mercedes sat just beyond an iron gate. "That one will do."

Laura said nothing, only expressing her disapproval with a heavy sigh. I continued on for another block, then pulled over to the curb and shut off the engine. I opened the door and told Laura I'd be back. I put one foot on the pavement as another thought came to me. "I know you're tempted to drive off without me right now, but I'd appreciate it if you didn't."

"If you get caught, I will," Laura said.

I got out and closed the door. The rain had stopped and was replaced by a dense fog; the more the better, as far as I was concerned. I backtracked the block and found the prospective Mercedes. The wrought-iron gate hung awkwardly on its hinges, broken some time ago by the look of the latch. I entered the property and approached the car. Upon closer inspection, it was a 1930 770 model; the type used by Hitler and his cronies, which gave me a great deal of pleasure in stealing it. The thing was battered and had a couple of bullet holes in it, probably in the owner's attempt at escaping the Soviet onslaught. Which was why, I figured, it sat outside in the elements. I imagined the owner had been some high Nazi official who no longer cared to maintain the thing.

The door was locked, but one good tug got it open. The sound alerted a dog in the neighborhood, and the barking prompted me to hurry. In two minutes, I succeeded in hot-wiring the car, and by the time I sat upright behind the wheel, a light in the upper floor of the house came on. I backed out at a quick pace and raced up to the army sedan.

Laura was waiting for me by the side of the car. Sigrid leaned on Laura's shoulder. She looked pained, but she was able to stand, which I took as a good sign. Laura helped Sigrid into the back, then got in with her. I took off down the street and looked in the rearview at Laura.

"How is she doing?"

"Same as she was a half hour ago," Laura said. "Maybe you should worry about where we're going."

"I'm working on it," I said.

"Well, work on it faster. We can't be running around town in a stolen car for hours while you figure it out."

"Are you snapping at me because I stole a Nazi's car?"

"I'm angry because you don't seem to care if Sigrid gets medical attention or not."

"Anywhere we could go for a doctor leaves a trail for them to follow," I said.

"Them," Laura said. "You mean the military police, the German agents, and whoever took potshots at us earlier?"

"It's too dangerous," Sigrid said, her voice barely audible above the thrum of the engine. She still lay on Laura's lap and was out of my sight. "I'm okay."

"Says the woman who can't even sit up," Laura said.

Sigrid groaned and huffed as she pushed herself upright.

"Sigrid, I didn't mean for you to do that," Laura said in a contrite tone. "Lie back down before you make things worse."

The woman ignored Laura, though she leaned against her for support. "I know of a place we can go that's safe."

I wasn't sure if we could trust her or her judgment. I figured Laura had the same qualms, and I met her gaze in the rearview mirror. She gave me a subtle nod.

"Are you sure it's not someplace Leiter's gang knows about?" I asked.

Sigrid chortled. "Leiter's gang. It was never Leiter's gang."

"Whoever's gang it is, do they know about this place you're talking about?"

"No. No one alive, anyway," Sigrid said.

"All right, just as long as it's not an area crawling with military police," I said.

"We have to get off the road soon," Laura said.

"I know a way we can avoid the patrols," Sigrid said.

"I'm all ears," I said.

Sigrid directed us over a forty-minute span. We sliced through the western fringes of the American sector, then went north, crossing into the British one. She faded a few times, and Laura had to revive her, all the while giving me an icy glare as if it were my fault we were in this situation. Maybe she was right. She was right. I wanted to say I warned her I liked to punch through things as opposed to going around them. But that was the child in me, still having the impulse to defend myself from my mother's verbal onslaughts whenever she been on a binge. Which happened all too frequently until her death when I was nine.

Sigrid deftly navigated us through a maze of streets that avoided patrols and checkpoints. After passing the Deutsche Oper Berlin, a behemoth opera house gutted by bombs, Sigrid pointed feebly at the upcoming side road and mumbled for me to make a final turn right. I did so, and we continued for a couple of blocks, passing buildings that were black skeletal shapes against a charcoal sky, until stopping in front of a building only partially damaged by fire.

After scanning the area, I got out and opened the back door. Laura had to rouse Sigrid before helping me get her out of the car. With our support, she put one wobbly foot in front of the other. We entered a lobby blackened by flames. It was as if the charred remains absorbed the light from our flashlights, making it difficult to see our way past the rubble. The acrid odor of burned wood filled the air. Rats scurried in the darkness.

"Second floor," Sigrid said.

"Is this building stable?" Laura asked.

"It's still standing," Sigrid said.

"Is anyone else in this building?" I asked.

"An elderly woman on the fourth floor, but she's deaf," Sigrid said.

Laura and I took some of Sigrid's weight and mounted the spiral staircase. Fire had blackened the treads, and they creaked under our weight. On the second floor, fire had gutted the right half of the hallway, while the left had been spared. Sigrid pointed at the last door on the left. We shuffled over to the hallway window overlooking the courtyard. Sigrid felt along the window frame head and brought down a key. We followed her over to the apartment door. She unlocked it and pushed it open.

We entered a single room with a small bed against one wall. On the opposite side was the kitchenette, a sofa, and two chairs next to a square wooden table. Sigrid limped over to a tall chifforobe and opened the doors. I'd expected clothes on one side and linens on the other, and while the right half served as a clothes closet, the left side held a small arsenal: a STEN submachine gun, two Webley revolvers, a long-bladed knife used by British commandos, and a pair of binoculars.

"Everything a woman needs to make a cozy home," Laura said.

Sigrid managed a half smile and opened a small drawer and removed a box of ammunition for the Webleys. "This was a safe house when I worked as a Soviet agent. I shared it with a partner, but no one else knows about this place."

"Where's your partner now?" I asked.

"He was murdered by an unknown assailant," Sigrid said as she loaded rounds into the revolver's cylinder. "That was almost two years ago." She eyed us with a furrowed brow. "Don't think I work for them now. I hate the Russians." Her legs wobbled, her hands shook, making it hard for her to insert the rounds.

I went over to her and offered to help. She handed me the pistol. I loaded it, snapped the cylinder in place, and gave it back to her. "Why don't you sit down before you fall down?"

"We don't have time," she said. She took two steps and collapsed.

I caught her in mid-fall and helped her across the room. I lowered her onto the sofa, where she fell against the back cushion. She flinched in pain and put her hand on her rib cage while breathing heavily. The bruises on her face and neck had turned purple, and one eye was almost swollen shut.

Laura asked her for permission to get a better look at her injuries. Sigrid bit her bottom lip from the pain and nodded. Laura got her coat open and unbuttoned her blouse. She had bruises all across her torso.

"We have to get her to a doctor," Laura said.

"No!" Sigrid said. "We have to hurry."

"Sigrid," Laura said, "you may have damaged organs or internal bleeding that could get worse if you don't get medical care."

"This isn't the first time I've been beaten," Sigrid said. "I know what to look for."

"Why are you in such a hurry and risking your health?" Laura asked.

Tears formed in Sigrid's eyes as she stared at the ceiling. "They broke me. I tried to resist, but I couldn't anymore."

"Who broke you?" Laura asked.

"The man you killed and Ahmet," Sigrid said.

"Ahmet's the bartender?" I asked.

Sigrid nodded and lifted her head in alarm. "They made me tell them where Mike is hiding. They must be on their way now. We have to stop them."

Laura and I looked at each other with a mix of relief and concern. Mike was still alive but now being hunted by Pfeffer and his gang of cutthroats.

"So, you lied about not seeing Mike for a couple of weeks," I said.

"I didn't want you forcing me to go back there. Now, we

must." She tried to stand, but her eyes widened in pain. She sucked in her breath and fell back.

"Sigrid, you're in no shape to go anywhere," Laura said. "Just tell us where we can find him, and we'll go."

Sigrid slid down the sofa back and curled up in a fetal position. "I'll only say if you take me with you." She let out a long breath and became still.

Laura gently nudged her shoulder. "Sigrid?" No response. She had passed out.

Laura looked at me. "If she's bleeding internally, she could die. No telling what damage was done to her liver or kidneys. Mason, we've got to figure out some way of getting her care."

"If we take her to a German hospital, they'll see how badly she's been beaten and call the police, no matter what we say. The police will then take her into custody and arrest us. And you can imagine what would happen if we took her to an American military hospital."

"Then we find a doctor," Laura said, raising her voice.

It was after three in the morning. Finding a doctor seemed impossible. Plus, even if I did find one, I didn't know one I could trust. Then someone came to mind.

I pulled on my coat and belted my pistol. "I'll be back as soon as I can."

38

I decided to take back streets to avoid any patrols. Otherwise, the passenger car would stick out like a sore thumb on the deserted roads. While my destination wasn't far, it was in one of the densest parts of the British sector. That made me particularly nervous, because if the Brits stopped me with a stolen car, they'd put me back in the slammer and throw away the key.

After some trial and error, I found the row of buildings, parked, and got out. It was below freezing, with clear skies and a three-quarter moon. The silvery light made the disfigured buildings seem more forsaken, the shadows starker.

I walked up to the former clothing store and knocked on the door. Lights came on in several windows. In my haste, I hadn't considered that there would be more than one individual living in the building. A moment later, the door opened and a man who looked to be about eighty peered at me using a candle-powered lantern. He glared at me while clasping a ratty blanket over his shoulders.

"Sorry to bother you at this hour…" I began in German.

"I don't sleep," the man said. "But you disturbed me all the same. State your business and get out of here."

"Yes, sir. I need to speak to Doctor Lehmann. It's urgent."

He turned his head and used one eye to study me. "You're not from here, are you?"

I knew I spoke German with an Americanized Bavarian accent, which he obviously detected. "No, sir, I'm—"

"No foreigners," he said and tried to close the door in my face.

"Emil," a man said from the shadows of the corridor. "I'll handle it."

Emil grunted and stepped aside to let the speaker forward. Much to my relief, it was Lehmann. He started to speak, then noticed the old man still hovered just inside the door. He said something to the man I couldn't hear, then came back to the door. He leaned out and peered down the street both ways. "Where's my car?"

"Uh, I'm having the fuel pump replaced," I said.

He eyed me with suspicion but then let it go.

"Doctor, I need your help," I said. "We have a German woman who's been badly injured. She needs medical attention."

"It's four o'clock in the morning," he said. "Take her to the hospital."

"I can't," I said, not wanting to divulge more.

He studied me with his piercing eyes for a long moment. "I'll dress and be down in a minute."

Five minutes later, he exited the building wearing his overcoat and carrying his doctor's bag. He gave me a look that said plenty; he wasn't happy about me coming there in the middle of the night. But I knew he would be the type of doctor to honor his Hippocratic oath.

He followed me to the Mercedes and stopped to survey the oversized luxury car. "Should I ask whose car this is?"

"No," I said and got behind the wheel.

Lehmann gave me a chiding look, then joined me. His disapproving manner, much like my grandfather had expressed most of my early childhood, made my blood boil. I could usually let that kind of thing roll off my back, but I respected Lehmann, which made the rebuke harder to take. I kept my mouth shut and my eyes on the road, started up the car and drove off.

"Who are you?" he asked after a few blocks. "You said you were a former policeman, but nothing else."

"What you really want to know is, what is an American civilian doing in occupied Berlin?" I said.

As I took random turns to watch for a tail, I told him briefly about my time in the Chicago Police and the army. That my friend in the CIC, who had gotten me out of several jams, needed my help. "The woman is my friend's fiancé," I said, lying to him for some reason. "The two of them were trying to track down Germans working for the Soviets. She was beaten for what she knows and is in bad shape."

"But that's not all the story, is it?" he said.

"No, but the less you know, the safer you are," I said.

Lehmann fell quiet after that last revelation. He seemed to shrink in his seat as he stared out the window.

"I'm sorry about getting you involved," I said. "But the woman needs a doctor, and you're the only one I could think of."

Lehmann said nothing until I pulled over to the curb in front of the apartment building. "I'll help this woman, but my life is complicated enough without getting involved in your intrigue." He opened the car, then hesitated. "This is the last time we talk. And you will return my car as soon as it's repaired."

We crossed the street and entered the building. When we reached the second floor, Laura was waiting for us by the open door. I introduced her to the doctor, who seemed charmed by her beauty and grace, even lingering a moment before asking to see the patient. Sigrid lay in the same fetal position as when I'd left. She seemed almost lifeless when Lehmann started examining the cuts and bruises on her face. His touch startled her out of her sleep, and she let out a yelp. Lehmann's gentle words calmed her.

Laura and I stood back to let the doctor work. I leaned close to her and whispered, "Don't mention the car."

She looked surprised and pointed at Lehmann. "The Opel is his car? The one now probably impounded by the CID?"

I shushed her with my finger. To change the subject, I tilted my head toward Sigrid. "How is she?"

"She slept the whole time," Laura said. "She talked a little in her sleep, mumbling Mike's name."

Lehmann looked up at us. "Could you give us some privacy?"

Laura and I stepped out into the hallway and stood by the window overlooking the courtyard.

"Mike's being hunted, and we can't do anything about it," she said.

I had the same thoughts, but Laura voicing them made my stomach tie in knots. More to appease my own fears, I said, "He's managed to evade capture up until now. He can do it again."

Laura raised an eyebrow. "You don't believe that any more than I do. We have to get Mike's location from Sigrid, whether she's able to go or not."

"Knowing where he *might* be hiding is only half the battle."

"That's more than what we had before. Don't tell me you're having second thoughts."

"This isn't us just going up against a pack of wolves. We'll have to contend with the Soviet army. Not to mention the CID looking for us. And no telling what shape Mike might be in when we find him. Would he be able to walk? Or even move?"

"Whatever we come up with, we have to do it fast," Laura said. "We're running out of time."

"We have to do this smart, or we'll never get out of there."

"So, what's your plan, professor?"

I gave her a sideways glance to show I didn't find that amusing. "First, we'll need a guide to get us there and back undetected."

"That means waiting until Sigrid recovers, and that could take days, weeks!"

"We go tomorrow at noon," a woman said behind us.

We both turned to see Sigrid leaning against the open door of the apartment. Lehmann stood behind her. He shook his head in exasperation and went back inside. Laura and I walked up to Sigrid. She pushed herself off the doorframe and glared at us in defiance.

"It may not look like it, but I can do it," she said.

I walked past her and went inside to talk to Lehmann. He was muttering to himself as he leaned over the sofa and packed his doctor's bag.

"What did you find, Doctor?" I asked.

"She's a brave girl," Lehmann said. "She's in pain but refuses to show it. The only thing I could offer her was aspirin, but she even declined that."

"That doesn't answer my question," I said. "She wants to go with us to rescue our friend."

Lehmann finished packing and stood with his bag in his hand. "The only thing you care about is if she'll slow you down."

My temper flared, but I suppressed it. "You're wrong if you think I'm not concerned about her welfare. My best friend is in love with her. I'm not about to risk her life."

Laura and Sigrid came into the room. Lehmann glanced at Sigrid. "She can tell you," he said and walked past me.

I grabbed his arm to stop him. "I want to hear from you."

"Unhand me, please," the doctor said.

I released his arm, though Lehmann remained where he was. "Her left eye orbit and zygomatic arch—her cheekbone—are fractured. Her right eye is damaged, and she could lose sight in that eye without medical care. Two of her teeth are about to fall out. She has several severe bruises on her torso in the area around her liver and kidneys, and a cracked rib. Without an x-ray, I can't tell if there's internal bleeding. If the bleeding is profuse or doesn't stop, or she exerts herself, she could die. Now, I would appreciate a ride home."

"I'll take him," Laura said and held out her hand for the keys. "Less likely they'll stop me driving around at five in the morning."

I fished the keys out of my pocket and handed them to her. Lehmann walked out the front door without saying another word. Laura leaned in and lowered her voice. "You need to convince Sigrid that our chances are better if we go alone."

"I'm right here," Sigrid said. "My ears work just fine."

Laura ignored her and left. Sigrid used the wall as a support and stared at me. The weight of everything that had unfolded during the long day threatened to knock me over, and I let gravity pull me into one of the chairs.

"Relax," I said. "You don't need to prove you can stand."

"You're not going to convince me to stay behind."

"I worry your body is going to decide that for you," I said. "And in the middle of our mission."

Sigrid walked over to the sofa and used the arm to gently lower herself to the cushions. "I'll take full responsibility. If I can't go on, you will leave me behind."

"Neither of us would do that."

Sigrid groaned in frustration. "You are very stubborn."

"I think you've got us beat. Why risk your life when Laura and I can do this on our own?"

Sigrid took a moment to answer. "It's my fault Mike is in trouble. I told him of my suspicion that a small group of Gehlen's men were double agents, and that the leader might be a former SD sadist."

"Wilhelm Pfeffer," I said. She nodded. "You only *suspected* his identity?" I asked with skepticism.

She furrowed her brow. "I've never met the man or seen pictures of him. I only overheard Ernst Leiter talking about it. What I'm trying to say is that because I told Mike all this, he started an investigation. It didn't take long for the gang to suspect I leaked the information to him, and they went after me. I barely escaped by going into the Soviet sector. I knew of some safe houses there from my days working for the Soviets."

"And Mike followed you," I said.

"I didn't know that at the time."

"Is Mike in one of those houses?"

She smiled at my feeble attempt to get some information out of her. I appreciated she was still mentally sharp while suffering so much pain. She'd been trained well, and I wouldn't underestimate her again.

"When Mike called me in Boston for help, he said he'd been wounded in the leg. What shape was Mike in when you left? Will he be able to walk?"

"I doubt it," she said. "A veterinarian patched him up and said he suspected the bullet had fractured his tibia."

"If he was in that kind of shape, why did you leave him?" I tried to keep a neutral tone, but it still came out as an accusation.

Sigrid clamped her jaw so hard the muscles popped. She threw daggers with her glare. "That's enough. If we're going to do this in a couple of hours, I need some rest. Instead of using your energy for insults, I advise you to do the same."

With that, she lay down on the sofa and closed her eyes. In a minute, she began to snore, not unlike Laura's. The sound slowly took me under its spell, and I dreamed of being in a space void of light, the sound of gunfire ringing in my ears. Even in that unconscious state, I had the wherewithal to wonder if I was experiencing my past or my future.

39

As the U-Bahn train stopped at the Zoologischer Garten station, a conductor came through the cars announcing that this was the terminus due to servicing issues on the Soviet side farther down the line. Whether that was the real issue, or the Soviets had shut down that entry point for reasons unknown, it didn't matter to us. We'd planned to get off the train there, and the crush of exiting passengers would help to obscure us from prying eyes. Especially when Sigrid still looked like she'd stuck her head in a hornet's nest despite the gobs of makeup Laura had applied to mask the bruising. She'd already drawn looks from the passengers in our proximity, though no one inquired about her well-being; a battered woman was not an uncommon sight. Abuse from drunken soldiers, thieves praying on the vulnerable, or vengeful neighbors occurred with some frequency.

I led the way while trying to spot anyone who might be a threat. Sigrid, who barely reached my shoulders, followed close behind, with Laura taking up the rear. We stayed in a single line as if traveling separately. Laura and I had backpacks over tattered clothes taken from Sigrid's closet. She and a male colleague had left them there when it was a Soviet safe house. Our long overcoats concealed the weapons we'd raided from the arsenal in her wardrobe. Sigrid's coat also hid the tight bandages Laura had tied around her ribcage to alleviate some of the pain from her cracked ribs.

Sigrid gave me verbal directions, steering me toward a far corner of the underground station and in the opposite direction of the rest of the crowd. It was the lunch hour, and with the seven cars unloading at the same time, it felt like we were salmon swimming upstream.

We made it to the end, and Sigrid told me to enter a service door in the corner. I glanced behind for any danger. We appeared to be in the clear. The doorjamb had been ripped out of its casing, and the impacts of bullets dented the surface of the door. Lingering evidence of the violence between the Soviets and defending Nazis during the Battle of Berlin. I opened the door, and we entered a long, dark hallway.

We illuminated our flashlights and continued down a dank corridor slightly wider than my shoulders. The concrete walls were pockmarked by more bullets, and the electrical conduit had been replaced in several spots where explosions had gouged the walls and ceiling. It was obvious that an intense firefight had occurred in the tight space. The corpses were no longer there, but it felt like we moved through an empty coffin, a notion heightened by my nagging claustrophobia.

"How far?" I asked, my voice going up a pitch from my nerves.

"Fifty meters," Sigrid said.

Those fifty meters felt like a mile. Finally, my flashlight beam fell upon a man-sized hole opening up to a black void. Rancid sewer odors and the sound of trickling water wafted up from the sizeable gap in the concrete wall. I looked at Sigrid to see if we had arrived, and she nodded.

"Careful," she said. "It's about two meters to the bottom."

I climbed down, and my boots disappeared into the shallow sludge. The disturbance stirred up a cloud of foul air. I helped

Sigrid, then Laura, and surveyed the area with the flashlight. Sigrid explained earlier that she had used this way of crossing between east and west many times, but she'd failed to warn us that we'd smell like a backed-up toilet once we reached our destination.

Sigrid put her hand against the tunnel wall to support her weight. I pointed the flashlight beam at the ceiling, and the reflected light threw a soft glow on Sigrid. "Are you okay to continue?"

She nodded and pointed to a spot behind me. "That way."

I looked in the direction of her finger. The tunnel took a left turn about thirty feet from where we stood. Sigrid had said there were many turns in the system and would take us about three hours to reach our destination.

"Are you guys ready for this?" I asked, the question serving as a last offer to turn back.

Laura moved forward without a response, and Sigrid followed. The tunnel served both as a wastewater and storm drain and was a good fifteen feet wide and high, allowing us to walk together. I chose the middle, letting the women hug the sides and avoid the worst of the fetid sludge. The larger size of the tunnel helped dissipate my claustrophobia. My mind now clear, I could concentrate on the task at hand.

Without Sigrid, it would have been impossible to proceed. The first twenty minutes consisted of numerous turns and junctions of two or three pipes going in different directions. I kept one eye on Sigrid for signs of fatigue or crippling pain, but if she suffered from either, she didn't show it.

At the end of those twenty minutes, we entered a much larger storm drain tunnel. The water level was almost knee deep and freezing. The farther we went, the faster the flow. My feet became numb, and my leg muscles cramped. I drew strength from memories from the war, when I barely survived a snowy forced march from one Nazi POW camp to another. I don't know what Sigrid used to keep going. She and Laura were both unsteady on their feet, leaning forward and swinging their arms, displaying grim expressions, as they summoned their wills to continue.

Sigrid approached a metal ladder attached to the left tunnel wall. We gathered around it, and Sigrid clasped a rung above her head and tried to lift herself. Her arms shook from the effort. She could barely lift her legs. She stopped to catch her breath and tried again. I put my hand on her shoulder.

She smiled in embarrassment. "It seems my legs are too cold to work."

"I'll pull you up," I said and put my flashlight in my pocket. I climbed the eight rungs and crawled into the adjoining pipe. I checked the area with my flashlight. A couple of rats scurried away into the darkness, causing the hairs on my arms to stand up. I'd had plenty of unpleasant encounters with rats from the Nazi camps. Those memories and the moldy ceiling hovering just above my head brought back my claustrophobia. I pushed the feelings down, turned, and lowered my hand for Sigrid.

She took it, and I lifted her as her feet fumbled on the slippery metal rungs. Pulling on her arms must have extended her rib cage, and she cried out in pain. I got her to the top, and she fell to her knees. I turned to help Laura, who had made it halfway. She, too, had stopped to catch her breath.

"I can't feel my feet," she said.

I gave her a boost, and she made it to the top. She immediately checked on Sigrid, while I verified that the rats—or anything that creeped or crawled, for that matter—had vamoosed. My chest constricted as I peered into that darkness. I looked at my watch and guessed we had another hour and a half before reaching the surface again. I hoped I could keep myself in control until then.

40

The power in the flashlight batteries was about gone, the light reduced to a dim orange glow, which aptly symbolized our fading strength. We were resting underneath an access tunnel leading upward and an extensive park called Volkspark Friedrichshain. The ladder required a forty-foot climb, and since we'd arrived two hours before sunset, we'd decided to take a break before ascending and facing whatever awaited us on the surface. Sigrid lay back against the wall and had quickly fallen asleep. Laura sat across from me on a prominent part of the pipe and away from the near-frozen sludge. She was awake but looked bone-tired. The stress from my claustrophobia had dulled my senses, and despite the overwhelming desire to climb out of this stinking purgatory, I'd agreed to camp out and rest.

I held my watch under the light beam. It was 5:15 p.m. The sun had set about an hour ago, and it would be full night outside. We were getting a late start, but I'd let Sigrid sleep a little longer.

Sigrid opened one eye and looked at me as if knowing what I was thinking. "We still have another hour aboveground before we get to our destination." She pushed herself to her feet and brushed off what dirt she could from her backside. "You shouldn't have let me sleep so long."

"You needed it," I said.

Laura and I stood, gathered the canteens and what was left of our food, and checked our weapons. We hoisted our backpacks and shouldered the STEN guns. Sigrid was already at the ladder with her submachine gun at the ready. She put a foot on the first rung and began to climb. I was next in case we ran into trouble as soon as we exited. About a third of the way up, my flashlight went out and plunged me into darkness. The dim light from Sigrid's and Laura's flashlights were the only references I had to where I was. The claustrophobia crept back in and threatened to block out all my reasoning.

"Are you okay?" Laura asked beneath me. She put a hand on my heel.

Her touch gave me some comfort, and I started to climb again. Sigrid stopped, her breathing heavy and quick. She made a grunting noise, which I thought was her strength giving out, but then I heard metal grinding against concrete. Fresh air poured into the confined space.

I fought the urge to rush the opening and waited patiently for Sigrid to survey the area before crawling out of the hole. "Clear," she whispered into the hole, "but we have to move fast."

I bounded up the last few rungs and pushed myself up and out of the manhole. I took in gulps of fresh air while offering Laura my hand. She took it and used my help to climb out.

We were standing in the center of a concrete plaza that formed a shallow bowl. A damaged classical-style pavilion and an inoperative fountain stood at one end. Sigrid tapped my arm before rushing over an embankment and into a row of shrubs and sparse trees. Laura followed her, while I shoved the iron cover back in place. As it came to a rest, it made a loud hollow thud. I looked around just as a pair of Soviet soldiers entered the plaza. I stayed low and raced over the embankment to join Laura and Sigrid.

We remained close to the ground and peered through the branches. The soldiers chattered and smoked as they came closer. They moved at a leisurely pace, unaware of our presence. I kept one hand on my brass knuckles and the other on my knife tucked in my boot, just in case. They passed out of sight.

There were voices and laughter in the near distance and the sound of traffic farther away. Close behind us and to the left were two wide intersecting streets that formed the park's western boundary. To our right was a dense woodland area segmented by winding paths and various statues and small fountains. Half the ground was covered in bomb craters. The few trees that had survived the war lost their leaves weeks ago. We couldn't count on much cover as we moved.

Sigrid pointed at an area to our right and slightly behind me. Rising above the treetops were the gargantuan ruins of a double-turreted flak tower. "We head in that direction."

After a last survey of the area, we headed out. Moving quickly, we stuck to the trees and avoided the paths. At a hundred yards we began skirting a line of trees that abutted a wide swath of cleared land surrounding the destroyed flak tower. The immense structure was split down the middle, with the center portion higher than the ends. It looked like a ghoulish fortress that had been cleaved in two by a subterranean giant. A small-scale locomotive with attached mining cars stood at the base where, under the glare of a single work light, a handful of workers were unloading rubble collected from the nearby ruins.

Sigrid stopped and squatted down, prompting us to do the same.

"Bombs couldn't have done that," Laura said, her eyes glued to the monstrosity.

"The Soviets blew it up after the war," Sigrid said. "Now they use it as a place to dump rubble." She pointed toward the opposite end. "We have to cross the field. Otherwise, we'll be too close to the street."

Between us and the tower ruins was a good eighty yards. "That's a lot of open ground to cross," I said.

"We're dressed like everyone else, so we shouldn't have a problem," Sigrid said.

Laura looked unsure and turned to me for an opinion. She was right to be skeptical. I still didn't know how much I could trust Sigrid. "Looks like we don't have a choice," I said.

We stood and moved across the field at a leisurely pace, paralleling the front of the flak tower. The workers paid us no mind. Neither did the strolling couple coming in the opposite direction. A handful of kids played soccer on an improvised field near a small pond. I didn't worry until we came in sight of a broad boulevard running along the southern edge of the park.

A small group of vendors had set up a black-market site just before the street. Whatever they were selling was attracting a sizable gathering of Russian soldiers and men in somber attire. I guessed that at least a few of them were secret police. One man in a long, black overcoat looked our way as he wandered among the line of makeshift booths.

"We should go around that crowd," I said.

Laura and Sigrid followed me in a left turn. I glanced over my shoulder at the customers. The man who had eyeballed us was now sixty yards behind and keeping pace.

"We've picked up a tail," I said.

"We'll try to lose him in the cemetery up ahead," Sigrid said.

I wanted to ask "Then what?" but she wouldn't have more of a clue than I did. The cemetery was visible through the damaged trees. It was a small three-sided piece of ground with humble gravestones. Beyond that was a hospital that had suffered near destruction from the bombings and the Battle of Berlin. The wide boulevard to our right was lined with heavily damaged buildings and promised to be the best option for a quick getaway.

"We cross the cemetery, then get to the other side of the boulevard and lose him in that bombed-out neighborhood," I said.

"If we change direction again, he'll be even more suspicious," Laura said.

"Right now, we're going farther away from our destination," Sigrid said. "I say we risk it."

We entered the cemetery by a hole in the low brick wall, crossed the sixty feet of ground, and climbed over the opposite wall that was nothing but a jumbled pile of brick and mortar. We turned south, moving between the cemetery and the hospital. I resisted the temptation to look back at our pursuer and kept going.

We reached the wide boulevard and crouched near a pile of stones. Apparently, it was a vital artery, because there were Soviet trucks, armored personnel carriers, and sedans with uniformed drivers zooming by at regular intervals. To get across was going to take some good timing and a bit of luck.

A convoy of Soviet vehicles was rumbling past us, then the street looked clear of vehicles. As the last armored car crossed in front of us, I said, "Let's go."

As we took our first steps onto the roadway, someone called out to us in Russian. It was the man in the long overcoat who'd been following us, and whatever he said made Sigrid break into a run. Laura and I did the same. We dashed across the road, dodging a pack of cyclists as we did so, and made a beeline for a perpendicular street that pierced the neighborhood of ruins. Several dozen local Germans walked along the sidewalks or stood over barrel fires for warmth. A crew of workers were finishing up for the day, securing a wooden crane, or packing their tools. Our pursuer was not far behind us. I didn't understand Russian, but it seemed obvious he was yelling commands for us to stop.

All eyes followed us. Some people cowered in fear; others

gave us sympathetic stares. I figured we weren't the only people they'd seen branded as enemies of the state and pursued by authorities. How many times had this happened in a day? In a week? The answer was in their faces.

We made it to the perpendicular street and took a sharp left at the next block. The buildings along this narrow road still stood but were burned-out hulks. A handful of pedestrians scurried out of the way. Behind us, the man had yet to turn the corner.

"In here," I said and dashed for a gap in the wall of a building to our right.

We plunged into darkness, me in the lead. We kept going deeper into the gutted lobby until a mound of rubble blocked our way. The rapid footsteps from the long-coated man echoed loudly in the narrow street. Then the footsteps stopped. Through one of the bare window frames, we could see the man standing in the middle of the street as he searched for any sign of our presence.

I cursed under my breath and coaxed Laura and Sigrid to keep moving. Maybe we could get lucky and continue moving through building interiors until discovering a way out. Almost blind in the darkness, we had a difficult time navigating the rubble without tripping or causing further collapse of the structure.

Sigrid hissed a curse and tumbled over something. She cried out in pain when she hit the ground and several pieces of concrete tumbled after her.

Laura and I turned toward the noise. Sigrid must have fallen behind, and we hadn't noticed. We hurried back the way we'd come. We reached the spot in time to see Sigrid struggling with the man in black. He was trying to drag her toward the street. He saw us and pulled out his pistol.

Laura and I ducked behind the rubble. The man fired twice. The bullets struck the concrete near our position.

The sound of Sigrid's struggles prompted us to look out from our hiding place and saw her fighting with the man. His and Sigrid's abrupt movements made it impossible for me to get a clean shot, and I fired twice, hitting the concrete structure above the man's head.

He tried to use Sigrid as a shield, but she squirmed out of his grasp. The man's eyes went wide with shock and fear, and he sprinted for the street. Laura fired once but missed, hitting a concrete pillar instead. The next instant, the man was on the street and racing away. I ran in pursuit, but by the time I got out onto the street, the man disappeared around the far corner.

Laura came out of the building with Sigrid propped on one shoulder. Sigrid grimaced in pain with each step. I went over and put my shoulder under Sigrid's other arm. She pushed both of us away and stood on her own. Her legs wobbled; her chest heaved as she took in air.

"Are you sure you can go on?" I asked her.

She clenched her jaw as if mustering her strength. "Follow me."

41

Laura, Sigrid, and I walked three abreast as we weaved through a hellscape of shattered buildings. To complete the nightmare, the shadowy light played tricks on my sight, transforming civilians into phantoms as they wandered the sidewalks or carved out shelters in the rubble.

I'm sure we made a similar impression on the locals, all three of us trudging along from exhaustion and caked in mud, with Sigrid hugging her ribs with one arm and using the other to propel her forward like a corpse that had risen from the dead. Laura had begun to limp, not badly, but I worried it would get worse. The only advantage to our appearance was that no one paid much attention to us. We were just another group of Berliners bereft of home and possessions seeking refuge for the night.

Sigrid had finally told us that Mike's location lay in an area to the southwest of our position and about a kilometer from the Spree River. To avoid being picked up by the Soviet patrols, we headed east, intending to loop around to the south and our destination. My hope was that the Soviets would search for us along the Spree River and the neighborhoods near the American sector.

We turned right onto a side street, and a broad boulevard came into view. I slowed my pace, and we came to a stop.

"We should find a way of going around that street," I said.

"Not possible," Sigrid said in a breathless voice. "That's Frankfurter Allee. We would have to go into the city center to avoid it. Or try crossing using the train tracks. But that means another kilometer out of our way."

Crossing such a busy street was risky, but when I looked at Laura's and Sigrid's exhausted faces, I knew we were running out of time, out of energy, let alone luck.

"All right," I said. "We cross one at a time and meet up a block south."

As we approached the boulevard, my heart started pumping ice. A T-34 tank was parked on the opposite side of the road. Jeeps rolled by with three or four soldiers. The buildings along the broad roadway still stood, though most had lost their windows and roofs, and the walls were pockmarked by bullets and shells like they had suffered from a mortal pox.

We got to the corner and peered around it. Soldiers manned the sidewalks at hundred-foot intervals, though they seemed more interested in talking and smoking than being vigilant. We ducked back when another pair of Jeeps raced by.

Sigrid made a move toward the intersection, but I put my hand on her arm to stop her. Sigrid yanked her arm away and glowered at me.

"They're looking for us as a group," I said. "We cross one at a time, and Laura goes first."

"Why?" she asked. "You don't trust I will wait for you?"

"No, I don't," I said. I said to Laura, "If I don't make it, keep going."

Laura looked at me. "Just see that you do, or I'll murder you myself." She checked to see if her submachine gun was well concealed and headed out. She stepped out onto the sidewalk in a leisurely fashion and looked left and right, waited for a passing sedan before proceeding. I slid up to the corner and watched the reactions of the soldiers as Laura crossed. She exaggerated her limp just enough to appear like a local down on her luck and tired from a long day of labor.

Despite her muddy clothes, dirty face, and tousled hair, two soldiers whistled and called out to her in heavily accented German. One took a couple of steps toward her, but Laura covered one nostril and blew out mucus with the other in his direction. She then coughed and spit out phlegm. The soldier looked like he'd bit into a lemon, turned, and walked away.

"That's my girl," I said under my breath.

Laura made it to the other side and entered a narrow side street. When she disappeared into the shadows, Sigrid stepped forward. I figured her zombie-like walk would discourage the wolves in uniform, but the same soldier approached Sigrid. He purred at her in bad German. Wild-eyed, she yelled at him in Russian. Whatever she said, it did the trick. Once again, the soldier returned to his post after giving her an obscene gesture.

Across the boulevard, five men in workmen's overalls were heading in my direction. They only gave Sigrid a cursory glance as they smoked and talked in loud voices, mostly exchanging teasing insults at one another, letting off steam after a hard day's work. I tilted my hat forward, lowered my head, and stepped out of the shadows.

I was too busy watching the soldiers beyond the brim of my hat to notice a Russian army staff car barreling down on me. The car's horn startled me. The driver swerved right, as if trying to run me down. I froze as the car's grill seemed to block out my field of view. At the last minute, it veered away from me and rocketed past. The soldiers chuckled, but the German workers gave me sympathetic looks as we crossed paths. It had drawn the soldiers' attention, but they must have figured I'd experienced enough humiliation for the moment, and they went back to smoking and gabbing. I let out a breath of relief when I set foot on the side street.

I couldn't see either of the women and quickened my pace. I bolted around the corner to find Sigrid with her back against the wall, her mouth wide open, her face twisted in pain. Laura was working furiously on the bandages cinched around Sigrid's rib cage.

"I can't breathe," Sigrid said between gasps for air.

"It's not any tighter than it was," Laura said to me. "It could be she panicked, or it's simply from exhaustion." She continued to loosen the wrap while using a soothing voice to encourage Sigrid to take deep breaths and try to calm down.

Laura tied off the bandage and buttoned up her blouse, and Sigrid slowly got herself under control. A moment passed, then Sigrid gritted her teeth and pushed herself off the wall. "We have to go."

"We can wait a couple of minutes," I said.

"I won't be able to move if I rest any longer," Sigrid said. "We're not far."

Sigrid led the way, and after ten minutes and a series of zigzag turns, we came to an intersection of two modest streets. She stopped us and hugged the corner building to our left. We all peered out from the wall. The perpendicular street ran for another block before ending at a four-lane road divided by a median. A single Soviet Jeep passed by on the wider road, which was the only sign of activity.

"He's in that one at the corner," Sigrid said and pointed toward what appeared to be an abandoned bank, a stately neo-classical building that had been disfigured and blackened by war. The walls and austere edifice remained, but the domed roof had collapsed into the interior. Its neighbors looked as if a strong breeze would bring down their brick walls. "We can get in through a rear entrance and avoid the main street."

I resisted the urge to sprint toward the building. We were finally close to achieving what we'd traveled so far and risked so much to do.

Rescue our friend.

42

The three of us crept down the street, watching the shadows. We stuck to the north side, where the buildings had suffered the greatest amount of damage. I could almost trace the path of a bomber as it dropped its payload, hitting one side and sparing the other. No one moved, not even the wind. There was no sound at all except for Sigrid's labored breathing and our shoes on the debris-strewn pavement. There was something disturbing about the absence of life under the moonless sky.

The lack of activity around the building meant either Pfeffer's gang either had not yet arrived or already left. Just before reaching the building, the suspense was too much, and we trotted the rest of the way. We turned down the small alley behind the bank and mounted the steps to the rear entrance. I spotted it at the last moment and skidded to a halt. I held out my arms to block Laura and Sigrid from stepping over the threshold of the doorless entry.

A foot above the ground, someone had rigged a tripwire across the opening. At best, it was a warning system against intruders. At worst, an explosive booby trap. As I helped Laura and Sigrid step over the wire, I wondered how many more devices we might encounter as we went deeper into the ruins.

The interior was much larger than it appeared from the street. It was sixty feet to the main entrance, while the width of the building extended into the darkness. Thick columns held up nothing but a portion of the brick and sandstone roof. The rest lay on the floor in heaps pierced by twisted iron framework.

Sigrid pointed to the marble and cast-iron staircase. "Up there," she whispered.

With a flight of approximately thirty treads, the staircase ended at what appeared to be only a fragment of the second floor. If there had been a third floor, it was gone. If Mike was "upstairs" as Sigrid said, I didn't see where he could be, aside from clinging to the ceiling. I looked at Laura to see if she was as confused as I was. She raised an eyebrow and shrugged.

Sigrid put a finger to her lips and moved toward the stairs, prompting us to do the same. We caught up to her and pointed our flashlights at the floor to avoid tripping over the debris or more booby traps. We had to climb over piles of brick and iron at several points. Sigrid refused any help, making me hold my breath each time she had to slink over another obstacle.

Several feet from the base of the staircase, the metallic click of a cigarette lighter stopped us. It came from above. We doused our flashlights, and I looked up to see the orange glow of a cigarette lighter coming from somewhere to the right of the return wall on the second floor. We all crouched down and froze.

The voices of two men speaking in German echoed down the stairs, but I couldn't make out what they were saying. We had our answer; Pfeffer's gang had already arrived. Two of them were up there, and maybe more. I cursed myself for not checking the front entrance for others. I fished the brass knuckles out of my pocket and pulled the knife from my boot. I signaled Laura to back me up with her pistol in case things got out of hand. She nodded, and we crept up the stairs. Laura stayed three steps behind me. Sigrid remained below.

I took two steps at a time to minimize the noise and got within six feet of the landing. The staircase led up to a hallway, or what was left of one. To the right, there couldn't have been more than ten feet of floor before the collapsing roof had sheared off the rest. On the left, I could only see a few feet of hallway and had to assume there was a single, intact office at the end of it. Mike had to be there.

I was close enough to hear the one guy puffing on his cigarette. He was right around the corner. The second guy was the problem; I had no clue where he was. I picked up a fist-sized chunk of concrete, handed it to Laura, and made a motion for her to throw it out into the lobby.

She looked alarmed at my request but took it. I coiled my body and tensed my muscles, then counted down from three with my fingers. I made a fist, and Laura tossed the concrete. It took two long seconds for it to land. It clattered and bounced before stopping on the floor below.

Shoes shuffled on rough concrete. Two shadows emerged from the short hallway and rushed toward me, a big man in front, with his partner rolling off the return wall. I launched up and forward. Neither of them had expected me.

I slammed the brass knuckles into the big man's jaw. He stumbled sideways, then tried to grab me. I deflected his charge, and he screamed as he tumbled the thirty feet to the ground floor. I twisted and lunged to my left and jammed the seven-inch blade of the Ka-Bar into the second man's chest. He cried out as he fell against the wall and slid to the ground.

I turned toward the office, anticipating an attack from that direction. Nothing but darkness. The only sound was the death throes of the man I'd stabbed.

Laura was gasping at the violence, and I looked down at her. "Are you okay?"

Laura had tears in her eyes and averted my gaze. She wordlessly followed Sigrid into the room as dark as a coal mine.

I let the two women move on ahead. Laura would need some time to get over the shock of being up close to that kind of violence. After a moment, I strode into the office and stood next to the women. We used our flashlights to search the sizeable room. A lone desk stood against one wall amid the dust, dirt, and detritus. Laura rapped my arm to get my attention. Her flashlight beam had landed on a motionless body lying on a tattered mattress at the back left corner of the room.

"Mike," Sigrid yelled and rushed toward it.

Laura and I did the same and stopped at the foot of the mattress. Forester was covered in sweat. His hands and legs were bound, and a rag was jammed in his mouth. Sigrid dropped to her knees, pulled the gag out of his mouth, and checked his pulse. Laura and I took our submachine guns from our shoulders, knelt next to Sigrid. I cut the ropes binding him.

Sigrid tapped Forester's cheek with her open hand. "Mike? Mike?" Forester didn't react. She touched his forehead. "He's so hot."

"Probably an infection," Laura said and pulled back the blankets covering his clothed body. A stench of rotting meat rose into the air. Bloodstains covered an area of his left leg just below the knee.

Forester's eyes popped wide, and he sucked in air. He saw Sigrid leaning into his face and reached out to her. He mouthed words but no sounds came out.

Sigrid kissed him on the lips and said, "Your friends are here."

He moved his eyes and smiled. "What took you so long?" he asked in a raspy voice. He took Laura's hand and closed his eyes in relief.

I moved over to get closer to him. "Sorry, buddy. We ran into a few obstacles."

"And they're not finished with us yet," Laura said. She took my knife from my hand and cut Forester's left pant leg.

Sigrid opened her canteen and put it to Forester's lips. He took hungry sips. His eyes and cheeks were sunken into his skull. I remembered him as a muscular man, but his torso looked like the scarecrow from the *Wizard of Oz* after his stuffing had been pulled out.

Laura shined a light on Forester's leg and hissed as if she had felt the pain. "It's infected all right. He's got blood poisoning, and it's moved up to his thigh."

"Mike, we've got to get out of here fast," I said. "You think you can move?"

"It's that or die," he said.

Sigrid went over to the tattered desk and retrieved his overcoat. She pocketed some of the medication and bandages left on there as well.

I put his arms around my neck. "Are you ready?"

"As I'll ever be," he said and locked his hands.

I lifted him enough to get my hands on his back and pulled him up. Laura helped me by lifting him by his arms. He moaned and wheezed with the effort, but didn't cry out in pain. I turned while holding him and put my shoulder under his armpit. Laura did the same. We moved slowly at first, letting him get his blood flowing and remind his legs how to move. Sigrid grabbed up my STEN gun and her backpack and followed us toward the door.

"Those obstacles wouldn't happen to be Leiter and his men, would it?" Forester asked between breaths of air.

"Leiter's no longer around, but the rest of his gang is," I said. "Well, minus one at the Rote Lantern and two out in the hallway."

"The SS commander you were investigating," Laura said, "Wilhelm Pfeffer is leading them now."

"I would have preferred Leiter," Forester said. "Pfeffer is a sadist." He stopped and faced me. "If I don't make it, there's something you've got to know now." I tried to get him moving, but he batted my hand away. "No, listen. They're using the AFN radio station to send messages."

"Who is?" I asked.

"The Soviets, Leiter's gang, and whoever is running things on the U.S. side. They use dedications to songs to send messages in code broadcasted at fifteen-thirty hours. Alerts of information to pass on, times and locations for the exchanges. I was on my way to the AFN when Heissmeyer tried to assassinate me. I'm sure someone knew I was hot on Hodgson's trail and tried to stop me."

"Hodgson was the contact?" Laura asked.

Forester shook his head. "Hodgson's just the errand boy. I'm sure if you put enough pressure on him, he'll spill everything."

"Hate to break it to you, buddy, but Hodgson was blown up two days ago," I said. "I'm sure whoever ordered the bomb was controlling Hodgson and keeping Leiter's gang under control."

"Boys, we have to hurry," Laura said. "The rest of the gang is on their way."

"I couldn't figure how they knew about this place," Forester said.

Laura and I didn't respond, but after a moment, Sigrid said, "I told them."

Forester stiffened; his steps faltered.

Sigrid came around to face him, but he wouldn't look at her. "I'm sorry, darling," she said.

"They tortured her for the information," Laura said.

Pain filled Forester's eyes. He wrapped his arms around Sigrid, and they held each other tight.

"We'll have plenty of time for that once we get out of here," I said. "Right now, all our concentration should be on how to get to the American sector."

We made it to the top of the stairs. Sigrid took the lead. Laura and I helped Forester. He moved as if his legs were made of rubber, but some of his coordination was returning. He took the next steps under more of his own power.

"We can't go back the way we came," Sigrid said. "Our only option is to use one of the bridges across the Spree. It's about a half kilometer."

"You used the sewer system to Volkspark Friedrichshain?" Forester asked Sigrid. When she nodded, he said, "It's the safest way back. I can make it."

"Except that we exchanged fire with a Soviet MGB agent," I said. "Now, they're looking for us."

"Is there anyone you haven't pissed off?" Forester asked me.

"You mean other than the CID, the CIC, and G-2?" I asked.

Forester chuckled, but it was cut short when he was seized by a coughing fit. We reached the ground floor and stopped to let him get his cough under control.

A pop of a small explosive was followed by a groan like a tree falling behind us. A man crying out in alarm came a split second later.

"The tripwire!" Forester said.

43

We all turned to see the bottom half of a marble column tumble to the floor. The shock of the impact caused a portion of the second floor, still hanging on by a thread, to fall onto the two men who were trying to enter the building via the rear entrance. One man was on the ground and motionless. The other man was dazed and on his knees. He saw us and tried to aim his pistol in our direction.

"They're here," Sigrid yelled. She swung around with the STEN submachine gun and fired a burst in the man's direction. One round clipped him in the hip. He dropped and writhed in agony.

"Get down!" Laura yelled.

Gunfire erupted from the front entrance. Laura instantly returned fire with her submachine gun, causing the shooters to retreat onto the portico. The rest of us dived for cover behind a pile of rubble.

Sigrid tossed me the STEN and helped Forester find better cover. Laura and I kept the shooters at bay, but we only had so much ammunition, and there were at least four men outside.

"They'll try to go around back," I yelled over the gunfire.

Sigrid was already keeping watch on the rear entrance, with Forester lying next to her. She gestured toward me. "Give me the STEN."

I tossed her the submachine gun and pulled out my .45. I turned my attention back to the front. "The Russians are going to show up any minute after all this gunfire." I said to Sigrid, "You and Mike make your way to the back entrance. We'll cover you."

As Sigrid and Forester moved from one rubble pile to the next, Laura and I fired anytime one of the shooters showed their faces. Laura popped out an empty magazine and loaded the spare. "Last one," she said.

I glanced back and saw that Sigrid and Forester had made it to the rear entrance. "Let's go."

She and I fired a burst, then darted from pile to pile and stopped only to shoot a couple rounds to keep our pursuers at bay. By the time we dropped behind the third pile, there were only two shooters left at the front door. The other two were plainly going around the building to cut us off. I tapped Laura's arm, and we sprinted for the rear.

We reached the rear entrance. Forester was just outside the door, out of breath and leaning against the wall. Sigrid was at the bottom step. I rushed past her and looked down the street toward the front of the building. Two men were hunkered low and moving toward us. I fired at them, but they managed to drop to the ground and fire back.

Behind us, a Soviet army sedan roared up the street and veered into the alley. The two shooters on the ground fired at the sedan, leaving the two occupants confused about who was a threat and who wasn't.

Laura and Sigrid charged at the vehicle with their submachine guns, forcing the sedan to stop. I came at them from the side. Sigrid yelled at them in Russian, and the two Soviet MPs got out of the car and held their hands in the air.

Sigrid pointed toward the opposite end of the street and

barked something in Russian while holding her submachine gun on them. They hurried away with their hands still in the air. Sigrid helped Forester into the back seat, while Laura got in the front passenger's seat.

I fired at the two shooters hugging the side of the building one more time before jumping into the driver's seat. I slammed the car in reverse, backed out onto the street, and headed away from the boulevard.

Bullets hit the back window and struck the trunk. A round pierced the windshield. Another blew off the passenger's side-view mirror. Just as I turned left, three pursuing cars appeared in the rearview mirror.

"Our only chance to cross the Spree is the Shilling Bridge," Sigrid said. "It's the last one still intact."

"I'm going to need more than a name," I yelled.

"South, south!" she yelled.

I was too disoriented and distracted to know in that moment which way was south. Sigrid yelled for me to turn left at the last minute. I turned too fast, and the car fishtailed. The tires screeched, then grabbed the road. I gave it some gas and took off.

The three vehicles chasing us made the same turn seconds later. The passenger in the lead car took potshots at us. Most of the rounds missed, but one struck the back window, shattering it, the pieces falling on the back seat.

Sigrid turned in her seat and returned fire.

I zigzagged as much as I could in the two-lane street. That kept the cars from teaming up or passing me. But a block later, the street widened into four lanes. The lead sedan gained on us, while a Soviet-style Jeep tried to come up alongside the first.

The ruins of buildings raced by. High piles of rubble had been stacked on the edges of the roadway, and the street surface was pitted from bombs. That gave me an idea.

I increased my speed and headed straight for one of the larger craters.

"I hope you know what you're doing," Laura said.

I said nothing as I calculated our approach. The crater loomed in the foreground. We were so close, I could see the bottom, eight feet below.

Laura held on tight and sucked in her breath. I swerved at the very last minute. The front tire glided past the edge, but the back left tire missed the mark. The car dipped and bucked, but momentum carried the car out of the precipice.

The driver in the lead sedan wasn't so lucky. He tried to avoid it, but it was too late. The sedan spun and the back end dropped into the crater. The driver's side slammed into the opposing wall. One down and two more to go.

The lead Jeep clipped the front end of the first, then overcompensated and took a sideways bounce off a parked car. The impacts were too much for the car or the driver. It slowed to a crawl. The third sedan zoomed past its two companions.

We had a city block lead now. Ours and the pursuers' vehicle were matched in horsepower, and the third pursuer could only keep pace. In a desperate move, the front passenger fired his pistol.

Sigrid took aim through the broken back window and unloaded the rest of the submachine gun's magazine at the charging car. Steam gushed from the hood of the pursuers' car, and it slowed down.

Our cheers of success were cut short when we approached the tunnel where the street passed under a series of railroad tracks. Two Soviet sedans were parked at the entrance, with four Russian MPs clustered around and ready to fire at us.

"We're dead if we stop," I said and mashed the accelerator to the floor.

Laura leaned out the window and fired her pistol. The MPs dived behind the sedans for safety.

"Hold on!" I yelled and aimed for the walkway to the right of the sedans.

The front right wheel hit the curb. The car bounced onto the sidewalk. I nearly lost control as it swerved. The left fender scraped against the tunnel wall. My door sideswiped one of the MPs' sedans. The metal screeched as it ripped past.

The MPs recovered and fired several shots before scrambling for their cars.

"How much farther?" I asked.

"Turn right when the road ends," Sigrid said and leaned forward to look over my shoulder. "There," she said and pointed down the street.

I looked in the rearview mirror. Three blocks behind, and the two Russian MP sedans were racing toward us.

I took the turn onto a four-lane road that paralleled the Spree. Through the ruined buildings, I caught glimpses of the river's far shore. We came up quickly to the intersection for the bridge, and I was about to turn, when Laura blurted out, "Don't turn! Keep going!"

I pressed down on the gas, and we zoomed past the intersection. I could see why Laura had stopped me from turning. Four Russian military vehicles, including two armored cars, had formed an impenetrable barrier across the bridge entrance.

A blast of wind presaged the torrential rain that pelted the windshield. A blessing and a curse. It might help blind our pursuers, but it did the same to me. Any more speedy turns and we could wind up becoming part of the ruins.

I hit the steering wheel in frustration and checked the rearview mirror again. The Jepp from the shoot-out joined the two MP cars. "What now?" I asked, my rising panic coming through in my voice.

Sigrid took a moment to think. "The next few bridges are too damaged to cross. Not even for someone on foot. There's one that has been repaired enough for pedestrians, but that's almost to the center of town."

"We're not doing that," Laura said.

"Well, somebody think of something," I said.

The speedometer needle was pinned against the end of the gauge. The engine whined from the strain and running on fumes.

Four streets later, we passed another bridge that had been blown up by the retreating Germans to prevent the Soviets from crossing the river. We were out of options. I ran through the possible solutions in my head. None of them avoided a frozen gulag or a firing squad.

Forester leaned forward and held onto the back of the seat for stability. "The next bridge, the Jannowitzbrücke."

"That bridge is half in the water," Sigrid said, her voice rising a pitch in her panic.

"We do it on foot," Forester said. "I've done it. No one expects a crossing that way. It's unguarded."

"You can barely walk," Sigrid said. "Now you want to climb on girders?"

"It's our only option," he said.

We were all silent for a moment. If Forester's idea had any chance of us making it across, then we had to take it.

44

I checked on our pursuers one last time. They were about two hundred yards back. Only their headlights were visible in the heavy rain. We would have very little time to park, get out, and climb on the bridge before they were on us. At least the darkness was on our side. I doused the car lights. Laura braced herself against the dashboard.

I saw the arched-shaped superstructure of riveted steel rising above the ruins that hugged the river's edge. I reduced my speed only enough to turn onto the road leading to the bridge without flipping the car. I hit the brakes and skidded to a stop under the trestlework of the elevated train tracks.

We all jumped out and ran toward the stricken bridge. The arch remained, but the roadway it supported had collapsed into the river. We climbed down several blocks of concrete to reach the lower girder. Laura got on first. Holding on to the crossbeams, she slowly made her way out over the river.

I sighed in relief when the three pursuing vehicles raced past the intersection. The relief would be fleeting, as I knew they'd quickly realize their mistake and come back.

Sigrid climbed on next and tried to help Forester, but he was having a tough time raising his wounded leg. Sigrid pulled while I hoisted him. He panted and grimaced from the pain, but managed to clamber onto the girder alongside Sigrid. They edged along, taking a sideways step, then used their hands to pull their upper bodies as they descended the arch. It would be a slow process, and we had little time.

I climbed on right after Forester and kept a hand on his back to keep him from falling. He already gasped for air, and his legs shook. If falling onto the collapsed roadway didn't kill us, the icy water would.

My heart jacked into overdrive when our pursuers tore around the corner and skidded to a halt under the railroad bridge. Most of them charged the sedan we'd stolen with their weapons drawn. I hoped they wouldn't suspect we'd be crazy enough to cross the collapsed bridge.

I got up beside my friend and nudged him. "Sorry, buddy, but we've got to get the lead out."

Forester looked at the men rushing toward the bridge. He cursed and began moving faster. Laura had passed the halfway point, but Sigrid and Forester lagged behind. The girder arched upward at a steep angle before leveling out, and Forester was having a tough time pulling himself up while keeping his shoes from slipping on the wet steel. Sigrid was trying to hold on to the cross beams while pulling Forester along.

Some men searched along the concrete wall bordering the shoreline. Others used their flashlights to illuminate the river and fallen roadway. A couple of beams began sweeping the bridge as they searched for us. Moments later, one beam landed on me, and the men started yelling in Russian. I didn't need Sigrid to tell me what they were saying. A few gunshots told the entire story. Bullets clanked against the steel structure or ripped through the air around me. I figured the poor light, the rain, and the eighty yards between us hindered their aim.

Three of the MPs climbed onto the arch in pursuit.

A bullet hit the girder next to Forester's hand. He flinched, then lost his footing, nearly falling and taking Sigrid with him. The pursuers were gaining on us. Something had to be done to speed things up.

I grabbed Forester's arm and tucked myself in between him and the steel structure. Bullets pinged around us as I hoisted him on my back. He clasped his hands against my chest. He was as tall as I was and used his feet to take some of his own weight and propel us along.

I didn't bother checking on the men climbing after us. I concentrated all my efforts on keeping a firm hold on the crossbeams and moving us along.

Laura made it to the embankment on the other side. I could barely make her out in the darkness, but I heard her pistol fire. The Russians' bullets no longer flew around us, which meant they were shooting at Laura. The idea she might get hit gave me the urgency to move faster.

Forester grunted in pain, and his legs dangled in the air.

"Are you all right, buddy?" I yelled over the gunfire.

"Just worry about not falling, would you?" he said.

"We'll make it," I said, but the words sounded hollow.

"Yeah? Well, even if we do, we still have a good three hundred yards of Soviet territory to go through."

"That's not helping, pal," I said.

We were on the downward slope of the arch, which proved to be just as tough as going up. Mist had settled on the girder, and with Forester's weight pushing me instead of me lifting him, it took all my strength to keep from slipping. The rain kept getting into my eyes, blinding me.

Sigrid leaped the last few feet off the girder and onto the concrete embankment. She, too, opened fire on the MPs on the bridge. I glanced at the horizon beyond the west bank, thinking that the gunfire would surely bring more Russian MPs. Nothing was in sight but the jagged shapes of buildings. Blocks and blocks of them. Referred to as the Print and Publishing District, it was on several U.S. and British Army maps as a point of interest. A tourist destination for witnessing destruction on a grand scale, a sprawling monument to the horrors of war.

I hurried the last few yards, using some of the downward momentum to carry me the rest of the way. Sigrid and Laura were at the base, and they took most of Forester's weight as I climbed down to the ground.

Forester teetered on his feet. He bent over and took in deep breaths between grunts of pain. I took his arm and wrapped it around my shoulders, taking most of his weight.

"I've seen you take the pain before," I said to him. "You've got to do it again."

Forester clamped his mouth shut and nodded. We stood facing a wide boulevard that once fed onto the destroyed bridge. Sirens sounded in the distance from somewhere on this side of the river. The Russian MPs had gotten word to their comrades.

"We have to get off this boulevard," I said. "Our best bet is to go into those ruins." I gestured toward the graveyard of brick and stone in the near distance.

"I know this area," Forester said. "We go left."

Laura led the way under Forester's directions. She still had some ammunition left in her STEN gun, and she kept a vigilant eye on our surroundings.

With her head bent from sheer exhaustion, Sigrid dragged her feet as she held her rib cage with one arm while the other hung by her side. Forester was doing his best, but had to rely more and more on my support. I knew at some point I'd have to hoist him onto my back, but carrying him over the bridge had drained me.

I needed to save the rest of my strength for the inevitable run for our lives.

45

The sirens were getting closer, and we increased our straggling pace. In moments, we entered the most damaged part of the city I'd seen yet. Piles of rubble twice the height of a man loomed over us. The remnants of the buildings resembled jagged buttes forming a canyon in the western U.S. Signs in German and Russian warned of the danger of entering the structures. A few had been cordoned off with postings of future demolitions.

There were no discernible landmarks or street signs, and without Forester's knowledge of the area, we would have been lost. He steered us through a maze of small streets as police sirens echoed around us. I figured they would try to cut us off from entering the American sector by setting up checkpoints along any major artery that crossed the direct path to the border. Forester must have considered the same thing and kept us moving in small streets or alleys to avoid any checkpoints. We turned left down a street almost impassable by the rubble, then our first obstacle came into sight. A wide avenue separated by a median.

We approached the avenue with caution and bunched

together in the remnants of a corner building. To my surprise, the Russians hadn't yet set up barricades along this section of the street. Russian MPs were gathering farther down, but not in our immediate area.

We ducked back into the ruins when a Russian Jeep slowly cruised past. The Jeep's passenger used a spotlight to search the buildings. I let out my breath when it finally moved on.

"We make a run for it?" I asked.

Everyone agreed, and we gathered in the street. I leaned out to keep watch on the soldiers. From what I could tell through the veil of rain, they were spreading out and slowly coming our way.

"Go," I said, and Laura and Sigrid began trotting across the street, but Forester spasmed in pain when he tried to cross. I pulled him back and bent to offer my back. "Ready to go for a ride?"

Forester glowered at me, then climbed on. "You're never going to let me forget this, are you?"

"Not a chance," I said, and I took off. There was nothing I could do about any soldiers or vehicles that might be approaching, and I kept my focus on the dark street. Halfway across, my muscles cramped, and my back screamed at me.

I lurched into the darkness and fell sideways against the wall. Forester got off with Laura's and Sigrid's help. Five years ago, I could have carried him for miles, but after that sprint, I had to take deep breaths and push my spine against the wall to relieve my back muscles.

Laura put her hands on my chest. Her touch eased some of the pain. "Are you going to be okay?"

I nodded and pushed off the wall.

"We've got maybe four blocks," Forester said.

The notion that we were near the American sector gave me strength, even with the idea that my mug was on a most-wanted poster tacked up on the CID wall.

Forester pointed straight ahead. "The next big street we come to is the border."

Laura and I walked together, with Sigrid helping Forester at our side. We were all dead tired and limping along. I didn't think it was possible, but the deeper we went into the neighborhood, the more destruction we encountered. I couldn't imagine how Berlin would ever recover.

We had just passed a second street in silence when two pairs of headlights came on, blinding us. Five men got out of the cars and advanced up to the front fenders. I didn't need to see the lead man's face. I could tell by his posture, his back bent slightly backward as if, despite his modest stature, he looked down his nose at his inferiors … it was Wilhelm Pfeffer. The other four were who was left of his gang. Light gleamed off the metal of their guns, but they didn't open fire.

"Major Forester," Pfeffer said. "Once I heard you had eluded my men at the bank, I knew you would pass through this point. A mutual friend informed us that you would come through here when you were looking for Sigrid. He gave us permission to kill you. Much to my embarrassment, we only wounded you in the leg."

I made a mental note to ask Forester what "mutual friend" might have betrayed him. If we ever got out of there alive.

"I appreciate you being a man of habit," Pfeffer said. "It has saved us a great deal of trouble." One of Pfeffer's men pulled back the charger on his submachine gun. "Drop your weapons and lie on the ground."

Even if we could get a few rounds off before Pfeffer and his men returned fire, the risk was too great. Then it came to me. They could have gunned us down the moment we'd stepped out onto the street. They were just as scared of the Soviets as we were.

I spun on my heels and raised my .45 into the air. Audible gasps from my companions preceded me pulling the trigger. I fired three times. It sounded like small bombs going off in the otherwise silent street and reverberated off the walls.

"Run!" I yelled.

Two blocks behind us, Russian soldiers appeared with their rifles aimed in our direction. They fired as we ran for the nearest gutted building. Bullets whizzed by our heads or pierced Pfeffer's cars with metallic thwacks.

I pulled Forester along as I looked to my right. Pfeffer and his men were running for cover from the Russian bullets as they fired at us.

Laura breached the gaping hole that was once a department store entrance. Sigrid staggered in right behind her. I pushed Forester inside, and I dived in after him. I grabbed his coat and pulled him to his feet, but he yanked out of my grasp.

"Manhandle me again, and I'll cut off your hands," he said and looked like he meant it.

His hostility was a good sign. He was full of adrenaline, which overrode his weakened state. We scrambled over the rubble and headed for the opposite side. The darkness was complete. Forester had the only gun-free hands, and I gave him my flashlight to light our way.

Footsteps to our right meant Pfeffer and his men were moving parallel to us in the adjacent building to cut us off. Outside, heavy boots slapped the wet asphalt as the Russians raced to hunt us down. I hoped they were after Pfeffer and his men as well; Soviet intelligence agents would know they were collaborators, but not the pursuing Russian MPs.

We came up to a solid wall of brick and frantically searched for a way out.

"This way," Forester said with his flashlight trained on a metal door.

It took several shoves to get it to open. I poked my head out. The alley was empty. I stepped out and kept watch while the others exited the building.

"Come on," Forester said and hurried for a hole in the adjacent wall.

I let the others crawl inside, then I did the same. The upper floors and roof were gone. Rain poured in and pooled in the center of the space. We sloshed through the freezing water, moving through the building, hoping to get to the next street or alley.

"If we keep moving parallel to the border, we'll never get out of here," I said.

Several shots rang out. Sigrid cried out and fell, face first, into the pooled water.

"Sigrid!" Forester yelled with a melancholy that chilled my spine. He let go of the flashlight. It hit a concrete slab and went out. He ran back to her and dropped to his knees.

Laura and I turned toward the sound of the gunfire. The silhouettes of two of Pfeffer's men stood on either side of the hole with pistols aimed at the interior. Forester dropping the flashlight was the only thing that had saved us. The shooters couldn't see us. One of the men put his foot inside, and I opened fire. Laura followed suit. The man fell to the ground without uttering a sound. The second man fired wildly into the blackness with his submachine gun.

Laura kept the shooter pinned just outside the opening while I rushed over to Forester. He sat in the water, rocking and cradling Sigrid's lifeless body in his arms. He seemed impervious to the deafening explosions and whizzing bullets.

I squatted next to him. "Mike, she's gone," I said in a calm voice. "We've got to keep moving."

He grabbed the 9mm pistol that Sigrid had dropped and walked toward the second shooter. I got up and put my hand on his shoulder. "Mike, she wouldn't want you to sacrifice your life…"

He shrugged it away and kept on moving. Laura saw what was going on and stood to block him. "Laura, get out of my way."

Forester's voice was so menacing that Laura did what he said. He raised the pistol and marched forward despite his wounded leg. He and the second gunman exchanged fire, neither one hitting their mark.

Loud voices made the shooter turn to the street. He fired a brief burst in that direction. Rifle fire from the Russian soldiers followed immediately, and the man went down. Three soldiers appeared near the hole and examined the body.

Forester stopped, turned, and came toward us.

Laura moved up next to him and said in a soft voice. "Mike," was all she said. But it had the desired effect on him. He let his gun arm drop to his side, and he leaned on her for support.

I rushed up to them and helped get Forester moving. Side by side, we blindly headed for the opposite wall. I glanced back. A soldier stepped inside, but an eruption of gunfire coming from somewhere up the street got them running toward the sound. Hope couldn't express what I felt, more like a desperate prayer that the Russians would be tied up with Pfeffer and his men and overlook us.

Maybe, just maybe, we could get out of there.

46

The building's far wall was half gone, and I couldn't see how the remaining structure could possibly be standing. We charged through the hole onto another narrow side street.

The hairs on the back of my neck stood up. A single man, taller than our German pursuers, stood stock-still in the middle of the street. He was just a silhouette, but light from somewhere glinted off his nickel-plated revolver with a long barrel. In that split second of panic, my mind focused on the shining metal and the pearl handle nestled in the man's gloved hand.

"Move!" I yelled, and we sprinted for the neighboring building.

He opened fire in rapid succession. A round ripped through my overcoat and stung my shoulder blade. Laura cried out in pain and held up a bleeding hand.

Pfeffer and his men joined the silhouetted shooter and opened fire as well.

We fired back as we ran, suppressing the worst of their volley. Russian rifle fire made Pfeffer and his men scatter, and I took a moment to thank our lucky stars that the Russians were hot on our heels.

We blew past a charred door of a neighboring building. It was nothing but a shell composed of four jagged walls. The lack of a roof let ambient light into the space, making it a little easier to find our way through the ruins.

The sounds of Jeeps and boots on the ground seemed to surround us, diminishing my hopes that we could escape the Soviet sector. I brushed away any thoughts of what might happen to us if we were captured. The same thoughts must have assaulted Forester's mind, because he hopped along on his good leg with a speed I hadn't seen in him since we left the bank. I'd seen the same impulse to survive in other men during my time in the war. Men who seemed to be on death's door and found a sudden burst of energy in order to survive.

"We turn right once we clear this building," Forester yelled. "A block and we're home."

That gave us all a boost. We bounded over small piles of bricks or dashed around bigger ones. An opening in the opposite wall was our target. Shots rang out behind us, a submachine gun and pistols. Pfeffer and the remainder of his gang had entered the same building in hot pursuit.

Without slowing down, we charged out of a wide hole in the wall and cut right on the street. The block ahead of us looked much the same as the others, except this time we saw the signs announcing we would be entering the American sector.

Russian voices yelled some distance behind us. Heavy footsteps came from the building five seconds after we'd exited. Pfeffer and his men were catching up. I waited for a gunshot and the impact of a bullet. There was nothing left to do but run.

From the intersection delineating the sector border, searchlights and car headlights flashed on, blinding us. If the Russians had cut us off, we were doomed. We ran on regardless, heading for the lights. As we got closer, cheering and yelling erupted from the silhouettes. I couldn't believe my ears, my eyes. Like fans urging athletes across the finish line, American soldiers encouraged us on.

The race wasn't over yet. Pfeffer and his men hadn't opened fire, but they were gaining on us. Obviously, their goal now was to stop us before we reached the safety of our border, as there were strict rules forbidding armed American soldiers to cross the line to help us.

Fifty yards to go. The cheering kept us going. We poured on our last ounce of energy, regardless of the legal trouble that awaited us on the other side.

Two Russian Jeeps came roaring up the intersecting street to cut us off. A dozen soldiers ran toward us, yelling at us in Russian. My heart dropped into my stomach, and I wanted to scream out in utter frustration. We'd been so close.

Still, we kept running.

The Russians were just about on us when two dozen American soldiers breached the invisible barrier and formed two lines, creating an gap for us. They were risking an open fight that might cause a greater conflict, but they held the line and blocked off the Russian MPs.

As we entered the gap, several fistfights broke out among the opposing sides. A heavy machine gun fired a deafening burst from the American side. The brawls ceased.

Breathless, Laura, Forester, and I crossed into the American sector.

Forester collapsed. Laura and I bent forward with our hands on our knees and took in air. My legs shook. Despite the cold, I was covered in sweat. Hands were on us. Voices congratulated us. I tried to straighten, but a sharp pain radiated out from my shoulder blade to my spine. Despite the discomfort, I stood upright and thanked the soldiers and shook a half dozen hands.

I then turned to Laura, who grimaced in pain. A medic was treating her left hand. "How is it?" I asked her.

"Feels like a truck ran over it."

I hugged her for a long moment, then we watched the American soldiers pull back behind the border. The Russian soldiers were yelling and making obscene gestures. The Americans were happy to return the favor.

A half block down the street from where we'd come, Pfeffer and his remaining two men stood staring at us. The silhouetted shooter with the chrome pistol stood behind them, then disappeared into the ruins. A Russian MP officer was barking at Pfeffer, but he ignored them as he glared at me with murder in his eyes. The MP officer had his policemen surround the three and escort them away.

Laura and I watched until they disappeared.

The medic finished bandaging Laura's hand and stepped away. Laura kissed me on the cheek and went over to Forester, who was now lying on a stretcher. She knelt, leaned into him, and held his hand.

I turned to go to them when someone said, "I don't know whether to pat you on the back or kick your ass."

It was Wilson.

"Man, you have a way of ruining a victory party," I said.

"We have a lot to talk about," Wilson said. "You left a trail of destruction that was pretty easy to follow."

"Did you go by the Rote Lantern?"

Wilson's mouth gave me a lopsided smile. "We did. The Turk who runs the bar is in custody. I figured from the mess in the basement that you'd been there and rescued Sigrid." He looked around. "Where is she, by the way?"

"She didn't make it," I said and pointed toward the Soviet sector. "We had to leave her about five blocks back."

"I'm sorry for Forester. Tough break."

I looked Wilson in the eye. "Me leaving a trail. Is that how you knew where to wait for us?"

"That wasn't me," Wilson said and used his thumb to point

behind him. I looked in the direction he'd indicated. "He was first on the scene and called us over."

It was Ellenberg. He stepped up and stood next to Wilson.

"Hardin let you off your leash?"

"Now, is that any way to talk?" Ellenberg said. "I just saved your hide."

I grunted a response, thinking it was wiser to keep my opinions to myself. "Before you clap me in irons, I'd like to say goodbye to my friend."

"Oh, he's not going far," Ellenberg said. "We have a load of questions for him, too."

Wilson told me to go ahead, and I went over and squatted next to Laura and Forester. His skin was pasty and drawn. Laura wiped tears from his eyes. He tried to smile, but it went nowhere. He would recover from the wounds, but the pain of losing Sigrid would never go away. He lifted his hand and put it on my arm in a silent thanks.

"We'll be seeing you around," I said.

The two medics lifted his stretcher and slid it into the back of the ambulance. As we watched the ambulance drive away, Wilson, Ellenberg, and four MPs came over to us. The MPs pulled out two pairs of handcuffs.

Wilson waved them off and said to us, "Consider yourselves under arrest."

47

It was midmorning at the 279th Station Hospital, though the dark clouds and heavy rain gave the impression we had woken up in a timeless purgatory. I was sitting up in my hospital room bed watching Laura shoveling in another serving of hospital food with her good hand. She'd already finished the first tray the nurse had brought for us.

My back ached. According to the doctor, a bullet had gouged out a ribbon of skin, starting a millimeter from the spine and extending to the lower tip of my shoulder blade. That extra millimeter saved me from living the rest of my life in a wheelchair. Another scar to add to my carcass. Like one of those strange modern art paintings, I had small circles, slashes, and a few star-shaped ones from stab wounds all presented on a fleshy canvas.

A bullet had taken a small chunk out of the side of Laura's hand near the little finger. The surgeon had done some reconstruction using tissue from her thigh, but she would have to go through a couple more sessions to complete the repair.

I couldn't get enough of watching her finish the few bites of what the nurse had said was beef stew, but we both had our doubts there was much cow involved. We had survived the night. More importantly, Laura had survived, and I liked to think the child we'd lost in Jerusalem had become her guardian angel. Maybe the kid was watching out for me, too.

Two armed guards stood outside the door. No handcuffs, but we were under house arrest. I supposed Forester was in a similar situation in the critical care wing. I asked the nurses and doctors for updates, but none offered any information. I wouldn't say we'd jumped out of the frying pan and into the fire, but all three of us were in deep water hot enough to burn.

Laura pushed aside her plate and wiped her mouth with the napkin. "Hospital food is bad everywhere in the world."

"You only came to that conclusion after two bowlfuls?" I asked.

Laura grunted and wiped her mouth. "I see your sarcasm didn't suffer from the trauma."

"Hand me my backpack, would you?" I asked her.

She leaned over, picked up the pack, and laid it on my bed. "Another look at Hodgson's notes?"

I fished the notepad out of the pack and cracked it open. "We have something to go on after what Mike said."

Laura sat on the edge of the bed so we could examine it together. I leafed through the first few pages and found the first phrase, "Martin and Nancy 4th anniversary."

"Mike said they were using AFN song dedications to relay drop points."

I pointed to another one of the strange phrases, "Quincy and his six siblings."

"I would imagine it would go something like, 'Quincy dedicates this song to his six siblings,' or something like that."

Laura pointed to another one on the opposite page. "Mel dedicates this to the one he loves."

I turned back to the first phrase. "Martin dedicates this next song to his wife Nancy on their fourth anniversary."

Laura flipped more pages. "All of them have numbers and names."

I leafed through several pages, reading each of the dedications. "A lot of names with M, N, P, or O."

"We isolate out the numbers and the first letter in the names, then figure out the code," Laura said.

"I'm hoping it's simpler than that," I said.

Someone knocked on the door. Laura grabbed the notepad and slid it off the bed.

"Yeah, come in," I said.

Wilson and Ellenberg entered. Wilson said, "Glad to see you two are on the mend."

"We'll both be doing even better when you let us out of here," Laura said.

They both gave her a cursory smile and stepped into the center of the room.

"How's Forester?" I asked.

"He got out of surgery a couple of hours ago," Wilson said. "They managed to save the leg and pumped him full of penicillin, but he's still fighting to get the infection under control. Whoever operated on him in the Soviet sector missed a bullet fragment and only treated him with sulpha powder. Not to mention the unsanitary conditions. The docs think that's why it got reinfected."

"Lucky you two found him when you did," Ellenberg said.

"Now, how about you tell us everything that went on last night," Wilson said. "How you got there. What did you see?"

Laura and I took turns recounting our little adventure into Sovietland. From using the sewers to the altercation with the secret police and the soldiers. The German agents showing up at the bank building, to the ensuing run for our lives. We intentionally left out what Forester had said about the coded messages broadcasted by the AFN.

"Did Forester say or do anything to suggest he was there as a Soviet asset?" Ellenberg asked.

"Of course not," Laura said. "Don't tell me you guys still think Mike is a traitor."

"He's still under investigation for that, yes," Ellenberg said.

"We already established that Forester was probing a splinter group from Gehlen's organization," I said. "He was sure the members of the group were all double agents and working for the Soviets. And the guy leading them was none other than Wilhelm Pfeffer."

Ellenberg raised an eyebrow. "That name sounds familiar."

"That's because he's on every Allied wanted list for war crimes," I said.

"It seems absurd the guy could walk around Berlin with impunity," Wilson said. "You have any proof?"

"We're the evidence," Laura said. "He nearly killed us twice, and both times in the Soviet sector."

"You guys saw him last night," I said. "He was one of the three chasing us. The last of his gang. They were carted off by the Russians. How much you want to bet they'll resurface and work exclusively for them?"

"Are you sure about this?" Ellenberg asked in a somber tone.

I hesitated. "The two witnesses who confirmed it are dead."

Laura added, "But that's who Major Forester suspected was leading the gang, and they framed him for it."

"He's no longer suspected of murder," Wilson said, "but the espionage charges haven't gone away."

"Those accusations have got to be coming from the same intelligence officer who's been shielding Pfeffer and his gang," I said.

"Do you have any proof of that?" Ellenberg asked in an exasperated tone.

"You keep coming back to that," Wilson said. "But I wonder if it's all made up to let Forester off the hook."

My anger flared, and I jumped out of bed despite the pain radiating from everywhere. "You're just pissed about us slipping out of CID headquarters and making you look bad."

Ellenberg held up his hands. "Everyone calm down." He walked up to me and gestured toward the bed. "Why don't you lie back down before you bust your stitches?"

Ellenberg said it in a way that persuaded me to do what he asked. He was different, more in control and confident. "You're not a junior officer in the CIC, are you?"

He glanced at Wilson before answering. "Let's say I'm in nonmilitary intelligence."

"The Office of Special Operations," I said.

Ellenberg smiled. "I'm not at liberty to discuss it further."

"I know because I had a run-in with you guys before. In Vienna."

He tried to maintain a neutral expression, but he licked his lips as he figured out what to say next. It was brief yet enough.

"What is the Office of Special Operations?" Laura asked.

"The clandestine arm of the newly formed Central Intelligence Agency," I said to Laura and turned back to Ellenberg. "And you've been tasked with rooting out U.S. double agents in intelligence. Is that why you were shadowing Hardin?"

Ellenberg said nothing, though he allowed a modest smile to speak for him.

Astonished, Wilson looked at Ellenberg. "That's why you don't operate like a junior officer. If you've been investigating turncoat intelligence officers, what have you got on Forester?"

Ellenberg shrugged.

"He's not at liberty to discuss it," I said in a sarcastic tone.

"Just what you have," Ellenberg said to Wilson.

"If he really is a double agent," I said, "why would he risk his life to get to the American sector when he could have requested asylum from the Soviets?"

"Conversely," Ellenberg said, "why would Forester risk everything and run to the Soviet sector just to save his girlfriend? I don't buy it. He had another reason."

"We didn't exactly have time to discuss it. We were too busy trying to stay alive."

Laura shifted in her seat but said nothing to refute my statement. She asked Ellenberg, "You remember the night Colonel McCormick took Greta Schaller and the money, right?" When he said yes, she continued, "Just before she was taken away, she said that the money was not for Hodgson."

Ellenberg stuck out his lower lip. "Interesting."

"That's the best you have?" Laura asked.

"It's odd Schaller turned it into a guessing game," Ellenberg said. "Why didn't she come out and say who it was for?"

"Hardin's goons pulled her out of the room before she could tell me more," Laura said.

"Let's ask her now," Wilson said. "Where is she?"

"Why don't you ask McCormick?" I asked. "He's the one who took her."

Ellenberg shoved his hands in his pockets and rocked back on his heels. "According to McCormick, G-2 turned her over to the provost marshal in Frankfurt. She'll be charged with aiding and abetting Hodgson's spying activities."

"You'd better verify that story," I said. "She could just as well wind up floating in the Spree River."

"You suspect McCormick now?" Ellenberg said.

"I suspect everybody," I said.

Laura said to Ellenberg, "How did you know where to wait for us?"

Ellenberg locked his eyes on her and seemed to be weighing what he could reveal. "From Forester's notes. He mentions going into that neighborhood in search of the supposed German double agent. Once Wilson put together that you'd rescued Sigrid, I surmised she led you two into the Soviet sector to find

Forester. When all the shooting started, it was a matter of putting two and two together."

"In other words, you made a lucky guess," I said.

Ellenberg shrugged.

"Then there's McCormick," Laura said. "He refused to let us leave Berlin and threatened us with jail time unless we brought in Major Forester. He's the one who took Greta Schaller to prevent her from talking and kept the money he'd given Hodgson for doing his dirty work."

"He's a lieutenant-colonel and head of Berlin's G-2," Wilson said. "We're not about to confront a high-ranking officer without any evidence."

From my time as a CID investigator, I knew that, on paper, we were authorized to investigate anyone in the army regardless of rank, but in reality, high-ranking officers were off limits unless caught in the act of a crime. And even then, it was tough to convince a provost marshal to bring charges against those in lofty positions of power.

"So, we're back to square one," I said.

"Until we get Forester to confess," Ellenberg said.

I opened my mouth to protest when Wilson held up his hand to stop me. "This debate is getting us nowhere," he said. "No more talk. You and Laura concentrate on recuperating. We can take this up later."

An awkward silence fell on the room. It seemed Wilson and Ellenberg were done with the interrogation. For now. They started to go.

"I've got one more thing to ask you," I said to Wilson. He stopped, and Ellenberg did as well. "Not you," I said, eyeing Ellenberg.

Wilson tilted his head at Ellenberg, who scowled at me before exiting the room.

When I was sure Ellenberg was out of listening range, I asked Wilson, "Did you bring them?"

He reached into his satchel and pulled out a handful of folded maps. "I did, but I'll be damned if I know what you intend to do with these."

I tilted my head toward Laura. She shifted through my backpack and put the notepad and the sheet of tracing paper on the bed.

"I found this sheet of dots hidden in Hodgson's office's desk drawer," I said.

Wilson furrowed his brow. "You what?" He was angry, but his curiosity seemed to get the better of him, and he stepped forward. He tossed the maps onto the bed in front of me.

"Before we were attacked at the bank," I said, "Forester told us he'd discovered that the coordinates for document drops were sent out using dedications for songs played at the AFN radio station."

Laura and I pointed out the truncated messages in Hodgson's notepad and explained that the dedications all contained a name and number, which were sent out at the same time of day. "We think the first letter of the names and the number correspond to grid positions on a map."

I opened the first one, a map showing all of Berlin, and laid the tracing paper on top of it. The paper covered only half the area represented on the map. I discarded that one and moved to the next. It was a map for tourists, which was too small and lacked grid lines. My frustration grew, and I went through the next three maps in quick succession. The sixth was of the American sector delineated by thick lines. There were grid lines with numbers and letters, and circled numbers designating U.S. military installations, hotels, clubs, and recreational venues. I felt a surge of excitement when the dots matched up perfectly with many of the circled numbers.

"Ladies and gentlemen, we have a winner," I said.

Wilson leaned in to get a better look. Laura called out some of the dedications' letters and numbers, while I searched the locations using the grid. Each time, they corresponded with one point of interest on the map.

"And you think those are clandestine drop points?" Wilson asked.

"Why else would he hide the tracing paper and transmit the locations in code at a designated hour?" I asked.

"Assuming your theory is correct, we know how they passed on secret documents, but that doesn't let Forester off the hook," Wilson said. "Or the American officer who might be behind the betrayal."

I tapped on the map. "This is how we catch some fish."

48

The driver of our squad car pulled up to the entrance of the Femina Nightclub. It was in the middle of a block-long building that was a modern take on institutional ugly. And while most of the neighboring buildings had sustained damage, remarkably, the five-story behemoth had escaped a similar fate. A rollicking club since the twenties, the Femina was considered one of the hottest places in town. I'd expected big lights and flickering neon, but the marquee over the doors resembled something hanging over an average department store.

I got out, and the driver rushed around the front of the car to open Laura's door. She looked like a starlet ready to walk the red carpet for a movie opening. Wilson had somehow acquired a woman's pearl-colored cashmere overcoat and a sapphire-blue raw silk dress. Her hair was done up in waves and small curls. She concealed her bandaged hand in a pocket, which made her look like she was posing for the cover of a fashion magazine.

Wilson had provided me with an army officer's uniform that sported colonel insignias. It felt strange being in army greens again. It was too tight across the shoulders and tormented the bullet wound's stitching across my back, but I was focused on our mission and gave it little thought.

I joined Laura on the sidewalk. Wilson got out of the front passenger's seat, then leaned into the car to give the driver instructions that I couldn't make out. He wore business attire fit for a banker.

A second sedan pulled up behind us. Two junior CID investigators got out, both in dress uniforms. They paused at the curb and talked with Wilson. Then one of the investigators nodded and peeled off, heading inside at a fast clip. Wilson motioned for us to enter, but before we could make it to the front doors, Ellenberg intercepted us.

He wore a gray silk suit and a dark gray wool overcoat, but as dapper as the threads were, they made him look like a college kid playing dress-up. I couldn't tell if he was faking it or was genuinely surprised to see us. "I didn't expect they'd let you out of the hospital without an armed escort."

"We promised Wilson to be good," Laura said.

"Yeah, we wouldn't miss the show for anything," I said.

Ellenberg gave us a cordial smile, though his eyes looked for a clue as to what I meant by that last statement. "I reserved a big table overlooking the ballroom," he said. "Why don't we sit together?"

"Lead the way," Laura said.

We went through the glass double doors and into a large space of marble walls and floors and accented in gold-plated aluminum, with art déco lamps and statuettes of lithe women draped in diaphanous fabrics. It was a big night at the Femina. Tommy Dorsey and his band were the top billing. No doubt the ballroom would be packed in an hour or so, and despite our early arrival, people were already streaming into the club.

To the right was the cloakroom. To the left an entrance to a modest-sized bar, where an ample-proportioned female crooner in a red sequined dress belted out a throaty number. I headed that way, but Wilson tapped on my shoulder and tilted his head toward a bank of elevators.

We moved across the lobby and waited for an elevator. Two men in drab suits walked up to Ellenberg. The three of them stepped aside and consulted in hushed tones. Then the two men split away and headed for a staircase at the opposite side of the lobby.

"You expecting trouble?" Wilson asked Ellenberg when he rejoined us.

"Just being prepared," Ellenberg said. "We might get lucky tonight."

A soft ping announced the elevator's arrival. The four of us and a half dozen concert goers crammed into the car. I scanned our fellow passengers' faces. I didn't put it past our potential target to send his minions to avoid or cause trouble.

The elevator car jerked to a stop. Swing music flooded in as the doors opened. We stepped out into the main ballroom. A stage big enough for a thirty-piece swing band was at the far end and overlooked a sizable dance floor. The opening act was a twenty-piece band formed of musicians turned soldiers of army units from all over occupied Germany. Tables, crammed together in anticipation of the large crowds, surrounded the dance floor on three sides. Above us, a balcony ringed the entire space and was wide enough to accommodate additional tables, two deep.

The OMGUS's big Christmas bash wasn't scheduled for another couple of weeks, but the place was already decked out in holiday decorations: an enormous Christmas tree by the far corner of the room; pine garlands lining the stage, the proscenium, and the balcony railings; oversized ornaments hanging from the ceiling.

Ellenberg led the way to the right and up a flight of stairs to the balcony. A woman in a sparkly, skin-tight bodice and billowing skirt greeted us at the top of the stairs and escorted us to a circular table where the balcony took a ninety-degree turn. Ellenberg said something to the woman I couldn't hear over the music.

The four of us sat facing the main floor. I was close to the railing, with Laura next to me. Wilson sat on Laura's other side. Ellenberg sat opposite me, leaving the middle chair, with less of an optimal view, unoccupied. Aside from the tables directly beneath us, we could survey the entire ballroom and bar.

Being an hour early, half of the reserved tables were still empty. A dozen well-dressed couples danced to the music, while young hostesses clad in the same sparkly outfits escorted patrons to available tables. Of the approximately two hundred already in attendance, most of the men were in uniform. Half were American. British soldiers were second, then a handful of French.

Sitting together near the far corner of the dance floor were around three dozen Soviet officers sporting chests full of metals, along with another dozen bloated-faced Russian officials. The majority of the group were accompanied by women young enough to be their daughters. It wasn't uncommon for the Soviets to go to the western bars or attend events in the other sectors. The official Soviet doctrine was to condemn decadent Western culture, but they sure showed up for the fun that was lacking on their side of the city.

I tilted my head at the Soviet contingent and asked Ellenberg, "You recognize any of them?"

"None of the top brass," Ellenberg said. "You've got some military and state intelligence officers down there, but it's the ones you don't see that concern me."

Laura leaned toward me and said in my ear, "What if our fish tries to make contact with one of them?"

I didn't have a good answer and said nothing. Laura and I were taking a risk with a plan that could easily be a dud. Then we'd wind up back in hot water, and Forester would face a court-martial as a traitor. Laura and I exchanged nervous glances.

Earlier that day, Laura and I had come up with a dedication for a song using Hodgson's code. It had been broadcast out at the appointed time: "Henry dedicates this song to his wife of ten years and urgently awaits her arrival at nine" to the song "Don't Sit Under the Apple Tree." Particularly poignant for this occasion were the lyrics about being true to someone and fearing that they're bound to stray, their plans will fade away.

Now, it was a matter of time to know if the quarry had taken the bait.

The band was playing one of Glenn Miller's big hits, "Moonlight Cocktails." Laura swayed in her seat to the beguiling tune.

It crossed my mind to ask her to dance, but I quickly changed my mind.

McCormick had just entered the ballroom. A stately woman about his same age walked next to him with her hand on his arm. They were both dressed to the nines, him in his dress uniform and her with a black sequined dress. Two other gray-haired couples accompanied them, and one of the men was the deputy commander of the local military government.

Laura squeezed my hand. Out of the corner of my eye, I noticed Wilson and Ellenberg sit up straight while one of the tight-bodiced women escorted McCormick and his party across the room. The colonel stopped to let the ladies sit first at a table, which happened to be one row over from the Soviet contingent. He turned slowly to scan the ballroom, then returned to his entourage. He seemed to be in a jovial mood, and the entire party guffawed as they took their seats. His devil-may-care attitude made me wonder if I was all wrong about him being the big fish. Then again, a skilled agent could deceive most attentive observers.

Laura squeezed my hand twice, and this time it wasn't nervousness, but a signal. I looked at where she had furtively glanced. It was at the bar, and it took me a minute to spot what she wanted me to see through the ever-growing crowd of thirsty drinkers.

My gaze locked in on the pumpkin-headed man, Dietrich. Pfeffer's henchman and one of the last of his gang had just bellied up to the bar.

49

Dietrich's back was to us, and he kept his head low, his attention on the activity behind the bar. I only looked a minute, not wanting Wilson or Ellenberg to notice. I glanced at them to see their reactions, but they were focused on McCormick.

I exchanged looks with Laura. I subtly shook my head, and she nodded. We wouldn't point out Dietrich in case he was the contact as opposed to the Soviets.

I returned my attention to McCormick. A waiter was serving drinks, while McCormick pumped his arms as if telling another gut buster. The party erupted in another round of laughter.

"Where is our waiter?" Laura asked impatiently. "I'm ready for a stiff drink."

Wilson pointed toward the far end of the balcony. "He's down there handling a big group."

A shadow loomed over the table, and a tall man sat in the last available chair. If he was trying for a dramatic entrance, he'd succeeded. A sizzle ran down my spine, and Laura suppressed a chirp.

Hardin grinned at us through the pipe clenched in his teeth.

"Well, the gang's all here." He removed the pipe and expanded his grin. "You all should see the surprised look on your faces."

If Hardin had taken our bait, he didn't act like it. He extended his spine to look over the balcony railing. "A lot of Russkis down there. You people think you'll catch a traitor by watching those Reds get soused on vodka?"

"Get lost, Hardin," Ellenberg said.

"Now, is that any way to treat a fellow intelligence officer?" Hardin said, feigning offense. "I see you've latched onto these three now. Are you kissing their asses as enthusiastically as you did mine?" He looked at me as he thrusted his thumb at Ellenberg. "You know, this clown was so sure you and your girlfriend were here to join Forester in his espionage schemes that he hounded me for weeks to get you two thrown out of the country. I told him I didn't see that in your background. A self-righteous pain in the ass, sure, but a spy for the other side? Nah. I said to myself, now there's a man who works hard to get into all sorts of trouble. Just not the traitor kind." He'd said it with a jovial expression, but there was a predatory sound to his words.

I looked from Hardin to Ellenberg, then back again. "If you two represent the best American intelligence has to offer, then heaven help the United States."

Ellenberg shot me an angry glare, but Hardin gave me another toothy grin. "If anyone hasn't thanked you yet, I want to congratulate you on bringing back Forester to face a courtmartial."

Laura, Wilson, and Hardin broke into a three-way argument about Forester's guilt, which then broke out into a debate about the quality of American intelligence. I wasn't listening, because out of the corner of my eye, I noticed Ellenberg was silent and staring at something intently on the ballroom level.

I went slowly through the process of getting out a cigarette and lighting it to mask my curiosity about what had captured Ellenberg's fixed attention. My gaze locked onto Dietrich, the gunsel. The man had turned his back to the bar and was scanning the tables and dance floor. His fingers tapped the bar as if impatient. It seemed that whoever he was planning to contact, they had failed to show up at the appointed time. But what I found more interesting is he seemed completely oblivious to McCormick's presence or the Soviets. Then his focus shifted to the balcony, and he turned his head from left to right as he scrutinized the guests. It was hard to tell from the distance between the bar and our table, but it seemed to me he paused for a split second on Ellenberg. I turned my head away before he spotted me.

Laura noticed me facing the wall. "Looking for the waiter? I've been trying to catch his eye for a while now."

I twisted in my chair to search for the waiter when I caught sight of Ellenberg's two men. They'd taken up posts against the back wall of the balcony and thirty feet from our table. I thought they were supposed to fan out and wait at strategic points. Maybe they were waiting for Ellenberg's signal to arrest McCormick? Hardin? Wilson? Or Laura and me. What did he have up his sleeve?

I turned to Ellenberg. He had rejoined the intelligence debate, though he glanced at me for a moment. He displayed a cool demeanor, but his leg bounced under the table, and his fingers picked at the tablecloth. The first time I'd seen Hardin and him together, he had squirmed in Hardin's presence. Despite him being much higher in the intelligence food chain, Ellenberg acted like Hardin had all the power. Hardin was a master manipulator and a blowhard, and he probably tried to lord over most people. Me included. But Ellenberg was a pushover. Me? All I had to do was imagine giving Hardin a punch in the kisser. Worked every time.

I checked on Dietrich. He faced the bar again and appeared to be nursing a beer. He was certainly waiting for someone. I put my arms on the table to give myself a hoist. "I'm tired of waiting for the waiter. What is everyone having? First round's on me."

Everyone told me what they wanted except for Hardin, who had brought his martini to the table. Laura gave me a quizzical look as I stood. Since everyone's eyes were on me, I gave her a noncommittal smile. I didn't want to convey anything that might betray my actual intentions. I nodded at Ellenberg's men as I passed, then headed down the stairs. I used a group of five people lingering near the bottom to conceal myself from Dietrich's sight and made a loop out of the room, then in again to keep people between me and pumpkin head.

The bar took a ninety-degree turn at the close end and extended fifteen feet to the wall. Customers were two deep. I wedged half my body between two couples, using them to hide myself from Dietrich's view. I waved at the bartender. He came up, and I yelled out my drink order.

Peering between the couple's heads, I watched Dietrich. He would glance at the room, then go back to his drink. He'd rotated his glass on the counter or rapped his knuckles on the bar's surface in his impatience. He never looked over at McCormick or the Russians. The bartender was arranging my drinks on a tray when Dietrich turned again and looked up toward our table on the balcony. It was only for a moment, and when he returned to his drink, he muttered something with a snarl.

He wasn't there for McCormick or the Soviets, but somebody at our table.

The bartender brought me the tray of drinks. I leaned in as I passed him the money. "See that bubble-headed fellow with a permanent frown on his face about twenty feet down?"

The bartender glanced behind him and looked back at me with a wary expression. "Yeah."

"Tell him his friend is waiting to see him upstairs," I said.

"Why don't you tell him yourself?"

"You see that bruise on the side of his head?" I asked. The

bartender glanced at Dietrich. "That was me," I said and slipped him ten bucks. "That'll save everyone from another nasty brawl."

He pocketed the cash. "I'll give you a moment to get out of sight."

I thanked him and took a similar roundabout path back to the staircase. Moments later, I laid the tray on our table and passed around the drinks. "It's getting packed down there," I said. "I doubt we're going to see much of the waiter."

"Then I'll get the next round," Wilson said.

There was a pause in the conversation while we all took sips of our drinks. The volume of the music rose to compete with the ever-increasing din of conversation and laughter. Laura kept checking me for signs of what I was thinking. She could read me like a book and must have seen something on my face that said I was up to no good.

Ellenberg would shift his gaze between everyone at the table, then sneak peeks down at the ballroom level. Hardin and Wilson were as busy as I was in surveying the guests flowing into the ballroom.

The army band finished their set with a lively version of "St. Louis Blues March." They said goodnight, and everyone applauded while they gathered their instruments. Moments later, the thirty-odd musicians of Tommy Dorsey's band walked on stage to an even bigger round of applause.

I checked on McCormick. He was yucking it up with his companions and seemed half lit. Either he was a consummate actor at faking his inebriation, or it was all genuine. Ellenberg's men hadn't moved from their previous positions at the wall. Sitting at the end of the table near the railing, I had a partial view of the staircase. My heart rate was up in anticipation of Dietrich's arrival. I didn't have to wait long.

Dietrich's enormous head breached the level of the floor as he finished the last few steps to the balcony. He would definitely recognize Laura and me, but there was no hiding from him now. The question was, what would he do once he spotted us?

Laura squeezed my hand when she saw Dietrich lumbering our way. Wilson peered at him over the edge of his beer mug and glanced at me as if knowing that I'd set this up when I went to the bar.

Hardin's back was to the man, but Ellenberg froze with his glass of bourbon halfway to his mouth. It lasted a heartbeat, but it was enough for Hardin to notice, and he turned his head to see what had unnerved the man. He turned back to the table and eyed his martini.

Dietrich kept his gaze straight ahead as he approached us, and though no one at the table looked directly at the man, I could tell everyone was tracking his movement. It was like we were all playing a high-stakes poker game, where no one dared betray their hand and tried to guess what cards the others were holding.

The big man passed the table and was no longer in my line of sight. Hardin had the only vantage point, and he kept one eye on the gunsel's progress. By his eye movement, I could tell our pumpkin-headed friend had continued all the way around the balcony without stopping.

The Tommy Dorsey band broke into "Opus One," bouncy and loud. To break the silence, I gulped down the last of my beer and smacked the mug on the table. Laura quickly finished her Manhattan and pushed the glass toward the center of the table.

"Which of you gentleman would like to get another round?" Laura asked.

Wilson eyed me, then stood. "I promised I'd get the next one." He swept his index finger around the table. "The same for everyone?"

We all agreed, and Wilson headed for the stairway. He took his time and wove through groups of guests standing with drinks in their hands. I lost sight of him and figured that was his intention.

I figured Dietrich was heading back our way when Hardin had to twist his torso to keep an eye on the man. Laura kicked me under the table and tilted her head in Hardin's direction. His contortions had forced his jacket open. Tucked in his shoulder holster was a nickel-plated revolver with a seven-and-a-half-inch barrel and pearl grips. Suddenly I regretted having to leave my .45 in the care of an MP at the hospital.

A long minute later, Dietrich came into my view, and I watched him move toward the stairs. His pace was easy, though his posture was stiff as if on high alert. He paused for a moment at the top of the steps, then committed to descending the staircase.

If anything went south, Wilson was the only one with a weapon between the three of us. And my concern grew when he had yet to appear at the bar. He'd had plenty of time to navigate the crowds. In fact, enough time had passed for him to place his order and come back with the drinks. I watched to see if Dietrich had returned to his position at the bar, but he, too, was nowhere to be seen.

"You two are awfully quiet," Hardin said to Laura and me.

I tilted my head at his suit coat. "I was just remembering where I saw that pistol in your shoulder holster before."

Hardin unconsciously put his arms to his side to close his jacket and conceal the pistol.

I continued. "You don't see many Colt Single Actions in nickel and ivory handle floating around."

"It was my father's. He was a career army cavalry and fought in the First World War. So what?"

"The thing is, I saw the very same type of pistol in the hand of someone taking potshots at us on the Soviet side of the border. It took a chunk out of my darling's hand and left a gash across my back. I couldn't make out the shooter, but I sure noticed the pistol."

Hardin returned a smile. His eyes were fixed on mine. But while he remained calm, Ellenberg fidgeted in his seat.

I continued. "I found it odd that Mr. Ellenberg here knew exactly where we'd try to cross into the American sector. And what a strange coincidence that someone with a pearl-handled revolver was waiting for us in the Soviet sector, just a block away from where Pfeffer tried to cut us off. The same spot someone told him to wait in ambush to murder Forester. And odder still, both those locations were indicated on a map we found in Hodgson's office. Locations that matched music dedications broadcasted from the AFN station."

"Are you seriously trying to accuse either of us of being traitors?" Ellenberg asked. "Because it's not going to work—"

"We're not finished," Laura said, interrupting. "You both knew to come for us moments after that bomb took Hodgson's life. Knew that you'd find Greta Schaller and the suitcase of money."

I said, "We had AFN broadcast a message using Hodgson's code to call for a clandestine meeting here. Tonight. And look who showed up? Then Dietrich, one of Pfeffer's gunmen, comes looking for you two when he got the message. Is he your courier? I figure you used Pfeffer's gang to send over stolen documents to the Soviets."

Hardin glanced at Ellenberg. There seemed to be a silent message passed between them, which made Ellenberg's eyes twitch with nervous tension. Hardin then leaned forward. "Dietrich might have fallen for your ruse, but not us. That message you sent over AFN airwaves was too obvious. A clumsy setup. It was, however, the best opportunity to get you two out in the open." He pulled out his pistol and extended it under the table, presumably pointing in Laura's or my direction. "Now we're going to walk out of here calmly and quietly."

50

"You plan to shoot your way past Wilson and his MPs?" I asked.

"Wilson won't be helping you out this evening," Ellenberg said and nodded his head toward the two men who had accompanied him to the nightclub. They approached the table and stood on either side of Laura and me. Two other tuxedoed men made their presence known by moving to cover the staircase. How many other men Hardin or Ellenberg had in place, I didn't know.

"Get up slowly," Hardin said.

Shooting us in a ballroom full of military personnel would be an insane thing to do unless Hardin and Ellenberg had an exit strategy in place. Calling out for help might disrupt their plans, but it risked one of them losing their cool and opening fire, killing innocent people. Possibly killing Laura.

I squeezed Laura's hand, signaling her to follow my lead. I rose from the table, as did she. Hardin tucked his gun hand inside his suit jacket and stood. Ellenberg did the same and flashed a Walther PPK tucked in his belt before making the first move toward the stairs.

To add a surreal touch to our dire predicament, the orchestra started playing "Santa Claus is Comin' to Town." The crowds were in peak merriment; the alcohol flowed freely. Everyone was singing or bouncing to the rhythms or trying to talk over the brass section. No one paid any attention to our little party moving slowly past the tables and weaving around clusters of people standing, belly laughing, and backslapping.

Ellenberg's men were only inches behind us with their pistols pressed into our backs. When we reached the stairs, the two men standing guard at the top—whether Hardin's or Ellenberg's—turned and led the group down the steps. I kept looking for an opportunity to escape, but the four guards knew what they were doing. We were boxed in tight.

The two lead men pushed through the swinging doors, and we caught an open elevator. I could still hear the music and the din of the crowd when the doors closed, and the car descended to the ground floor. We exited the elevator and entered the lobby. Aside from a few latecomers and those leaving early, the space was empty; the music subdued.

"Hold up here," Hardin said.

We all stopped, and Hardin ordered two of his men to handcuff us, while another one patted me down. He found the Ka-Bar knife in my boot but missed the brass knuckles. They were of no use with my hands bound behind my back, but it gave me a little comfort to know they were still there.

As a man finished cuffing me, I asked Hardin, "Where's Wilson? What have you done with him?"

"Not your worry," Hardin said. "But if you must know, Dietrich is taking care of him."

I struggled against the man's grasp to face Hardin, my face hot, my eyes blazing.

"Go ahead," Hardin said. "Say you're going to kill me as soon as you get out of this jam." He paused as if daring me to mouth those words. "The whole purpose of this daring ploy is to make sure you or Mrs. Talbot never have that opportunity."

I turned away with my back to the man holding me. I relaxed somewhat against his grasp. He let off slightly on the pressure on my wrists. I jammed the heel of my shoe onto the top of the man's foot. He cried out and lost control of me.

Just as I broke free of his grasp, one of the men in front spun around and slugged me in the stomach. The blow knocked the wind out of me. A jolt of pain radiated through my entire torso. My knees buckled. I heard Laura call my name and curse out the men. A few of the people in the lobby cried out.

"These two are under arrest," Hardin said to the onlookers. "This one was trying to escape."

Hardin's gorillas lifted me by the armpits and forced me toward the door.

"They're abducting us," Laura said to the bystanders. "Help us."

Hardin held up his CIC badge as we crossed the last few feet of the lobby. The people backed away or rushed toward the ballroom. I regained control of my diaphragm and sucked in air. The doors opened. The blast of cold air revived me, but dread crept in when I saw that Wilson's MPs, the ones who had been there when we first entered, were gone. In their place were two army staff cars. I figured one of them was the same that had chased Laura and me from Wilson's house to CID headquarters. Four men in suits stood by the vehicles, awaiting our arrival.

"You seem disappointed," Ellenberg said to me. "Did you expect Wilson's men to save you? Dietrich persuaded Wilson to dismiss them."

I tried to get in Ellenberg's face, but the two men escorting me seized my shoulders and neck and began shoving me out the door.

We were halfway out when a commanding voice said behind us, "Hold it right there."

The group stopped. I could turn my head enough to see

Colonel McCormick standing on the opposite side of the lobby with three MPs at his side. "Release those two, now."

Hardin said, "Colonel, I'm arresting them for spying for the Soviets. You have no authority to order me to release them."

"You're gravely mistaken," McCormick said. "General Ort, the divisional commander, has given me the green light to arrest you."

Hardin revealed his pistol and aimed it at McCormick. Ellenberg did the same, as did the four men. "I'm afraid we have the advantage, Colonel. And by the time you can get your forces together, we'll be in the Soviet sector."

While maintaining their aim toward the lobby, our captors pushed through the doors. McCormick remained where he was while his MPs held their weapons at their sides.

Just as we stepped onto the sidewalk, one of the four men by the staff cars yelled out, "Take cover!" The four men spun around and aimed their pistols in both directions. A dozen MPs and soldiers were rushing toward us from both ends of the street fifty yards distant. Hardin's men by the staff cars opened fire, and McCormick's men followed suit. The four men holding Laura and me went for their guns, releasing us in the process.

One, then two, of Hardin's men fell after being hit. The others crouched in shooting stances or got between the two sedans. Laura and I bent low and sought cover against the building's wall. Hardin was pinned between the two open car doors and firing. Ellenberg was more concerned with making himself as small as possible, but when he saw us make a run for it, he came after us.

With my hands still cuffed, I bent low and charged, shoulder first, and rammed into Ellenberg's torso. He let out a sharp bark as the air was forced out of his lungs. I straightened and head-butted him in the face. He went down.

Ellenberg lay sprawled on the sidewalk and seemed too stunned to get up. His jacket was open, revealing a set of keys clipped to his belt.

"Laura!" I yelled over the gun blasts and gestured toward Ellenberg. "The keys!"

She raced forward and put her back against Ellenberg's waist to get at the key fob.

Ellenberg started to come to. I kicked him just behind the ear to keep him subdued.

Hardin came out of nowhere and grabbed me by my overcoat. I tried to kick him in the groin, but I missed the mark.

He kneed me, shoved me to the pavement, and raised his gun to shoot. Laura cried out, and I braced for the impact.

Two gun barrels came within inches of Hardin's head. At the same moment, the shooting around us stopped.

"You're under arrest," McCormick said to Hardin. "Drop the gun or I'll open up your skull."

After a moment's hesitation, Hardin lowered his weapon. The two MPs with McCormick pinned his arms and handcuffed him. Another two of McCormick's MPs handcuffed Ellenberg, while the third helped Laura to her feet. The other soldiers and MPs under McCormick's command were disarming the men at the staff cars. A handful of army sedans, two ambulances, and a three-quarter-ton truck pulled up in front of the club.

I hurried over to the MP, who had just unlocked Laura's cuffs and urged him to remove mine. Once I was free of the handcuffs, I grabbed Ellenberg by the lapels. "Where's Wilson?" I yelled, getting in his face. "Where's Dietrich?"

He had a tough time focusing on me. I shook him. "Wilson! Where is he?"

The two MPs pulled me away from Ellenberg. I broke free from their grasp and rushed up to McCormick. "Sir, there's another conspirator. A German double agent. He abducted Investigator Wilson. They've got to still be in the building somewhere."

McCormick turned to Hardin. "If you don't want a murder rap, then tell us where the chief is."

"Dietrich could have gone anywhere," Hardin said with a tone of defiance.

McCormick raised an eyebrow, then said to an MP sergeant, "Get them to the CID and have whoever's in charge book them both for espionage and murder."

The sergeant pulled Hardin away by the elbow, but Hardin resisted and turned to McCormick. "Try the basement."

McCormick signaled for the MP sergeant to go look for Wilson and Dietrich. The sergeant ordered two of his men to go with him, and they charged inside.

"Colonel," I said. "Let me go search for my friend. Please."

He studied me for a long moment. "You're not under arrest." He tilted his head toward the building.

I took off running, burst through the glass doors and raced across the lobby. The sergeant and MPs headed for a door leading to the basement, but I hesitated.

"How did Wilson give orders to his men?" Laura asked, coming up behind me.

"Not from the basement," I said. "And he couldn't show up at the front doors with Dietrich restraining him."

I'd noticed a staircase in the far-left corner when we'd first arrived.

"That's what I thought, too," Laura said. "He must have given the orders to his MPs from a window on a higher floor."

"You should hang back on this one," I said. "The only weapon we have between us is a pair of brass knuckles."

"It's going to take the two of us to take down that bull," she said.

I knew not to argue with her and motioned for us to head for the stairs. We bounded up the steps, then slowed when we approached the third floor so as not to make too much noise. At the top, we found ourselves in a wide hallway serving what appeared to be offices. Some doors were closed, some were open. None of the ceiling lights were on, leaving the place in a dim light. I stopped Laura and pointed to my ear, telling her we should listen.

Our heavy breathing and hubbub out on the street were the only sounds. I got out the brass knuckles and slipped them onto my right hand, then I motioned for us to creep forward. We passed offices left and right with doors open. They seemed to have been empty for some time, with a layer of dust on the floors and blinds askew.

The offices overlooking the street were at the end of the hallway, and we increased our pace, ignoring the closed doors. Near the last two offices, I heard a gasping sound.

"That's Wilson!" I said.

We hurried to the last office on the right. My chest constricted when I saw Wilson leaning against the far wall with blood soaking his suit coat and shirt.

"Arnie!" I said and rushed over to him.

His eyes were wide in his panic. He wheezed as he tried to take in gulps of air.

Laura checked the wound. "Knife wound. Probably punctured his lung."

I got in close to Wilson and asked him, "Did Dietrich do this? Where is he?"

Wilson met my gaze, though it looked like he was about to pass out. He pointed to a corner of the room hidden by the open door. I spun around, thinking Dietrich had set a trap. Instead, the man lay on his stomach. His eyes stared at nothing. Blood still trickled from the long gash in his neck.

"Pfeffer," Wilson said barely above a whisper. "Back way."

Pfeffer had been there and executed Dietrich, and he was trying to escape using a back exit.

"Stay with Arnie," I said and raced for the door, ignoring Laura's warnings.

51

I hit the second floor landing floor at full speed and entered the ballroom. The servers' entrance to the kitchen was just inside the doorway and to the right of the bar. Even at that short distance, my frenzied run caused a stir with those clustered near the entrance. Several men shouted at me to stop, but I ignored them and blew through the swinging doors, nearly taking out a waiter with a full tray of food. The kitchen bustled with cooks and waiters in a large space that rivaled the lobby.

I stopped to get my bearings. I looked toward the back wall. There, a man with a black homburg hat moved through a sea of white-uniformed cooks. The path between cleared for a moment. The outburst I'd caused from some of the cook staff prompted the man to turn. His eyes went wide in alarm when he recognized me.

"Pfeffer!" I yelled.

He spun on his heels and darted for the back door. I broke into a run, dodging the tangle of employees. I lost sight of Pfeffer in the chaos, but just above the heads, I saw the back door swing closed.

I sprinted for the door, ricocheting off a man-sized rolling cart as I went. I grabbed a metal tray off the cart and slammed into the door. It flew open, but an instinct told me to freeze at the threshold. If Pfeffer waited in ambush, he could be to the left or right of the door. I chose the right.

I held the tray with both hands and swung it at head height as I stepped out into the alley. My swing missed, but it had surprised Pfeffer. He jerked back to avoid the blow. That left him vulnerable.

I caught his knife hand and jerked him by the arm from his place of hiding. He struck me twice across the jaw as we struggled for control of the knife. I suppressed the pain, brought up my leg, and slammed his arm against my thigh. I heard bone crack, and the knife dropped to the concrete with a clang. He screamed.

Now desperate, he lunged forward and kneed me in the crotch. My body froze from the electrical shock of agony. He struck me again across the jaw.

Rage took over. Adrenaline overrode my pain. I growled and backhanded his jaw with my brass knuckles. Stunned, he stumbled. I brought my arm back and swung with everything I had. I caught him again in the jaw. I felt bone shatter.

He fell to his knees. He was down, but I kept hitting him in the face until he dropped to his side. Still, I didn't stop. I struck him again and again, and I wouldn't have stopped, except two pairs of powerful hands grabbed me from behind and dragged me off him.

MPs the size of heavyweight boxers pinned me. They spun me around, pushed my face into the wall.

"Chief Investigator Wilson," I said. "He's on the third floor and bleeding out."

"He's being taken care of," the older of the two MPs said as he jammed my face into the brick. The younger MP forced my hands behind my back and handcuffed my wrists.

An ambulance raced up the alley and stopped near the back

door. The MPs turned me around again in time to watch two medics exit the ambulance and load Pfeffer, a mangled and bloody mess, onto a stretcher. He would survive, but his face would never be the same. And I took satisfaction that, if they didn't hang him, he would sit out the rest of his life behind bars.

"Thanks," I said to the two MPs. "You kept me from getting a murder rap."

A military police staff car rolled up alongside the ambulance. An MP master sergeant got out of the front passenger's seat. Laura exited the back and ran for me, but the master sergeant stopped her from embracing me.

"Are you okay?" she asked.

I nodded. "What about Arnie?"

She paused for a moment then looked at me with a pained expression. "He has a chance. But a slim one."

A Jeep roared up the alley with McCormick. He jumped out and walked up to us with a self-satisfied smile. "Release him," McCormick said to the MPs. As the older MP complied, McCormick said to me. "When I saw the four of you at the balcony table, I was prepared to arrest all of you. Of course, that was before Hardin tried to take you and Mrs. Talbot at gunpoint."

"The man they're putting in the ambulance is Wilhelm Pfeffer," I said. "A Nazi war criminal and a double agent."

McCormick looked back at the ambulance driving away. "Yes, I know. Supposed to be working for Gehlen."

It took me a moment to put the pieces together. "You didn't arrest him earlier because you wanted him to lead you to his American handlers."

"And he did."

"With us as bait," Laura said in a sharp tone.

"Why not?" I said. "Everyone else was doing it."

"But this time, the bait hooked the fishermen," McCormick said and walked away.

"I take it, with everything that's happened, you'll exonerate Major Forester," Laura yelled at the retreating colonel.

No response.

"Are we still under arrest?" I asked him.

Without turning to us, he said, "We'll talk more later. In the meantime, I advise having that wound of yours looked at."

Laura sucked in her breath and touched my back. She brought her hand forward with blood on her fingers. "Your jacket is soaked. Those stitches opened up."

I opened my mouth, then slammed it shut when Laura pointed her finger at me like a weapon. "Don't say it."

52

Forester opened one bleary eye when Laura knocked on the doorway of his hospital room.

"Are you up for company?" Laura asked.

"Come on in," Forester said in a raspy voice. He tried to lift his head as we approached the bed, but he gave up with a grimace.

Laura gave him a peck on the cheek, and I took his hand for a long moment. We found chairs and sat near his bed. A nurse had repaired the stitches in my back, and they stung when I tried to sit back. With half-lidded eyes, Forester glanced at the hospital gown I wore over my pants and the bruises on my jaw and knuckles. He did the same for Laura's bandaged hand.

"I hope the other guys are worse off," Forester said.

We told him about what had happened at the Femina Nightclub, and the arrests of Hardin and Ellenberg.

He furrowed his brow at the news. "Ellenberg, I didn't know that well. But Hardin. My partner. I must be slipping because I never saw that coming."

Laura told him about how Pfeffer had murdered his henchman, Dietrich, and Pfeffer had been arrested. "Mason left Pfeffer in a bloody mess, if that makes you feel a little better."

It didn't. Forester's expression remained dark. We let him take a moment to mourn Sigrid. He looked up at the ceiling and let out a fluttering sigh. A moment passed, then he turned his attention back to us. "I heard Investigator Wilson didn't make it."

We'd only received the news ten minutes earlier, and hearing it again made the knot in my chest grow tighter.

Forester tapped my forearm to make sure I focused on what he was about to say. "You would have been completely justified if you'd killed Pfeffer."

"It's better he hangs with a broken face," I said.

"What's the doc say about when you'll be getting back on your feet?" Laura asked.

"They're not saying," Forester said. "Sooner than later, if I have anything to do about it." His gave us a feeble smile. "How can I thank you guys enough? I heard some about your exploits." He nodded his head at us. "Obviously, you two put your lives on the line for me. I hope those wounds aren't too serious."

We both said they were nothing, though Laura would have some work ahead of her to get back full use of her hand.

She must have read my mind, because she said, "At least I'm a righty."

Forester smiled, but it was brief. "Honestly, what can I ever do to repay you?"

"Mike," I said, "you saved my life more than once, as you pointed out on the phone. Call it even."

"What about you?" he asked Laura.

"Just make it a point to come visit us in Boston once you're back on your feet," Laura said. "I'll take that as payment."

"So, you guys are going back?"

I looked at Laura. We hadn't discussed it. But I could tell by the look in her eyes that she was ready.

I guess I was too.

"Before you answer that, we should talk," a man said in a deep baritone voice.

McCormick came into the room with a captain, who I assumed was a member of his staff. The colonel went over to Forester and shook his hand. "You've been exonerated of any wrongdoing, and any entries of those accusations on your record have been expunged."

Forester shook the man's hand one more time. "Thank you for telling me, Colonel."

"I want you to get well so you can return to duty as soon as possible," McCormick said. "We need good men in the Berlin CIC office. Now more than ever." His aide grabbed a chair near the empty bed and placed it alongside ours. The colonel sat with an audible groan. "It's been a long couple of days. It's never easy throwing fellow intelligence officers in the stockade."

"Are they talking?" I asked.

"They're both singing all right," McCormick said. "But different tunes. Ellenberg claims Hardin manipulated him, but Hardin says Ellenberg recruited him. From our investigation, their interrogation statements, and looking at their finances, they were in it for the money. Piles of money at first. Then less and less, because once the Soviets had their hooks in them, they threatened to expose them if they didn't do more spying for less. The two of them got desperate. Then things started to get out of control."

"That's where framing Forester comes in," Laura said.

McCormick nodded. "That and doing away with any loose ends."

"Like Hodgson and Leiter," I said.

"Yes," McCormick said. "Seems Leiter was having cold feet about working for the Soviets."

"Where does Pfeffer figure into all this?" Laura asked.

"The Soviets already had him in their pocket. They looked past his war crimes because of his connections to German intelligence and his intense hatred of us and the Brits for bombing Dresden into rubble. Hardin used his rank in the CIC to give

Pfeffer and his gang fake IDs and carte blanche passes to move around the city."

"Pfeffer's gang was associated with the Gehlen Organization," I said. "I thought it was a bad idea using ex-Nazis as U.S. intelligence assets."

"The Gehlen Organization has produced some of the only real intelligence we've gotten on the Soviets," McCormick said. "While the Reds get better and better with their intelligence, Washington keeps changing their minds about who's in charge. We're losing experienced men, and you end up with hacks like Hardin and Ellenberg. That's why we're so eager to have Major Forester off the bench and in play."

Laura put her hand on Forester's arm and smiled at him. Silence fell on the room for a moment, then she looked up at McCormick with a serious expression. "So, let's get to the bad news. What did you mean when you said 'we have to talk'?"

McCormick grinned at us both like a bank manager denying us a loan. He then keyed in on me. "We, I, would like for you to come work for us. We keep losing good men because they're being mustered out and sent back to the States. In their place, we're getting green recruits. And with your qualifications, you could be an excellent asset. You were G-2 during the war, your fluency in German—"

I held up my hands. "Wait, wait," I said, trying to talk over Forester's peals of laughter. "I can spare you the rest of your pitch. I'm not interested. Plus, the army's accusations against me haven't been expunged. I was forced to resign after all the trouble I stirred up as a CID investigator."

"The army would like to reverse that decision," McCormick said. "Come back to G-2 or, since we've lost Arnold Wilson, and Cuthbert's in prison, I'd like to see you join up with the CID. The remaining investigators in the detachment are still wet behind the ears. It would be a real asset to them if you took up the reins."

I was speechless. It seemed as if all the air in the room had been sucked out of it. The only sound was the buzz of the fluorescent lights and the bustle in the hallway.

McCormick cleared his throat, breaking the silence. "The alternative is not what you might think. Take my offer, and you will both avoid any criminal charges. Clean slates, as it were."

"What?" I said, incredulous. "We shut down a German spy ring, captured a Nazi war criminal, and saved Forester from a travesty of justice. And you want to charge us?"

"Let's break it down for you," McCormick said. "Kidnapping, breaking and entering, assault and battery, grand theft, and withholding vital evidence in a criminal case. I could go on, but you get the picture." He turned to Laura. "I talked to a friend of mine at United Press. Since their key reporter, Walter Cronkite, left for their Moscow bureau, they need someone to cover the remaining Nuremberg trials. The UP guy was quite anxious to speak to you about assignments. There's also the tensions going on here with the Soviets. My guess is the Commies are about to do something drastic. Considering your experience as a war correspondent, I thought the brewing situation might be right up your alley."

I held up my hand to make a point. "Before I even think about us staying, you have to do one thing for me."

"If I can do it, I will," McCormick said.

"I borrowed a car from a German guy who's down on his luck. The car is his pride and joy. Almost perfect condition. And I—"

"And you managed to get it shot up," McCormick said. "Yes, I know about that. I'll have some crackerjack guys in the motor pool fix it up better than you found it." He paused. "So, do we have a deal?"

Laura took my hand. Her touch was soft and comforting, and I imagined she was dealing with many of the same conflicting thoughts as I was. I looked at her. Her face expressed a mix of emotions. We had sought adventure and an escape from the ordinary. But now that the option to go home seemed to be threatened, it felt more important than ever.

I slumped in my chair and thought to myself ...

Well, Mason, this is another fine mess you've gotten us into.

THE END

ALSO BY JOHN A CONNELL

The Mason Collins Series:

Madness in the Ruins (Book #1)

It is the winter, 1945. Munich is in ruins, and a savage killer is stalking the city.

U.S. Army investigator Mason Collins is determined to stop the madman, but he gets more than he's bargained for when the murderer makes him a target. Now it's a high-stakes duel, and to win it Mason must bring into deadly play all that he values: his partner, his career—even his life.

Haven of Vipers (Book #2)

While investigating a rash of murders, Mason discovers a web of coconspirators more dangerous than anything he's ever encountered.

Witnesses and evidence disappear, someone on high is stifling the investigation, and Mason must feel his way in the darkness if he is going to find out who in town has the most to gain—and the most to lose…

Bones of the Innocent (Book #3)

Summer, 1946. Just as assassins from a shadowy organization close in for the kill, a flamboyant stranger offers Mason a way out: He must accompany the stranger to Morocco to investigate the abductions of teenage girls. Girls that vanished without a trace.

Once Mason lands in Tangier, he discovers that nothing—or no one—is what it seems. This playground for the super rich is called the wickedest city in the world, and he realizes those who could help him the most harbor a terrible secret.

To Kill A Devil (Book #4)

1946, Vienna. When a shadowy organization fails to assassinate Mason Collins, they go after his colleagues, his friends, and the love of his life. Mason knows the only way to stop the killings is to cut off the head of the snake.

But tracking down the man responsible appears to be an unsurmountable task; everyone speaks his name with awe and fear, but no one knows if he's real or a gangland myth. Mason, desperate for answers, abandons his strict moral code, leading him down a very dark path, and to succeed in hunting one devil, he makes a pact with another.

Where the Wicked Tread (Book #5)

It is 1947. Mason is on the hunt for the Gestapo commander who, during the war, executed a little girl Mason had sworn to protect. He's tracked the man to the notorious Italian route for escaping Nazi war criminals.

The problem is the man is fleeing justice with several other Nazi fugitives, and it finally becomes clear that the only way to stop them and get his man is through one final showdown.

Mason is ready to make the ultimate sacrifice for retribution, for forgiveness, to exorcise his demons. But first he has to survive.

Upon A Bloodstained Land (Book #6)

Mason joins Laura, the love of his life, in Jerusalem. She's pregnant with his child, and his priority is to get them out of the volatile region. But then a skilled assassin picks up their trail. To keep Laura safe, he decides the best option is to run, then tragedy strikes, putting Laura in the hospital with her life hanging by a thread.

Enraged, Mason vows to hunt down those responsible. But how can he hunt for killers in a war zone? Who does he turn to when he can't tell friend from foe?

A Standalone Historical Crime Thriller:

Good Night, Sweet Daddy-O

1958 San Francisco

Struggling jazz musician, Frank Valentine, suffers a midnight beating, leaving his left hand paralyzed. Jobless, penniless, and desperate, Frank agrees to join his best friend, George, and three other buddies to distribute a gangster's heroin for quick money.

What he doesn't know is that George has far more dangerous plans…

Inexperienced in the ways of crime, Frank quickly slips deeper and deeper into the dark vortex of San Francisco gangsters, junkies, and murderers for hire. To make things worse, Frank's newfound love, a mysterious, dark-haired beauty, is somehow connected to it all.

And when it becomes clear that a crime syndicate is bent on his destruction, Frank realizes that the easy road out of purgatory often leads to hell.

AUTHOR'S NOTES

History inspires each of my Mason Collins stories, and At Their Own Peril is no different. War-torn Berlin, with its blocks-long ruins and a hub of international spies, provided a dramatic background for Mason and Laura's latest adventure. I endeavored to portray the city as it was in November of 1947. The challenge was that Berlin had been ravaged by relentless Allied bombing raids and the Battle of Berlin between the German Army and the Soviets.

Needless to say, Berlin has changed immensely in the almost 80 years since the end of World War Two. However, I was able to find maps, photos, documents, and testaments that provided me with a solid base with which to describe what it might have been like to be there in 1947, from the neighborhoods, down to the streets and buildings. Most of the locations, from the military installations and recreational fields, to the clubs, bridges, and other landmarks, as well as the street names of that time, are as accurate as I could make them. Only the hotels and houses Mason and Laura visited are of my own invention.

Virtually all the characters populating the story also sprung from my imagination, including one of the main antagonists,

Wilhelm Pfeffer. While he is fictitious, he is an amalgam of several real Nazi war criminals who perpetrated the atrocities attributed to him.

The Gehlen Organization did exist, as did Reinhard Gehlen (though he does not make an appearance in this story). After the war, Gehlen, a former general in Wehrmacht intelligence, recruited ex-Nazi intelligence officers to spy on the Soviets for the U.S. Because the Soviets were dominating the espionage game, U.S. intelligence looked the other way when it came to the Gehlen and his associates' Nazi pasts. This was due, in part, to the constant reorganization of the American intelligence agencies which had left American espionage efforts in a confused and inefficient state. The Gehlen Organization was one of the only effective groups spying on the Soviets, though it was later discovered that Soviet operatives and Germans sympathetic to Soviet Union had infiltrated the organization almost from its beginnings.

The formation of the CIA was created in the fall of 1947, only months before At Their Own Peril begins, but it was still a fledgling organization. A separate entity within the CIA, the Office of Strategic Operations (OSO), was in charged with performing clandestine operations. The OSO would be folded into the CIA as we know it in the early 1950s.

If you're interested in further reading about Berlin in the post-WW2 era, the following is a list of the main sources that I leaned on heavily for facts and inspiration:

Online Sources:

There are numerous sources for the history, photographs and films on the web, but these are the two principal ones I turned to:

The U.S. Army's website: https://history.army.mil

A website assembled by army veterans: https://www.usarmygermany.com

Books and other publications:

After the Reich: From the Liberation of Vienna to the Berlin Airlift, Giles MacDonald

In the Ruins of the Reich, Douglas Botting

Endgame 1945: Victory, Retribution, Liberation, David Stafford

America's Secret Army: The Untold Story of the Counter Intelligence Corps, Ian Sayer & Douglas Botting

The City Becomes a Symbol: The U.S. Army in the Occupation of Berlin, 1945–1948, by William Stivers and Donald A. Carter

∼

Since my youth, I've wanted to step back in time and try to imagine what it would be like to walk in the shoes of someone from the past. Writing these stories has given me that opportunity, and I have loved every minute of it. I hope you've enjoyed walking in those shoes as much as I have.

ABOUT THE AUTHOR

John A. Connell writes spellbinding crime thrillers with a historical twist. His Mason Collins series follows the ex-military policeman to some of the most dangerous and turbulent places in the post-World War Two world. The series has garnered praise from such bestselling authors as Lee Child and Steve Berry. *Where the Wicked Tread* has been nominated for best e-book 2022 by International Thriller Writers, and *Madness in the Ruins* was a 2016 Barry Award nominee. Atlanta-born, John spends his time between the U.S. and France.

You can visit John online at: http://johnaconnell.com

Printed in Great Britain
by Amazon